Iain Banks is the author of three novels – THE WASP FACTORY, WALKING ON GLASS and THE BRIDGE – that have gained him a wide following and prompted Fay Weldon to describe him as 'the great white hope for contemporary British literature'. He is currently at work on a new novel.

Also by Iain Banks

THE WASP FACTORY
WALKING ON GLASS
THE BRIDGE

IAIN BANKS

Consider Phlebas

Futura

An Orbit Book

Copyright © Iain Banks, 1988

First published in Great Britain in 1987 by
Macmillan London Ltd,

This edition published in 1988 by
Futura Publications, a Division of
Macdonald & Co (Publishers) Ltd,
London & Sydney
Reprinted 1988 (twice)

ISBN 0 7088 3707 7

Reproduced, printed and bound in Great Britain by
Hazell Watson & Viney Limited
Member of BPCC plc
Aylesbury, Bucks, England

Futura Publications
A Division of
Macdonald & Co (Publishers) Ltd
Greater London House
Hampstead Road
London NW1 7QX
A member of Maxwell Pergamon Publishing Corporation plc

Idolatry is worse than carnage.

The Koran, 2: 190

Gentile or Jew
O you who turn the wheel and look to windward,
Consider Phlebas, who was once handsome and tall as you.

T. S. Eliot,
'The Waste Land', IV

to the memory of Bill Hunt

Prologue

The ship didn't even have a name. It had no human crew because the factory craft which constructed it had been evacuated long ago. It had no life-support or accommodation units for the same reason. It had no class number or fleet designation because it was a mongrel made from bits and pieces of different types of warcraft; and it didn't have a name because the factory craft had no time left for such niceties.

The dockyard threw the ship together as best it could from its depleted stock of components, even though most of the weapon, power and sensory systems were either faulty, superseded or due for overhaul. The factory vessel knew that its own destruction was inevitable, but there was just a chance that its last creation might have the speed and the luck to escape.

The one perfect, priceless component the factory craft did have was the vastly powerful – though still raw and untrained – Mind around which it had constructed the rest of the ship. If it could get the Mind to safety, the factory vessel thought it would have done well. Nevertheless, there was another reason – the real reason – the dockyard mother didn't give its warship child a name; it thought there was something else it lacked: hope.

The ship left the construction bay of the factory craft with most of its fitting-out still to be done. Accelerating hard, its course a four-dimensional spiral through a blizzard of stars where it knew that only danger waited, it powered into hyperspace on spent engines from an overhauled craft of one class, watched its birthplace disappear astern with battle-damaged sensors from a second, and tested outdated weapon units cannibalised from yet another. Inside its warship body, in narrow, unlit, unheated, hard-vacuum spaces, constructor drones struggled to install or complete sensors, displacers, field generators, shield disruptors, laserfields, plasma chambers, warhead magazines, manoeuvring units, repair systems and the thousands of other major and minor components required to make a functional warship.

Gradually, as it swept through the vast open reaches between the star systems, the vessel's internal structure changed, and it became less chaotic, more ordered, as the factory drones completed their tasks.

Several tens of hours out on its first journey, while it was testing its track scanner by focusing back along the route it had taken, the ship registered a single massive annihilation explosion deep behind it, where the factory craft had been. It watched the blossoming shell of radiation expand for a while, then switched the scanner field to dead ahead and pushed yet more power through its already overloaded engines.

The ship did all it could to avoid combat; it kept well away from the routes enemy craft would probably use; it treated every hint of any craft as a confirmed hostile sighting. At the same time, as it zigzagged and ducked and weaved and rose and fell, it was corkscrewing as fast as it could, as directly as it dared, down and across the strand of the galactic arm in which it had been born, heading for the edge of that great isthmus and the comparatively empty space beyond. On the far side, on the edge of the next limb, it might find safety.

Just as it arrived at that first border, where the stars rose like a glittering cliff alongside emptiness, it was caught.

A fleet of hostile craft, whose course by chance came close enough to that of the fleeing ship, detected its ragged, noisy emission shell, and intercepted it. The ship ran straight into their attack and was overwhelmed. Out-armed, slow, vulnerable, it knew almost instantly that it had no chance even of inflicting any damage on the opposing fleet.

So it destroyed itself, detonating the stock of warheads it carried in a sudden release of energy which for a second, in hyperspace alone, outshone the yellow dwarf star of a nearby system.

Scattered in a pattern around it, an instant before the ship itself was blown into plasma, most of the thousands of exploding warheads formed an outrushing sphere of radiation through which any escape seemed impossible. In the fraction of a second the entire engagement lasted, there were at the end some millionths when the battle-computers of the enemy fleet briefly analysed the four-dimensional maze of expanding radiation and saw that there was one bewilderingly complicated and unlikely way out of the concentric shells of erupting energies now opening like the petals of some immense flower between the star systems. It was not, however, a route the Mind of a small, archaic warship could plan for, create and follow.

By the time it was noticed that the ship's Mind had taken exactly that path through its screen of annihilation, it was too late to stop it from falling away through hyperspace towards the small, cold planet fourth out from the single yellow sun of the nearby system.

It was also too late to do anything about the light from the ship's exploding warheads, which had been arranged in a crude code, describing the vessel's fate and the escaped Mind's status and position, and legible to anybody catching the unreal light as it sped through the galaxy. Perhaps worst of all – and had their design permitted such a thing, those electronic brains would now have felt dismay – the planet the Mind had made for through its shield of explosions was not one they could simply attack, destroy or even land on; it was Schar's World, near the region of barren space between two galactic strands called the Sullen Gulf, and it was one of the forbidden Planets of the Dead.

1.

Sorpen

The level was at his top lip now. Even with his head pressed hard back against the stones of the cell wall his nose was only just above the surface. He wasn't going to get his hands free in time; he was going to drown.

In the darkness of the cell, in its stink and warmth, while the sweat ran over his brows and tightly closed eyes and his trance went on and on, one part of his mind tried to accustom him to the idea of his own death. But, like an unseen insect buzzing in a quiet room, there was something else, something that would not go away, was of no use, and only annoyed. It was a sentence, irrelevant and pointless and so old he'd forgotten where he had heard or read it, and it went round and round the inside of his head like a marble spun round the inside of a jug:

> The Jinmoti of Bozlen Two kill the hereditary ritual assassins of the new Yearking's immediate family by drowning them in the tears of the Continental Empathaur in its Sadness Season.

At one point, shortly after his ordeal had begun and he was only part-way into his trance, he had wondered what would happen if he threw up. It had been when the palace kitchens – about fifteen or sixteen floors above, if his calculations were correct – had sent their waste down the sinuous network of plumbing that led to the sewercell. The gurgling, watery mess had dislodged some rotten food from the last time some poor wretch had drowned in filth and garbage, and that was when he felt he might vomit. It had been almost comforting to work out that it would make no difference to the time of his death.

Then he had wondered – in that state of nervous frivolity which sometimes afflicts those who can do nothing but wait in a situation of mortal threat – whether crying would speed his death. In theory it would, though in practical terms it was irrelevant; but that was when the sentence started to roll round in his head.

9

The liquid, which he could hear and feel and smell all too clearly – and could probably have seen with his far from ordinary eyes had they been open – washed briefly up to touch the bottom of his nose. He felt it block his nostrils, filling them with a stench that made his stomach heave. But he shook his head, tried to force his skull even further back against the stones, and the foul broth fell away. He blew down and could breathe again.

There wasn't long now. He checked his wrists again, but it was no good. It would take another hour or more, and he had only minutes, if he was lucky.

The trance was breaking anyway. He was returning to almost total consciousness, as though his brain wanted fully to appreciate his own death, its own extinction. He tried to think of something profound, or to see his life flash in front of him, or suddenly to remember some old love, a long-forgotten prophecy or premonition, but there was nothing, just an empty sentence, and the sensations of drowning in other people's dirt and waste.

You old bastards, he thought. One of their few strokes of humour or originality had been devising an elegant, ironic way of death. How fitting it must feel to them, dragging their decrepit frames to the banquet-hall privies, literally to defecate all over their enemies, and thereby kill them.

The air pressure built up, and a distant, groaning rumble of liquid signalled another flushing from above. *You old bastards. Well, I hope at least you kept your promise, Balveda.*

The Jinmoti of Bozlen Two kill the hereditary ritual . . . thought one part of his brain, as the pipes in the ceiling spluttered and the waste splashed into the warm mass of liquid which almost filled the cell. The wave passed over his face, then fell back to leave his nose free for a second and give him time to gulp a lungful of air. Then the liquid rose gently to touch the bottom of his nose again, and stayed there.

He held his breath.

It had hurt at first, when they had hung him up. His hands, tied inside tight leather pouches, were directly above his head, manacled inside thick loops of iron bolted to the cell walls, which took all his weight. His feet were tied together and left to dangle inside an iron tube, also attached to the wall, which stopped him from taking any weight on his feet and knees and at the same time prevented him from moving his legs more than a hand's breadth out from the wall or to either side. The tube ended just above his knees; above it there was only a thin and dirty loincloth to hide his ancient and grubby nakedness.

He had shut off the pain from his wrists and shoulders even while the four burly guards, two of them perched on ladders, had secured him in place. Even so he could feel that niggling sensation at the back of his skull which told him that he *ought* to be hurting. That had lessened gradually as the level of waste in the small sewercell had risen and buoyed up his body.

He had started to go into a trance then, as soon as the guards left, though he knew it was probably hopeless. It hadn't lasted long; the cell door opened again within minutes, a metal walkway was lowered by a guard onto the damp flagstones of the cell floor, and light from the corridor washed into the darkness. He had stopped the Changing trance and craned his neck to see who his visitor might be.

Into the cell, holding a short staff glowing cool blue, stepped the stooped, grizzled figure of Amahain-Frolk, security minister for the Gerontocracy of Sorpen. The old man smiled at him and nodded approvingly, then turned to the corridor and, with a thin, discoloured hand, beckoned somebody standing outside the cell to step onto the short walkway and enter. He guessed it would be the Culture agent Balveda, and it was. She came lightly onto the metal boarding, looked round slowly, and fastened her gaze on him. He smiled and tried to nod in greeting, his ears rubbing on his naked arms.

'Balveda! I thought I might see you again. Come to see the host of the party?' He forced a grin. Officially it was his banquet; he was the host. Another of the Gerontocracy's little jokes. He hoped his voice had shown no signs of fear.

Perosteck Balveda, agent of the Culture, a full head taller than the old man by her side and still strikingly handsome even in the pallid glow of the blue torch, shook her thin, finely made head slowly. Her short, black hair lay like a shadow on her skull.

'No,' she said, 'I didn't want to see you, or say goodbye.'

'You put me here, Balveda,' he said quietly.

'Yes, and there you belong,' Amahain-Frolk said, stepping as far forward on the platform as he could without overbalancing and having to step onto the damp floor. 'I wanted you tortured first, but Miss Balveda here'—the minister's high, scratchy voice echoed in the cell as he turned his head back to the woman—'pleaded for you, though God knows why. But that's where you belong all right; murderer.' He shook the staff at the almost naked man hanging on the dirty wall of the cell.

Balveda looked at her feet, just visible under the hem of the long, plain grey gown she wore. A circular pendant on a chain around her neck glinted in the light from the corridor outside. Amahain-Frolk had stepped back beside her, holding the shining staff up and squinting at the captive.

'You know, even now I could almost swear that was Egratin hanging there. I can . . .' He shook his gaunt, bony head. '. . . I can hardly believe it isn't, not until he opens his mouth, anyway. My God, these Changers are dangerous frightening things!' He turned to Balveda. She smoothed her hair at the nape of her neck and looked down at the old man.

'They are also an ancient and proud people, Minister, and there are very few of them left. May I ask you one more time? Please? Let him live. He might be—'

The Gerontocrat waved a thin and twisted hand at her, his face distorting in a grimace. 'No! You would do well, Miss Balveda, not to keep asking for this . . . this assassin, this murderous, treacherous . . . *spy*, to be spared. Do you think we take the cowardly murder and impersonation of one of our Outworld ministers lightly? What damage this . . . *thing* could have caused! Why, when we arrested it two of our guards died just from being *scratched*! Another is blind for life after this monster spat in his eye! However,' Amahain-Frolk sneered at the man chained to the wall, 'we took those teeth out. And his hands are tied so that he can't even scratch himself.' He turned to Balveda again. 'You say they are few? I say good; there will soon be one less.' The old man narrowed his eyes as he looked at the woman. 'We are grateful to you and your people for exposing this fraud and murderer, but do not think that gives you the right to tell us what to do. There are some in the Gerontocracy who want nothing to do with *any* outside influence, and their voices grow in volume by the day as the war comes closer. You would do well not to antagonise those of us who do support your cause.'

Balveda pursed her lips and looked down at her feet again, clasping her slender hands behind her back. Amahain-Frolk had turned back to the man hanging on the wall, wagging the staff in his direction as he spoke. 'You will soon be dead, impostor, and with you die your masters' plans for the domination of our peaceful system! The same fate awaits them if they try to invade us. We and the Culture are—'

He shook his head as best he could and roared back, 'Frolk, you're

12

an idiot!' The old man shrank away as though hit. The Changer went on, 'Can't you see you're going to be taken over anyway? Probably by the Idirans, but if not by them then by the Culture. You don't control your own destinies any more; the war's stopped all that. Soon this whole sector will be part of the front, unless you *make* it part of the Idiran sphere. I was only sent in to tell you what you should have known anyway – not to cheat you into something you'd regret later. For God's sake, man, the Idirans won't *eat* you—'

'Ha! They look as though they could! Monsters with three feet; invaders, killers, infidels . . . You want us to link with them? With three-strides-tall-monsters? To be ground under their *hooves*? To have to worship their false gods?'

'At least they have a God, Frolk. The Culture doesn't.' The ache in his arms was coming back as he concentrated on talking. He shifted as best he could and looked down at the minister. 'They at least think the same way you do. The Culture doesn't.'

'Oh no, my friend, oh no.' Amahain-Frolk held one hand up flat to him and shook his head. 'You won't sow seeds of discord like that.'

'My God, you stupid old man,' he laughed. 'You want to know who the real representative of the Culture is on this planet? It's not her,' he nodded at the woman, 'it's that powered flesh-slicer she has following her everywhere, her knife missile. She might make the decisions, it might do what she tells it, but it's the real emissary. That's what the Culture's about: machines. You think because Balveda's got two legs and soft skin you should be on her side, but it's the Idirans who are on the side of life in this war—'

'Well, you will shortly be on the other side of *that*.' The Gerontocrat snorted and glanced at Balveda, who was looking from under lowered brows at the man chained to the wall. 'Let us go, Miss Balveda,' Amahain-Frolk said as he turned and took the woman's arm to guide her from the cell. 'This . . . *thing's* presence smells more than the cell.'

Balveda looked up at him then, ignoring the dwarfed minister as he tried to pull her to the door. She gazed right at the prisoner with her clear, black-irised eyes and held her hands out from her sides. 'I'm sorry,' she said to him.

'Believe it or not, that's rather how I feel,' he replied, nodding. 'Just promise me you'll eat and drink very little tonight, Balveda. I'd like to think there was one person up there on my side, and it might as well be my worst enemy.' He had meant it to be defiant and funny, but it sounded only bitter; he looked away from the woman's face.

'I promise,' Balveda said. She let herself be led to the door, and the blue light waned in the dank cell. She stopped right at the door. By sticking his head painfully far out he could just see her. The knife missile was there, too, he noticed, just inside the room; probably there all the time, but he hadn't noticed its sleek, sharp little body hovering there in the darkness. He looked into Balveda's dark eyes as the knife missile moved.

For a second he thought Balveda had instructed the tiny machine to kill him now – quietly and quickly while she blocked Amahain-Frolk's view – and his heart thudded. But the small device simply floated past Balveda's face and out into the corridor. Balveda raised one hand in a gesture of farewell.

'Bora Horza Gobuchul,' she said, 'goodbye.' She turned quickly, stepped from the platform and out of the cell. The walkway was hoisted out and the door slammed, scraping rubber flanges over the grimy floor and hissing once as the internal seals made it watertight. He hung there, looking down at an invisible floor for a moment before going back into the trance that would Change his wrists, thin them down so that he could escape. But something about the solemn, final way Balveda had spoken his name had crushed him inside, and he knew then, if not before, that there was no escape.

. . . by drowning them in the tears . . .

His lungs were bursting! His mouth quivered, his throat was gagging, the filth was in his ears but he could hear a great roaring, see lights though it was black dark. His stomach muscles started to go in and out, and he had to clamp his jaw to stop his mouth opening for air that wasn't there. Now. No . . . *now* he had to give in. Not yet . . . surely now. Now, now, now, any second; surrender to this awful black vacuum inside him . . . he had to breathe . . . *now*!

Before he had time to open his mouth he was smashed against the wall – punched against the stones as though some immense iron fist had slammed into him. He blew out the stale air from his lungs in one convulsive breath. His body was suddenly cold, and every part of it next to the wall throbbed with pain. Death, it seemed, was weight, pain, cold . . . and too much light . . .

He brought his head up. He moaned at the light. He tried to see, tried to hear. What was happening? Why was he breathing? Why was he so damn *heavy* again? His body was tearing his arms from their sockets; his wrists were cut almost to the bone. Who had *done* this to him?

Where the wall had been facing him there was a very large and ragged hole which extended beneath the level of the cell floor. All the ordure and garbage had burst out of that. The last few trickles hissed against the hot sides of the breach, producing steam which curled around the figure standing blocking most of the brilliant light from outside, in the open air of Sorpen. The figure was three metres tall and looked vaguely like a small armoured spaceship sitting on a tripod of thick legs. Its helmet looked big enough to contain three human heads, side by side. Held almost casually in one gigantic hand was a plasma cannon which Horza would have needed both arms just to lift; the creature's other fist gripped a slightly larger gun. Behind it, nosing in towards the hole, came an Idiran gun-platform, lit vividly by the light of explosions which Horza could now feel through the iron and stones he was attached to. He raised his head to the giant standing in the breach and tried to smile.

'Well,' he croaked, then spluttered and spat, 'you lot certainly took your time.'

2.

The Hand of God 137

Outside the palace, in the sharp cold of a winter's afternoon, the clear sky was full of what looked like glittering snow.

Horza paused on the warshuttle's ramp and looked up and around. The sheer walls and slim towers of the prison-palace echoed and reflected with the booms and flashes of continuing fire-fights, while Idiran gun-platforms cruised back and forth, firing occasionally. Around them on the stiffening breeze blew great clouds of chaff from anti-laser mortars on the palace roof. A gust sent some of the fluttering, flickering foil towards the stationary shuttle, and Horza found one side of his wet and sticky body suddenly coated with reflecting plumage.

'Please. The battle is not over yet,' thundered the Idiran soldier behind him, in what was probably meant to be a quiet whisper. Horza turned round to the armoured bulk and stared up at the visor of the giant's helmet, where he could see his own, old man's face reflected. He breathed deeply, then nodded, turned and walked, slightly shakily, into the shuttle. A flash of light threw his shadow diagonally in front of him, and the craft bucked in the shock wave of a big explosion somewhere inside the palace as the ramp closed.

By their names you could know them, Horza thought as he showered. The Culture's General Contact Units, which until now had borne the brunt of the first four years of the war in space, had always chosen jokey, facetious names. Even the new warships they were starting to produce, as their factory craft completed gearing up their war production, favoured either jocular, sombre or downright unpleasant names, as though the Culture could not take entirely seriously the vast conflict in which it had embroiled itself.

The Idirans looked at things differently. To them a ship name ought to reflect the serious nature of its purpose, duties and resolute use. In the huge Idiran navy there were hundreds of craft named after the same heroes, planets, battles, religious concepts and impressive adjectives. The light cruiser which had rescued Horza was the 137th vessel to be called *The Hand of God*, and it existed concurrently with over a hundred other craft in the navy using the same title, so its full name was *The Hand of God 137*.

Horza dried in the airstream with some difficulty. Like everything else in the spaceship it was built on a monumental scale befitting the size of the Idirans, and the hurricane of air it produced nearly blew him out of the shower cabinet.

The Querl Xoralundra, spy-father and warrior priest of the Four Souls tributory sect of Farn-Idir, clasped two hands on the surface of the table. It looked to Horza rather like a pair of continental plates colliding.

'So, Bora Horza,' boomed the old Idiran, 'you are recovered.'

'Just about,' nodded Horza, rubbing his wrists. He sat in Xoralundra's cabin in *The Hand of God 137*, clothed in a bulky but comfortable space suit apparently brought along just for him. Xoralundra, who was also suited up, had insisted the man wear it because the warship was still at battle stations as it swept a fast and low-powered orbit around the planet of Sorpen. A Culture GCU of the Mountain class had been confirmed in the system by Naval Intelligence; the *Hand* was in on its own, and they couldn't find any trace of the Culture ship, so they had to be careful.

Xoralundra leaned towards Horza, casting a shadow over the table. His huge head, saddle-shaped when seen from directly in front, with the two front eyes clear and unblinking near the edges, loomed over the Changer. 'You were lucky, Horza. We did not come in to rescue you out of compassion. Failure is its own reward.'

'Thank you, Xora. That's actually the nicest thing anybody's said to me all day.' Horza sat back in his seat and put one of his old-looking hands through his thin, yellowing hair. It would take a few days for the aged appearance he had assumed to disappear, though already he could feel it starting to slip away from him. In a Changer's mind there was a self-image constantly held and reviewed on a semi-subconscious level, keeping the body in the appearance willed. Horza's need to look like a Gerontocrat was gone now, so the mental picture of the minister he had impersonated for the Idirans was fragmenting and dissolving, and his body was going back to its normal, neutral state.

Xoralundra's head went slowly from side to side between the edges of the suit collar. It was a gesture Horza had never fully translated, although he had worked for the Idirans and known Xoralundra well since before the war.

'Anyway. You are alive,' Xoralundra said. Horza nodded and drummed his fingers on the table to show he agreed. He wished the Idiran chair he was perched on didn't make him feel so much like a child; his feet weren't even touching the deck.

'Just. Thanks, anyway. I'm sorry I dragged you all the way in here to rescue a failure.'

'Orders are orders. I personally am glad we were able to. Now I must tell you why we received those orders.'

Horza smiled and looked away from the old Idiran, who had just given him something of a compliment; a rare thing. He looked back and watched the other being's wide mouth – big enough, thought Horza, to bite off both your hands at once – as it boomed out the precise, short words of the Idiran language.

'You were once with a caretaker mission on Schar's World, one of the Dra'Azon Planets of the Dead,' Xoralundra stated. Horza nodded. 'We need you to go back there.'

'Now?' Horza said to the broad, dark face of the Idiran. 'There are only Changers there. I've told you I won't impersonate another Changer. I certainly won't kill one.'

'We are not asking you to do that. Listen while I explain.' Xoralundra leant on his back-rest in a way almost any vertebrate – or even anything like a vertebrate – would have called tired. 'Four standard days ago,' the Idiran began – then his suit helmet, which was lying on the floor near his feet, let out a piercing whine. He picked up the helmet and set it on the table. '*Yes?*' he said, and Horza knew enough about the Idiran voice to realise that whoever was bothering the Querl had better have a good reason for doing so.

'We have the Culture female,' a voice said from the helmet.

'Ahh . . .' Xoralundra said quietly, sitting back. The Idiran equivalent of a smile – mouth pursing, eyes narrowing – passed over his features. 'Good, Captain. Is she aboard yet?'

'No, Querl. The shuttle is a couple of minutes out. I'm withdrawing the gun-platforms. We are ready to leave the system as soon as they are all on board.'

Xoralundra bent closer to the helmet. Horza inspected the aged skin on the back of his hands. 'What of the Culture ship?' the Idiran asked.

'Still nothing, Querl. It cannot be anywhere in the system. Our computer suggests it is outside, possibly between us and the fleet.

21

Before long it must realise we are in here by ourselves.'

'You will set off to rejoin the fleet the instant the female Culture agent is aboard, without waiting for the platforms. Is that understood, Captain?' Xoralundra looked at Horza as the human glanced at him. 'Is that understood, Captain?' the Querl repeated, still looking at the human.

'Yes, Querl,' came the answer. Horza could hear the icy tone, even through the small helmet speaker.

'Good. Use your own initiative to decide the best route back to the fleet. In the meantime you will destroy the cities of De'aychanbie, Vinch, Easna-Yowon, Izilere and Ylbar with fusion bombs, as per the Admiralty's orders.'

'Yes, Qu—' Xoralundra stabbed a switch in the helmet, and it fell silent.

'You got Balveda?' Horza asked, surprised.

'We have the Culture agent, yes. I regard her capture, or destruction, as of comparatively little consequence. But only by our assuring the Admiralty we would attempt to take her would they contemplate such a hazardous mission ahead of the main fleet to rescue you.'

'Hmm. Bet you didn't get Balveda's knife missile.' Horza snorted, looking again at the wrinkles on his hands.

'It destructed while you were being put aboard the shuttle which brought you up to the ship.' Xoralundra waved one hand, sending a draught of Idiran-scented air across the table. 'But enough of that. I must explain why we risked a light cruiser to rescue you.'

'By all means,' Horza said, and turned to face the Idiran.

'Four standard days ago,' the Querl said, 'a group of our ships intercepted a single Culture craft of conventional outward appearance but rather odd internal construction, judging by its emission signature. The ship was destroyed easily enough, but its Mind escaped. There was a planetary system near by. The Mind appears to have transcended real space to within the planetary surface of the globe it chose, thus indicating a level of hyperspatial field management we had thought – hoped – was still beyond the Culture. Certainly such spaciobatics are beyond us for the moment. We have reason to believe, due to that and other indications, that the Mind involved is one from a new class of General Systems Vehicles the Culture is developing. The Mind's capture would be an intelligence coup of the first order.'

The Querl paused there. Horza took the opportunity to ask, 'Is this thing on Schar's World?'

'Yes. According to its last message it intended to shelter in the tunnels of the Command System.'

'And you can't do anything about it?' Horza smiled.

'We came to get you. That is doing something about it, Bora Horza.' The Querl paused. 'The shape of your mouth tells me you see something amusing in this situation. What would that be?'

'I was just thinking . . . lots of things: that that Mind was either pretty smart or very lucky; that *you* were very lucky you had me close by; also that the Culture isn't likely to sit back and do nothing.'

'To deal with your points in order,' Xoralundra said sharply, 'the Culture Mind was both lucky and smart; we were fortunate; the Culture can do little because they do not, as far as we know, have any Changers in their employ, and certainly not one who has served on Schar's World. I would also add, Bora Horza,' the Idiran said, putting both huge hands on the table and dipping his great head towards the human, 'that *you* were more than a little lucky yourself.'

'Ah yes, but the difference is that I believe in it.' Horza grinned.

'Hmm. It does you little credit,' observed the Querl. Horza shrugged.

'So you want me to put down on Schar's World and get the Mind?'

'If possible. It may be damaged. It may be liable to destruct, but it is a prize worth fighting for. We shall give you all the equipment you need, but your presence alone would give us a toe-hold.'

'What about the people already there? The Changers on caretaker duty?'

'Nothing has been heard from them. They were probably unaware of the Mind's arrival. Their next routine transmission is due in a few days, but, given the current disruption in communications due to the war, they may not be able to send.'

'What . . .' Horza said slowly, one finger describing a circular pattern on the table surface which he was looking at, '. . . do you know about the personnel in the base?'

'The two senior members have been replaced by younger Changers,' the Idiran said. 'The two junior sentinels became seniors, remaining there.'

'They wouldn't be in any danger, would they?' Horza asked.

'On the contrary. Inside a Dra'Azon Quiet Barrier, on a Planet of the Dead, must rank as one of the safest places to be during the current hostilities. Neither we nor the Culture can risk causing the Dra'Azon any offence. That is why they cannot do anything, and we can only use you.'

'If,' Horza said carefully, sitting forward and dropping his voice slightly, 'I can get this metaphysical computer for you—'

'Something in your voice tells me we approach the question of remuneration,' Xoralundra said.

'We do indeed. I've risked my neck for you lot long enough, Xoralundra. I want out. There's a good friend of mine on that Schar's World base, and if she's agreeable I want to take her and me out of the whole war. That's what I'm asking for.'

'I can promise nothing. I shall request this. Your long and devoted service will be taken into account.'

Horza sat back and frowned. He wasn't sure if Xoralundra was being ironic or not. Six years probably didn't seem like very long at all to a species that was virtually immortal; but the Querl Xoralundra knew how often his frail human charge had risked all in the service of his alien masters, without real reward, so perhaps he was being serious. Before Horza could continue with the bargaining, the helmet shrilled once more. Horza winced. All the noises on the Idiran ship seemed to be deafening. The voices were thunder; ordinary buzzers and bleepers left his ears ringing long after they stopped; and announcements over the PA made him put both hands to his head. Horza just hoped there wasn't a full-scale alarm while he was on board. The Idiran ship alarm could cause damage to unprotected human ears.

'What is it?' Xoralundra asked the helmet.

'The female is on board. I shall need only eight more minutes to get the gun—'

'Have the cities been destroyed?'

'. . . They have, Querl.'

'Break out of orbit at once and make full speed for the fleet.'

'Querl, I must point out—' said the small, steady voice from the helmet on the table.

'Captain,' Xoralundra said briskly, 'in this war there have to date been fourteen single-duel engagements between Type 5 light cruisers and Mountain class General Contact Units. All have ended in victory for the enemy. Have you ever seen what is left of a light cruiser after a GCU has finished with it?'

'No, Querl.'

'Neither have I, and I have no intention of seeing it for the first time from the inside. Proceed at once.' Xoralundra hit the helmet button again. He fastened his gaze on Horza. 'I shall do what I can to secure your release from the service with sufficient funds, if you succeed.

24

Now, once we have made contact with the main body of the fleet you will go by fast picket to Schar's World. You will be given a shuttle there, just beyond the Quiet Barrier. It will be unarmed, although it will have the equipment we think you may need, including some close-range hyperspace spectographic analysers, should the Mind conduct a limited destruct.'

'How can you be certain it'll be "limited"?' Horza asked sceptically.

'The Mind weighs several thousand tonnes, despite its relatively small size. An annihilatory destruct would rip the planet in half and so antagonise the Dra'Azon. No Culture Mind would risk such a thing.'

'Your confidence overwhelms me,' Horza said dourly. Just then the note of background noise around them altered. Xoralundra turned his helmet round and looked at one of its small internal screens.

'Good. We are under way.' He looked at Horza again. 'There is something else I ought to tell you. An attempt was made, by the group of ships which caught the Culture craft, to follow the escaped Mind down to the planet.'

Horza frowned. 'Didn't they know better?'

'They did their best. With the battle group were several captured chuy-hirtsi warp animals which had been deactivated for later use in a surprise attack on a Culture base. One of these was quickly fitted out for a small-scale incursion on the planet surface and thrown at the Quiet Barrier in a warp-cruise. The ruse did not succeed. On crossing the Barrier the animal was attacked with something resembling gridfire and was heavily damaged. It came out of warp near the planet on a course which would take it in on a burn-up angle. The equipment and ground force it contained must be considered defunct.'

'Well, I suppose it was a good try, but a Dra'Azon must make even this wonderful Mind you're after look like a valve computer. It's going to take more than that to fool it.'

'Do you think you will be able to?'

'I don't know. I don't *think* they can read minds, but who knows? I don't *think* the Dra'Azon even know or care much about the war or what I've been doing since I left Schar's World. So they probably won't be able to put one and one together – but again, who knows?' Horza gave another shrug. 'It's worth a try.'

'Good. We shall have a fuller briefing when we rejoin the fleet. For now we must pray that our return is without incident. You may want to speak to Perosteck Balveda before she is interrogated. I have

25

arranged with the Deputy Fleet Inquisitor that you may see her, if you wish.'

Horza smiled, 'Xora, nothing would give me greater pleasure.'

The Querl had other business on the ship as it powered its way out of the Sorpen system. Horza stayed in Xoralundra's cabin to rest and eat before he called on Balveda.

The food was the cruiser autogalley's best impression of something suitable for a humanoid, but it tasted awful. Horza ate what he could and drank some equally uninspiring distilled water. It was all served by a medjel – a lizard-like creature about two metres long with a flat, long head and six legs, on four of which it ran, using the front pair as hands. The medjel were the companion species of the Idirans. It was a complicated sort of social symbiosis which had kept the exosocio faculties of many a university in research funds over the millennia that the Idiran civilisation had been part of the galactic community.

The Idirans themselves had evolved on their planet Idir as the top monster from a whole planetful of monsters. The frenetic and savage ecology of Idir in its early days had long since disappeared, and so had all the other homeworld monsters except those in zoos. But the Idirans had retained the intelligence that made them winners, as well as the biological immortality which, due to the viciousness of the fight for survival back then – not to mention Idir's high radiation levels – had been an evolutionary advantage rather than a recipe for stagnation.

Horza thanked the medjel as it brought him plates and took them away again, but it said nothing. They were generally reckoned to be about two thirds as intelligent as the average humanoid (whatever that was), which made them about two or three times dimmer than a normal Idiran. Still, they were good if unimaginative soldiers, and there were plenty of them; something like ten or twelve for each Idiran. Forty thousand years of breeding had made them loyal right down to the chromosome level.

Horza didn't try to sleep, though he was tired. He told the medjel to take him to Balveda. The medjel thought about it, asked permission via the cabin intercom, and flinched visibly under a verbal slap from a distant Xoralundra who was on the bridge with the cruiser captain. 'Follow me, sir,' the medjel said, opening the cabin door.

In the companionways of the warship the Idiran atmosphere became more obvious than it had been in Xoralundra's cabin. The smell of

Idiran was stronger and the view ahead hazed over – even seen through Horza's eyes – after a few tens of metres. It was hot and humid, and the floor was soft. Horza walked quickly along the corridor, watching the stump of the medjel's docked tail as it waggled in front of him.

He passed two Idirans on the way, neither of whom paid him any attention. Perhaps they knew all about him and what he was, but perhaps not. Horza knew that Idirans hated to appear either over-inquisitive or under-informed.

He nearly collided with a pair of wounded medjel on AG stretchers being hurried along a cross-corridor by two of their fellow troopers. Horza watched as the wounded passed, and frowned. The spiralled spatter-marks on their battle armour were unmistakably those prod-uced by a plasma bolt, and the Gerontocracy didn't have any plasma weapons. He shrugged and walked on.

They came to a section of the cruiser where the companionway was blocked by sliding doors. The medjel spoke to each of the barriers in turn, and they opened. An Idiran guard holding a laser carbine stood outside a door; he saw the medjel and Horza approaching and had the door open for the man by the time he got there. Horza nodded to the guard as he stepped through. The door hissed shut behind him and another one, immediately in front, opened.

Balveda turned quickly to him when he entered the cell. It looked as though she had been pacing up and down. She threw back her head a little when she saw Horza and made a noise in her throat which might have been a laugh.

'Well, well,' she said, her soft voice drawling. 'You survived. Congratulations. I did keep my promise, by the way. What a turn-around, eh?'

'Hello,' Horza replied, folding his arms across the chest of his suit and looking the woman up and down. She wore the same grey gown and appeared to be unharmed. 'What happened to that thing around your neck?' Horza asked.

She looked down, at where the pendant had lain over her breast. 'Well, believe it or not, it turned out to be a memoryform.' She smiled at him and sat down cross-legged on the soft floor; apart from a raised bed-alcove, this was the only place to sit. Horza sat too, his legs hurting only a little. He recalled the spatter-marks on the medjel's armour.

'A memoryform. Wouldn't have turned into a *plasma* gun, by any chance, would it?'

27

'Amongst other things.' The Culture agent nodded.

'Thought so. Heard your knife missile took the expansive way out.' Balveda shrugged.

Horza looked her in the eye and said, 'I don't suppose you'd be here if you had anything important you could tell them, would you?'

'Here, perhaps,' Balveda conceded. 'Alive, no.' She stretched her arms out behind her and sighed. 'I suppose I'll have to sit out the war in an internment camp, unless they can find somebody to swap. I just hope this thing doesn't go on too long.'

'Oh, you think the Culture might give in soon?' Horza grinned.

'No, I think the Culture might win soon.'

'You must be mad.' Horza shook his head.

'Well . . .' Balveda said, nodding ruefully, 'actually I think it'll win eventually.'

'If you keep falling back like you have for the last three years, you'll end up somewhere in the Clouds.'

'I'm not giving away any secrets, Horza, but I think you might find we don't do too much more falling back.'

'We'll see. Frankly I'm surprised you kept fighting this long.'

'So are our three-legged friends. So is everybody. So are we, I sometimes think.'

'Balveda,' Horza sighed wearily, 'I still don't know why the hell you're fighting in the first place. The Idirans never were any threat to you. They still wouldn't be, if you stopped fighting them. Did life in your great Utopia really get so boring you needed a war?'

'Horza,' Balveda said, leaning forward, 'I don't understand why *you* are fighting. I know Hiedohre is in—'

'Hei*bohre*,' Horza interjected.

'OK, the goddamn asteroid the Changers live in. I know it's in Idiran space, but—'

'That's got nothing to do with it, Balveda. I'm fighting for them because I think they're right and you're wrong.'

Balveda sat back, amazed. 'You . . .' she began, then lowered her head and shook it, staring at the floor. She looked up. 'I really *don't* understand you, Horza. You must know how many species, how many civilisations, how many systems, how many individuals have been either destroyed or . . . throttled by the Idirans and their crazy goddamned religion. What the hell has the Culture ever done compared to *that*?' One hand was on her knee, the other was displayed in front of Horza, clawed into a strangling grip. He watched her and smiled.

28

'On a straight head count the Idirans no doubt do come out in front, Perosteck, and I've told them I never did care for some of their methods, or their zeal. I'm all for people being allowed to live their own lives. But now they're up against you lot, and that's what makes the difference to me. Because I'm against you, rather than for them, I'm prepared—' Horza broke off for a moment, laughing lightly, self-consciously. '. . . Well, it sounds a bit melodramatic, but sure – I'm prepared to die for them.' He shrugged. 'Simple as that.'

Horza nodded as he said it, and Balveda dropped the outstretched hand and looked away to one side, shaking her head and exhaling loudly. Horza went on, 'Because . . . well, I suppose you thought I was just kidding when I was telling old Frolk I thought the knife missile was the real representative. I wasn't kidding, Balveda. I meant it then and I mean it now. I don't care how self-righteous the Culture feels, or how many people the Idirans kill. They're on the side of life – boring, old-fashioned, biological life; smelly, fallible and short-sighted, God knows, but *real* life. You're ruled by your machines. You're an evolutionary dead end. The trouble is that to take your mind off it you try to drag everybody else down there with you. The worst thing that could happen to the galaxy would be if the Culture wins this war.'

He paused to let her say something, but she was still sitting with her head down, shaking it. He laughed at her. 'You know, Balveda, for such a sensitive species you show remarkably little empathy at times.'

'Empathise with stupidity and you're halfway to thinking like an idiot,' muttered the woman, still not looking at Horza. He laughed again and got to his feet.

'Such . . . bitterness, Balveda,' he said.

She looked up at him. 'I'll tell you, Horza,' she said quietly, 'we're going to win.'

He shook his head. 'I don't think so. You wouldn't know how to.'

Balveda sat back again, hands spread behind her. Her face was serious. 'We can learn, Horza.'

'Who from?'

'Whoever has the lesson there to teach,' she said slowly. 'We spend quite a lot of our time watching warriors and zealots, bullies and militarists – people determined to win regardless. There's no shortage of teachers.'

'If you want to know about winning, ask the Idirans.'

Balveda said nothing for a moment. Her face was calm, thoughtful, perhaps sad. She nodded after a while. 'They do say there's a danger

29

. . . in warfare,' she said, 'that you'll start to resemble the enemy.' She shrugged. 'We just have to hope that we can avoid that. If the evolutionary force you seem to believe in really works, then it'll work through us, and not the Idirans. If you're wrong, then it deserves to be superseded.'

'Balveda,' he said, laughing lightly, 'don't disappoint me. I prefer a fight. . . . You almost sound as though you're coming round to my point of view.'

'No,' she sighed. 'I'm not. Blame it on my Special Circumstances training. We try to think of everything. I was being pessimistic.'

'I'd got the impression SC didn't allow such thoughts.'

'Then think again, Mr Changer,' Balveda said, arching one eyebrow. 'SC allows all thoughts. That's what some people find so frightening about it.'

Horza thought he knew what the woman meant. Special Circumstances had always been the Contact section's moral espionage weapon, the very cutting edge of the Culture's interfering diplomatic policy, the élite of the élite, in a society which abhorred élitism. Even before the war, its standing and its image within the Culture had been ambiguous. It was glamorous but dangerous, possessed of an aura of roguish sexiness – there was no other word for it – which implied predation, seduction, even violation.

It had about it too an atmosphere of secrecy (in a society that virtually worshipped openness) which hinted at unpleasant, shaming deeds, and an ambience of moral relativity (in a society which clung to its absolutes: life/good, death/bad; pleasure/good, pain/bad) which attracted and repulsed at once, but anyway excited.

No other part of the Culture more exactly represented what the society as a whole really stood for, or was more militant in the application of the Culture's fundamental beliefs. Yet no other part embodied less of the society's day-to-day character.

With war, Contact had become the Culture's military, and Special Circumstances its intelligence and espionage section (the euphemism became only a little more obvious, that was all). And with war, SC's position within the Culture changed, for the worse. It became the repository for the guilt the people in the Culture experienced because they had agreed to go to war in the first place: despised as a necessary evil, reviled as an unpleasant moral compromise, dismissed as something people preferred not to think about.

SC really did try to think of everything, though, and its Minds were reputedly even more cynical, amoral and downright sneaky than those which made up Contact; machines without illusions which prided themselves on thinking the thinkable to its ultimate extremities. So it had been wearily predicted that just this would happen. SC would become a pariah, a whipping-child, and its reputation a gland to absorb the poison in the Culture's conscience. But Horza guessed that knowing all this didn't make it any easier for somebody like Balveda. Culture people had little stomach for being disliked by anybody, least of all their fellow citizens, and the woman's task was difficult enough without the added burden of knowing she was even greater anathema to most of her own side than she was to the enemy.

'Well, whatever, Balveda,' he said, stretching. He flexed his stiff shoulders within the suit, pulled his fingers through his thin, yellow-white hair. 'I guess it'll work itself out.'

Balveda laughed mirthlessly. 'Never a truer word . . .' She shook her head.

'Thanks, anyway,' he told her.

'For what?'

'I think you just reinforced my faith in the ultimate outcome of this war.'

'Oh, just go away, Horza.' Balveda sighed and looked down to the floor.

Horza wanted to touch her, to ruffle her short black hair or pinch her pale cheek, but guessed it would only upset her more. He knew too well the bitterness of defeat to want to aggravate the experience for somebody who was, in the end, a fair and honourable adversary. He went to the door, and after a word with the guard outside he was let out.

'Ah, Bora Horza,' Xoralundra said as the human appeared out of the cell doorway. The Querl came striding along the companionway. The guard outside the cell straightened visibly and blew some imaginary dust off his carbine. 'How is our guest?'

'Not very happy. We were trading justifications and I think I won on points.' Horza grinned. Xoralundra stopped by the man and looked down.

'Hmm. Well, unless you prefer to relish your victories in a vacuum, I suggest that the next time you leave my cabin while we are at battle stations you take your—'

Horza didn't hear the next word. The ship's alarm erupted.

The Idiran alarm signal, on a warship as elsewhere, consists of what sounds like a series of very sharp explosions. It is the amplified version of the Idiran chest-boom, an evolved signal the Idirans had been using to warn others in their herd or clan for several hundred thousand years before they became civilised, and produced by the chest-flap which is the Idiran vestigial third arm.

Horza clapped his hands to his ears, trying to shut out the awful noise. He could feel the shock waves on his chest, through the open neck of the suit. He felt himself being picked up and forced against the bulkhead. It was only then that he realised he had shut his eyes. For a second he thought he had never been rescued, never left the wall of the sewercell, that this was the moment of his death and all the rest had been a strange and vivid dream. He opened his eyes and found himself staring into the keratinous snout of the Querl Xoralundra, who shook him furiously and, just as the ship alarm cut off and was replaced by a merely painfully intense whine, said very loudly into Horza's face, 'HELMET!'

'Oh shit!' said Horza.

He was dropped to the deck as Xoralundra let him go, turned quickly, and scooped a running medjel off the floor as it tried to get past him. 'You!' Xoralundra bellowed. 'I am the spy-father Querl of the fleet,' he shouted into its face and shook the six-limbed creature by the front of its suit. 'You will go to my cabin immediately and bring the small space helmet lying there to the port-side stern emergency lock. As fast as possible. This order supersedes all others and cannot be countermanded. Go!' He threw the medjel in the right direction. It landed running.

Xoralundra flipped his own helmet over from its back-hinged position, then opened the visor. He looked as though he was about to say something to Horza, but the helmet speaker crackled and spoke, and the Querl's expression changed. The small noise stopped and only the continuing wail of the cruiser's alarm was left. 'The Culture craft was hiding in the surface layers of the system sun,' Xoralundra said bitterly, more to himself than to Horza.

'In the *sun*?' Horza was incredulous. He looked back at the cell door, as though somehow it was Balveda's fault. 'Those bastards are getting smarter all the time.'

'Yes,' snapped the Querl, then turned quickly on one foot. 'Follow me, human.' Horza obeyed, starting after the old Idiran at a run, then bumping into him as the huge figure stopped in its tracks. Horza watched the broad, dark, alien face as it swivelled round to look over his head at the Idiran trooper still standing stiffly at the cell door. An expression Horza could not read passed over Xoralundra's face.

'Guard,' the Querl said, not loudly. The trooper with the laser carbine turned. 'Kill the woman.'

Xoralundra stamped off down the corridor. Horza stood for a moment, looking first at the rapidly receding Querl, then at the guard as he checked his carbine, ordered the cell door to open, and stepped inside. Then the man ran down the corridor after the old Idiran.

'Querl!' gasped the medjel as it skidded to a stop by the airlock, the suit helmet held in front of it. Xoralundra swept the helmet from its grasp and fitted it quickly over Horza's head.

'You will find a warp attachment in the lock,' the Idiran told Horza. 'Get as far away as possible. The fleet will be here in about nine standard hours. You shouldn't have to do anything; the suit will summon help on a coded IFF response. I, too—' Xoralundra broke off as the cruiser lurched. There was a loud bang and Horza was blown off his feet by a shock wave, while the Idiran on his tripod of legs hardly moved. The medjel which had gone for the helmet yelped as it was blown under Xoralundra's legs. The Idiran swore and kicked at it; it ran off. The cruiser lurched again as other alarms started. Horza could smell burning. A confused medley of noises that might have been Idiran voices or muffled explosions came from somewhere overhead. 'I too shall try to escape,' Xoralundra continued. 'God be with you, human.'

Before Horza could say anything the Idiran had rammed his visor down and pushed him into the lock. It slammed shut. Horza was thrown against one bulkhead as the cruiser juddered mightily. He looked desperately round the small, spherical space for a warp unit, then saw it and after a short struggle unclamped it from its wall magnets. He clamped it to the rear of his suit.

'Ready?' a voice said in his ear.

Horza jumped, then said, 'Yes! Yes! Hit it!'

The airlock didn't open conventionally; it turned inside out and threw him into space, tumbling away from the flat disc of the cruiser in a tiny galaxy of ice particles. He looked for the Culture ship, then told himself not to be stupid; it was probably still several trillion kilometres away. That was how divorced from the human scale modern warfare had become. You could smash and destroy from unthinkable distances, obliterate planets from beyond their own system and provoke stars into novae from light-years off . . . and still have no good idea why you were really fighting.

With one last thought for Balveda, Horza reached until he found

c.p.—3

33

the control handle for the bulky warp unit, fingered the correct buttons on it, and watched the stars twist and distort around him as the unit sent him and his suit lancing away from the stricken Idiran spacecraft.

He played with the wrist-set for a while, trying to pick up signals from *The Hand of God 137*, but got nothing but static. The suit spoke to him once, saying 'Warp/unit/charge/half/exhausted.' Horza kept a watch on the warp unit via a small screen set inside the helmet.

He recalled that the Idirans said some sort of prayer to their God before going into warp. Once when he had been with Xoralundra on a ship which was warping, the Querl had insisted that the Changer repeat the prayer, too. Horza had protested that it meant nothing to him; not only did the Idiran God clash with his own personal convictions, the prayer itself was in a dead Idiran language he didn't understand. He had been told rather coldly that it was the gesture that mattered. For what the Idirans regarded as essentially an animal (their word for humanoids was best translated as 'biotomaton'), only the behaviour of devotion was required; his heart and mind were of no consequence. When Horza had asked, what about his immortal soul? Xoralundra had laughed. It was the first and only time Horza had experienced such a thing from the old warrior. Whoever heard of a mortal body having an immortal soul?

When the warp unit was almost exhausted, Horza shut it off. Stars swam into focus around him. He set the unit controls, then threw it away from him. They parted company, he moving slowly off in one direction, while the unit spun off in another; then it disappeared as the controls switched it back on again to use the last of its power leading anybody following its trace away in the wrong direction.

He calmed his breathing down gradually; it had been very fast and hard for a while, but he slowed it and his heart deliberately. He accustomed himself to the suit, testing its functions and powers. It smelled and felt new, and looked like a Rairch-built device. Rairch suits were meant to be among the best. People said the Culture made better ones, but people said the Culture made better everything, and they were still losing the war. Horza checked out the lasers the suit had built in and searched for the concealed pistol he knew it ought to carry. He found it at last, disguised as part of the left forearm casing, a small plasma hand gun. He felt like shooting it at something, but there was nothing to aim at. He put it back.

He folded his arms across his bulky chest and looked around. Stars were everywhere. He had no idea which one was Sorpen's. So the

Culture ships could hide in the photospheres of stars, could they? And a Mind – even if it was desperate and on the run – could jump through the bottom of a gravity-well, could it? Maybe the Idirans would have a tougher job than they expected. They were the natural warriors, they had the experience and the guts, and their whole society was geared for continual conflict. But the Culture, that seemingly disunited, anarchic, hedonistic, decadent mélange of more or less human species, forever hiving off or absorbing different groups of people, had fought for almost four years without showing any sign of giving up or even coming to a compromise.

What everybody had expected to be at best a brief, limited stand, lasting just long enough to make a point, had developed into a whole-hearted war effort. The early reverses and first few megadeaths had not, as the pundits and experts had predicted, shocked the Culture into retiring, horrified at the brutalities of war but proud to have put its collective life where usually only its collective mouth was. Instead it had just kept on retreating and retreating, preparing, gearing up and planning. Horza was convinced the Minds were behind it all.

He could not believe the ordinary people in the Culture really wanted the war, no matter how they had voted. They had their communist Utopia. They were soft and pampered and indulged, and the Contact section's evangelical materialism provided their conscience-salving good works. What more could they want? The war had to be the Minds' idea; it was part of their clinical drive to clean up the galaxy, make it run on nice, efficient lines, without waste, injustice or suffering. The fools in the Culture couldn't see that one day the Minds would start thinking how wasteful and inefficient the humans in the Culture themselves were.

Horza used the suit's internal gyros to steer himself, letting him look at every part of the sky, wondering where, in that light-flecked emptiness, battles raged and billions died, where the Culture still held and the Idiran battle fleets pressed. The suit hummed and clicked and hissed very quietly around him: precise, obedient, reassuring.

Suddenly it jolted, steadying him without warning and jarring his teeth. A noise uncomfortably like a collision alarm trilled violently in one ear, and out of the corner of his eye Horza could see a microscreen set inside the helmet near his left cheek light up with a holo red graph display.

'Target/acquisition/radar,' the suit said. 'Incoming/increasing.'

3.

Clear Air Turbulence

'What!' roared Horza.

'Target/acqui—' the suit began again.

'Oh shut up!' Horza shouted, and started punching buttons on the suit's wrist console, twisting this way and that, scanning the darkness around him. There ought to have been a way of getting a head-up display on the inside of the helmet visor to show him what direction the signals were coming from, but he hadn't enough time to familiarise himself completely with the suit, and he couldn't find the right button. Then he realised he could probably just ask. 'Suit! Give me a head-up on the transmission source!'

The top left edge of the visor flashed. He turned and tipped until a winking red dot positioned itself on the transparent surface. He hit the wrist buttons again, and the suit hissed as it evacuated gas from its sole-nozzles, sending him shooting away under about one gravity. Nothing appeared to change apart from his weight, but the red light went out briefly, then came back on. He swore. The suit said:

'Target/acquisition—'

'I *know*,' Horza told it. He unslung the plasma pistol from his arm and readied the suit lasers. He cut the gas jets, too. Whatever it was coming after him, he doubted he'd be able to outrun it. He became weightless again. The small red light continued to flash on the visor. He watched the internal screens. The transmission source was closing on a curved course at about point zero-one lights, in real space. The radar was low frequency and not particularly powerful – all too low-tech to be either the Culture or the Idirans. He told the suit to cancel the head-up, brought the magnifiers down from the top of the visor and switched them on, aiming at where the radar source had been coming from. A doppler shift in the signal, still displayed on one of the helmet's small internal screens, announced that whatever was producing the transmission was slowing down. Was he going to be picked up rather than blown apart?

Something glinted hazily in the magnifiers' field. The radar switched off. It was very close now. He felt his mouth go dry, and his hands shook inside the heavy gloves of the suit. The image in the magnifiers seemed to explode with darkness, then he swept them back to the top of the helmet and looked out into the starfields and the inky night. Something tore across his vision, pure black, racing across the backdrop of sky in utter silence. He jabbed at the button which switched on the suit's needle radar and tried to follow the shape as it passed him, occluding stars; but he missed, so there was no way of telling how close it had come, or how big it was. He had lost track of it in the spaces between the stars when the darkness ahead of him flared. He guessed it was turning. Sure enough, back came the radar pulse.

'Ta—'

'Quiet,' Horza said, checking the plasma gun. The dark shape expanded, almost directly ahead. The stars around it wobbled and brightened in the lens effect of an imperfectly adjusted warp motor in cancel mode. Horza watched the shape come closer. The radar switched off again. He switched his own back on, the needle beam scanning the craft ahead. He was looking at the resulting image on an internal screen when it flickered and went out, the suit's hissings and hummings stopped, and the stars started to fade away.

'Sapping/effector/fi . . . re . . .' said the suit, as it and Horza went limp and unconscious.

There was something hard under him. His head hurt. He couldn't remember where he was or what he was supposed to be doing. He only just remembered his name. Bora Horza Gobuchul, Changer from the asteroid Heibohre, lately employed by the Idirans in their holy war against the Culture. How did that connect with the pain in his skull though, and the hard, cold metal under his cheek?

He had been hit hard. While he still couldn't see or hear or smell anything, he knew something severe had occurred, something almost fatal. He tried to remember what had happened. Where had he been last? What had he been doing?

The Hand of God 137! His heart leapt as he remembered. He had to get off! Where was his helmet? Why had Xoralundra deserted him? Where was that stupid medjel with his helmet? *Help!*

He found he couldn't move.

Anyway, it wasn't *The Hand of God 137*, or any Idiran ship. The deck was hard and cold, if it was a deck, and the air smelled wrong. He could hear people talking now, too. But still no sight. He didn't know if his eyes were open and he was blind, or if they were shut and he couldn't open them. He tried to bring his hands up to his face to find out, but nothing would move.

The voices were human. There were several. They were speaking the Culture's language, Marain, but that didn't mean much; it had grown increasingly common as a second language in the galaxy over the last few millennia. Horza could speak and understand it, though he hadn't used it since . . . since he had talked to Balveda, in fact, but before that not for a long time. Poor Balveda. But these people were chattering, and he couldn't make out the individual words. He tried to move his eyelids, and eventually felt something. He still couldn't think where he might be.

All this darkness . . . Then he remembered something about being in a suit, and a voice talking to him about targets or something. With a shock he realised he had been captured, or rescued. He forgot about trying to open his eyes and concentrated hard on understanding what the people near by were saying. He had used Marain just recently; he could do it. He had to. He had to know.

'. . . goddamn system for two weeks and all we get is some old guy in a suit.' That was one voice. Female, he thought.

'What the hell did you expect, a Culture starship?' Male.

'Well, shit, a *bit* of one.' The female voice again. Some laughter.

'It's a good suit. Riarch, by the look of it. Think I'll have it.' Another male voice. Tone of command; no mistaking it.

'. . .' No good. Too quiet.

'They adjust, idiot.' The Man again.

'. . . bits of Idiran and Culture ships would be floating all over the place and we could . . . that bow laser . . . and it's still fucked.' Woman, different one.

'Our effector won't have damaged it, will it?' Another male; young sounding, cutting across what the woman had said.

'It was on suck, not blow,' the captain said, or whatever he was. Who *were* these people?

'. . . of a lot less than grandad over there,' said one of the men. Him! They were talking about him! He tried not to show any sign of life. He only now realised that of course he was *out* of the suit, lying a few metres away from people probably standing around it, some with their backs to him. He was lying with one arm underneath his body, on his side, naked, facing them. His head still hurt and he could feel saliva dribbling from his half-open mouth.

'. . . weapon of some sort with them. Can't see it, though,' said the

41

Man, and his voice altered, as though he was changing position as he spoke. Sounded like they had lost the plasma gun. They were mercenaries. Had to be. Privateers.

'Can I have your old suit, Kraiklyn?' Young male.

'Well, that's that,' the Man said, his voice sounding as though he was getting up from a squatting position, or turning round. It seemed he had ignored the previous speaker. 'A bit of a disappointment maybe, but we did get this suit. Better get out now before the big boys show.'

'What now?' One of the females again. Horza liked her voice. He wished he could get his eyes open.

'That temple. Should be easy meat, even without the bow laser. Only about ten days from here. We'll do a little bit more funding-up on some of their altar treasures and then buy some heavy weaponry on Vavatch. We can all spend our ill-gotten gains there.' The Man – Krakeline or whatever his name was – paused. He laughed. 'Doro, don't look so frightened. This'll be simple. You'll be thankful I heard about this place, once we're rich. The goddamn priests don't even carry weapons. It'll be easy—'

'Easy out. Yeah, we know.' A woman's voice; the nice one. Horza was aware of light now. Pink in front of his eyes. His head was still sore but he was coming to. He checked out his body, consciously calling on the feedback nerves to gauge his own physical readiness. Below normal, and it wouldn't be perfect until the last effects of his geriatric appearance had faded away, in a few days – if he lived that long. He suspected they thought he was already dead.

'Zallin,' the Man said, 'dump that weed.'

Horza opened his eyes with a start as footsteps approached. The Man had been talking about *him*!

'Aah!' somebody cried nearby. 'He's not dead. His eyes are moving!' The footsteps suddenly halted. Horza sat up shakily, narrowing his eyes in the glare. He was breathing hard and his head swam as he raised it. His eyes focused.

He was in a brightly lit but small hangar. An old, weather-beaten shuttle craft filled about half of it. He was sitting almost against one bulkhead; near the other stood the people who had been talking. Halfway between him and the group stood a large, ungainly youth with very long arms and silver hair. As Horza had guessed, the suit he had been wearing lay prone on the floor at the feet of the group of humans. He swallowed and blinked. The youth with the silver hair stared at him and scratched nervously at one ear. He wore a pair of shorts and a frayed T-shirt. He jumped when one of the taller men in the group, in the voice Horza had decided was that of the captain, said, 'Wubslin,' (he turned to one of the other men) 'isn't that effector working properly?'

Don't let them talk about you as though you aren't here! He cleared his throat and spoke as loudly and as determinedly as he could. 'There's nothing wrong with your effector.'

'Then,' the tall man said, smiling thinly and arching one eyebrow, 'you should be dead.'

They were all looking at him, most with suspicion. The youth near him was still scratching his ear; he appeared puzzled, even frightened, but the rest just looked as though they wanted rid of him as quickly as possible. They were all humans, or close to; male and female; mostly dressed in either suits or bits of suits, or T-shirts and shorts. The captain, now moving through the group, closer to Horza, looked tall and muscular. He had a mass of dark hair combed back from his brow, a sallow complexion and something feral about his eyes and mouth. The voice suited him. As he came closer Horza saw that he was holding a laser pistol. The suit he wore was black, and its heavy boots rang on the naked metal deck. He advanced until he was level with the young man with the silver hair, who was fiddling with the hem of his T-shirt and biting his lip.

'Why aren't you dead?' the Man asked Horza quietly.

'Because I'm a lot fucking tougher than I look,' Horza said. The Man smiled and nodded.

'You must be.' He turned round and looked briefly back at the suit. 'What were you doing way out here in that?'

'I used to work for the Idirans. They didn't want the Culture ship to catch me, and they thought they might be able to rescue me later, so they threw me overboard to wait for the fleet. It'll be here in about eight or nine hours, by the way, so I wouldn't hang around.'

'Will it, now?' the captain said quietly, raising his eyebrow again. 'You seem very well informed, old man.'

'I'm not that old. This was a disguise for my last job – an agatic drug. It's wearing off. A couple of days and I'll be useful again.'

The Man shook his head sadly. 'No you won't.' He turned and started back towards the other people. 'Dump him,' he told the youth in the T-shirt. The youth started forward.

'Now wait a goddamned minute!' Horza shouted, scrambling to his feet. He backed against the wall, hands out, but the youth was coming straight at him. The others were looking either at him or at their captain. Horza swung forward and up with one leg, too fast for the young man with the silver hair. He caught him in the groin with his foot. The youth gasped and fell to the deck, clutching at himself. The Man had turned. He looked down at the youth, then at Horza.

'Yes?' he said. Horza got the impression he was enjoying it all. Horza pointed to the now kneeling youth.

'I told you – I can be useful. I'm pretty good in a fight. You can have the suit—'

'I've *got* the suit,' the captain said drily.

'So at least give me a chance.' Horza looked around them. 'You're mercenaries or something, right?' Nobody said anything. He could feel himself starting to sweat; he stopped it. 'Let me join. All I'm asking for's a chance. If I louse up first time, dump me then.'

'Why not dump you now and save the hassle?' The captain laughed, spreading his arms wide. Some of the others laughed too.

'A *chance*,' Horza repeated. 'Shit, it isn't much to ask.'

'I'm sorry.' The Man shook his head. 'We're overcrowded already.'

The silver-haired youth was looking up at Horza, his face twisted with pain and hate. The people in the group were smirking at Horza or talking quietly to each other and nodding at him, grinning. He was suddenly aware that he looked like just a skinny old man in the nude.

'Fuck it!' he spat, glaring right at the Man. 'Give me five days and I'll take *you* on anytime.'

The captain's eyebrows went up. For a second he might have looked angry, then he burst out laughing. He waved the laser at Horza. 'All right, old man. I'll tell you what we'll do.' He put his hands on his waist and nodded at the youth still kneeling on the deck. 'You can fight Zallin here. You feel up to a rumble, Zallin?'

'I'll kill him,' Zallin said, looking straight at Horza's throat. The Man laughed. Some of his black hair spilled out of the back lip of his suit.

'That's the idea.' He looked at Horza. 'I told you we're already overcrowded. You'll have to produce a vacancy.' He turned round to the others. 'Clear a space. And somebody get this old guy some shorts; he's putting me off my food.'

One of the women threw Horza a pair of shorts. He put them on. The suit had been lifted from the deck, and the shuttle rolled a couple of metres sideways until it clanged against the hull on the far side of the hangar. Zallin had finally risen from the deck and gone back to the others. Somebody sprayed anaesthetic on his genitals. *Thank goodness for non-retractables*, Horza thought. He was resting against the bulk-head, watching the group of people. Zallin was taller than any of them. His arms seemed to reach to his knees and they were as thick as Horza's thighs.

Horza saw the captain nod towards him, and one of the women walked over. She had a small, hard-looking face. Her skin was dark, and she had spiky fair hair. Her whole body looked slim and hard; she walked, Horza thought, like a man. As she got closer Horza saw she was lightly furred on her face, legs and arms, which the long shirt she wore revealed. She stopped in front of him and looked at him, from his feet to his eyes.

'I'm your second,' she said, 'whatever good that's supposed to do you.'

She was the one with the nice voice. Horza was disappointed, even through his fear. He waved one hand. 'My name's Horza. Thanks for asking.' *Idiot!* he told himself. *Tell them your real name, that's it. Why not tell them you're a Changer as well? Fool.*

'Yalson,' the woman said abruptly, and stuck her hand out. Horza wasn't sure if the word was a greeting or her name. He was angry with himself. As though he didn't have enough problems, he'd tricked himself into giving his real name. Probably it wouldn't matter, but he knew too well that it was the small slips, the seemingly inconsequential mistakes, that often made the difference between success and failure, even life and death. He reached out and clasped the woman's hand when he realised that was what he was supposed to do. Her hand was dry and cool, and strong. She squeezed his. She let go before he had time to squeeze back. He had no idea where she came from, so he didn't read too much into it. Where he came from that would have been a fairly specific sort of invitation.

'Horza, eh?' She nodded and put her hands on her hips in the same way as the captain had done. 'Well, good luck, Horza. I believe Kraiklyn thinks Zallin's the most expendable member of the crew, so he probably won't mind if you win.' She looked down at his slack-skinned paunch and rib-skinny chest, and her brow furrowed. '*If* you win,' she repeated.

'Thanks a lot,' Horza said, trying to suck in his belly and push out his chest. He gestured over to the others. 'They taking bets over there?' He tried to grin.

'Only on how long you'll last.'

Horza let the attempt at a grin fade. He looked away from the woman and said, 'You know, I could probably get this depressed even without your help. Don't let me stop you if you want to go and put some money down.' He looked back at the woman's face. He could see no compassion or even sympathy in it. She looked him up and down again, then nodded, turned on her heel and went back to the others. Horza swore.

'Right!' Kraiklyn clapped his gloved hands together. The group of people split up and moved around the sides of the hangar, lining two of them. Zallin was standing glaring at Horza from the far end of the cleared space. Horza pushed himself away from the bulkhead and shook himself, trying to loosen up and get ready.

'So, it's to the death, both of you,' Kraiklyn announced, smiling. 'No weapons, but I don't see any referees, so . . . anything goes. OK – begin.'

Horza made a little more room between himself and the bulkhead. Zallin was coming towards him, crouched, arms out like a pair of oversized mandibles on some enormous insect. Horza knew that if he used all his built-in weapons (and if he had them all; he had to keep reminding himself they'd taken out his venom-teeth on Sorpen), he could probably win without too much trouble, unless Zallin landed a lucky blow. But he was equally sure that if he did use the only effective weapon he had left – the poison glands under his fingernails – the others would guess what he was and he'd be dead anyway. He might have got away with using his teeth somehow and biting Zallin. The poison affected the central nervous system, and Zallin would have slowed down gradually; probably nobody would guess. But scratching him would be fatal for both of them. The poison contained in the sacs under Horza's nails paralysed muscles sequentially from the point of entry, and it would be obvious Zallin had been scratched by something other than ordinary nails. Even if the other mercenaries didn't regard this as cheating, there would be a good chance the Man, Kraiklyn, would guess Horza was a Changer, and have him killed.

A Changer was a threat to anybody who ruled by force, either of will or of arms. Amahain-Frolk had known that, and so would Kraiklyn. There was also a degree of human-basic revulsion reserved for Horza's species. Not only were they much altered from their original genetic stock, they were a threat to identity, a challenge to the individualism even of those they were never likely to impersonate. It had nothing to do with souls or physical or spiritual possession; it was, as the Idirans well understood, the behaviouristic copying of another which revolted. Individuality, the thing which most humans held more precious than anything else about themselves, was somehow

46

cheapened by the ease with which a Changer could ignore it as a limitation and use it as a disguise.

He had Changed into an old man, and that legacy still lay with him. Zallin was getting very close.

The youth lunged, using his huge arms like pincers and making an ungainly grab for Horza. Horza ducked and jumped to one side, faster than Zallin had anticipated. Before he could follow Horza round, the Changer had landed a kick on the youth's shoulder which had been aimed at his head. Zallin swore. So did Horza. He'd hurt his foot.

Rubbing his shoulder, the youth came forward again, almost casually at first, then suddenly swinging one long arm out, hand fisted, and very nearly catching Horza's face. The Changer felt the wind of the scything swing on his cheek. If the blow had landed, it would have finished the fight. Horza dummied one way, then leapt in the other direction, pivoting on one heel and lashing out again with a foot aimed between the youth's legs. It landed, but Zallin just smiled painfully and grabbed at Horza again. The spray must have deadened all feeling.

Horza circled the youth. Zallin was staring at him with a look of intense concentration on his face. His arms were still bowed out in front of him like pincers, and at their ends his fingers flexed every now and again, as though desperate for the feel of Horza's throat. Horza was hardly aware of the people standing around him, or the lights and fittings of the hanger. All he could see was the crouched, ready young man in front of him, with his massive arms and silvery hair, his frayed T-shirt and light shoes. The shoes squeaked on the metal deck as Zallin lunged again. Horza spun and flicked out with his right foot. It caught Zallin across his right ear, and the youth pranced away, rubbing his ear.

Horza knew he was breathing hard again. He was using up too much energy just staying at maximum tension, ready for the next attack, and in the meantime he just wasn't hurting Zallin enough. At this rate the youth would soon wear him down, even without coming at him. Zallin spread his arms again and advanced. Horza skipped to one side, his old muscles complaining. Zallin swivelled. Horza leapt forward, pivoting again on one foot and swinging the other heel at the youth's midriff. It connected with a satisfying thump, and Horza started to jump away, then realised his foot was caught. Zallin was holding it. Horza fell to the deck.

Zallin was swaying, one hand down at the base of his ribcage. He was gasping, almost doubled up, and staggering – Horza suspected he'd cracked a rib – but he held Horza's foot with the other hand. Twist and pull as he might, Horza couldn't loosen the grip.

He tried a sweat-pulse in his lower right leg. He hadn't done that since single-combat exercise in the Academy in Heibohre, but it was worth a try; anything was, if it had a chance of loosening that grip. It didn't work. Perhaps he had forgotten how to do it properly, or perhaps his artificially aged sweat glands were incapable of reacting that fast, but either way he was still trapped in the youth's grip. Zallin was recovering now from the blow Horza had landed. He shook his head, the hangar lights reflecting on his hair; then he took hold of Horza's foot with his other hand.

Horza was walking on his hands round the youth, one leg gripped, the other hanging down, trying to take some weight on the deck. Zallin stared at the Changer and whipped his hands round, as though trying to twist Horza's foot right off. Horza read the motion and was throwing his whole body round even as Zallin started the manoeuvre; he ended up back where he'd started, his foot held in Zallin's hands and his own palms crabbing across the deck as he tried to follow the movements of the youth. *I could go for his legs; sweep in and bite*, Horza thought, desperately trying to think of something. *The instant he starts to slow down I'd have a chance. They wouldn't notice. All I need is—* Then, of course, he remembered again. They had taken those teeth out. Those old bastards – and Balveda – were going to kill him after all, in Balveda's case from beyond the grave. As long as Zallin had his foot like this, the fight was only going to go one way.

What the hell, I'll bite him anyway. He surprised himself with the thought; it was conceived and acted upon before he had time really to consider it. The next thing he knew he had pulled on the leg which Zallin held and pushed as hard as he could with his hands, flinging himself between the youth's legs. He fastened his remaining teeth into the boy's right calf.

'AAH!' Zallin screamed. Horza bit harder, feeling the grip round his foot slacken slightly. He jerked his head up, trying to tear the youth's flesh. He felt as though his kneecap was going to explode and his leg would break, but he worried the mouthful of living flesh and punched up towards Zallin's body with all his might. Zallin let go.

Horza stopped biting instantly and threw himself away as the youth's hands came slamming down towards his head. Horza got to his feet; his ankle and knee were sore, but not seriously injured. Zallin was limping as he came forward, blood pouring from his calf. Horza changed tactics and pounced forward, striking the youth square in the

48

belly, beneath the rudimentary guard of his huge arms. Zallin put his hands to his stomach and lower ribcage and crouched reflexively. As Horza went past he turned and brought both hands down on Zallin's neck.

Normally the blow would have killed, but Zallin was strong and Horza was still weak. As the Changer steadied and turned he had to avoid colliding with some of the mercenaries lining the bulkhead; the fight had traversed the hangar, from one end to the other. Before Horza could get in another blow, Zallin was upright again, his face contorted with frustrated aggression. He screamed and rushed at Horza, who sidestepped neatly. But Zallin stumbled in his headlong rush, and by pure luck his head thumped into Horza's stomach.

The blow was all the more painful and demoralising for being unexpected. Horza fell and rolled, trying to send Zallin straight over the top, but the youth fell on him, pinning him to the deck. Horza wriggled, but nothing happened. He was trapped.

Zallin raised himself up on one palm and drew the other hand up behind him into a fist as he leered at the face of the man beneath him. Horza realised suddenly that there was nothing he could do. He watched that massive fist go up and back, his own body flattened, his arms pinned, and knew it was over. He'd lost. He got ready to move his head as fast as possible, out of the way of the bone-splintering punch he could see would be unleashed at any moment, and tried again to move his legs, but knew it was hopeless. He wanted to close his eyes, but knew he had to keep them open. *Maybe the Man will take pity. He must have seen I fought well. I was just unlucky. Maybe he'll stop it* . . .

Zallin's fist paused, like a guillotine blade raised to its highest point, just before release.

The blow never fell. As Zallin tensed, his other hand, taking the weight of his upper body on the deck, skidded; it went shooting out from under him as it slipped on some of the youth's own blood. Zallin grunted in surprise. As he fell towards Horza his body shifted, and the Changer could feel the weight pinning him lessen. He heaved himself out from underneath Zallin as the youth rolled. Horza rolled in the other direction, almost into the legs of the mercenaries who stood watching. Zallin's head hit the deck – not hard, but before the youth could react Horza threw himself onto Zallin's back, locking his hands round his neck and bringing the youth's silver-haired head back. He slid his legs down either side of Zallin's body, straddling him, and held him there.

Zallin went still, a gurgling noise coming from his throat where Horza's hands held him. He was more than strong enough to throw the Changer off, to roll on his back and crush him; but before he could have done anything, one flick of Horza's hands would have broken his neck.

Zallin was looking up at Kraiklyn, who stood almost right in front of him. Horza, too, lathered in sweat and gulping air, looked up into the dark, deep-set eyes of the Man. Zallin wriggled a little, then went motionless again when Horza tensed his forearms.

They were all looking at him – all the mercenaries, all the pirates or privateers or whatever they wanted to call themselves. They stood round the two walls of the hangar and they looked at Horza. But only Kraiklyn was looking into Horza's eyes.

'This doesn't have to be to the death,' Horza panted. He looked for a moment at the silver hairs in front of him, some of them plastered with sweat to the boy's scalp. He looked up at Kraiklyn again. 'I won. You can let the kid off next place you stop. Or let me off. I don't want to kill him.'

Something warm and sticky seemed to be seeping from the deck along his right leg. He realised it was Zallin's blood from the wound on his leg. Kraiklyn had a strangely distant look on his face. The laser gun, which he had holstered, was lifted easily back out of its holster into his left hand and pointed at the centre of Horza's forehead. In the silence of the hangar, Horza heard it click and hum as it was switched on, about a metre away from his skull.

'Then you'll die,' Kraiklyn told him, in a flat, even voice. 'I've no place on this ship for somebody who hasn't the taste for a little murder now and again.'

Horza looked into Kraiklyn's eyes, over the motionless barrel of the laser pistol. Zallin moaned.

The snap echoed round the metal spaces of the hangar like a gunshot. Horza opened his arms without taking his eyes off the mercenary chief's face. Zallin's limp body tumbled slackly to the deck and crumpled under its own weight. Kraiklyn smiled and put the gun back in its holster. It clicked off with a fading whine.

'Welcome aboard the *Clear Air Turbulence*.' Kraiklyn sighed and stepped over Zallin's body. He walked to the middle of one bulkhead, opened a door and went out, his boots clattering on some steps. Most of the others followed him.

'Well done.' Horza, still kneeling, turned at the words. It was the woman with the nice voice again, Yalson. She offered him her hand

50

once more, this time to help him up. He took it gratefully and got to his feet.

'I didn't enjoy it,' he told her. He wiped some sweat from his brow with his forearm and looked into the woman's eyes. 'You said your name was Yalson, right?'

She nodded. 'And you're Horza.'

'Hello, Yalson.'

'Hello, Horza.' She smiled a little. Horza liked her smile. He looked at the corpse on the deck. Blood had stopped flowing from the wound in one leg.

'What about that poor bastard?' he asked.

'Might as well dump him,' Yalson said. She looked over at the only other people left in the hangar, three thickly furred and identical heavy-set males in shorts. They stood in a group near the door the others had left by, looking at him curiously. All three had heavy boots on, as though they had just started to suit up and had been interrupted at the same moment. Horza wanted to laugh. Instead he smiled and waved.

'Hello.'

'Ah, those are the Bratsilakins,' Yalson said, as the three furry bodies waved dark grey hands at him, not quite in synch. 'One, Two and Three,' she continued, nodding at each one in turn. 'We must be the only Free Company with a clone group that's paranoid.'

Horza looked at her to see if she was serious, just as the three furry humans came over to him.

'Don't listen to a word she says,' one of them said, in a soft voice Horza found surprising. 'She's never liked us. We just hope that you're on *our* side.' Six eyes looked anxiously at Horza. He did his best to smile.

'You can depend on it,' he told them. They smiled back and looked from one to another, nodding.

'Let's get Zallin into a vactube. Probably dump him later,' Yalson said to the other three. She went over to the body. Two of the Bratsilakins followed her, and between the three of them they got the limp corpse to an area of the hangar deck where they lifted some metal planks up, opened a curved hatch, stuffed Zallin's body into a narrow space, then closed both hatch and deck again. The third Bratsilakin took a cloth from a wall panel and mopped up the blood on the deck. Then the hairy clone group headed for the door and the stairs. Yalson came up to Horza. She made a sideways gesture with her head. 'Come on. I'll show you where you can clean up.'

He followed her over the hangar deck towards the doorway. She turned round as they went. 'The rest have gone to eat. I'll see you in the mess if you're ready in time. Just follow your nose. Anyway, I have to collect my winnings.'

'Your winnings?' Horza said as they got to the doorway, where Yalson put her hand on what Horza assumed were lighting switches. She turned to him, looking into his eyes.

'Sure,' she said, and pressed one of the switches covered by her hand. The lights didn't change, but under his feet Horza could feel a vibration. He heard a hiss and what sounded like a pump running. 'I bet on you,' Yalson said, then turned and bounded up the steps beyond the door, two at a time.

Horza looked round at the hangar once and then followed her.

Just before the *Clear Air Turbulence* went back into warp and its crew sat down at table, the ship expelled the limp corpse of Zallin. Where it had found a live man in a suit, it left a dead youth in shorts and a tattered shirt, tumbling and freezing while a thin shell of air molecules expanded around the body, like an image of departing life.

4.

Temple of Light

The *Clear Air Turbulence* swung through the shadow of a moon, past a barren, cratered surface – its track dimpling as it skirted the top edge of a gravity well – and then down towards a cloudy, blue-green planet. Almost as soon as it passed the moon its course started to curve, gradually pointing the craft's nose away from the planet and back into space. Halfway through that curve the *CAT* released its shuttle, slinging it towards one hazy horizon of the globe, at the trailing edge of the darkness which swept over the planet surface like a black cloak.

Horza sat in the shuttle with most of the rest of the *CAT*'s motley crew. They were suited up, sitting on narrow benches in the cramped shuttle's passenger compartment in a variety of spacesuits; even the three Bratsilakins had slightly different models on. The only really modern example was the one Kraiklyn wore, the Rairch suit he had taken from Horza.

They were all armed, and their weapons were as various as their suits. Mostly they were lasers, or to be more exact what the Culture called CREWS – Coherent Radiation Emission Weapon Systems. The better ones operated on wavelengths invisible to the human eye. Some people had plasma cannons or heavy pistols, and one had an efficient-looking Microhowitzer, but only Horza had a projective rifle, and an old, crude, slow-firing one at that. He checked it over for the tenth or eleventh time and cursed it. He cursed the leaky old suit he'd been given, too; the visor was starting to mist up. This whole thing was hopeless.

The shuttle started to lurch and vibrate as it hit the atmosphere of the planet Marjoin, where they were going to attack and rob something called the Temple of Light.

It had taken the *Clear Air Turbulence* fifteen days to crawl across the twenty-one or so standard light-years that lay between the Sorpen system and that of Marjoin. Kraiklyn boasted that his ship could hit nearly twelve hundred lights, but that sort of speed, he said, was for emergencies only. Horza had taken a look at the old craft and doubted it would even get into four figures without its outboard warping engines pancaking the ship and everything in it all over the skies.

The *Clear Air Turbulence* was a venerable Hronish armoured-assault ship from one of the declining, later dynasties, and was built more for ruggedness and reliability than for performance and sophistication. Given the level of technical expertise possessed by its crew, Horza thought this was just as well. The ship was about a hundred metres long, twenty across the beam and fifteen high, plus – on top of the rear hull – a ten-metre-high tail. On either side of the hull the warp units bulged, like small versions of the hull itself, and connected to it by stubby wings in the middle and thin flying pylons swept back from just behind the craft's nose. The *CAT* was streamlined, and fitted with sprinter fusion motors in the tail, as well as a small lift engine in the nose, for working in atmospheres and gravity wells. Horza thought its accommodation left a lot to be desired.

He had been given Zallin's old bunk, sharing a two-metre cube – euphemistically termed a cabin – with Wubslin, who was the mechanic on the ship. He called himself the engineer; but after a few minutes' talk trying to pump him for technical stuff on the *CAT*, Horza realised that the thickset white-skinned man knew little about the craft's more complex systems. He wasn't unpleasant, didn't smell, and slept silently most of the time, so Horza supposed things could have been worse.

There were eighteen people on the ship, in nine cabins. The Man, of course, had one to himself, and the Bratsilakins shared one rather pungent one; they liked to leave the door to it open; everybody else liked to close the door as they went past. Horza was disappointed to find that there were only four women aboard. Two of them hardly ever showed themselves outside their cabin and communicated with the others mostly by signs and gestures. The third was a religious fanatic who, when not trying to convert him to something called the Circle of Flame, spent her time wired up in the cabin she shared with Yalson, spooling fantasy head-tapes. Yalson seemed to be the only normal female on board, but Horza found it difficult to think of her as a woman at all. It was she, however, who took on the job of introducing him to the others and telling him the things about the ship and its crew which he would need to know.

He had cleaned up in one of the ship's coffin-like wash-points, then followed his nose as Yalson had suggested to the mess, where he was more or less ignored, but some food was shoved in his direction. Kraiklyn looked at him once as he sat down, between Wubslin and a Bratsilakin, then didn't look at him again and continued talking about weapons and armour and tactics. After the meal Wubslin had shown Horza to their cabin, then left. Horza cleared a space on Zallin's bunk, hauled some torn sheets over his tired, aching, old-looking frame, and fell into a deep sleep.

When he woke he bundled up Zallin's few possessions. It was pathetic; the dead youth had a few T-shirts, shorts, a couple of little kilts, a rusty sword, a collection of cheap daggers in frayed sheaths and some large plastic micropage books with moving pictures, repeating and repeating scenes from ancient wars for as long as they were held open. That was about all. Horza kept the youth's leaky suit, though it was far too big and non-adjustable, and the badly maintained and ancient projectile rifle.

He carried the rest, wrapped in one of the more tatty bed sheets, down to the hangar. It was as it had been when he'd left it. Nobody had bothered to roll the shuttle back. Yalson was there, stripped to the waist, exercising. Horza stood in the doorway at the bottom of the steps, watching the woman work out. She spun and leapt, did backflips and somersaults, kicked her feet out and jabbed punches at the air, making small grunting noises with each sharp movement. She stopped when she saw Horza.

'Welcome back.' She stooped and picked up a towel from the deck, then started to rub it over her chest and arms, where sweat glistened in the golden down. 'Thought you'd croaked.'

'Have I been asleep long?' Horza asked. He didn't know what sort of time system they used on the ship.

'Two days standard.' Yalson towelled her spiky hair and draped the damp towel over her lightly furred shoulders. 'You look better for it, though.'

'I feel better,' Horza said. He hadn't had a look in a mirror or a reverser yet, but knew that his body was starting to come back to normal, losing the geriatric look.

'That Zallin's stuff?' Yalson nodded at the package in his hands. 'Yes.'

'I'll show you how to work the vactubes. We'll probably sling it when we next come out of warp.'

Yalson opened the deck and the tube hatch beneath, then Horza dropped Zallin's gear into the cylinder and Yalson closed it again. The

Changer liked the way Yalson smelled when he caught the scent of her warm, perspiring body, but somehow there was nothing in her attitude towards him to make him think they would ever become more than friends. He'd settle for a friend on this ship, though. He certainly needed one.

They went to the mess after that, to have something to eat. Horza was ravenous; his body demanded food to rebuild itself and put more bulk onto the thin shape it had assumed to impersonate the Gerontocracy of Sorpen's outworld minister.

At least, thought Horza, the autogalley works all right and the AG field seems smooth. The idea of cramped cabins, rotten food and a lumpy or erratic gravity field filled the Changer with horror.

'. . . Zallin didn't have any real friends,' Yalson said, shaking her head as she stuffed some food into her mouth. They were sitting in the mess together. Horza wanted to know if there was anybody on the ship who might want to avenge the youth he had killed.

'Poor bastard,' Horza said again. He put his spoon down and stared across the cluttered space of the low-ceilinged mess room for a second, feeling again that quick, decisive bone-snap through his hands, seeing in his mind's eye the spinal column sever, windpipe crumple, arteries compress – turning off the youth's life as though rotating a switch. He shook his head. 'Where did he come from?'

'Who knows?' Yalson shrugged. She saw the expression on Horza's face and added, between chews, 'Look, he'd have killed you. He's dead. Forget about him. Sure it's tough, but . . . anyway, he was pretty boring.' She ate some more.

'I just wondered if there was anybody I ought to send anything to. Friends or relations or—'

'Look, Horza,' Yalson said, turning to him, 'when you come on board this ship you don't have a past. It's considered very bad manners to ask anybody where they came from or what they've done in their lives before they joined. Maybe we've all got some secrets, or we just don't want to talk or think about some of the things we've done, or some of the things we've had done to us. But either way, don't try to find out. Between your ears is the only place on this crate you'll ever get any privacy, so make the most of it. If you live long enough, maybe somebody will want to tell you all about themselves – eventually, probably when they're drunk . . . but by that time you may not want them to. Whatever; my advice is just to leave it for the moment.'

Horza opened his mouth to say something, but Yalson went on, 'I'll tell you all I know now, just to save you asking.' She put her spoon down and wiped her lips with one finger, then turned in her seat to face him. She held up one hand. The tiny hairs of the light fur on her forearms and the back of her hands gave a golden outline to her dark skin. She stretched one finger out. 'One – the ship: Hronish; been around hundreds of years. At least a dozen not very careful owners. Currently without its bow laser since we blew it up trying to alter its wavelength pattern. Two –' She extended another finger. 'Kraiklyn: he's had this craft since any of us have known him. He says he won it in a game of Damage somewhere, just before the war. I know he plays the game but I don't know how good he is. Anyway, that's his business. Officially we're called the KFC, Kraiklyn's Free Company, and he's the boss. He's a pretty good leader and he isn't afraid to slug it out with the rest of the troops when it comes to the crunch. He leads from the front, and that makes him OK in my book. His gimmick is he never sleeps. He has a . . . ah . . .' Yalson frowned, obviously looking for the right words. '. . . an enhanced hemispherical task-division in his brain. One third of the time one half sleeps and he's a bit dreamy and vague; the other third of the time the other half sleeps and he's all logic and numbers and he doesn't communicate too well. The other third of the time, like when he's in action or whenever there's an emergency, both sides are awake and functioning. Makes it pretty hard to sneak up on him in his bunk.'

'Paranoid clones and a Man with a shift system in his skull,' Horza shook his head. 'OK. Go on.'

'Three –' Yalson said, 'we're not mercenaries. We're a Free Company. Actually we're just pirates, but if that's what Kraiklyn wants to call us, that's what we are. In theory anybody can join so long as they eat the food and breathe the air, but in practice he's a bit more selective than that, and he'd like to be even more so, I'll bet. Anyway. We've carried out a few contracts, mostly protection, a couple of escort duties for third-level places who've found themselves caught up in the war, but most of the time we just attack and steal wherever we think the confusion caused by the war makes us likely to get away with it. That's what we're on our way to do at the moment. Kraiklyn heard about this place called the Temple of Light on a just-about-level three planet in this neck of the woods and he reckons it'll be easy in, easy out – to use one of his favourite expressions. According to him it's full of priests and treasure; we shoot the former and grab the latter. Then we head for the Vavatch Orbital before the Culture blows it away and we buy something to replace our bow laser. I guess the prices should be pretty good. If we hang on long enough people will probably be trying to give the stuff away.'

'What's happening to Vavatch?' Horza asked. This wasn't something he'd heard about. He knew the big Orbital was in this part of the war zone, but he'd thought its condominium-style ownership would keep it out of the firing line.

'Didn't your Idiran friends tell you?' Yalson said. She dropped the hand with the outstretched fingers. 'Well,' she said, when Horza just shrugged, 'as you probably *do* know, the Idirans are advancing through the whole inward flank of the Gulf – the Glittercliff. The Culture seems to be putting up a bit of a fight for a change, or at least preparing to. It looked like they were going to come to one of their usual understandings and leave Vavatch as neutral territory. This religious thing the Idirans have about planets means they weren't really interested in the O as long as the Culture didn't try to use it as a base, and they promised they wouldn't. Shit, with these big fucking GSVs they're building these days they don't *need* bases on Os or Rings, or planets or anything else. . . . Well, all the various types and weirdos on Vavatch thought they were going to be just fine, thank you, and probably do very well out of the galactic fire-fight going on around them. . . . Then the Idirans announced they *were* going to take Vavatch over after all, though only nominally; no military presence. The Culture said they weren't having this, both sides refused to abandon their precious principles, and the Culture said, "OK, if you won't back down we're going to blow the place away before you get there." And that's what's happening. Before the Idiran battle fleets arrive the Culture's going to evacuate the whole damn O and then blast it.'

'They're going to *evacuate* an *Orbital*?' Horza said. This really was the first he'd heard of any of this. The Idirans had mentioned nothing about Vavatch Orbital in the briefings they had given him, and even once he was actually impersonating the outworld minister Egratin, most of what had been coming in from outside had been rumour. Any idiot could see that the whole volume around the Sullen Gulf was going to become a battle space hundreds of light-years across, hundreds tall and decades deep at least, but exactly what was going on he hadn't been able to find out. The war was shifting up a gear indeed. Still, only a lunatic would think of trying to move everybody off an Orbital.

Yalson nodded, all the same. 'So they say. Don't ask me where they're going to pull the ships from for that one, but that's what they say they're going to do.'

'They're crazy.' Horza shook his head.

'Yeah, well, I think they proved that when they went to war in the first place.'

'OK. Sorry. Go on,' Horza said, waving one hand.

'I've forgotten what else I was going to say,' Yalson grinned, looking at the three fingers she had extended as though they would give her a clue. She looked at Horza. 'I think that about covers it. I'd advise you to keep your head down and your mouth shut until we get to Marjoin, where this temple is, and still to keep your head down once we get there, come to think of it.' She laughed, and Horza found himself laughing with her. She nodded and picked up her spoon again. 'Assuming you come through OK, people will accept you more once you've been in a fire-fight with them. For now you're the baby on the ship, no matter what you've done in the past, and regardless of Zallin.'

Horza looked at her doubtfully, thinking about attacking anywhere – even an undefended temple – in a second-hand suit with an unreliable projectile rifle. 'Well,' he sighed, spooning more food from his plate, 'so long as you don't all start betting on which way I'll fall again. . . .'

Yalson looked at him for a second, then grinned, and went back to her food.

Kraiklyn proved more inquisitive about Horza's past, despite what Yalson had said. The Man invited Horza to his cabin. It was neat and tidy, with everything stowed and clamped or webbed down, and it smelt fresh. Real books lined one wall, and there was an absorber carpet on the floor. A model of the *CAT* hung from the ceiling, and a big laser rifle was cradled on another wall; it looked powerful, with a large battery pack and a beam-splitter device on the end of the barrel. It gleamed in the soft light of the cabin as though it had been polished.

'Sit down,' Kraiklyn said, motioning Horza to a small seat while he adjusted the single bed to a couch and flopped into it. He reached behind to a shelf and picked up two snifflasks. He offered one to Horza, who took it and broke the seal. The captain of the *Clear Air Turbulence* drew deeply on the fumes from his own bowl, then sipped a little of the misty liquid. Horza did the same. He recognised the substance but couldn't remember the name. It was one of those you could snort and get high on or drink and just be sociable; the active ingredients lasted only a few minutes at body temperature, and anyway were broken up rather than absorbed by most humanoid digestive tracts.

'Thanks,' Horza said.

'Well, you're looking a lot better than when you came on board,' Kraiklyn said, looking at Horza's chest and arms. The Changer had almost resumed his normal shape after four days of rest and heavy eating. His trunk and limbs had filled out to something approaching their fairly muscular usual and his belly had grown no larger. His skin had tautened and taken on a golden-brown sheen, while his face looked both firmer and yet more supple, too. His hair was growing in dark from the roots; he had cut off the yellow-white lankness of the Gerontocrat's sparse locks. His venom-teeth were also regrowing, but they would need another twenty days or so before they could be used.

'I feel better, too.'

'Hmm. Pity about Zallin, but I'm sure you could see my point.'

'Sure. I'm just glad you gave me the chance. Some people would have zapped me and thrown me out.'

'It crossed my mind,' Kraiklyn said, toying with the flask he held, 'but I sensed you weren't totally full of crap. Can't say I believed you about this ageing drug and the Idirans, at the time, but I thought you might make a fight of it. Mind you, you were lucky, right?' He smiled at Horza, who smiled back. Kraiklyn looked up at the books on the far wall. 'Anyway, Zallin was sort of dead weight; know what I mean?' He looked back at Horza. 'Kid hardly knew which end of his rifle to point. I was thinking of dropping him from the team next place we hit.' He took another gulp of the fumes.

'Like I say – thanks.' Horza was deciding that his first impression of Kraiklyn – that the Man was a shit – was more or less correct. If he had been going to drop Zallin anyway there was no reason for the fight to be to the death. Horza could have bunked down in the shuttle or the hangar, or Zallin could have. One more person wouldn't have made the *CAT* any more roomy for the time it took to get to Marjoin, but it wouldn't have been for all that long, and they weren't going to start using up all the air or anything. Kraiklyn had just wanted a show. 'I'm grateful to you,' Horza said, and raised the flask towards the captain briefly before inhaling again. He studied Kraiklyn's face carefully.

'So, tell me what it's like working for these guys with the three legs,' Kraiklyn said, smiling and resting one arm on a shelf at the side of the couch bed. He raised his eyebrows. 'Hmm?'

Ah-hah, thought Horza. He said, 'I didn't have much time to find

62

out. Fifty days ago I was still a captain in the marines on Sladden. Don't suppose you've heard of it?' Kraiklyn shook his head. Horza had been working on his story for the past two days, and knew that if Kraiklyn did check up he would find there was such a planet, its inhabitants were mostly humanoid and it had recently fallen under Idiran suzerainty. 'Well, the Idirans were going to execute us because we fought on after the surrender, but then I was hauled out and told I'd live if I did a job for them. They said I looked a lot like this old guy they wanted on their side; if they removed him, would I pretend to be him? I thought, what the hell. What have I got to lose? So I ended up on this Sorpen place with this ageing drug, impersonating a government minister. I was doing all right, too, until this Culture woman shows, blows my whole bloody act and nearly gets me killed. They were just about to bump me off when this Idiran cruiser came in to snatch her. They rescued me and captured her and they were making their way back to the fleet when they got jumped by a GCU. I got stuffed into that suit and thrown overboard to wait for the fleet.' Horza hoped his story didn't sound too rehearsed. Kraiklyn stared into the flask he held, frowning.

'I've been wondering about that.' He looked at Horza. 'Why should a cruiser go in by itself when the fleet was just behind it?'

Horza shrugged. 'Don't really know, myself. They hardly had time to debrief me before the GCU showed up. I guess they must have wanted that Culture woman pretty badly, and thought if they waited for the fleet to show, the GCU would have spotted it, picked up the woman and made a run for it.'

Kraiklyn nodded, looking thoughtful.

'Hmm. They must have wanted her awful bad. Did you see her?'

'Oh, I saw her all right. Before she dropped me in it, and afterwards.'

'What was she like?' Kraiklyn furrowed his brows and played with the flask again.

'Tall, thin, sort of good looking, but off-putting as well. Too damn smart for my liking. I don't know. . . . Not much different from any Culture woman I've seen. I mean, they all look different and so on, but she wouldn't have stood out.'

'They say they're pretty special, some of these Culture agents. Supposed to be able to . . . do tricks, you know? All sorts of special adaptations and fancy body chemistry. She do anything special you heard of?'

Horza shook his head, wondering where all this was leading. 'Not that I know of,' he said. Fancy body chemistry, Kraiklyn had said. Was the Man starting to guess? Did he think Horza was a Culture agent, or even a Changer? Kraiklyn was still looking at his drug flask. He nodded and said:

'About the only sort of woman I'd have anything to do with, one of these Culture ones. They say they really do have all these . . . alterations, you know?' Kraiklyn looked at Horza and winked as he inhaled the drug. 'Between the legs; the men have these souped-up balls, right? Sort of recirculating . . . And the women have something similar, too; supposed to be able to come for fucking hours. . . . Well, minutes, anyway . . .' Kraiklyn's eyes looked slightly glazed as his voice trailed off. Horza tried not to appear as scornful as he felt. *Here we go again*, he thought. He tried to count the number of times he'd had to listen to people – usually from third- or low fourth-level societies, usually fairly human-basic, and more often than not male – talking in hushed, enviously admiring tones about how It's More Fun in the Culture. Perversely coy for once, the Culture played down the extent to which those born into it inherited such altered genitalia.

Naturally, such modesty only increased everybody else's interest, and Horza occasionally became angry with humans who exhibited the sort of fawning respect the Culture's quasi-technological sexuality so often engendered. Coming from Kraiklyn, it didn't surprise him a bit. He wondered if the Man had had some cheap, Culture-imitative surgery himself. It wasn't uncommon. It wasn't safe, either. Too often such alterations were simply plumbing jobs, especially on males, and made no attempt to uprate the heart and the rest of the circulatory system – at least – to cope with the increased strain. (In the Culture, of course, that high performance was genofixed in.) Such mimicking of this symptom of the Culture's decadence had, quite literally, caused a lot of broken hearts. *I suppose we'll hear about those wonderful drug glands next*, Horza thought.

'. . . Yeah, and they have those drug glands,' Kraiklyn went on, eyes still unfocused, nodding to himself. 'Supposed to be able to take a hit of almost anything, any time they want. Just by thinking about it. Secrete stuff that makes them high.' Kraiklyn stroked the flask he held. 'You know, they say you can't rape a Culture woman?' He didn't seem to expect an answer. Horza stayed silent. Kraiklyn nodded again. 'Yeah, they've got class, those women. Not like some of the shit on this ship.' He shrugged and took another snort from the flask. 'Still . . .'

Horza cleared his throat and leant forward in his seat, not looking at Kraiklyn. 'She's dead now, anyway,' Horza said, looking up.

'Hmm?' Kraiklyn said absently, looking at the Changer.

'The Culture woman,' Horza said. 'She's dead.'

'Oh yes.' Kraiklyn nodded, then cleared his throat and said, 'So what do you want to do now? I'm sort of expecting you to come along on this temple caper. I think you owe us that, for the ride.'

'Oh yeah, don't worry,' Horza said.

'Good. After that, we'll see. If you shape up you can stay; otherwise we'll drop you off somewhere you want, within reason, like they say. This operation should be no problem: easy in, easy out.' Kraiklyn made a dipping, flying motion with his flattened hand, as though it was the model of the *CAT* which hung somewhere over Horza's head. 'Then we go to Vavatch.' He took another gulp from the fumes in the snifflask. 'Don't suppose you play Damage, hmm?' He brought the flask down, and Horza looked into the predatory eyes through the thin mist rising from the flask's neck. He shook his head.

'Not one of my vices. Never really got the chance to learn.'

'Yeah, I guess not. It's the only game.' Kraiklyn nodded. 'Apart from this . . .' He smiled and glanced about, obviously meaning the ship, the people in it and their occupation. 'Well,' Kraiklyn said, smiling and sitting up, 'I think I've already said welcome aboard, but you are welcome.' He leant forward and tapped Horza on the shoulder. 'So long as you realise who's boss, eh?' He smiled widely.

'It's your ship,' Horza said. He drank what remained of the flask's contents and put it on a shelf beside a portrait holocube which showed Kraiklyn standing in his black suit, holding the same laser rifle which was mounted on the wall above.

'I think we'll get on just fine, Horza. You get to know the others and train up, and we'll knock the shit out of these monks. What do you say?' The Man winked at him again.

'You bet,' Horza said, standing and smiling. Kraiklyn opened the door for him.

And for my next trick, thought Horza as soon as he was out of the cabin and walking down to the mess, *my impression of . . . Captain Kraiklyn!*

During the next few days he indeed got to know the rest of the crew. He talked to those who wanted to talk and he observed or carefully overheard things about those who didn't. Yalson was still his only friend, but he got on well enough with his room-mate, Wubslin, though the stocky engineer was quiet and, when not eating or working, usually asleep. The Bratsilakins had apparently decided that Horza probably wasn't against them, but they seemed to be reserving

65

their opinion about whether he was *for* them until Marjoin and the Temple of Light.

Dorolow was the name of the religious woman who roomed with Yalson. She was plump, fair skinned and fair haired, and her huge ears curved down to join onto her cheeks. She spoke in a very high, squeaky voice which she said was pretty low as far as she was concerned, and her eyes watered a lot. Her movements were fluttery and nervous.

The oldest person in the Company was Aviger, a smallish, weather-beaten man with brown skin and little hair. He could do surprisingly supple things with his legs and arms, like clasp his hands behind his back and bring them over his head without letting go. He shared a cabin with a man named Jandraligeli, a tall, thin, middle-aged Mondlidician who wore the scar-marks from his homeworld on his forehead with unrepentant pride and a look of perpetual disdain. He ignored Horza devoutly, but Yalson said he did this with every new recruit. Jandraligeli spent a lot of time keeping his old but well-maintained suit and laser rifle clean and sparkling.

Gow and kee-Alsorofus were the two women who kept themselves so much to themselves and were alleged to *do things* when alone in their cabin, which seemed to annoy the less tolerant of the Company males – that is, most of them. Both women were fairly young and had a rather poor grasp of Marain. Horza thought maybe that was all that kept them so isolated, but it turned out they were pretty shy anyway. They were of average height, medium build, and sharp-featured in grey skin, with eyes that were pools of black. Horza thought perhaps it was just as well they didn't look at people straight too often; with those eyes it could be an unsettling experience.

Mipp was a fat, sombre man with jet-black skin. He could pilot the ship manually when Kraiklyn wasn't aboard and the Company needed close support on the ground, or he could take over at the shuttle controls. He was supposed to be a good shot, too, with a plasma cannon or rapid projectile rifle, but he was prone to binges, getting dangerously drunk on a variety of poisonous liquids he procured from the autogalley. Once or twice Horza heard him throwing up in the next stall in the heads. Mipp shared a cabin with another drunkard, called Neisin, who was more sociable and sang a lot. He had, or had convinced himself he had, something terrible to forget, and although he drank more steadily and regularly than Mipp, sometimes when he'd had a bit more than usual he would go very quiet and then start crying in great, sucking sobs. He was small and wiry, and Horza wondered where he put all the drink, and where all the tears came from inside his compact, shaved head. Perhaps there was some sort of short circuit between his throat and his tear ducts.

Tzbalik Odraye was the ship's self-styled computer ace. Because he and Mipp together could, in theory, have overridden the fidelities Kraiklyn had programmed into the *CAT*'s non-sentient computer and then flown off in the ship, they were never allowed to stay on the craft together when Kraiklyn wasn't aboard. In fact, Odraye wasn't that well versed in computers at all, as Horza discovered through a little close but apparently casual questioning. However, the tall, slightly hunchbacked man with the long yellow-skinned face probably knew just about enough, Horza reckoned, to handle anything that went wrong with the ship's brains, which seemed to have been designed for durability rather than philosophical finesse. Tzbalik Odraye roomed with Rava Gamdol, who looked as though he came from the same place as Yalson, judging from his skin and light fur, but he denied this. Yalson was vague on the subject, and neither liked the other. Rava was another recluse; he had boarded off the tiny space around his top bunk and installed some small lights and an air fan. Sometimes he spent days at a time in this small space, going in with a container of water and coming out with another full of urine. Tzbalik Odraye did his best to ignore his room-mate, and always vigorously denied blowing the smoke from the pungent Cifetressi weed, which he smoked, through the ventilation holes of Rava's tiny cubicle.

The final cabin was shared by Lenipobra and Lamm. Lenipobra was the youngster of the Company; a gangly youth with a stutter and garish red hair. He had a tattooed tongue which he was very proud of and would display at every possible opportunity. The tattoo, of a human female, was in every sense crude. Lenipobra was the *CAT*'s best excuse for a medic and was rarely seen without a small screen-book which contained one of the more up-to-date pan-human medical textbooks. He proudly showed this to Horza, including a few of the moving pages, one of which showed in vivid colour the basic techniques for treating deep laser burns in the most common forms of digestive tracts. Lenipobra thought it looked like great fun. Horza made a mental note to try even harder not to get shot in the Temple of Light. Lenipobra had very long and skinny arms, and spent about a quarter of each day going about on all fours, though whether this was entirely natural to his species or merely affectation Horza could not discover.

Lamm was rather below average height, but very muscular and dense looking. He had double eyebrows and small horngrafts; the latter stuck out from his thinning but very dark hair above a face he usually did his best to make aggressive and threatening. He did comparatively little talking between operations, and when he did talk, it was usually about battles he had been in, people he had killed, weapons he had used, and so on. Lamm considered himself second-in-command on the ship, despite Kraiklyn's policy of treating everybody else as equals. Every now and again Lamm would remind people not to give him any problems. He was well armed and deadly, and his suit even had a nuclear device in it which he said he would set off sooner than be captured. The inference he seemed to hope people would make was that, if they upset him, he might just set off this fabled nuke in a fit of pique.

'What the hell are you looking at me for?' Lamm's voice said, in amongst the storm of static, as Horza sat in the shuttle, shaking and rattling inside his too-big suit. Horza realised he had been looking across at the other man, who was directly opposite. He touched the mike button on his neck and said:

'Thinking about something else.'

'I don't want you looking at me.'

'Us all got to look somewhere,' Horza said jokingly to the man in the matt-black suit and grey-visored helmet. The black suit made a gesture with the hand not holding a laser rifle.

'Well, don't fucking look at me.'

Horza let his hand drop from his neck. He shook his head inside the suit helmet. It fitted so badly it didn't move on the outside. He stared at the section of fuselage above Lamm's head.

They were going to attack the Temple of Light. Kraiklyn was at the controls of the shuttle, bringing it in low over the forests of Marjoin, still covered in night, heading for the line of dawn breaking over the packed and steaming greenery. The plan was that the *CAT* would come back in towards the planet with the sun very low behind it, using its effectors on any electronics the temple did have, and making as much noise and as many flashes as it could with its secondary lasers and a few blast bombs. While this diversion was absorbing any defensive capacity the priests might have, the shuttle would either head straight for the temple and let everybody off, or, if there was any hostile reaction, land in the forest on the night side of the temple and disgorge its small force of suited troops there. The Company would then disperse and, if they had the facility, use their AG to fly to the temple, or – as in Horza's case – just crawl, creep, walk or run as best they could for the collection of low, slope-sided buildings and short towers which made up the Temple of Light.

Horza couldn't believe they were going in without some sort of reconnaissance; but Kraiklyn, when tackled on this point during the pre-op briefing in the hangar, had insisted that that might mean giving up the element of surprise. He had accurate maps of the place and a good battle plan. As long as everybody stuck to the plan, nothing would go wrong. The monks weren't total idiots, and the planet had been Contacted and doubtless knew about the war going on around it. So, just in case the sect had hired any overhead observation, it was wiser not to attempt a look-see which might give the game away. Anyway, temples didn't change much.

Horza and several of the others hadn't been very impressed with this reading of the situation, but there was nothing they could do. So here they all sat, sweating and nervous and being shaken up like the ingredients of a cocktail in this clapped-out shuttle, slamming into a potentially hostile atmosphere at hypersonic speeds. Horza sighed and checked his rifle again.

Like his antique armour, the rifle was old and unreliable; it had jammed twice when he tested it on the ship using dummy shells. Its magnetic propulsor seemed to work reasonably, but, judging by the erratic spread of the bullets, its rifling field was next to useless. The shells were big – at least seven-millimetre calibre and three times that long – and the gun could hold only forty-eight at a time and fire them no faster than eight a second. Incredibly, the huge bullets weren't even explosive; they were solid lumps of metal, nothing else. To top it all, the weapon's sight was out; a red haze filled the small screen when it was turned on. Horza sighed.

'We're about three hundred metres above the trees now,' Kraiklyn's voice said from the shuttle flight deck, 'doing about one and a half sounds. The *CAT*'s just started its run-in. About another two minutes. I can see the dawn. Good luck, all.' The voice crackled and died in Horza's helmet speaker. A few of the suited figures exchanged glances. Horza looked over at Yalson, sitting on the other side of the shuttle about three metres away, but her visor was mirrored. He couldn't tell if she was looking at him or not. He wanted to say something to her, but didn't want to bother her over the open circuit in case she was concentrating, preparing herself. Beside Yalson, Dorolow sat, her gloved hand making the Circle of Flame sign over the top of her helmet visor.

Horza tapped his hands on the old rifle and blew through his mouth

69

at the mist of condensation forming on the top edge of his visor. It made it worse, just as he thought it might. Perhaps he should open his visor, now that they were inside the planet's atmosphere.

The shuttle shook suddenly as though it had clipped the top of a mountain. Everybody was thrown forward, straining their seat harnesses, and a couple of guns went sailing forward and up, to clatter off the shuttle ceiling before slamming back to the deck. People grabbed for the guns and Horza closed his eyes; he wouldn't have been at all surprised if one of these enthusiasts had left their safety catch off. However, the guns were retrieved without mishap, and people sat cradling them and looking about.

'What the hell was that?' the old man, Aviger, said, and laughed nervously. The shuttle began some hard manoeuvring, throwing first one half of the group on their backs while the people on the other side were suspended by their seat webbing, then flipping in the other direction and reversing the postures. Grunts and curses came over the open channel into Horza's helmet. The shuttle dipped, making Horza's stomach feel empty, floating, then the craft steadied again.

'Bit of hostile fire,' Kraiklyn's clipped tones announced, and all the suited heads started to look from side to side.

'What?'

'Hostile *fire*?'

'I knew it.'

'Oh-oh.'

'Fuck.'

'*Why* did I think as soon as I *heard* those fateful words, "easy in, easy out", that this was going—' began Jandriligeli in a bored, knowing drawl, only to be cut off by Lamm.

'Hostile fucking fire. That's all we need. Hostile fucking fire.'

'They *are* gunned up,' Lenipobra said.

'Shit, who isn't these days?' Yalson said.

'Chicel-Horhava, sweet lady; save us all,' muttered Dorolow, speeding up the tracings of the Circle over her visor.

'Shut the fuck up,' Lamm told her.

'Let's hope Mipp can distract them without getting his ass blown off,' Yalson said.

'Maybe we should call it off,' Rava Gamdol said. 'Think we ought to call if off? Do you think we should call it off? Does anybody—'

'NO!' 'YES!' 'NO!' shouted three voices, almost in unison. Everybody looked at the three Bratsilakins. The two outer Brat-

70

silakins turned their helmets to look at the one in the middle, as the shuttle swooped again. The middle Bratsilakin's helmet turned briefly to each side. 'Oh, shit,' a voice said over the open channel, 'all right: NO!'

'I think maybe we should—' Rava Gamdol's voice started again.

Then Kraiklyn shouted, 'Here we go! Everybody ready!'

The shuttle braked hard, banking steeply one way, then the other, shuddering once and dipping. It bounced and shook, and for a second Horza thought they were crashing, but then the craft slid to a stop and the rear doors jawed open. Horza was on his feet with the rest of them, piling out of the shuttle and into the jungle.

They were in a clearing. At its far end a few branches and twigs were still tumbling from huge, heavy-looking trees where the shuttle had just seconds before torn through the edge of the forest canopy as it dipped in for the small area of level, grassy ground. Horza had time to see a couple of bright birds flying fast out of the trees near by and caught a glimpse of a blue-pink sky. Then he was running with the others, round the front of the shuttle where it still glowed dark red and vegetation beneath it smouldered, and on into the jungle. A few of the Company were using their AG, floating over the undergrowth between the moss-covered tree trunks, but hampered by creepers which hung like thick, flower-strewn ropes between the trees.

So far they still couldn't see the Temple of Light, but according to Kraiklyn it was just ahead of them. Horza looked round at the others on foot as they clambered over fallen trees covered in moss and swept past creepers and suspended roots.

'Fuck dispersing; this is too hard going.' It was Lamm's voice. Horza looked round and up, and saw the black suit heading vertically for the green mass of foliage above them.

'Bastard,' said a breathless voice.

'Yeah. B-b-bastard,' Lenipobra agreed.

'Lamm,' Kraiklyn said, 'you son of a bitch, don't break through up there. Spread out. Disperse, damn it!'

Then a shock wave Horza could feel through his suit blasted over them all. Horza hit the ground immediately and lay there. Another boom came through the hissing helmet speaker as it fed in the noise from outside.

'That was the *CAT* going over!' He didn't recognise the voice.

'You sure?' Somebody else.

'I saw it through the trees! It was the *CAT*!'

71

Horza got up and started running again.

'Black bastard nearly took my fucking head off. . . .' Lamm said.

There was light ahead of Horza, through the trunks and leaves. He heard some firing: the sharp crack of projectiles, the sucking *whoop* of lasers and the snap-*whoosh*-crash of plasma cannon. He ran to a small earth and shrub bank and threw himself down so that he could just see over the top. Sure enough, there was the Temple of Light, silhouetted against the dawn, all covered in vines and creepers and moss, with a few spires and towers sticking out above like angular tree trunks.

'There she is!' Kraiklyn shouted. Horza looked along the earth bank and saw a few of the Company, in the same prone position as he was. 'Wubslin! Aviger!' Kraiklyn shouted. 'Cover us with the plasmas. Neisin, you keep the micro on each side of the grounds – beyond, as well. Everybody else, follow me!'

More or less as one, they were off, over the tangled bank of mossy ground and bushes and down the other side, through light scrub and long, cane-like grass, the stalks covered in clinging, dark green moss. The mixture of ground cover came up to about chest height and made the going difficult, but it would be reasonably easy to duck down out of a line of fire. Horza waded through as best as he could. Plasma bolts sang through the air above them, lighting the dim stretch of ground between them and the sloping temple wall.

Distant fountains of earth and crashes he could feel through his feet told Horza that Neisin, sober the last two days, was laying down a convincing and, more importantly, accurate fire pattern with the Microhowitzer.

'There's a little gunfire from the upper left level,' the cool, unhurried voice of Jandraligeli said. According to the plan, he was supposed to be hiding high in the forest canopy watching the temple. 'I'm hitting it now.'

'Shit!' somebody yelled suddenly. One of the women. Horza could hear firing from ahead, though there were no flashes from the part of the temple he could see.

'Ha ha.' Jandraligeli's smug voice came through the helmet speaker. 'Got them!' Horza saw a puff of smoke over to the left of the temple. He was about halfway there by now, maybe closer. He could see some of the others not far away, to his left and right, pushing and striding through the cane grass and bushes with their rifles held high to one shoulder. They were all gradually getting covered in the dark green moss, which Horza supposed might be useful as camouflage (providing, of course, that it didn't turn out to be some horrible,

72

previously undiscovered sentient killer-moss . . . He told himself to stop being silly).

Loud crashes in the shrubbery around him, and smashed bits of cane and twigs fluttering past like nervous birds, sent him diving for the ground. The earth beneath him shuddered. He rolled over and saw flames lick the mossy stalks above; a flickering patch of fire lay directly behind him.

'Horza?' a voice said. Yalson's.

'OK,' he said. He got up to a crouch and started running through the grass, past bushes and young trees.

'We're coming in now,' Yalson said. She was up in the trees, too, along with Lamm, Jandraligeli and Neisin. According to the plan, all except Neisin and Jandraligeli would now start moving through the air on AG towards the temple. Although the anti-gravity units on their suits gave them an extra dimension to work with, they could be something of a mixed blessing; while a figure in the air tended to be harder to hit than one on the ground, it also tended to attract a lot more fire. The only other person in the Company with AG was Kraiklyn, but he said he preferred to use his for surprise or in emergencies, so he was still on the ground with the rest of them.

'I'm at the walls!' Horza thought it was Odraye's voice. 'This looks all right. The walls are really easy; the moss makes it—'

Horza's helmet speaker crackled. He wasn't sure if there was something wrong with his communicator or if something had happened to Odraye.

'—ver me while I'm—'

'—on you useless—' Voices clashed in Horza's helmet. He kept wading through the cane grass, and thumped the side of his helmet.

'—asshole!' The helmet speaker buzzed, then went silent. Horza swore and stopped, crouching down. He fumbled with the communicator controls at the side of the helmet, trying to coax the speaker back into life. His too-big gloves hindered him. The speaker stayed silent. He cursed again and got to his feet, pushing through the scrub and long grass to the temple wall.

'—rojectiles inside!' a voice yelled suddenly. 'This — . . . —cking simple!' He couldn't identify the voice, and the speaker went dead again immediately.

He arrived at the base of the wall; it slanted out of the scrub at about forty degrees and was covered in moss. Further along, two of the Company were clambering up it, almost at the top, about seven metres above. Horza saw a flying figure weaving through the air and disappearing over the parapet. He started climbing. The clumsily large suit made it more difficult than it should have been, but he got to the top without falling and jumped down from the parapet onto a broad wall-walk. A similar moss-covered wall sloped up to the next storey. To Horza's right the wall turned a corner beneath a stubby tower; to his left the wall-walk seemingly disappeared into a blank cross-wall. According to Kraiklyn's plan Horza was supposed to head along that way. There ought to be a door there. Horza jogged along towards the blank wall.

A helmet bobbed up from the side of the sloped wall. Horza started to duck and swerve, just in case, but first an arm waved from the same place, then both helmet and arm appeared, and he recognised the woman Gow.

Horza threw back the visor on his helmet as he ran, getting a faceful of jungle-scented Marjoin air. He could hear some rattling projectile fire from inside the temple, and the distant thud of an exploding Microhowitzer round. He ran up to a narrow entrance cut in the sloped wall, half covered by streamers of mossy growth. Gow was kneeling, gun ready, on the splintered remains of a heavy wooden door which had blocked the passageway beyond. Horza knelt beside her and pointed at his helmet.

'My communicator's out. What's been happening?'

Gow touched a button on her wrist, and her suit PA said, 'OK so far. No hurts. They on towers.' She pointed up. 'Them no fly go in. They enemy got projectile guns only, them fall back.' She nodded and kept glancing round through the doorway and into the dark passageway beyond. Horza nodded too. Gow tapped his arm. 'I tell Kraiklyn you go in, yes?'

'Yeah, tell him my communicator's out, OK?'

'Yeah, sure. Zallin same trouble had. You be safe, OK?'

'Yeah, you be safe, too,' Horza said. He stood up and entered the temple, scuffing over splinters of wood and fragments of sandstone scattered over the moss by the door's demolition. The dark corridor branched three ways. He turned back to Gow and pointed. 'Centre corridor, correct?'

The crouched figure, silhouetted against the light of the dawn, nodded and said, 'Yeah, sure. Go middle.'

Horza set off. The corridor was covered in moss. Every few metres dim yellow electric lights burned from the walls, casting murky pools of light which the dark moss seemed to absorb. Soft-walled, sponge-floored, the narrow passage made Horza shiver, though it wasn't cold.

He checked that his gun was ready to fire. He could hear no other sound apart from his own breathing.

He came to a T-junction in the corridor and took the right-hand branch. Some steps appeared and he ran up them, stumbling once as his feet tried to run out of his oversized boots; he put his hand out and jarred his arm on the step. Some moss came off the step and he caught a glimpse of something glinting underneath, in the dull yellow light cast by the wall lights. He recovered his balance, shaking his jarred arm as he continued up the steps and wondering why the temple's builders had made the steps out of what looked like glass. At the top of the steps he went down a short corridor, then up another flight of stairs, curving to the right and unlit. Considering its name, Horza thought, the temple was remarkably dark. He came out onto a small balcony.

The monk's cloak was dark, the same colour as the moss, and Horza didn't see him until the pale face turned towards him, along with the gun.

Horza threw himself to one side, against the wall to his left, and fired his gun from the hip at the same time. The monk's gun jerked upwards and let loose a fusillade of rapid fire at the ceiling as he collapsed. The shots echoed round the dark, empty space beyond the small balcony. Horza squatted by the wall, gun pointed at the dark, crumpled figure only a couple of metres away. He raised his head and in the gloom saw what was left of the monk's face, then relaxed slightly. The man was dead. Horza levered himself away from the wall and knelt by the balcony balustrade. Now he could see a large hall in the dim light of the few small globes which protruded from its roof. The balcony was about halfway up and along one of the longer walls, and, from what he could see, there was some sort of stage or altar at one end of the hall. The light was so dim he couldn't be sure, but he thought he saw shadowy figures on the floor of the hall, moving. He wondered if it was the Company and tried to recall seeing other doors or corridors on his way to the balcony; he was supposed to be down there, on that level, on the floor of the hall. He cursed his useless communicator and decided he would have to risk shouting down to the people in the hall.

He leant forward. Some shards of glass had fallen from the roof, where it had been hit by the monk's gun, and his suited knee crunched on the debris. Before he could open his mouth to shout down into the hall, he heard noises from beneath – a high-pitched voice speaking a language of squeaks and clicks. He went still, said nothing. It might just have been Dorolow's voice, he supposed, but why would she talk in anything other than Marain? The voice called again. He thought he heard another, but then laser and projectile fire erupted briefly from the opposite end of the hall from the altar. He ducked and in the lull heard something click behind him.

He spun round, tightening his finger on the trigger, but there was nobody there. Instead, a small round thing, about the size of a child's clenched fist, wobbled on the top of the balustrade and plonked down onto the moss about a metre away. He kicked at it with his foot and dived across the body of the dead monk.

The grenade detonated in mid-air, just under the balcony.

Horza jumped up while the echoes were still cracking back from the altar. He leapt into the doorway at the far end of the balcony, putting out one hand and grabbing the soft corner of the wall as he went past, spinning himself round as he fell to his knees. He reached out and grabbed the dead monk's gun from the corpse's slack grip, just as the balcony started to come away from the wall with a glassy, grinding noise. Horza shoved himself back into the corridor behind him. The balcony tipped bodily away into the empty space of the hall in a dully glittering cloud of fragments and fell with a great, shattering crash onto the floor below, taking the shadowy form of the dead monk fluttering with it.

Horza saw more of the shapes scatter in the darkness beneath him, and fired down with the gun he had just acquired. Then he turned and looked down the corridor he was now in, wondering if there was some way down to the hall floor, or even back outside. He checked the gun he had taken; it looked better than his own. He crouched and ran away from the doorway looking over the hall, putting his old rifle over his shoulder. The dimly lit corridor curved right. Horza straightened gradually as he left the doorway behind, and stopped worrying about grenades. Then it all started to happen in the hall behind him.

The first thing he knew was that his shadow was being thrown in front of him, flickering and dancing on the curving wall of the passage. Then a cacophony of noise and a stuttering burst of blast waves rocked him on his feet and assaulted his ears. He brought the helmet visor down quickly and crouched again as he turned back towards the hall and the bright flashes of light. Even through the helmet, he thought he could hear screams mixed in with the gunfire and explosions. He ran back and threw himself down where he had been before, lying looking out into the hall.

He put his head down as fast as he could and used his elbows to lever himself back the instant he realised what was happening. He wanted to run, but he lay where he was, stuck the dead monk's rifle round the corner of the doorway and sprayed fire in the general direction of the altar until the weapon stopped firing, keeping his helmet as far back from the doorway as possible, visor turned away. When that gun stopped he threw it away and used his own, until it jammed. He slid himself away after that, and ran off down the corridor, away from the opening of the hall. He didn't doubt that the rest of the Company would be doing the same thing, those that could.

What he had seen ought to have been incredible, but although he had looked only long enough for a single, hardly moving image to form on his retinas, he knew what he was seeing and what was happening. As he ran he tried to work out why the hell the Temple of Light had been laserproofed. When he came to a T-junction in the corridor he stopped.

He swung his rifle butt at the corner of the wall, through the moss; the metal connected, doubtless denting, but he felt something else give too. Using the weak light from the suit torch cells on either side of the visor, he looked at what lay underneath the moss.

'Oh God . . .' he breathed to himself. He struck at another part of the wall and looked again. He remembered the glint of what he'd thought was glass under the moss on the stairs, when he'd jarred his arm, and the crunching feeling under his knee on the balcony. He leant against the soft wall, feeling sick.

Nobody had gone to the extraordinary lengths of laserproofing an entire temple, or even one large hall. It would have been horrendously expensive and surely unnecessary on a stage-three planet anyway. No; probably the whole interior of the temple (he recalled the sandstone to which the outer door had been attached) had been built from blocks of crystal, and that was what was buried under all the moss. Hit it with a laser and the moss would vaporise in an instant, leaving the interior surfaces of the crystal beneath to reflect the rest of that pulse and any subsequent shots falling on the same place. He looked again at the second place he'd struck with the gun, looked deep into the transparent surface beyond, and saw his own suit lights shining dully back at him from a mirrored boundary somewhere inside. He pushed himself away and ran down the right-hand branch of the corridor, past heavy wooden doors, then down some curved steps towards a splash of light.

What he had seen in the hall was chaos, lit with lasers. A single glimpse, coinciding with several flashes, had burned an image into his

77

eyes he thought he could still half see. At one end of the hall, on the altar, monks were crouched, guns firing, their own guns flashing with chemical-explosive fire; around them burst dark explosions of smoke as moss vaporised. At the other end of the hall several of the Company stood or lay or staggered, their own shadows huge on the wall behind them. They were loosing off with everything they had, rifles strobing pulses off the far wall, and they were being hit by their own shots slamming back from the internal surfaces of crystal blocks they didn't even realise they were aiming at. At least two were blind already, judging by the way they were caught in poses of sightless blundering, arms out in front of them, guns firing from one hand.

Horza knew too well that his own suit, his visor especially, was not capable of stopping a laser hit, from either visible wavelength guns or X-rays. All he could do was get his head out of the way and loose off with what projectiles he had, hoping to get a few of the priests or their guards. He had probably been lucky he hadn't been hit even in the brief length of time he'd looked into the hall; now all he could do was get out. He tried shouting into the helmet mike, but the communicator was dead; his voice sounded hollow in the suit and he couldn't hear himself through the ear speaker.

He saw another shadowy shape ahead, a dim silhouette crouched low against the wall in the pool of daylight coming from another corridor. Horza threw himself into a doorway. The figure didn't move.

He tried his rifle; its knocks on the crystal walls seemed to have unjammed it. A burst of fire made the figure collapse slackly to the floor. Horza stepped out of the doorway and walked to it.

It was another monk, dead hand gripped round a pistol. His white face was visible in the light which came down another passageway. On the wall behind the monk there were the pockmarks of burned-off moss; clear, undamaged crystal showed through beneath. As well as the holes produced by Horza's burst of fire, the monk's tunic, now seeping with bright red blood, was covered with laser burns. Horza stuck his head round the corner, looking into the light.

Against the morning glow, framed in a slanting doorway, a suited form lay on the mossy floor, gun extended at the end of one hand so that it pointed down the passageway towards Horza. A heavy door lay at an angle behind, just hanging by one twisted hinge. *It's Gow*, Horza thought. Then he looked at the door again, thinking it looked wrong somehow. The door and the walls leading to it were scarred with laser burns.

He went up the corridor to the fallen figure and rolled it over so that he could see the face. His head swam for a second as he looked. It wasn't Gow; it was her friend, kee-Alsorofus, who had died here. Her blackened, cracked face stared out, dry-eyed, through the still clear visor of her helmet. He looked at the door and at the corridor. Of course: he was in another part of the temple. Same situation, but a different set of passageways, and a different person . . .

The woman's suit was holed, centimetres deep, in a few places; the smell of burned flesh leaked into Horza's ill-fitting suit, making him gag. He stood up, took kee-Alsorofus's laser, stepped over the slanted door and went out onto the wall-walk. He ran along it, round a corner, ducking once as a Microhowitzer shell landed too close to the temple's sloping walls and sent up a shower of flashing crystal fragments and ruddy chunks of sandstone. The plasma cannons were still firing from the forest, too, but Horza couldn't see any flying figures. He was looking for them when he suddenly sensed the suit to one side of him, standing in the angle of the wall. He stopped, recognising Gow's suit, and stood about three metres from her while she looked at him. She pushed the visor on her helmet up slowly. Her grey face and black, pit-like eyes fixed on the laser rifle he was carrying. The look on her face made him wish he had checked the gun was still switched on. He looked down at the gun in his hand, then at the woman, who was still staring at it.

'I—' He was going to explain.

'She killed, yeah?' The woman's voice sounded flat. She seemed to sigh. Horza drew in a breath, was about to start talking again, but Gow spoke in the same monotone. 'I thought I hear she.'

Suddenly she brought her gun hand up, flashing in the blue and pink of the morning sky. Horza saw what she was doing and started forward, reaching out instantly with one hand even though he knew he was too far away and too late to do anything.

'Don't!' he had time to shout, but the gun was already in the woman's mouth and an instant later, as Horza started to duck and his eyes closed instinctively, the back of Gow's helmet blew out in a single pulse of unseen light, throwing a sudden red cloud over the mossy wall behind.

Horza sat down on his haunches, hands closed round the gun barrel in front of him, eyes staring out at the distant jungle. *What a mess*, he thought, *what a fucking, obscene, stupid mess*. He hadn't been thinking of what Gow had just done to herself, but he looked round at the red stain on the angled wall and the collapsed shape of Gow's suit, and thought it again.

*   *   *

79

He was about to start back down the outer wall of the temple when something moved in the air above him. He turned and saw Yalson landing on the wall-walk. She looked at Gow's body once, then they exchanged what they both knew of the situation – what she had heard over the open communicator channel, what Horza had seen in the hall – and decided they would stay put until some of the others came out, or they gave up hope. According to Yalson only Rava Gamdol and Tzbalik Odraye were definitely dead after the fire-fight in the hall, but all three Bratsilakins had been there too, and nobody had heard anything from them after the open channel had become intelligible again and most of the screaming had stopped.

Kraiklyn was alive and well but lost; Dorolow lost too, sitting crying, maybe blinded; and Lenipobra, against all advice and Kraiklyn's orders, had entered the temple through a roof door and was heading down to try to rescue anybody he could, using only a small projectile pistol he'd been carrying.

Yalson and Horza sat back to back on the wall-walk, Yalson keeping the Changer informed on how things were going in the temple. Lamm flew overhead, heading for the jungle where he took one of the plasma cannons from the protesting Wubslin. He had just landed near by when Lenipobra announced proudly he had found Dorolow, and Kraiklyn reported he could see daylight. There was still no sound from the Bratsilakins. Kraiklyn appeared round a corner of the wall-walk; Lenipobra leapt into view, clutching Dorolow to his suit and bounding down over the walls in a series of great slow jumps as his AG struggled to lift both him and the woman.

They set off back to the shuttle. Jandraligeli could see movement on the road beyond the temple, and there was sniper fire coming from the jungle on either side. Lamm wanted to tear into the temple with the plasma cannon and vaporise a few monks, but Kraiklyn ordered the retreat. Lamm threw the plasma gun down and sailed off towards the shuttle alone, swearing loudly over the open channel on which Yalson was still trying to call the Bratsilakins.

They waded through the tall cane grass and bushes under the *whoosh*ing trails of plasma bolts, as Jandraligeli gave them cover. They had to duck occasionally as small-bore projectile fire tore through the greenery around them.

They sprawled in the hangar of the *Clear Air Turbulence*, beside the still warm shuttle as it clicked and creaked, cooling down again after its high-speed climb through the atmosphere.

Nobody wanted to talk. They just sat or lay on the deck, some with their backs against the side of the warm shuttle. Those who had been inside the temple were the most obviously affected, but even the others, who had only heard the mayhem over their suit communicators, seemed in a state of mild shock. Helmets and guns lay scattered about them.

'"Temple of Light",' Jandraligeli said eventually, and gave what sounded like a mixture of laugh and snort.

'Temple of fucking Light,' Lamm agreed.

'Mipp,' Kraiklyn said in a tired voice to his helmet, 'any signals from the Bratsilakins?'

Mipp, still on the *CAT*'s small bridge, reported that there was nothing.

'We ought to bomb that place to fuck,' Lamm said. 'Nuke the bastards.' Nobody replied. Yalson got up slowly and left the hangar, walking tiredly up the steps to the upper deck, helmet dangling from one arm, gun from the other, her head down.

'I'm afraid we've lost that radar.' Wubslin closed an inspection hatch and rolled out from underneath the nose of the shuttle. 'That first bit of hostile fire . . .' His voice trailed off.

'Least nobody's injured,' Neisin said. He looked at Dorolow. 'Your eyes better?' The woman nodded but kept her eyes closed. Neisin nodded, too. 'Actually worse, when people are injured. We were lucky.' He dug into a small pack on the front of his suit and produced a little metal container. He sucked at a nipple at the top and grimaced, shaking his head. 'Yeah, we were lucky. And it was fairly quick for them, too.' He nodded to himself, not looking at anybody, not caring that nobody seemed to be listening to him. 'See how everybody we've lost all shared the same . . . I mean they went in pairs . . . or threes . . . huh?' He took another slug and shook his head. Dorolow was near by; she reached over and held out her hand. Neisin looked at her in surprise, then handed the small flask to her. She took a swig and passed it back. Neisin looked around, but no one else wanted any.

Horza sat and said nothing. He was staring at the cold lights of the hangar, trying not to see the scene he had witnessed in the hall of the dark temple.

The *Clear Air Turbulence* broke orbit on fusion drive and headed for the outer edge of Marjoin's gravity well, where it could engage its warp motors. It didn't pick up any signals from the Bratsilakins and it didn't bomb the Temple of Light. It set a course for the Vavatch Orbital.

From radio transmissions they had picked up from the planet they worked out what had happened to the place, what had caused the monks and priests in the temple to be so well armed. Two nation states on the world of Marjoin were at war, and the temple was near the frontier between the two countries, constantly ready for attack. One of the states was vaguely socialist; the other was religiously inspired, the priests in the Temple of Light representing one sect of that militant faith. The war was partly caused by the greater, galactic conflict taking place around it, as well as being a tiny and approximate image of it. It was that reflection, Horza realised, which had killed the members of the Company, as much as any bounced laserflash.

Horza wasn't sure how he would sleep that night. He lay awake for a few hours, listening to Wubslin having quiet nightmares. Then the cabin door was tapped lightly. Yalson came in and sat on Horza's bunk. She put her head on his shoulder and they held each other. After a while she took his hand and led him quietly down the companionway, away from the mess – where a splash of light and distant music witnessed that the unsleeping Kraiklyn was unwinding with a drug flask and a holosound tape – down to the cabin which had been Gow's and kee-Alsorofus's.

In the darkness of the cabin, on a small bed full of strange scents and new textures, they performed the same old act, theirs – they both knew – an almost inevitably barren cross-matching of species and cultures thousands of light-years apart. Then they slept.

State of play: one

Fal 'Ngeestra watched the shadows of the clouds move on the distant plain, ten kilometres away horizontally and one vertically, and then, with a sigh, lifted her gaze to the line of snow-capped mountains on the far side of the open grassland. The mountain range was fully thirty kilometres from her eyes, but the peaks were sharp and distinct in the thin air which they invaded with their rock and brilliant icy whiteness. Even at that distance, through that much atmosphere, their glare startled the eye.

She turned away, walking along the broad flagstones of the lodge terrace with a stiff-legged gait unsuited to her lack of years. The trelliswork above her head was covered in bright red and white flowers and cast a regular pattern of shadows over the terrace beneath; she walked through light and shade, her hair dim then shining gold in turn as each halting step moved her from shadow to sunlight.

The gun-metal bulk of the drone called Jase appeared at the far end of the terrace, out of the lodge itself. Fal smiled when she saw it and sat down on a stone bench jutting out from the low wall which separated terrace from view. They were high up, but it was a hot and windless day; she wiped a little sweat from her forehead as the old drone floated along the terrace towards her, the slanting lines of sunlight passing over its body in a steady rhythm. The drone settled on the stones beside the bench, its broad, flat top about level with the crown of the girl's head.

'Isn't it a lovely day, Jase?' Fal said, looking back at the distant mountains again.

'It is,' Jase said. The drone had an unusually deep and full-toned voice, and made the most of it. For a thousand years or more Culture drones had had aura fields which coloured according to their mood – their equivalent of facial expression and body language – but Jase was old, made long before aura fields were thought of, and had refused to be refitted to accommodate them. It preferred either to rely on its voice to express what it felt, or to remain inscrutable.

85

'Damn.' Fal shook her head, looking at the far-away snow. 'I wish I was climbing.' She made a clicking noise with her mouth and looked down at her right leg, which stuck straight out in front of her. She had broken the leg eight days before, while climbing in the mountains on the other side of the plain. Now it was splinted up with a fine tracery of field-strands, concealed beneath fashionably tight trousers.

Jase ought, she thought, to have taken this as an excuse to lecture her again on the advisability of only climbing with a floater harness, or with a rescue drone near by, or at the very least on not climbing alone, but the old machine said nothing. She looked at it, her tanned face shining in the light. 'So, Jase, what have you got for me? Business?'

'I'm afraid so.'

Fal settled herself as comfortably as she could on the stone bench and crossed her arms. Jase stretched out a short force field from its casing to support the awkward-looking outstretched leg, though it knew that the splint's own fields were taking all the strain.

'Spit it out,' Fal said.

'You may recall an item from the daily synopsis eighteen days ago about one of our spacecraft which was cobbled together by a factory vessel in the volume of space Inside from the Sullen Gulf; the factory craft had to destruct, and later so did the ship it made.'

'I remember,' said Fal, who forgot little about anything, and nothing at all from a daily synopsis. 'It was a mongrel because the factory was trying to get a GSV Mind out of the way.'

'Well,' Jase said, its voice a little weary, 'we have a problem with that.'

Fal smiled.

The Culture, there could be no doubt, relied profoundly on its machines for both its strategy and tactics in the war it was now engaged in. Indeed, a case could be made for holding that the Culture was its machines, that they represented it at a more fundamental level than did any single human or group of humans within the society. The Minds that the Culture's factory craft, safe Orbitals and larger GSVs were now producing were some of the most sophisticated collections of matter in the galaxy. They were so intelligent that no human was capable of understanding just how smart they were (and the machines themselves were incapable of describing it to such a limited form of life).

From those mental colossi, down through the more ordinary but still sentient machines and the smart but ultimately mechanistic and predictable computers, right down to the smallest circuit in a micromissile hardly more intelligent than a fly, the Culture had placed its bets – long before the Idiran war had been envisaged – on the machine rather than the human brain. This was because the Culture saw itself as being a self-consciously rational society; and machines, even sentient ones, were more capable of achieving this desired state as well as more efficient at using it once they had. That was good enough for the Culture.

Besides, it left the humans in the Culture free to take care of the things that really mattered in life, such as sport, games, romance, studying dead languages, barbarian societies and impossible problems, and climbing high mountains without the aid of a safety harness.

A hostile reading of such a situation might lead to the idea that the discovery by the Culture's Minds that some humans were actually capable of matching and occasionally beating their record for accurately assessing a given set of facts would lead to machine indignation and blown circuits, but this was not the case. It fascinated those Minds that such a puny and chaotic collection of mental faculties could by some sleight of neuron produce an answer to a problem which was as good as theirs. There was an explanation, of course, and it perhaps had something to do with patterns of cause and effect which even the almost god-like power of the Minds had difficulty trying to fathom; it also had quite a lot to do with sheer weight of numbers.

There were in excess of eighteen trillion people in the Culture, just about every one of them well nourished, extensively educated and mentally alert, and only thirty or forty of them had this unusual ability to forecast and assess on a par with a well-informed Mind (of which there were already many hundreds of thousands). It was not impossible that this was pure luck; toss eighteen trillion coins in the air for a while and a few of them are going to keep landing the same side up for a long, long time.

Fal 'Ngeestra was a Culture Referer, one of those thirty, maybe forty, out of the eighteen trillion who could give you an intuitive idea of what was going to happen, or tell you why she thought that something which had already happened had happened the way it did, and almost certainly turn out right every time. She was being handed problems and ideas constantly, being both used and assessed herself. Nothing she said or did went unrecorded; nothing she experienced went unnoticed. She did insist, however, that when she was climbing, alone or with friends, she must be left to her own devices and not watched by the Culture's. She would take a pocket terminal with her to record everything, but she would not have a real-time link with any part of the Mind network on the Plate she lived on.

Because of that insistence she had lain in the snow with a shattered leg for a day and a night before a search party had discovered her.

The drone Jase started to give her the details of the flight of the nameless ship from its mother-craft, of its interception and self-destruction. Fal had turned her head, though, and was only half listening. Her eyes and mind were on the distant, snowy slopes, where she hoped she would be climbing again in a few days' time, once these stupid bones in her leg had thoroughly healed.

The mountains were beautiful. There were other mountains on the upslope side of the lodge terrace, reaching into the clear blue sky, but they were tame stuff indeed compared to those sharp, rearing peaks across the plain. She knew that was why they had put her in this lodge; they hoped she would climb those nearer mountains rather than take the trouble to hop into a flyer and head over the plain. It was a silly idea, though; they had to let her see the mountains, or she wouldn't be herself, and as long as she could see them she just *had* to climb them. Idiots.

On a planet, she thought, *you wouldn't be able to see them so well. You wouldn't be able to see the lower foothills, the way the mountains rise from the plain just so.*

The lodge, the terrace, the mountains and the plain were on an Orbital. Humans had built this place, or at least built the machines that built the machines that . . . Well, you could go on and on. The Plate of the Orbital was almost perfectly flat; in fact, vertically it was slightly concave, but as the internal diameter of the completed Orbital – properly formed only once all the individual Plates had been joined up and the last dividing wall was removed – would measure over three million kilometres, the curvature was a great deal less than on the convex surface of any human-habitable globe. So from Fal's raised vantage point she could see right to the base of the distant mountains.

Fal thought it must be very strange to live on a planet and have to look over a curve; so that, for example, you would see the top of a seaship appear over the horizon before the rest of it.

She was suddenly aware that she was thinking about planets because of something Jase had just said. She turned round and looked earnestly at the dark grey machine, playing back her short-term memory to recall exactly what it had just said.

'This Mind went *underneath* the planet in hyperspace?' she said. 'Then warped inside?'

'That was what it said it was trying to do when it sent the coded message in its destruct pattern. As the planet is still there it must have succeeded. Had it failed, at least half a per cent of its mass would have reacted with the planet's own material as though it was antimatter.'

'I see.' Fal scratched at one cheek with a finger. 'I thought that wasn't supposed to be possible?' Her voice contained the question. She looked at Jase.

'What?' it said.

'Doing . . .' She scowled at not being immediately understood and waved one hand impatiently. '. . . Doing what it did. Going under something so big in hyperspace and then bouncing over. I was told even we couldn't do that.'

'So was the Mind in question, but it was desperate. The General War Council itself decided that we should try to duplicate the feat, using a similar Mind and a spare planet.'

'What happened?' Fal asked, grinning at the idea of a 'spare' planet.

'No Mind would even consider the idea; far too dangerous. Even the eligible ones on the War Council demurred.'

Fal laughed, gazing up at the red and white flowers curled round the trelliswork overhead. Jase, which deep down was a hopeless romantic, thought her laughter sounded like the tinkling of mountain streams, and always recorded her laughs for itself, even when they were snorts or guffaws, even when she was being rude and it was a dirty laugh. Jase knew a machine, even a sentient one, could not die of shame, but it also knew that it would do just that if Fal ever guessed any of this. Fal stopped laughing. She said:

'What does this thing actually look like? I mean you never see them by themselves, they're always in something . . . a ship or whatever. And how did it – what did it use to warp with?'

'Externally,' Jase said in its usual, calm, measured tones, 'it is an ellipsoid. Fields up, it looks like a very small ship. It's about ten metres long and two and a half in diameter. Internally it's made up of millions of components, but the most important ones are the thinking and memory parts of the Mind proper; those are what make it so heavy because they're so dense. It weighs nearly fifteen thousand tonnes. It is fitted with its own power, of course, and several field generators, any of which could be pressed into service as emergency motors, and indeed are designed with this in mind. Only the outer envelope is constantly in real space, the rest – all the thinking parts, anyway – stay in hyperspace.

'Assuming, as we must, that the Mind did what it said it was going to do, there is only one possible way it could have accomplished the task, given that it does not have a warp motor or Displacer.' Jase paused as Fal sat forward, her elbows on her knees, her hands clenched under her chin. It saw her shifting her weight on her backside and a tiny grimace appear fleetingly on her face. Jase decided she was getting uncomfortable on the hard stone bench, and ordered one of the lodge drones to bring some cushions. 'The Mind does have an internal warping unit, but it is supposed to be used only to expand microscopic volumes of the memory so that there is more space around the sections of information – in the form of third-level elementary particle-spirals – which it wants to change. The normal volume limit on that warping unit is less than a cubic millimetre; somehow the ship Mind jury-rigged it so that it would encompass its entire body and let it appear within the planet's surface. A clear air space would be the logical place to go for, and the tunnels of the Command System seem an obvious choice; that is where it said it would head for.'

'Right,' Fal said, nodding. 'OK. Now, what are – oh . . .'

A small drone carrying two large cushions appeared at her side. 'Hmm, thanks,' Fal said, levering herself up with one hand and placing one cushion beneath her, the other at her back. The small drone floated off to the lodge again. Fal settled herself. 'Did you ask for these, Jase?' she asked.

'Not me,' Jase lied, secretly pleased. 'What were you going to ask?'

'These tunnels,' Fal said, leaning forward more comfortably this time. 'This Command System. What is it?'

'Briefly, it consists of a winding, paired loop of twenty-two-metre-diameter tunnels buried five kilometres deep. The whole system is several hundred kilometres in length. The trains were designed to be the wartime mobile command centres of a state which once existed on the planet, when it was at the intermediate-sophisticated stage-three phase. State-of-the-art weaponry at the time was the fusion bomb, delivered by transplanetary guided rocket. The Command System was designed to—'

'Yes.' Fal waved her hand quickly. 'Protect, keep mobile so they couldn't be blown up. Right?'

'Yes.'

'What sort of rock cover did they have?'

'Granite,' Jase said.

'Batholithic?'

'Just a second,' Jase said, consulting elsewhere. 'Yes. Correct: a batholith.'

90

'A batholith?' Fal said, eyebrows raised. 'Just one?'

'Just one.'

'This is a slightly low-G world? Thick crust?'

'Both.'

'Uh-huh. So the Mind's inside these. . . .' She looked along the terrace, not really seeing anything, but in her mind's eye looking down kilometres of dark tunnels (and thinking there might be some pretty impressive mountains above them: all that granite; low-G; good climbing territory). She looked at the machine again. 'So what happened? It's a Planet of the Dead; did the natives eventually do it to themselves?'

'With biological weapons, not nukes, to the last humanoid, eleven thousand years ago.'

'Hmm.' Fal nodded. Now it was obvious why the Dra'Azon had made Schar's World one of their Planets of the Dead. If you were a pure-energy superspecies long retired from the normal, matter-based life of the galaxy, and your conceit was to cordon off and preserve the odd planet or two you thought might serve as a fitting monument to death and futility, Schar's World with its short and sordid history sounded like the sort of place you'd put pretty near the top of your list.

Something occurred to her. 'How come the tunnels haven't sealed up again over all that time? Five klicks' worth of pressure . . .'

'We don't know,' Jase sighed. 'The Dra'Azon have not been very forthcoming with information. It is possible the System's engineers devised a technique for withstanding the pressure over such a period. This is unlikely, admittedly, but then they were ingenious.'

'Pity they didn't devote a little more ingenuity to staying alive rather than conducting mass slaughter as efficiently as possible,' Fal said, and made a little snorting noise.

Jase felt pleasure at the girl's words (if not the snort), but at the same time detected in them a tinge of that mixture of contempt and patronising smugness the Culture found it so difficult not to exhibit when surveying the mistakes of less advanced societies, even though the source civilisations of its own mongrel past had been no less fallible. Still, the underlying point held; experience as well as common sense indicated that the most reliable method of avoiding self-extinction was not to equip oneself with the means to accomplish it in the first place.

'So,' Fal said, looking down as she tapped her one good heel on the grey stones, 'the Mind's in the tunnels; the Dra'Azon's on the outside. What's the Quiet Barrier limit?'

'The usual half-distance to the nearest other star: three hundred

91

and ten standard light-days in the case of Schar's World at the moment.'

'— And . . .?' She held out her hand to Jase and raised her head and her eyebrows. Flower shadows moved on her neck as the gentlest of breezes started and ruffled the blossoms on the trelliswork above her head. 'What's the problem?'

'Well,' Jase said, 'the reason the Mind was allowed in at all was because—'

'In distress. Right. Go on.'

Jase, who had stopped being annoyed by Fal's interruptions the first time she had brought it a mountain flower, went on, 'There is a small base on Schar's World, as there is on almost all the Planets of the Dead. As usual it is staffed from a small, nominally neutral, non-dynamic society of some galactic maturity—'

'The Changer,' Fal broke in, quite slowly, as though guessing the answer to a puzzle which had been troubling her for hours and ought to have been simple. She looked through the flower-strewn trellis, to a blue sky where a few small white clouds were moving slowly. She looked back to the machine. 'I'm right, aren't I? That Changer guy who . . . and that Special Circumstancer – Balveda – and the place where you have to be senile to rule. They're Changers on Schar's World and this bloke—' She broke off and frowned. 'But I thought he was dead.'

'Now we're not so sure. The last message from the GCU *Nervous Energy* seemed to indicate he might have escaped.'

'What happened to the GCU?'

'We don't know. Contact was lost while it was trying to capture rather than destroy the Idiran ship. Both are presumed lost.'

'Capture it, eh?' Fal said tartly. 'Another show-off Mind. But that's it, isn't it? The Idirans might be able to use this guy – what's his name? Do we know?'

'Bora Horza Gobuchul.'

'Whereas we don't have any Changers.'

'We do, but the one we have is on the other side of the galaxy on an urgent job not connected with the war; it would take half a year to get her there. Besides, she has never been to Schar's World; the tricky part about this problem is that Bora Horza Gobuchul has.'

'Ho-*ho*,' Fal said.

'In addition, we have unconfirmed information that the same Idiran fleet which knocked out the fleeing ship also tried unsuccessfully to follow the Mind to Schar's World with a small landing force. Thus the

Dra'Azon concerned is going to be suspicious. It might let Bora Horza Gobuchul through, as he has served before with the caretaker staff on the planet, but even he is not certain to gain entry. Anybody else is very doubtful indeed.'

'Of course the poor devil might be dead.'

'Changers are not notoriously easy to kill, and besides, it would seem unwise simply to count on that possibility.'

'And you're worried he might get to this precious Mind and bring it back to the Idirans.'

'It could just happen.'

'Just supposing it *did* happen, Jase,' Fal said, screwing up her eyes and leaning forward to look at the machine, 'so what? Would it really make any difference? What would happen if the Idirans did get their hands on this admittedly resourceful kid Mind?'

'Assuming that we are going to win the war . . .' Jase said thoughtfully, '. . . it could lengthen the proceedings by a handful of months.'

'And how many's that supposed to be?' Fal said.

'Somewhere between three and seven, I suppose. It depends whose hand you're using.'

Fal smiled. 'And the problem is that the Mind can't destruct without making this Planet of the Dead even more dead than it is already, in fact without making it an asteroid belt.'

'Exactly.'

'So maybe the little devil shouldn't have bothered saving itself from the wreck in the first place, and should have just gone down with the ship.'

'It's called the instinct to survive.' Jase paused while Fal nodded, then it went on, 'It's programmed into most living things.' It made a show of weighing the girl's injured leg in its field-held grip. 'Though, of course, there are always exceptions. . . .'

'Yes,' Fal said, giving what she hoped was a condescending smile, 'very droll, Jase.'

'So you see the problem.'

'I see the problem,' Fal agreed. 'Of course we could force our way in there, and blow the place to smithereens if necessary, and to hell with the Dra'Azon.' She grinned.

'Yes,' Jase conceded, 'and put the whole outcome of the war in jeopardy by antagonising a power whose haziest unknown quantity is the exact extent of its immensity. We could also surrender to the Idirans, but I doubt we'll do that either.'

'Well, so long as we're considering all the options.' Fal laughed.
'Oh yes.'

'OK, Jase, if that's all – let me think about this lot for a while,' Fal
'Ngeestra said, sitting up straight on the bench and stretching and
yawning. 'It sounds interesting.' She shook her head. 'This is lap-of-
the-gods stuff, though. Let me have . . . anything you think might be
relevant. I'd like to concentrate on this bit of the war for a while; all
the information we've got on the Sullen Gulf . . . all I can handle,
anyway. OK?'

'OK,' Jase said.

'Hmm,' Fal murmured, nodding vaguely, her eyes unfocused. 'Yes
. . . all we've got on that general area . . . I mean volume . . .' She
waved her hand round in a circle, in her imagination encompassing
several million cubic light-years.

'Very well,' Jase said, and retreated slowly from the girl's gaze. It
floated back down the terrace in the shafts of sunlight and shade,
towards the lodge, under the flowers.

The girl sat by herself, rocking backwards and forwards on her
haunches and humming quietly, her hands at her mouth again and her
elbows on her knees, one of which was bent, and one of which was
straight.

Here we are, she thought, *killing the immortal, only just stopping short
of tangling with something most people would think of as a god, and here
am I, eighty thousand light-years away if I'm a metre, supposed to think of
a way out of this ridiculous situation. What a joke . . . Damn. I wish
they'd let me be a Field Referer, out there where the action is, instead of
sitting it out back here, so far away it takes two years just to get there. Oh
well.*

She shifted her weight and sat sideways on the seat so that her
broken leg lay along the bench, then turned her face to the mountains
glittering on the far side of the plain. She rested her elbow on the stone
parapet, her hand supporting her head as her eyes drank in the view.

She wondered whether they really had kept their word about not
watching her when she went climbing. She wouldn't put it past them
to have kept a small drone or micromissile or something near by, just
in case anything did happen, and then – after the accident, after she'd
fallen – left her lying there, frightened, cold and in pain, just to
convince her they were doing no such thing, and to see the effect it had
on her, as long as she wasn't in any real danger of dying. She knew,
after all, the way their Minds worked. It was the sort of thing she
would consider doing, if she was in charge.

Maybe I should just pack it in; leave. Tell them to shove their war. Trouble is . . . I like all this. . . .

She looked at one of her hands, golden brown in a beam of sunlight. She opened and closed it, looking at the fingers. *Three . . . to seven . . .* She thought of an Idiran hand. *Depending . . .*

She looked back, over the shadow-strewn plain towards the distant mountains, and sighed.

5.

Megaship

Vavatch lay in space like a god's bracelet. The fourteen-million-kilometre hoop glittered and sparkled, blue and gold against the jet-black gulf of space beyond. As the *Clear Air Turbulence* warped in towards the Orbital, most of the Company watched their goal approach on the main screen in the mess. The aquamarine sea, which covered most of the surface of the artefact's ultradense base material, was spattered with white puffs of cloud, collected in huge storm systems or vast banks, some of which seemed to stretch right across the full thirty-five-thousand-kilometre breadth of the slowly turning Orbital.

Only on one side of that looped band of water was there any land visible, hard up against one sloped retaining wall of pure crystal. Although, from the distance they were watching, the sliver of land looked like a tiny brown thread lying on the edge of a great rolled-out bolt of vivid blue, that thread was anything up to two thousand kilometres across; there was no shortage of land on Vavatch.

Its greatest attraction, however, was and had always been the Megaships.

'Don't you have a religion?' Dorolow asked Horza.

'Yes,' he replied, not taking his eyes away from the screen on the wall above the end of the main mess-room table. 'My survival.'

'So . . . your religion dies with you. How sad,' Dorolow said, looking back from Horza to the screen. The Changer let the remark pass.

The exchange had started when Dorolow, struck by the beauty of the great Orbital, expressed the belief that even though it was a work of base creatures, no better than humans, it was still a triumphant testimony to the power of God, as God had made Man, and all other souled creatures. Horza had disagreed, genuinely annoyed that the woman could use even something so obviously a testament to the power of intelligence and hard work as an argument for her own system of irrational belief.

Yalson, who was sitting beside Horza at the table, and whose foot was gently rubbing the Changer's ankle, put her elbows on the plastic surface beside the plates and beakers. 'And they're going to blow it away in four days' time. What a fucking waste.'

Whether or not this would have worked as a subject-changing parry, she did not get a chance to find out, because the mess PA crackled once and then came clear with the voice of Kraiklyn, who was on the bridge: 'Thought you might like to see this, people.'

The view of the distant Orbital was replaced by a blank screen onto which there then appeared a message in flashing letters.

WARNING/SIGNAL/WARNING/SIGNAL/WARNING/SIGNAL/WARNING: ATTENTION ALL CRAFT! VAVATCH ORBITAL AND HUB WITH ALL ANCILLARY UNITS WILL BE DESTROYED REPEAT DESTROYED MARAINTIME A/4872.0001 EXACT (EQUIVALENT G-HUB TIME 00043.2909.401: EQUIVALENT LIMB THREE TIME 09.256.8: EQUIVALENT IDIRTIMERELATIVE QU'URIBALTA 359.0021: EQIVALENT VAVATCHTIME SEG 7TH.4010.5) BY NOVALEVEL HYPER-GRIDINTRUSION AND SUBSEQUENT CAM BOMBARDMENT. SENT BY *ESCHATOLOGIST* (TEMPORARY NAME), CULTURE GENERAL SYSTEMS VEHICLE. TIMED AT A/4870.986: MARAINBASE ALLTRANS ... SIGNAL SECTION END ... SIGNAL REPETITION NUMBER ONE OF SEVEN FOLLOWS: .... WARNING/SIGNAL/WARNING/ SIGNAL/WARNING ...

'We just ran through that message shell,' Kraiklyn added. 'See you later.' The PA crackled again, then was silent. The message faded from the screen and the Orbital filled it again.

'Hmm,' Jandraligeli said. 'Brief and to the point.'

'Like I said.' Yalson nodded at the screen.

'I remember . . .' Wubslin said slowly, staring at the band of brilliant blue and white on the screen, 'when I was very young one of my teachers floated a little toy metal boat on the surface of a bucketful of water. Then she lifted the bucket by the handle and held me up against her chest with her other arm, so that I was facing the same way she was. She started to go round and round, faster and faster, letting the spin send the bucket out away from her, and eventually the bucket was straight out, the surface of the water in it at ninety degrees to the floor, and I was held there with this great big adult hand across my belly and everything spinning around me and I was watching this little toy boat, which was still floating on the water, even though the water was straight up and down in front of my face, and my teacher said, "You remember this if you're ever lucky enough to see the Megaships of Vavatch." '

'Yeah?' Lamm said. 'Well, they're about to let the fucking handle go.'

'So let's just hope we're not still on the surface when they do,' Yalson said.

Jandraligeli turned to her, one eyebrow up: 'After that last fiasco, dear, *nothing* would surprise me.'

'Easy in, easy out,' Aviger said, and the old man laughed.

The haul from Marjoin to Vavatch had taken twenty-three days. The Company had gradually recovered from the effects of the abortive attack on the Temple of Light. There were a few small sprains and grazes; Dorolow had been blind in one eye for a couple of days, and everybody had been quiet and withdrawn, but by the time Vavatch came into sight they were all starting to get so bored with life on board ship, even with less of them on it, that they were looking forward to another operation.

Horza kept the laser rifle which kee-Alsorofus had used, and carried out what rudimentary repairs and improvements the *CAT*'s limited engineering facilities would allow him to effect to his suit. Kraiklyn was full of praise for the one he had taken from Horza; it had lifted him out of the worst of the trouble in the hall of the Temple of Light, and, although it had still taken some heavy fire pulses, it was hardly marked, let alone damaged.

Neisin had said he'd never liked lasers anyway and wouldn't use one again; he had a perfectly good rapid-firing light projectile rifle, and lots of ammunition. He would carry that in future when he wasn't using the Microhowitzer.

Horza and Yalson had started sleeping together every night in what was now their cabin, the one the two women had occupied. During the long days of the voyage they had grown closer but spoken comparatively little, for new lovers. Both seemed to want it that way. Horza's body had completed its regeneration after its impersonation of the Gerontocrat, and there was no longer any trace or sign of that role left on him. But while he told the Company that he was now the way he had always looked, he had in fact moulded his body to look like that of Kraiklyn. Horza was a little taller and fuller-chested than his neutral normal, and his hair was darker and thicker. His face, of

101

course, he could not yet afford to Change, but under its light-brown surface it was ready. A short trance and he could pass for the captain of the *Clear Air Turbulence*; perhaps Vavatch would give him the opportunity he needed.

He had thought long and hard about what to do now that he was part of the Company, and relatively safe, but cut off from his Idiran employers. He could always just go on his own way, but that would let down Xoralundra, whether the old Idiran was alive or dead. It would also be running away from the war, from the Culture and the part he had chosen to play against it. In addition, at first, there was the idea Horza had been toying with anyway, even before he had heard that his next task was to involve going to Schar's World, and that was the idea of returning to an old love.

Her name was Sro Kierachell Zorant. She was what they called a dormant Changer, one who had no training in and no desire to practise Changing, and had accepted the post on Schar's World partly as a relief from the increasingly warlike atmosphere in the Changers' home asteroid of Heibohre. That had been seven years before, when Heibohre was already within what was generally recognised as being Idiran space, and when many Changers were already employed by the Idirans.

Horza was sent to Schar's World partly because he was being punished and partly for his own protection. A group of Changers had plotted to fire up the ancient asteroid's power-plants and take it out of Idiran space, make their home and their species neutral again in the war they could see was becoming inevitable. Horza had discovered the plot and killed two of the conspirators. The court of the Academy of Military Arts on Heibohre – its ruling body in all but name – had compromised between popular feeling on the asteroid, which wanted Horza punished for taking other Changers' lives, and the gratitude it felt towards Horza. The court had a delicate task, considering the not wholehearted support the majority of Changers gave to staying where they were and therefore within the Idiran sphere of influence. By sending Horza to Schar's World with instructions to stay there for several years – but not punishing him otherwise – the court hoped to make all concerned feel their own particular view had carried the day. To the extent that there was no revolt, that the Academy remained the ruling force in the asteroid, and that the services of Changers were in demand as never before since the formation of their unique species, the court had succeeded.

In some ways, Horza had been lucky. He was without friends or influence; his parents were dead; his clan was all but defunct save for him. Family ties meant a lot in the Changer society, and with no influential relatives or friends to speak for him Horza had perhaps escaped more lightly than he had a right to expect.

Horza cooled his heels on Schar's World's snows for less than a year before leaving to join the Idirans in their fight against the Culture, both before and after it was officially termed a war. During that time he had started a relationship with one of the four other Changers there: the woman Changer Kierachell, who disagreed with almost everything Horza believed, but had loved him, body and mind, despite it all. When he left, he knew it had hurt her much more than it had hurt him. He had been glad of the companionship and he liked her, but he hadn't felt anything like what humans were supposed to feel when they talked of love, and by the time he left he was starting, just starting, to grow bored. He told himself at the time that that was the way life was, that he would only hurt her more in the end by staying, that it was partly for her sake he was leaving. But the expression in her eyes the last time he'd looked into them had not been something he enjoyed thinking about, for a long time.

He had heard she was still there, and he thought of her and had fond memories; and the more he had risked his life and the more time had elapsed, the more he wanted to see her again; the more a quieter, less dangerous sort of existence appealed to him. He had imagined the scene, imagined the look in her eyes when he came back to her. . . . Maybe she would have forgotten about him, or even be committed to some relationship with the other Changers at the base on Schar's World, but Horza didn't really think so; he thought of such things only as a sort of insurance.

Yalson made things a little difficult, perhaps, but he was trying not to build too much into their friendship and coupling, even though he was fairly sure it was only those two things to her as well.

So he would impersonate Kraiklyn if he could, or at least kill him and just take over, and hope he could get round the comparatively crude identity fidelities built into the *CAT*'s computer, or get somebody else to do so. Then he would take the *Clear Air Turbulence* to Schar's World, rendezvous with the Idirans if he could, but go in anyway, assuming Mr Adequate – the pet name the Changers on the Schar's World base had for the Dra'Azon being which guarded the planet – would allow him through the Quiet Barrier after the Idirans' botched attempt to fool it with a hollowed-out chuy-hirtsi. He would, if at all possible, give the rest of the Company the chance to back out.

One problem was knowing when to strike at Kraiklyn. Horza was hoping that an opportunity would arise on Vavatch, but it was hard to make definite plans because Kraiklyn didn't seem to have any of his own. He had simply talked of 'opportunities' on the Orbital, which were 'bound to arise' due to its impending destruction, whenever he had been asked during the journey.

'That lying bastard,' Yalson said, one night when they were about halfway to Vavatch from Marjoin. They were lying together in what was now their cabin, in the darkness of the ship night, in about a half-G on the cramped bedspace.

'What?' Horza said. 'Don't you think he's going to Vavatch after all?'

'Oh, he's going there all right, but not because there are unknown possibilities for a successful job. He's going for the Damage game.'

'What Damage game?' Horza asked, turning to her in the darkness where her naked shoulders lay on his arm. He could feel their soft down against his skin. 'You mean a big game? A real one?'

'Yeah. The Ring itself. Last I heard it was only a rumour, but it makes more sense every time I think about it. Vavatch is a certainty, provided they can get a quorum together.'

'The Players on the Eve of Destruction.' Horza laughed gently. 'You think Kraiklyn means to watch or play?'

'He'll try to play, I suppose; if he's as good as he says he is, they might even let him, as long as he can raise the stake. That's supposed to be how he won the *CAT* – not off anybody in a Ring game, but it must have been pretty heavy company if they were gambling ships. But I guess he'd be prepared to watch if it came to it. I bet that's why we're all going on this little holiday. He might try and come up with some sort of excuse, or fabricate some op, but that's the real reason: Damage. Either he's heard something or he's making an intelligent guess, but it's so fucking obvious. . . .' Her voice died away, and Horza felt her head shake on his arm.

'Isn't one of the Ring regulars—?' he said.

'Ghalssel.' Now Horza could feel the light, short-haired head nod against the skin of his arm. 'Yeah, he'll be there, if he possibly can be. He'd burn out the motors on the *Leading Edge* to get to a major Damage game, and the way things have been hotting up in this neck of the woods recently, presenting all those wonderful easy-in, easy-out opportunities, I can't imagine him being far away.' Yalson's voice sounded bitter. 'Myself, I think Ghalssel's the subject of Kraiklyn's wet dreams. Thinks the guy's a fucking hero. Shit.'

'Yalson,' Horza said into the woman's ear, her hair tickling his nose, 'one: how does Kraiklyn have wet dreams if he doesn't sleep? And two: what if he has these cabins bugged?'

Her head turned towards him quickly. 'So fucking what? I'm not afraid of him. He knows I'm one of the most reliable people he's got; I shoot straight and I don't fill my pants when it starts getting hot. I also think Kraiklyn's the best excuse for a leader we've got on the ship or are likely to get, and he knows that. Don't you worry about me. Anyway . . .' He felt her shoulders and head move again, and knew she was looking at him. 'You'd settle it up if I got shot in the back, wouldn't you?'

The thought had never occurred to him.

'Wouldn't you?' she repeated.

'Well, of course I would,' he said. She didn't move. He could hear her breathing.

'You would, wouldn't you?' Yalson said. He brought his arms up and took her by the shoulders. She was warm, the down on her skin was soft, and the muscles and flesh underneath, over her slim frame, were strong and firm.

'Yes, I would,' he said, and only then realised that he meant it.

It was during this time, between Marjoin and Vavatch, that the Changer found out what he wanted to know about the controls and fidelities of the *Clear Air Turbulence*.

Kraiklyn wore an identity ring on the small finger of his right hand, and some of the locks in the *CAT* would work only in the presence of that ring's electronic signature. The control of the ship depended on an audio-visual identity link; Kraiklyn's face was recognised by the craft's computer, as was his voice when he said, 'This is Kraiklyn.' It was that simple. The ship had once had a retina recognition lock as well, but it had malfunctioned long before and been removed. Horza was pleased; copying somebody's retina pattern was a delicate and tricky operation, requiring, amongst a lot of other things, the careful growth of lasing cells around the iris. It almost made more sense to go for a total genetic transcription, where the subject's own DNA became the model for a virus which left only the Changer's brain – and, optionally, gonads – unaltered. That wouldn't be necessary to impersonate Captain Kraiklyn, however.

Horza found out about the ship's fidelities when he asked the Man for a lesson on how to fly the vessel. Kraiklyn had been reluctant at first, but Horza had not pressed him, and had answered a few of

Kraiklyn's apparently casual questions about computers, which followed this request, with feigned ignorance. Seemingly convinced that teaching Horza how to fly the *CAT* would not carry the risk of him taking over the ship, Kraiklyn relented, and allowed Horza to practise piloting the craft on manual, using the rather crude controls in simulator mode under Mipp's instruction while the craft went on its way through space towards Vavatch on autopilot.

'This is Kraiklyn,' the ship PA announced to the mess, a few hours after they ran through the Culture transmission warning of the Orbital's destruction. They were sitting around after a meal, drinking or inhaling, relaxing or, in Dorolow's case, making the Circle of Flame sign on her forehead and saying the Prayer of Thanks. The big Orbital was still on the mess screen and had grown much larger, almost filling it with its inner surface daylight side, but everybody had grown a little blasé about it and now gave it only the occasional glance. All the remaining Company were there, save for Lenipobra and Kraiklyn himself. They looked at each other or the PA speaker when Kraiklyn spoke. 'I've got a job for us, something I just had confirmed. Wubslin, you get the shuttle ready. I'll meet the rest of you in the hangar in three ship hours, suited up, team. And don't worry; this time there'll be no hostiles. This time it really is you-know-what in *and* out.' The speaker crackled, then went silent. Horza and Yalson exchanged looks.

'So,' Jandraligeli said, leaning back in his chair and putting his hands behind his neck. The scar marks on his face deepened slightly as he put on an expression of thoughtfulness. 'Our esteemed leader has again found us something to employ our slight talents?'

'Better not be in another fuckin' temple,' Lamm growled, scratching the small horn grafts where they joined his head.

'How are you going to find a temple on Vavatch?' Neisin said. He was slightly drunk, talking more than he normally did when with the others. Lamm turned his face towards the smaller man, a few seats away and on the other side of the table.

'You'd better just sober up, friend,' he said.

'Seaships,' Neisin told him, taking the nippled cylinder from the table in front of him. 'Nothing but big goddamned seaships on that place. No temples.' He closed his eyes, put his head back and drank.

'There might', Jandraligeli said, 'be temples on the ships.'

'There might be a fucking drunk on this spaceship,' Lamm said, watching Neisin. Neisin looked at him. 'You'd better sober up fast,

106

Neisin,' Lamm continued, pointing with one finger at the smaller man.

'Think I'll head for the hangar,' Wubslin said, standing and walking out of the mess.

'I'm going to see if Kraiklyn wants a hand,' Mipp said, leaving in the opposite direction, through another door.

'Think we could *see* any of those Megaships yet?' Aviger was looking back at the screen. Dorolow looked up at it, too.

'Don't be fucking stupid,' Lamm told him. 'They aren't that big.'

'They're *big*,' Neisin said, nodding to himself and the small cylinder. Lamm looked at him, then at the others, and shook his head. 'Yeah,' Neisin said, 'they're pretty big.'

'They're actually no more than a few kilometres long,' sighed Jandraligeli, sitting back in his chair and looking thoughtful, emphasising the scar marks still further. 'So you won't see them from this far out. But they certainly are large.'

'And they just go round and round the whole Orbital?' Yalson said. She already knew, but she would rather have the Mondlidician talking than Lamm and Neisin arguing. Horza smiled to himself. Jandraligeli nodded.

'For ever and ever. It takes them about forty years to go right round in a circle.'

'Don't they ever stop?' Yalson asked. Jandraligeli looked at her and raised an eyebrow.

'It *takes* them several years just to get to full *speed*, young lady. They weigh about a billion tonnes. They never stop; they just keep going round in circles. Full-size liners go on excursions and act as tenders, and they use aircraft, too.'

'Did you know,' Aviger said, looking round those still seated at the table and leaning forward with his elbows tightly folded, 'you actually weigh less on a Megaship? It's because they go round in the opposite direction from the way the Orbital spins.' Aviger paused and frowned. 'Or is it the other way round?'

'Oh fuck,' Lamm said, shaking his head violently, then getting up and leaving.

Jandraligeli frowned. 'Fascinating,' he said.

Dorolow smiled at Aviger, and the old man looked round the others nodding. 'Well, whatever; it's a fact,' Aviger declared.

'Right.' Kraiklyn placed one foot up on the shuttle's rear ramp and put his hands on his hips. He wore a pair of shorts; his suit stood ready to be put on, opened down the chest front like a discarded insect skin, just behind him. 'I told you we've got a job. This is what it is.' Kraiklyn paused, looked at the Company, standing or sitting or leaning on guns and rifles throughout the hangar. 'We're going to hit one of the Megaships.' He paused, apparently waiting for a reaction. Only Aviger looked surprised and in any way excited; the rest, with only Mipp and the recently woken Lenipobra absent, seemed unimpressed. Mipp was on the bridge; Lenipobra was still struggling to get ready in his cabin.

'Well,' Kraiklyn said, annoyed, 'you all know that Vavatch is going to get blown away by the Culture in a few days. People have been getting everything they can off the place, and the Megaships are all abandoned now apart from a few wrecking and salvage teams. I guess all the valuables are off them. But there is one ship called the *Olmedreca*, where a couple of the teams had a little argument. Some careless person let off a little nuke, and now the *Olmedreca*'s got a damn great hole in one side. It's still afloat and it's still scrubbing off speed, but, because the nuke went off on one side and that hole hasn't done a lot for the ship's streamlining, it's started going round in a big curve, and it's getting closer to the outside Edgewall all the time. The last transmission I picked up, nobody was sure whether it would hit before the Culture starts blasting or not, but they don't seem happy to take the chance, so it looks like there isn't anybody on board.'

'You want us to go onto it,' Yalson said.

'Yeah, because I've been on the *Olmedreca*, and I think I know something people will have forgotten in the rush to get off: bow lasers.'

A few of the Company looked sceptically from one to another.

'Yeah, Megaships have bow lasers – especially the *Olmedreca*. It used to sail through stretches of the Circlesea a lot of the other ships didn't go through, places where there was a lot of floating weeds or icebergs; it couldn't exactly manoeuvre out of the way so it had to be able to destroy anything in its path, and have the firepower to do it. The *Olmedreca*'s front armament would put a few fleet battleships to shame. That thing could frazzle its way through an iceberg bigger than it was itself, and blast islands of floatweed out of the water so big that people used to think it was attacking the Edgeland. My guess – and it's an educated one because I've been reading between the lines of the outcoming signals – is that nobody's remembered about all that weaponry, and so we're going to go for it.'

'What if this ship hits the wall while we're on board?' Dorolow said. Kraiklyn smiled at her.

'We're not blind, are we? We know where the wall is and we know where . . . we'll be able to *see* where the *Olmedreca* is. We'll go down, take a look, and then if we decide we have the time, we'll remove a few of the smaller lasers. . . . Hell, just one would do. I'm going to be down there, too, you know, and I'm not going to risk my own neck if I can see the Edgewall looming up, am I?'

'We taking the *CAT*?' Lamm said.

'Not over the top. The Orbital's got just enough mass to make the warp a tricky proposition, and the fusions would get zapped by the Hub auto-defences; they'd think our motors were meteorites or something. No – we'll leave the *CAT* here unmanned. I can always control it remotely from my suit if there's an emergency. We'll use the shuttle's FFD; force fields work fine on an Orbital. Oh, that's one thing I shouldn't really have to remind you about; *don't* try to use your AG on the place, OK? Anti-gravity works against mass, not spin, so you'd end up taking an unexpected bath if you jumped over the side expecting to fly round to the bows.'

'What do we do after we get this laser, if we get it?' Yalson said. Kraiklyn frowned briefly. He shrugged.

'Probably the best thing is to head for the capital. Its called Evanauth . . . a port where they used to build the Megaships. It's on the land, of course. . . .' He smiled, looking at some of the others.

'Yeah,' Yalson said. 'But what do we do once we get there?'

'Well . . .' Kraiklyn looked hard at the woman. Horza kicked her heel with his toe. Yalson glared round at the Changer while Kraiklyn spoke. 'We might be able to use the port facilities – in space, that is, on the underside of Evanauth – to mount the laser. But anyway, I'm sure the Culture will be prompt, so we might even just go to sample the last days of one of the most interesting combined ports of call in the galaxy. And its last nights, I might add.' Kraiklyn looked at several of the others, and there was some laughter and a few remarks. He stopped smiling and looked at Yalson again. 'So it could be quite interesting, don't you think?'

'Yeah. All right. You're the boss, Kraiklyn.' Yalson grinned, then put her head down. Under her breath, to Horza, she hissed, 'Guess where the Damage game is?'

'Won't this big seaship go right through the wall and wreck the Orbital anyway, before the Culture does anything?' Aviger was saying. Kraiklyn smiled condescendingly and shook his head.

'I think you'll find the Edgewalls are up to it.'

'Ho! I hope so!' Aviger laughed.

'Well, don't worry about it,' Kraiklyn reassured him. 'Now, somebody give Wubslin a hand to run a final check on the shuttle. I'm going up to the bridge to make sure Mipp knows what to do. We'll be setting off in about ten minutes.' Kraiklyn stepped back and into his suit, gathering it up and putting his arms into the sleeves. He fastened the main chest latches, picked up his helmet and nodded to the Company as he walked by them and up the steps out of the hangar.

'Were you trying to annoy him?' Horza asked Yalson. She turned to the Changer.

'Ah, I just wanted to give him a hint that I could see through him; he doesn't fool me.'

Wubslin and Aviger were checking the shuttle. Lamm was fiddling with his laser. Jandraligeli stood with arms crossed, his back resting against the hangar bulkhead near the door, eyes raised to the ceiling lights, a bored expression on his face. Neisin was talking quietly to Dorolow, who saw the small man as a possible convert to the Circle of Flame.

'You reckon Evanauth is where this Damage game's going to be?' Horza asked. He was smiling. Yalson's face looked very small inside the big, still open neck of her suit, and very serious.

'Yes I do. That devious bastard probably invented the whole goddamn op on this Megaboat thing. He's never told *me* he'd been to Vavatch before. Lying bastard.' She looked at Horza, punched him in the suit belly, making him laugh and dance back. 'What are you smiling at?'

'You,' Horza laughed. 'So what if he wants to go and play a game of Damage? You keep saying it's his ship and he's the boss and all that crap, but you won't let the poor guy have a bit of fun.'

'So why doesn't he admit it?' Yalson nodded sharply at Horza. 'Because he doesn't want to share any of his winnings, that's why. The rule is we divide *everything* we make, sharing it out according to—'

'Well, I can see his point if that's what it is,' Horza said reasonably. 'If he wins in a Damage game it's all his own work; nothing to do with us.'

'That's *not* the point!' Yalson yelled. Her mouth was set in a tight line, her hands were on her hips; she stamped her feet.

'OK,' Horza said, grinning. 'So when you bet on me to win my fight with Zallin, why didn't you give all your winnings right back again?'

'That's different—' Yalson said in exasperation. But she was interrupted.

'Hey, hey!' Lenipobra came bounding down the steps into the

hangar as Horza was about to say something. Both he and Yalson turned to the younger man as he skipped up to them, fastening his suit gloves to the cuffs. 'D-d-did you see that message earlier?' He looked excited and didn't seem to be able to keep still; he kept rubbing his gloved hands together and shuffling his feet. 'Novagrade g-gridfire! Wow! What a spectacle! I *love* the C-Culture! *And* a C-C-CAM dusting – hoo-wee!' He laughed, doubled at the waist, slapped both hands on the hangar deck, bounced up and smiled at everybody. Dorolow scratched her ears and looked puzzled. Lamm glared at the youth over the barrel of his rifle, while Yalson and Horza looked at each other, shaking their heads. Lenipobra went dancing and shadow-boxing up to Jandraligeli, who raised one eyebrow and watched the gangly young man prancing about in front of him.

'The weaponry of the end of the universe, and this young idiot is practically coming in his pants.'

'Aw, you're just a spoilsport, Ligeli,' Lenipobra said to the Mondlidician, stopping dancing and dropping his punching arms to turn away and slouch off towards the shuttle. As he passed Yalson and Horza he muttered, 'Yalson, what the hell is C-CAM anyay?'

'Collapsed Anti-Matter, kid.' Yalson smiled as Lenipobra kept on walking. Horza laughed soundlessly as the young man's head nodded inside the open neck of his suit. He walked into the open rear of the shuttle.

The *Clear Air Turbulence* rolled. The shuttle left the hangar and flew along the underside of the Vavatch Orbital, leaving the spacecraft flying underneath like a tiny silver fish under the hull of some great dark ship.

On a small screen, fitted at one end of the shuttle's main compartment since its last outing, the suited figures could watch the seemingly endless curve of ultradense base material stretching off into the dark distance, lit by starlight. It was like flying upside-down over a planet made of metal; and of all the sights the galaxy held which were the result of conscious effort, it was one bested for what the Culture would call *gawp value* only by a big Ring, or a Sphere.

The shuttle crossed a thousand kilometres of the smooth undersurface. Then suddenly above it there was a wedge of darkness, a slant of something which looked even smoother than the base material, but which was clear, transparent and angling out from the base itself and slicing into space like the edge of a crystal knife for two thousand kilometres: the Edgewall. This was the wall bordered by sea, on the

111

far side of the Orbital from the thread of land they had seen on their approach in the *CAT*. The first ten kilometres of the flat curve were dark as space; their mirror surface showed only when stars reflected on them, and looking at that perfect image the mind could spin, seeing for what looked like light-years when in fact the surface was only a few thousand metres away.

'God, that thing's big,' Neisin whispered. The shuttle continued to rise, and above it there appeared through the wall a glow of light, a shining expanse of blue.

Into sunlight, hardly filtered through the transparent wall, the shuttle climbed in empty space beside the Edgewall. Two kilometres away there was air, even if it was thin air, but the shuttle climbed in nothing, angling out along with the wall as it sloped towards its line of summit. The shuttle crossed that knife-edge, two thousand kilometres up from the base of the Orbital, then started to follow the slope of wall back down on the inside; it passed through the Orbital's magnetic field, a region where small magnetised particles of artificial dust blocked out some of the sun's rays, so making the sea below it cooler than elsewhere on the world, producing Vavatch's different climates. The shuttle continued to fall: through ions, then thin gases, finally into thin and cloudless air, shuddering in a coriolis jetstream. The sky above turned from black to blue. The Orbital of Vavatch, a fourteen-million-kilometre hoop of water seemingly hung naked in space, spread out before the falling craft like some vast circular painting.

'Well, at least we're in daylight,' Yalson said. 'Let's just hope our captain's information about exactly where this wonderful ship is turns out to be accurate.' The screen showed clouds. As the shuttle fell and flew, it was coming down onto a false landscape of water vapour. The clouds seemed to stretch for ever, along the curved inside surface of the Orbital, which even from that height looked flat, then sweeping up into the black sky above. Only much further away could they see the blue expanse of real ocean, though there were hints of smaller patches closer to hand.

'Don't worry about the cloud,' Kraiklyn said over the cabin speaker. 'That'll shift as the morning wears on.'

The shuttle was still dropping, still flying forward through the thickening atmosphere. After a while they started going through the first few very high altitude clouds. Horza shifted slightly in his suit; ever since the *CAT* had matched velocities and curve with the big Orbital, and turned off its own AG, the craft and the Company had been under the same fake gravity of the construction's spin – slightly more, in fact, because they were stationary relative to the base but further out from it. Vavatch, whose original builders had come from a higher-G planet, was spun to produce about twenty per cent more 'gravity' than the accepted human average which the *CAT*'s generator was set for. So Horza, like the rest of the Company, felt heavier than he was used to. His suit was chafing already.

Clouds filled the cabin screen with grey.

'There it is!' Kraiklyn shouted, not trying to keep the excitement from his voice. He had been quiet for almost a quarter of an hour, and people had started to get restless. The shuttle had banked a few times, this way and that, apparently searching for the *Olmedreca*. Sometimes the screen had been clear, showing layers of cloud beneath; sometimes it hazed over with grey again as they entered another bank or pillar of vapour. Once it had iced over. 'I can see the topmost towers!'

The Company crowded forward in the cabin, getting out of their seats and coming closer to the screen. Only Lamm and Jandraligeli stayed sitting down.

'About fucking time,' Lamm said. 'How the hell do you have to look all this time for something four K long?'

'It's easy when you've no radar,' Jandraligeli said. 'I'm just thankful we didn't *hit* the damn thing while we were flying through those awful clouds.'

'Shit,' Lamm said, and inspected his rifle again.

'. . . Look at that,' Neisin said.

In a wasteland of clouds, like some vast canyon torn in a planet made of vapour, through kilometres of levels and in a space so long and wide that even in the clear air between the piled clouds the view simply faded rather than ended, the *Olmedreca* moved.

Its lower levels of superstructure were quite hidden, invisible in the ocean-hugging bank of mist, but from its unseen decks rose immense towers and structures of glass and light metal, rearing hundreds of metres into the clear air. Seemingly unconnected, they moved slowly and smoothly over the flat surface of the low bank of cloud like pieces on an endless game board, casting dim and watery shadows on the opaque top of the mist as the sun of Vavatch's system shone through layers of cloud ten kilometres above.

As those huge towers moved through the air, they left behind them wisps and strands of vapour, ruffled from the mist's smooth top by the passage of the great ship beneath. In the small, clear spaces that the towers and higher levels of superstructure left in the mist, lower levels could be seen: walkways and promenades, the linked arches of a monorail system, pools and small parks with trees, even a few pieces of equipment like small flyers and bits of tiny, doll's-house-like furniture. As the eye and brain grasped the scene, they could, from that height, make out the overall bulge in the surface of the cloud that the ship made – an area of slight uplift in the mist four kilometres long and nearly three wide, and shaped like a stubby pointed leaf or an arrowhead.

The shuttle came lower. The towers, with their glinting windows, their suspended bridges, flyer pads, ariels, railings, decks and flapping awnings, sailed by alongside, silent and dark.

'Well,' Kraiklyn's voice said in a businesslike way, 'looks like we'll have a bit of a walk to the bows, team. I can't take us under this lot. Still, we're a good hundred kilometres away from the Edgewall, so we've got plenty of time. The ship isn't heading straight for it anyway. I'll put us down as close as I can.'

'Fuck. Here we go,' Lamm said angrily. 'I might have known.'

'A long walk in this gravity is just what I need,' Jandraligeli said.

'It's *vast*!' Lenipobra was still staring at the screen. 'That thing is *huge*!' He was shaking his head. Lamm got up from his seat, pushed the youth out of the way and banged on the door of the shuttle flight deck.

'What is it?' Kraiklyn said over the cabin speaker. 'I'm looking for a place to put down. If that's you, Lamm, just sit down.'

Lamm stared at the door with a look first of surprise, then of annoyance. He snorted and went back to his seat, shoving past Lenipobra again. 'Bastard,' he muttered, then put his helmet visor down and turned it to mirror.

'Right,' Kraiklyn said. 'We're putting down.' Those still standing sat again, and in a few seconds the shuttle bumped carefully down. The doors jawed and a cold gust of air entered through them. They filed out slowly, into the wide views of the silent, rock-steady Megaship. Horza sat in the shuttle waiting for the rest to go, then saw Lamm watching him. Horza stood and gave a mock bow to the dark-suited figure.

'After you,' he said.

'No,' Lamm said. 'You first.' He nodded his head to one side towards the open doors. Horza went out of the shuttle, followed by Lamm. Lamm always made a point of being last out of the shuttle; it was lucky for him.

114

They stood on a flyer landing pad, near the base of a large rectangular tower of superstructure, perhaps sixty metres tall. The decks of the tower soared into the sky above, while over the surface of the cloud bank in front, and to all sides of the pad, towers and small bulges in the mist showed where the rest of the ship was, though where it ended it was impossible to tell now that they were so low down. They couldn't even see where the nuke had gone off; there was no list, not a tremor to reveal that they were really on a damaged ship travelling over an ocean, not standing in a deserted city with clouds moving smoothly past.

Horza joined some of the others by a low restraining wall at the edge of the pad, looking down about twenty metres to a deck just visible now and again through the thin surface of the mist. Streamers of vapour flowed across the area below in long sinuous waves, sometimes revealing, sometimes obscuring a deck covered with patches of earth planted with small bushes, with little canopies and chairs scattered about and small tent-like buildings on the surface. It all looked deserted and forlorn, like a resort in winter, and Horza shivered inside his suit. Ahead of them, the view led to an implied point about a kilometre away, where a few small, skinny towers poked out of the cloud bank, near the unseen bows of the craft.

'Looks like we're heading into even more cloud,' Wubslin said, pointing in the direction they were heading. There a great canyon wall of cloud hung in the air, stretching from one side of the horizon to the other, and higher than any tower on the Megaship. It shone for them in the increasing sunlight.

'Maybe it'll go away as it gets warmer,' Dorolow said, not sounding convinced.

'If we hit that lot we can forget about these lasers,' Horza said, looking round from the rest towards the shuttle, where Kraiklyn was talking to Mipp, who was to stay on guard at the shuttle craft while the rest went forward to the bows. 'With no radar we'll have to lift off before we go into the cloud bank.'

'Maybe— ' Yalson began.

'Well, I'm going to take a look down there,' Lenipobra said, bringing his visor down and putting one hand on the low parapet. Horza looked across at him.

Lenipobra waved. 'See you at the b-bows; ya-hoo!'

He vaulted cleanly over the parapet and started to fall towards the deck five storeys below. Horza had opened his mouth to shout, and started forward to grab the youth, but, like the rest of them, he had realised too late what Lenipobra was doing.

One second he was there, the next he had leapt over.

'No!'

'Leni—!' Those not already looking down rushed to the parapet; the tiny figure was tumbling. Horza saw it and hoped that somehow it could pull up, stop, do something. The scream started in their helmets when Lenipobra was less than ten metres from the deck below; it ended abruptly the instant the spread-eagled figure crashed onto the border of a small earthed area. It bounced slackly for about a metre over the deck, then lay still.

'Oh my God . . .' Neisin suddenly sat down, took off his helmet and put his hand to his eyes. Dorolow put her head down and started to unfasten her helmet.

'What the hell was that?' Kraiklyn was running over from the shuttle, Mipp behind him. Horza was still looking over the parapet, down at the still, doll-like figure crumpled on the deck below. Mist thickened around it as the wisps and streamers grew thicker for a while.

'Lenipobra! Lenipobra!' Wubslin shouted into his helmet microphone. Yalson turned away and swore to herself softly, turning off her transmit intercom. Aviger stood, shaking, his face blank inside his helmet visor. Kraiklyn skidded to a halt at the parapet, then looked over.

'Leni—?' He looked round at the others. 'Is that—? What *happened*? What was he doing? If any of you were fooling—'

'He jumped,' Jandraligeli said. His voice was shaky. He tried to laugh. 'Guess kids these days just can't tell their gravity from their rotating frame of reference.'

'He *jumped*?' Kraiklyn shouted. He grabbed Jandraligeli by the suit collar. 'How could he *jump*? I *told* you AG wouldn't work, I *told* you all, when we were in the hangar. . . .'

'He was *late*,' Lamm broke in. He kicked at the thin metal of the parapet, failing to dent it. 'The stupid little bastard was *late*. None of us thought to tell him.'

Kraiklyn let go of Jandraligeli and looked around the rest.

'It's true,' Horza said. He shook his head. 'I just didn't think. None of us did. Lamm and Jandraligeli were even complaining about having to walk to the bows when Leni was in the shuttle, and you mentioned it, but I suppose he just didn't hear.' Horza shrugged. 'He was excited.'

He shook his head.

116

'We all fucked up,' Yalson said heavily. She had turned her communicator back on. Nobody spoke for a while. Kraiklyn stood and looked round them, then went to the parapet, put both hands on it and looked down.

'Leni?' Wubslin said into his communicator, looking down too. His voice was quiet.

'Chicel horhava,' Dorolow made the Circle of Flame sign, closed her eyes and said, 'Sweet lady, accept his soul in peace.'

'Wormshit,' Lamm swore, and turned away. He started firing the laser at distant, higher parts of the tower above them.

'Dorolow,' Kraiklyn said, 'you, Wubslin and Yalson head down there. See what . . . ah, shit . . .' Kraiklyn turned round. 'Get down there. Mipp, you drop them a line or the medkit, whatever. The rest of us . . . we're going forward to the bows, all right?' He looked around them, challenging. 'You might want to go back, but that just means he's died for nothing.'

Yalson turned away, switching off her transmit button again.

'Might as well,' Jandraligeli said. 'I suppose.'

'Not me,' Neisin said. 'I'm not. I'm staying here, with the shuttle.' He sat with his head bowed between his shoulders, his helmet on the deck. He stared at the deck and shook his head. 'Not me. No sir, not me. I've had it for today. I'm staying here.'

Kraiklyn looked at Mipp and nodded at Neisin. 'Look after him.' He turned to Dorolow and Wubslin. 'Get going. You never know; you might be able to do something. Yalson – you, too.' Yalson wasn't looking at Kraiklyn but she turned and followed Wubslin and the other woman when they set off to find a way down to the lower deck.

A crash they felt through their soles made them all jump. They turned round to see Lamm, a distant figure against the far-away clouds, firing up at flyer-pad supports five or six decks above, the invisible beam licking flame around the stressed metal. Another pad gave way, flapping and spinning like a huge playing-card, smashing into the level they stood on with another deck-quivering thump. 'Lamm!' Kraiklyn burst out. '*Stop* that!'

The black suit with the raised rifle pretended not to hear, and Kraiklyn lifted his own heavy laser and flicked the trigger. A section of deck five metres in front of Lamm ruptured in flame and glowing metal, heaving up, then collapsing back down, a blister of gases blowing out from it rocking Lamm off his feet so that he staggered and almost fell. He steadied and stood, visibly shaking with rage, even from that distance. Kraiklyn still had the gun pointing towards him.

117

Lamm straightened and shouldered his own gun, coming back almost at a saunter, as though nothing had happened. The others relaxed slightly.

Kraiklyn got them all together; then they set off, following Dorolow, Yalson and Wubslin to the inside of the tower and a broad sweeping spiral of carpeted staircase which led down, into the Megaship the *Olmedreca*.

'Dead as a fossil,' Yalson's voice said bitterly in their helmet speakers, when they were about halfway down. 'Dead as a god-damned fossil.'

When they passed them on their way to the bows, Yalson and Wubslin were waiting by the body for the winch line Mipp was lowering from above. Dorolow was praying.

They crossed over the deck level Lenipobra had died on, down into the mist and along a narrow gangway with nothing but empty space on either side. 'Just five metres,' Kraiklyn said, using the light needle radar in his Rairch suit to plumb the depths of vapour below them. The mist was getting slowly thinner as they went on, up again onto another deck, now clear, then down again, by outside stairs and long ramps. The sun was hazily visible a few times, a red disc which sometimes brightened and sometimes dimmed. They crossed decks, skirted swimming pools, traversed promenades and landing pads, went past tables and chairs, through groves and under awnings, arcades and arches. They saw towers above them through the mist, and a couple of times looked down into huge pits carved out of the ship and lined with yet more decks and opened areas, from the bottom of which they thought they could hear the sea. The swirling mist lay in the bottom of such great bowls like a broth of dreams.

They stopped at a line of small, open, wheeled vehicles with seats and gaily striped awnings for roofs. Kraiklyn looked around, getting his bearings. Wubslin tried starting the vehicles, but none of the small cars were working.

'There are two ways to go here,' Kraiklyn said, frowning as he looked forward. The sun was briefly bright above, turning the vapour over them and to each side golden with its rays. The lines of some unknown sport or game lay drawn out on the deck under their feet. A tower forced out of the mist to one side, the curls and whorls of mist moving like huge arms, dimming the sun again. Its shadow cut across the path in front of them. 'We'll split up.' Kraiklyn looked around. 'I'll go that way with Aviger and Jandraligeli. Horza and Lamm, you

118

go that way.' He pointed to one side. 'That's leading down to one of the side prows. There ought to be something there; just keep looking.' He touched a wrist button. 'Yalson?'

'Hello,' Yalson said over the intercom. She, Wubslin and Dorolow had watched Lenipobra's body being winched up to the shuttle and then left, following the rest.

'Right,' Kraiklyn said, looking at one of the helmet screens, 'you're only about three hundred metres away.' He turned and looked back the way they had come. A collection of towers, some kilometres away, were strung out behind them now, mostly starting at higher levels. They could see more and more of the *Omedreca*. Mist streamed quietly past them in the silence. 'Oh yeah,' Kraiklyn said, 'I see you.' He waved.

Some small figures on a distant deck at the side of one of the great mist-filled bowls waved back. 'I see you, too,' Yalson said.

'When you get to where we are now, head over to the left for the other side prow; there are subsidiary lasers there. Horza and Lamm will—'

'Yeah, we heard,' Yalson said.

'Right. We'll be able to bring the shuttle closer, maybe right down to wherever we find anything soon. Let's go. Keep your eyes open.' He nodded at Aviger and Jandraligeli, and they went forward. Lamm and Horza looked at each other, then set off in the direction Kraiklyn had indicated. Lamm motioned to Horza to switch off his communicator transmit and open his visor.

'If we'd waited we could have put the shuttle down where we wanted to in the first place,' he said with his own visor open. Horza agreed.

'Stupid little bastard,' Lamm said.

'Who?' asked Horza.

'That kid. Jumping off the goddamned platform.'

'Hmm.'

'Know what I'm going to do?' Lamm looked at the Changer.

'What?'

'I'm going to cut that stupid little bastard's tongue out, that's what I'm going to do. A tattooed tongue should be worth something, shouldn't it? Little bastard owed me money anyway. What do you think? How much do you think it'd be worth?'

'No idea.'

'Little bastard . . .' Lamm muttered.

The two men tramped along the deck, angling away from the dead-ahead line they had taken previously. It was difficult to tell where exactly they were heading, but according to Kraiklyn it was towards one of the side prows, which stuck out like enormous outriggers attached to the *Olmedreca* and formed harbours for the liners which had shuttled to and from the Megaship in its heyday, on excursions, or working as tenders.

They passed where there had evidently been a recent fire-fight; laser burns, smashed glass and torn metal littered an accommodation section of the ship, and torn curtains and wall hangings flapped in the steady breeze of the great ship's progress. Two of the small wheeled vehicles lay smashed on their sides near by. They crunched over the debris and kept walking. The other two groups were heading forward, too, making reasonable progress according to their reports and chatter. Ahead of them there still lay the enormous bank of cloud they had seen earlier; it wasn't growing any thinner or lower, and they could only be a couple of kilometres from it now, though distances were hard to estimate.

'We're here,' Kraiklyn said eventually, his voice crackling in Horza's ear. Lamm turned his transmit channel on.

'What?' He looked, mystified, at Horza, who shrugged.

'What's keeping you two?' Kraiklyn said. 'We had further to walk. We're at the main bows. They stick further out than the bit you're on.'

'The hell you are, Kraiklyn,' Yalson broke in from the other team, which was supposed to be heading for the opposite set of side prows.

'What?' Kraiklyn said. Lamm and Horza stopped to listen to the exchange over their communicators. Yalson spoke again:

'We've just come to the edge of the ship. In fact I think we're a bit out from the main side . . . on some sort of wing or buttress. . . . Anyway, there's no side prow around here. You've sent us in the wrong direction.'

'But you . . .' Kraiklyn began. His voice died away.

'Kraiklyn, dammit, you've sent us towards the bow and *you're* on a side prow!' Lamm yelled into his helmet mike. Horza had been coming to the same conclusion. That was why they were still walking and Kraiklyn's team had reached the bows. There was silence from the *Clear Air Turbulence*'s captain for a few seconds, then he said:

'Shit, you must be right.' They could hear him sigh. 'I guess you and Horza had better keep going. I'll send somebody down in your direction once we've had a quick look round here. I think I can see some sort of gallery with a lot of transparent blisters where there might be some lasers. Yalson, you head back to where we split up and tell me when you get there. We'll see who comes up with something useful first.'

'Fucking marvellous,' Lamm said, stamping off into the mist. Horza followed, wishing the ill-fitting suit didn't rub so much.

The two men walked on. Lamm stopped to investigate some state rooms which had already been looted. Fine materials snagged on broken glass floated like the cloud around them. In one apartment they saw rich wooden furniture, a holosphere lying broken in a corner and a glass-sided water tank the size of a room, full of rotting, brilliantly coloured fish and fine clothes, floating together on the surface like exotic weeds.

Over their communicators Horza and Lamm heard the others in Kraiklyn's group find what they thought was a door leading to the gallery where – they hoped – they would find lasers behind the transparent bubbles they had seen earlier. Horza told Lamm they had best not waste their time, and so they left the state rooms and went back out onto the deck to continue heading forward.

'Hey, Horza,' Kraiklyn said, as the Changer and Lamm walked along the deck and into a long tunnel lit by dim sunlight coming through mist and opaque ceiling panels. 'This needle radar's not working properly.'

Horza answered as they walked. 'What's wrong?'

'It isn't going through cloud, that's what's wrong.'

'I never really got a chance to . . . What do you mean?' Horza stopped in the corridor. He felt something wrong in his guts. Lamm kept walking, away from him, down the corridor.

'It's giving me a reading off that big cloud in front, right the way along and about half a K up.' Kraiklyn laughed. 'It isn't the Edgewall, that's for sure, and I can *see* that's a cloud, and it's closer than the needle says it is.'

'Where are you now?' Dorolow broke in. 'Did you find any lasers? What about that door?'

'No, just a sort of sun lounge or something,' Kraiklyn said.

'Kraiklyn!' Horza shouted. 'Are you sure about that reading?'

'I'm sure. The needle says—'

'Sure isn't much fucking sun to lounge—' somebody broke in, though it sounded as if it was accidental and they didn't know their transmit was on. Horza felt sweat start out on his brow. Something was wrong.

'Lamm!' he shouted. Lamm, thirty metres away down the cor-

121

ridor, turned as he walked and looked back. 'Come back!' Horza shouted. Lamm stopped.

'Horza, there can't be anything—'

'Kraiklyn!' This time it was Mipp's voice, calling from the shuttle. 'There was somebody else here. I just saw another craft take off somewhere behind where we landed; they've gone now.'

'OK, thanks Mipp,' Kraiklyn said, his voice calm. 'Listen, Horza, from what I can see from here, the bows where you are have just gone into the cloud, so it is a cloud. . . . Shit, we can all see it's a goddamn cloud. Don't—'

The ship shuddered under Horza's feet. He rocked. Lamm looked at him, puzzled. 'Did you feel that?' Horza shouted.

'Feel what?' Kraiklyn said.

'Kraiklyn?' It was Mipp again. 'I can see something. . . .'

'Lamm, get back here!' Horza shouted, through the air and into his helmet mike together. Lamm looked around him. Horza thought he could feel a continuing tremor in the deck below.

'What did you feel?' Kraiklyn said. He was starting to get annoyed.

Yalson chipped in, 'I thought I felt something. Nothing much. But listen, these things aren't supposed to . . . they aren't supposed to—'

'Kraiklyn,' Mipp said more urgently, 'I think I can see—'

'Lamm!' Horza was backing off now, back down the long tunnel of corridor. Lamm stayed where he was, looking hesitant.

Horza could hear something, a curious growling noise; it reminded him of a jet engine or a fusion motor heard from a very long distance away, but it wasn't either. He could feel something under his feet, too – that tremor, and there was some sort of pull, a tug that seemed to be dragging him forward, towards Lamm, towards the bows, as though he was in a weak field, or—

'Kraiklyn!' Mipp yelled. 'I can! There is! I – you – I'm—' he spluttered.

'Look, will you all just calm down?'

'I can feel something . . .' Yalson began.

Horza started running, pounding back down the corridor. Lamm, who had started to walk back, stopped and put his hands on his hips when he saw the other man running, away from him. There was a distant roaring noise in the air, like a big waterfall heard from far down a gorge.

'I can feel something too, it's as if—'

'What was Mipp yelling about?'

'We're crashing!' Horza shouted as he ran. The roaring was coming closer, growing stronger all the time.

'Ice!' It was Mipp. 'I'm bringing the shuttle! Run! It's a wall of ice! Neisin! Where are you? Neisin! I've got—'

'What!'

'*ICE?*'

The roaring noise grew; the corridor around Horza started to groan. Several of the opaque roof panels fractured and fell to the floor in front of him. A section of wall suddenly sprang out like an opening door and he just avoided running into it. The noise filled his ears.

Lamm looked round, and saw the end of the corridor coming towards him; the whole end section was closing off steadily with a grinding roar, advancing towards him at about running speed. He fired at it but it didn't stop; smoke poured into the corridor. He swore, turned and ran, following Horza.

People were yelling and shouting from all over now. There was a babble of tiny voices in both Horza's ears, but all he could really hear was the thundering noise behind him. The deck beneath his feet bucked and trembled, as though the whole gigantic ship was a building caught in an earthquake. The plates and panels which made up the corridor walls were buckling; the floor rose up in places; more roof panels shattered and fell. All the time the same sapping force was pulling him back, slowing him down as though he was in a dream. He ran out into daylight, heard Lamm not far behind.

'Kraiklyn, you stupid motherfucking son of a bitch's bastard!' Lamm screamed.

The voices yammered in his ear; his heart pounded. He threw each foot forward with all his might, but the roaring was coming closer, growing stronger. He ran past the empty state rooms where the soft materials blew, the roof was starting to fold in on the apartments and the deck was tilting; the holosphere they had seen earlier came rolling and bouncing out of the collapsing windows. A hatch near Horza blew out in a gust of pressured air and flying debris; he ducked as he ran, felt splinters strike his suit. He skidded as the deck under him banged and leapt. Lamm's steps came pounding behind him. Lamm continued to scream abuse at Kraiklyn over the intercom.

The noise behind him was like a gigantic waterfall, a big rock-slide, like a continuous explosion, a volcano. His ears ached and his mind reeled, stunned by the volume of the racket. A line of windows set in the wall ahead of him went white, then exploded towards him, throwing particles at his suit in a series of small hard clouds. He put his head down again, he headed for the doorway.

'Bastard bastard bastard!' Lamm bellowed.

'—not stopping!'

'—over here!'

'Shut up, Lamm.'

'Horzaaa . . . !'

Voices screamed in his ear. He was running on carpet now, inside a broad corridor; open doors were flapping, light fittings on the ceiling were vibrating. Suddenly a deluge of water swept across the corridor in front of him, twenty metres away, and for a second he thought he was at sea level, but knew he couldn't be; when he ran over the place where the water had been he could see and hear it frothing and gurgling down a broad spiral stairwell, and only a few dribbles were falling from overhead. The tugging of the slowly decelerating ship seemed less now, but the roar of noise was still all around him. He was weakening, running in a daze, trying to keep his balance as the long corridor vibrated and twisted around him. Now a rush of air was flowing past him; some sheets of paper and plastic flapped past him like coloured birds.

'—bastard bastard bastard—'

'Lamm—'

There was daylight ahead, through a glassed-over sun deck of broad windows. He jumped through some big-leaved plants growing in large pots and landed in a group of flimsy chairs set round a small table, demolishing them.

'—fucking stupid bast—'

'Lamm, shut up!' Kraiklyn's voice broke in. 'We can't hear—'

The line of windows ahead went white, cracking like ice then bursting out; he dived through the space, to skid over the fragments scattered on the deck beyond. Behind him, the top and bottom of the shattered windows started to close slowly, like a huge mouth.

'You bastard! You motherfu—'

'Dammit, change channels! Go to—'

He slipped on the shards of glass, almost falling.

Only Lamm's voice sounded through his helmet now, filling his ears with oaths which were mostly drowned in the smothering roar of the endless wreck behind. He looked back, just for a second, to see Lamm throwing himself between the jaws of the crumpling windows; he careened over the deck, falling and rolling, then rising again, still holding his gun, as Horza looked away. It was only at that point he realised he no longer had his own gun; he must have dropped it, but he couldn't remember where or when.

Horza was slowing down. He was fit and strong, but the above-standard pull of Vavatch's false gravity and the badly fitting suit were taking their toll.

He tried, as he ran in something like a trance, as his breath streamed back and forth through his wide-open mouth, to imagine how close they had been to the bows, for how long that immense weight of ship behind would be able to compress its front section as its billion-tonne mass rammed into what must – if it had filled the cloud bank they had seen earlier – be a massive tabular iceberg.

As though in a dream, Horza could see the ship about him, still wrapped in clouds and mist but lit from above by the wash of golden sunlight. The towers and spires seemed unaffected, the whole vast structure still sliding forward towards the ice as the kilometres of Megaship behind them pressed forward with the vessel's own titanic momentum. He ran by game courts, past tents of billowing silver, through a pile of musical instruments. Ahead there was a huge tiered wall of more decks, and above him were bridges, swaying and thrashing as their bow-ward supports, out of sight behind him, came closer to the advancing wave of wreckage and were consumed. He saw the deck to one side drop away into airy, hazy nothing. The deck under his feet started to rise, slowly, but for fifteen metres or more in front of him; he was fighting his way up a slope growing steeper all the time. A suspension bridge to his left collapsed, wires flailing; it disappeared into the golden mist, the noise of its fall lost in the crushing din assaulting his ears. His feet started to slide on the tilt of deck. He fell, landed heavily on his back and turned, looking behind him.

Against a wall of pure white towering higher than the *Olmedreca*'s tallest spire, the Megaship was throwing itself to destruction in a froth of debris and ice. It was like the biggest wave in the universe, rendered in scrap metal, sculpted in grinding junk; and beyond and about it, over and through, cascades of flashing, glittering ice and snow swept down in great slow veils from the cliff of frozen water beyond. Horza stared at it, then started to slide down towards it as the deck tilted him. To his left a huge tower was collapsing slowly, bowing to the breaking wave of compacted wreckage like a slave before a master. Horza felt a scream start in his throat as he saw decks and railings, walls and bulkheads and frames he had only just run past start to crumple and smash and come towards him.

He rolled over sliding shards and skidding fragments to the buckling rail at the edge of the deck, grabbed at the rails, caught them, heaved with both arms, kicked with one foot, and threw himself over the side.

He fell only one deck, crashing into sloped metal, winding himself. He got to his feet as fast as he could, sucking air through his mouth and swallowing as he tried to get his lungs to work. The narrow deck he was on was also buckling, but the fold-point was between him and the wall of towering, grinding wreckage; he slipped and slid away from it down the sloping surface as the deck behind him rose into a peak. Metal tore, and girders crashed out of the deck above like broken bones through skin. A set of steps faced him, leading to the deck he'd just jumped from, but to an area that was still level. He scrambled up to the level deck, which only then started to tip, canting away from the wave front of debris as its front edge lifted, crumpling.

He ran down the increasing slope, water from shallow ornamental pools cascading around him. More steps: he hauled himself towards the next deck.

His chest and throat seemed filled with hot coals, his legs with molten lead, and all the time that awful, nightmarish pull came from behind, dragging him back towards the wreckage. He stumbled and gasped his way from the top of the steps past the side of a broken, drained swimming pool.

'Horza!' a voice yelled. 'Is that you? Horza! It's Mipp! Look up!'

Horza lifted his head. In the mist, thirty metres above him, was the *CAT*'s shuttle. He waved weakly at it, staggering as he did so. The shuttle lowered itself through the mist ahead of him, its rear doors opening, until it was hovering just over the next deck above.

'I've opened the doors! Jump in!' Mipp shouted. Horza tried to reply, but could produce no sound apart from a sort of rasping wheeze; he staggered on, feeling as though the bones in his legs had turned to jelly. The heavy suit bumped and crashed around him, his feet slipped on the broken glass which covered the thrumming deck under his boots. Yet more steps towered ahead, leading to the deck where the shuttle waited. 'Hurry up, Horza! I can't wait much longer!'

He threw himself at the steps, hauled himself up. The shuttle wavered in the air, swivelling, its open rear ramp pointing at him, then away. The steps beneath him shuddered; the noise around him roared, full of screams and crashes. Another voice was shouting in his ears but he couldn't make out the words. He fell onto the upper deck, lunged forward for the shuttle ramp a few metres away; he could see the seats and lights inside, Lenipobra's suited body slumped in one corner.

126

'I can't wait! I've—' Mipp shouted above the scream of the wreckage and the other shouting voice. The shuttle started to rise. Horza threw himself at it.

His hands caught the lip of the ramp just as it rose level with his chest. He was hoisted from the deck, swinging under outstretched arms and looking forward under the shuttle's fuselage belly as the craft forced its way up into the air.

'Horza! Horza! I'm sorry,' Mipp sobbed.

'You've got me!' Horza yelled hoarsely.

'What?'

The shuttle was still climbing, passing decks and towers and the thin horizontal lines of monorail tracks. All Horza's weight was taken by his fingers, hooked in their gloves over the edge of the ramp door. His arms ached. 'I'm hanging onto the goddamn ramp!'

'You bastards!' screamed another voice. It was Lamm. The ramp started to close; the jerk almost broke Horza's grip. They were fifty metres up and climbing. He saw the top part of the doors jawing down towards his fingers.

'Mipp!' he yelled. 'Don't close the door! Leave the ramp where it is and I'll try to get in!'

'OK,' Mipp said quickly. The ramp stopped angling up, halting at about twenty degrees. Horza began swinging his legs from side to side. They were seventy, eighty metres up, facing away from the wave of wreckage and heading slowly away from it.

'You black bastard! Come back!' Lamm bellowed.

'I can't, Lamm!' Mipp cried. 'I can't! You're too close!'

'You fat *bastard*!' Lamm hissed.

Light flickered around Horza. The underside of the shuttle blazed in a dozen places as laser fire hit it. Something slammed into Horza's left foot, on the sole of his boot, and his right leg was kicked out as his leg burned with pain.

Mipp screamed incoherently. The shuttle started to gather speed, heading back over the Megaship and diagonally across it. The air roared around Horza's body, slowly tearing his grip away. 'Mipp, slow down!' he shouted.

'Bastard!' Lamm yelled agin. The mist to one side glowed as a fan of short-lived beams incandesced within it, then the laser fire shifted and the shuttle sparkled again, cracking with five or six small explosions around the front and nose section. Mipp howled. The shuttle increased speed. Horza was still trying to swing one leg onto the sloped ramp, but the clawed fingers of his gloves were slowly scraping

127

along the roughened surface as his body was slipstreamed back behind the speeding craft.

Lamm screamed – a high, gurgling sound which went through Horza's head like an electric shock, until the noise snapped off suddenly, replaced for an instant by sharp cracking, breaking noises.

The shuttle raced over the surface of the crashing Megaship, a hundred metres up. Horza felt the strength ebbing from his fingers and arms. He looked through the helmet visor at the interior of the shuttle only a few metres away as, millimetre by millimetre, he slipped away from it.

The interior flashed once, then an instant later blazed white, blindingly, unbearably. His eyes closed instinctively, and a burning yellow light came through his eyelids. His helmet speakers made a sudden, piercing, inhuman noise, like a machine screaming, then cut out altogether. The light faded slowly. He opened his eyes.

The shuttle interior was still brightly lit, but it was smouldering now, too. In the turbulent air whirling in from the open rear doors, wisps of smoke were tugged from scorched seats, singed straps and webbing, and the crisped black skin on Lenipobra's exposed face. Shadows seemed to be burnt onto the bulkhead in front.

Horza's fingers, one by one, came to the edge of the ramp.

My God, he thought, looking at the scorch marks and the smoke, *that maniac had a nuke after all*. Then the shock wave hit.

It slapped him forward, over the ramp and into the shuttle, just before it hit the machine itself, throwing it bucking and bouncing about the sky like a tiny bird caught in a storm. Horza was rattled about the interior from side to side, trying desperately to grab hold of something to stop himself falling back out through the open rear doors. His hand found some straps and fisted round them with the last of his strength.

Back through the doors, through the mist, a huge rolling fireball was climbing slowly into the sky. A noise like every clap of thunder he had ever heard vibrated through the hot, hazed interior of the fleeing machine. The shuttle banked, throwing Horza against one set of seats. A big tower flashed by the open rear doors, blocking out the fireball as the shuttle continued to turn. The rear doors seemed to try to close, then jammed.

Horza felt heavy and hot inside his suit, as the heat from the bomb's flash seeped through from the surfaces which had been exposed to the initial fireball. His right leg hurt badly, somewhere below the knee. He could smell burning.

As the shuttle steadied and its course straightened, Horza got up and limped forward to the door set in the bulkhead, where the outlines of the seats and Lenipobra's slumped body – now spread-eagled near the rear doors – were burnt in frozen shadows onto the off-white surface of the wall. He opened the door and went through.

Mipp was in the pilot's seat, hunched over the controls. The monitor screens were blank, but the view through the thick, polarised glass of the shuttle's windscreen showed cloud, mist, some towers sliding underneath and open sea beyond, covered with yet more cloud. 'Thought you . . . were dead. . . .' Mipp said thickly, half turning towards Horza. Mipp looked wounded, crouched in his seat, hunchbacked, eyelids drooped. Sweat glistened on his dark brow. There was smoke in the flight deck, acrid and sweet at once.

Horza took his helmet off and fell into the other seat. He looked down at his right leg. A neat, black-rimmed hole about a centimetre across had been punched through the back of the suit calf, matched by a larger and more ragged hole on the side. He flexed the leg and winced; just a muscle burn, already cauterised. He could see no blood.

He looked at Mipp. 'You all right?' he asked. He already knew the answer.

Mipp shook his head. 'No,' he said, in a soft voice. 'That lunatic hit me. Leg, and my back somewhere.'

Horza looked at the back of Mipp's suit, near where it rested against the seat. A hole in the bowl of the seat led to a long, dark scar on the suit surface. Horza looked down at the flight-deck floor. 'Shit,' he said. 'This thing's full of holes.'

The floor was pitted with craters. Two were directly under Mipp's seat; one laser shot had caused that dark scar on the side of the suit, the other must have hit Mipp's body.

'Feels like that bastard shot me right up the ass, Horza,' Mipp said, trying to smile. 'He did have a nuke, didn't he? That's what went off. Blew all the electrics away. . . . Only the optic controls still working. Useless damn shuttle . . .'

'Mipp, let me take over,' Horza said. They were in cloud now; only a vague coppery light showed through the crystal screen ahead. Mipp shook his head.

'Can't. You couldn't fly this thing . . . with it in this shape.'

'We've got to go back, Mipp. The others might have—'

'Can't. They'll all be dead,' Mipp said, shaking his head and gripping the controls tighter, staring through the screen. 'God, this thing's dying.' He looked round the blank monitors, shaking his head slowly. 'I can feel it.'

'Shit!' Horza said, feeling helpless. 'What about radiation?' he said suddenly. It was a truism that in any properly designed suit, if you survived the flash and blast, you'd survive the radiation; but Horza wasn't sure that his was a properly designed suit. One of the many instruments it lacked was a radiation monitor, and that was a bad sign in itself. Mipp looked at a small screen on the console.

'Radiation . . .' He shook his head. 'Nothing serious,' he said. 'Low on neutrons . . .' he grimaced with pain. 'Pretty clean bomb; probably not what that bastard wanted at all. He should take it back to the shop. . . .' Mipp gave a small, strangled, despairing laugh.

'We have to go back, Mipp,' Horza said. He tried to imagine Yalson, running away from the wreckage with a better start than he and Lamm had had. He told himself she'd have made it, that when the bomb had gone off, she'd have been far enough away not to be injured by it, and that the ship would finally stop, the metal glacier of wreckage slowing and halting. But how would she or any of the others get off the Megaship, if any of them had survived? He tried the shuttle's communicator, but it was as dead as his suit's.

'You won't raise them,' Mipp said, shaking his head. 'You can't raise the dead. I heard them; they cut off, while they were running. I was trying to tell them—'

'Mipp, they changed channels, that was all. Didn't you hear Kraiklyn? They swapped channels because Lamm was shouting so much.'

Mipp crouched in his seat, shaking his head. 'I didn't hear that,' he said after a moment. 'That wasn't what I heard. I was trying to tell them about the ice . . . the size of it; the height.' He shook his head again. 'They're dead, Horza.'

'They were well away from us, Mipp,' Horza said quietly. 'At least a kilometre. They probably survived. If they were in shadow, if they'd run when we did . . . They were further back. They're probably alive, Mipp. We've got to go back and get them.'

Mipp shook his head. 'Can't, Horza. They must be dead. Even Neisin. Went off for a walk . . . after you had all gone. Had to leave without him. Couldn't raise him. They must be dead. All of them.'

'Mipp,' Horza said, 'it wasn't a very *big* nuke.'

Mipp laughed, then groaned. He shook his head again. 'So what? You didn't see that ice, Horza; it was—'

Just then the shuttle lurched. Horza looked quickly to the screen,

130

but there was only the glowing light of the cloud they were flying through, all around them. 'Oh God,' Mipp whispered, 'we're losing it.'

'What's wrong?' Horza asked. Mipp shrugged painfully.

'Everything. I think we're dropping, but I've no altimeter, no airspeed indicator, communicator or nav gear: nothing. . . . Running rough because of all these holes and the doors being open.'

'We're losing height?' Horza asked, looking at Mipp.

Mipp nodded. 'You want to start throwing things out?' he said. 'Well, throw things out. Might get us more height.' The shuttle lurched again.

'You're serious,' Horza said, starting to get out of the seat. Mipp nodded.

'We're dropping. I'm serious. Damn, even if we did go back we couldn't take this thing over the Edgewall, not even with one or two of us just . . .' Mipp's voice trailed off.

Horza levered himself painfully out of his seat and through the door.

In the passenger compartment there was smoke, mist and noise. The hazy light streamed through the doors. He tried to tear the seats from the walls, but they wouldn't move. He looked at Lenipobra's broken body and burned face. The shuttle lurched; for a second Horza felt lighter inside his suit. He grabbed Lenipobra's suit by the arm and hauled the dead youth to the ramp. He pushed the corpse over the ramp, and the limp husk fell, vanishing into the mist below. The shuttle banked one way, then the other, almost throwing Horza off his feet.

He found some other bits and pieces: a spare suit helmet, a length of thin rope, an AG harness and a heavy gun tripod. He threw them out. He found a small fire extinguisher. He looked round but there didn't seem to be any flames and the smoke hadn't got any worse. He held onto the extinguisher and went through to the flight deck. The smoke appeared to be clearing there, too.

'How are we doing?' he asked. Mipp shook his head.

'Don't know.' He nodded at the seat Horza had been sitting in. 'You can unlock that from the deck. Throw it out.'

Horza found the latches securing the seat to the deck. He undid them and dragged the seat through the door, to the ramp, and threw it out along with the extinguisher.

'There are catches on the walls, near this bulkhead,' Mipp called, then grunted with pain. He went on, 'You can detach the wall seats.'

Horza found the catches, and pushed first one line of seats, then the other, complete with straps and webbing, along the rails fixed to the shuttle interior, until they rolled out, bouncing on the ramp edge and then spinning away into the glowing mist. He felt the shuttle bank again.

The door between the passenger compartment and the flight deck slammed shut. Horza went forward to it; it was locked.

'Mipp!' he shouted.

'Sorry, Horza,' Mipp's voice came weakly from the other side of the door. 'I can't go back. Kraiklyn would kill me if he isn't dead already. But I couldn't find them. I just couldn't. It was only luck I saw you.'

'Mipp, don't be crazy. Unlock the door.' Horza shook it. It wasn't strong; he could break his way through it if he had to.

'Can't, Horza. . . . Don't try to force the door; I'll point her nose straight down; I swear it. We can't be that high above the sea anyway. . . . I can hardly keep her flying as it is. . . . If you want, try closing the doors manually. There should be an access panel somewhere on the rear wall.'

'Mipp, for God's sake, where are you *going*? They're going to blow the place up in a few days. We can't fly for ever.'

'Oh, we'll ditch before that,' Mipp's voice came from behind the closed door. He sounded tired. 'We'll ditch before they blow the Orbital up, Horza, don't you worry. This thing's dying.'

'But where are you *going*?' Horza repeated, shouting at the door.

'Don't know, Horza. The far side maybe . . . Evanauth . . . I don't know. Just away. I—' There was a thump as though something had fallen to the floor, and Mipp cursed. The shuttle juddered, heeling over briefly.

'What is it?' Horza asked anxiously.

'Nothing,' Mipp said. 'I dropped the medkit, that's all.'

'Shit,' Horza said under his breath, and sat down, back against the bulkhead.

'Don't worry, Horza, I'll . . . I'll . . . do what I can.'

'Yes, Mipp,' Horza said. He got to his feet again, ignoring the ache of exhaustion in both legs and the stabbing pain in his right calf, and went to the rear of the shuttle. He looked for an access panel, found one and prised it open. It revealed another fire extinguisher; he threw it out, too. On the other wall the panel led to a hand crank. Horza twisted the grip. The doors started to close slowly, then jammed. He strained at the lever until it snapped; he swore and threw it out as well.

Just then the shuttle came clear of the mist. Horza looked down and saw the ruffled surface of a grey sea where slow waves rolled and broke. The bank of mist lay behind them, an indeterminate grey curtain beneath which the sea disappeared. The sunlight slanted across the layered mist, and hazy clouds filled the sky.

Horza watched the broken handle tumble down towards the sea, becoming smaller and smaller; it stroked a mark of white across the water, then it was gone. He reckoned they were about one hundred metres above the sea. The shuttle banked, forcing Horza to grab the side of the door; the craft turned to head almost parallel to the cloud bank.

Horza went to the bulkhead and banged on the door. 'Mipp? I can't get the doors closed.'

'It's all right,' the other man replied faintly.

'Mipp, open the door. Don't be crazy.'

'Leave me alone, Horza. Leave me alone, understand?'

'God-*damn*,' Horza said to himself. He went back to the open doors, buffeted by the wind curling back in from the slipstream. They seemed to be heading away from the Edgewall, judging by the angle of the sun. Behind them lay nothing but sea and clouds. There was no sign of the *Omedreca* or any other craft or ship. The seemingly flat horizon to either side disappeared into a haze; the ocean gave no impression of being concave, only vast. Horza tried to stick his head round the corner of the shuttle's open door to see where they were going. The rush of air forced his head back before he could take a proper look, and the craft lurched again slightly, but he had an impression of another horizon as flat and featureless as that on either side. He got further back into the shuttle and tried his communicator, but there was nothing from his helmet speakers; all the circuits were dead; everything seemed to have been knocked out by the electro-magnetic pulse from the explosion on the Megaship.

Horza considered taking the suit off and throwing it out, too, but he was already cold, and if he took the suit off he'd be virtually naked. He would keep the device on unless they started losing height suddenly. He shivered, and his whole body ached.

He would sleep. There was nothing he could do for now, and his body needed rest. He considered Changing, but decided against it. He closed his eyes. He saw Yalson, as he had imagined her, running on the Megaship, and opened his eyes again. He told himself she was all right, just fine, then closed his eyes once more.

Maybe by the time he woke they would be out from under the layers of magnetised dust in the upper atmosphere, in the tropical or even just temperate zones, rather than the arctic region. But that would probably mean only that they would finally ditch in warm water, not cold. He couldn't imagine Mipp or the shuttle holding together long enough to complete a journey right across the Orbital.

. . . assume it was thirty thousand kilometres across; they were making perhaps three hundred per hour. . . .

His head full of changing figures, Horza slipped into sleep. His last coherent thought was that they just weren't going fast enough, and probably couldn't. They would still be flying over the Circlesea towards land when the Culture blew the whole Orbital into a fourteen-million-kilometre halo of light and dust. . . .

Horza woke rolling around inside the shuttle. In the first few blurred seconds of his waking he thought he had already tumbled out of the rear door of the shuttle and was falling through the air; then his head cleared and he found himself lying spread-eagled on the floor of the rear compartment, watching the blue sky outside tilt as the shuttle banked. The craft seemed to be travelling more slowly than he remembered. He could see nothing from the rear view out of the doors except blue sky, blue sea and a few puffy white clouds, so he stuck his head round the side of the door.

The buffeting wind was warm, and over in the direction the shuttle was banking lay a small island. Horza looked at it incredulously. It was tiny, surrounded by smaller atolls and reefs showing pale green through the shallow water, and it had a single small mountain sticking up from concentric circles of lush green vegetation and bright yellow sand.

The shuttle dipped and levelled, straightening on its course for the island. Horza brought his head back in, resting the muscles of his neck and shoulder after the exertion of holding his head out in the slipstream. The shuttle slowed yet more, dipping again. A slight juddering vibrated through the craft's frame. Horza saw a torus of lime-coloured water appear in the sea behind the shuttle; he stuck his head round the side of the door again and saw the island just ahead and about fifty metres below. Small figures were running up the beach which the shuttle was approaching. A group of the humans were heading across the sand for the jungle, carrying what looked like a huge pyramid of golden sand on a sort of litter or stretcher, held on poles between them.

Horza watched the scene slide by underneath. There were small fires on the beach, and long canoes. At one end of the beach, where the trees cut down towards the water, there squatted a broad-backed, shovel-nosed shuttle, perhaps two or three times the size of the *CAT*'s. The shuttle flew over the island, through some vague grey pillars of smoke.

The beach was almost clear of people; the last few, who looked thin and almost naked, ran into the cover of the trees as though afraid of the craft flying over them. One figure lay sprawled on the sand near the module. Horza caught a glimpse of one human figure, more fully clothed than the others, not running but standing and pointing up towards him, pointing towards the shuttle flying over the island, with something in his hand. Then the top of the small mountain appeared just underneath the open shuttle door, blocking off the view. Horza heard a series of sharp reports, like small, hard explosions.

'Mipp!' he shouted, going to the closed door.

'We've had it, Horza,' Mipp said weakly from the other side. There was a sort of despairing jocularity in his voice. 'Even the natives aren't friendly.'

'They looked frightened,' Horza said. The island was disappearing behind. They weren't turning back, and Horza felt the shuttle speeding up.

'One of them had a gun,' Mipp said. He coughed, then moaned.

'Did you see that shuttle?' Horza asked.

'Yeah, I saw it.'

'I think we should go back, Mipp,' Horza said. 'I think we ought to turn round.'

'No,' Mipp said. 'No, I don't think we ought to. . . . I don't think that's a good idea, Horza. I didn't like the look of the place.'

'Mipp, it looked *dry*. What more do you want?' Horza looked at the view through the rear doors; the island was nearly a kilometre away already and the shuttle was still increasing speed, gaining height all the time.

'Got to keep going, Horza. Head for the coast.'

'Mipp! We'll never get there! It'll take us four days at least and the Culture's going to blow this place apart in three!'

There was silence from the far side of the door. Horza shook its light, grubby surface with his hand.

'Just leave it, Horza!' Mipp screamed. Horza hardly recognised the man's hoarse, shrill voice. 'Just leave it! I'll kill us both, I swear!'

The shuttle suddenly tilted, pointing its nose at the sky and its open doors at the sea. Horza started to slide back, his feet slipping on the shuttle's floor. He jammed the suit fingers into the wall slot the seats had been attached to, hanging there as the shuttle started to stall in its steep climb.

'All right, Mipp!' he shouted. 'All right!'

The shuttle fell, side-slipping, throwing Horza forward and against the bulkhead. He was suddenly heavy as the craft bottomed out of its short dive. The sea slithered underneath, only fifty or so metres below.

'Just leave me *alone*, Horza,' Mipp's voice said.

'OK, Mipp,' Horza said. 'OK.'

The shuttle rose a little, gaining altitude and increasing speed. Horza went back, away from the bulkhead which separated him from the flight deck and Mipp.

Horza shook his head and went to stand by the open door, looking back towards the island with its lime shallows, grey rock, green-blue foliage and band of yellow sand. It all slowly shrank, the frame of the open shuttle doors filling with more and more sea and sky as the island lost itself in the haze.

He wondered what he could do, and knew there was only one course of action. There had been a shuttle on that island; it could hardly be in a worse state than the one he was in now, and their chances of being rescued at the moment were virtually nil. He turned round to look at the flimsy door leading to the flight deck, still holding onto the edge of the rear door, the warm buffeting air spilling in around him.

He wondered whether just to charge straight in or to try to reason with Mipp first. While he was still thinking about it the shuttle gave a shudder, then started to fall like a stone towards the sea.

6.

The Eaters

Horza was weightless for a second. He felt himself caught by the eddying wind swirling through the rear doors, drawing him towards them. He grabbed at the channel in the wall he had held onto earlier. The shuttle dipped its nose, and the roar of the wind increased. Horza floated, his eyes closed, his fingers jammed into the wall slot, waiting for the crash; but instead the shuttle levelled out again, and he was back on his feet.

'Mipp!' he shouted, staggering forward to the door. He felt the craft turning and glanced out through the rear doors. They were still falling.

'It's gone, Horza,' Mipp said faintly. 'I've lost it.' He sounded weak, calmly despairing. 'I'm turning back for the island. We won't get there, but . . . we're going to hit in a few moments. . . . You'd best get down by this bulkhead and brace yourself. I'll try to put her down as soft as I can. . . .'

'Mipp,' Horza said, sitting down on the floor with his back to the bulkhead, 'is there anything I can do?'

'Nothing,' Mipp said. 'Here we go. Sorry, Horza. Brace yourself.'

Horza did exactly the opposite, letting himself go limp. The air roaring through the rear doors howled in his ears; the shuttle shook underneath him. The sky was blue. He caught a glimpse of waves. . . . He kept just enough tension in his back to keep his head against the bulkhead surface. Then he heard Mipp shout; not words – just a shout of fear, an animal noise.

The shuttle crashed, slamming into something, forcing Horza hard back against the wall, then releasing him. The craft raised its nose slightly. Horza felt light for a moment, saw waves and white spray through the open rear doors, then the waves went, he saw sky, and closed his eyes as the shuttle's nose dipped again.

The craft smashed into the waves, crashing to a stop in the water. Horza felt himself squashed into the bulkhead as though by the foot of some gigantic animal. The wind was forced out of him, blood roared, the suit bit at him. He was shaken and flattened, and then, just as the impact seemed to be over, another shock sledge-hammered into his back and neck and head, and suddenly he was blind.

The next thing he knew there was water everywhere about him. He was gasping and spluttering, striking out in the darkness and hitting his hands off hard, sharp, broken surfaces. He could hear water gurgling, and his own choked breath frothing. He blew water out of his mouth and coughed.

He was floating in a bubble of air, in darkness, in warm water. Most of his body seemed to be aching, each limb and part clamouring with its own special message of pain.

He felt gingerly round the small space he was trapped in. The bulkhead had collapsed; he was – at last – in the flight-deck area with Mipp. He found the other man's body, crushed between seat and instrument panel, trapped and still, half a metre under the surface of the water. His head, which Horza could feel by reaching down between the seat head-rest and what felt like the innards of the main monitor screen, moved too easily in the neck of the suit, and the forehead had been crushed.

The water was rising higher. The air was escaping through the smashed nose of the shuttle, floating and bobbing bow-up in the sea. Horza knew he would have to swim down and back through the shuttle's rear section and out through the rear doors, otherwise he'd be trapped.

He breathed as deeply as he could, despite the pain, for about a minute, while the rising water level gradually forced his head into the angle between the top of the craft's instrument panel and the flight-deck ceiling. He dived.

He forced his way down, past the wreckage of the crushed seat Mipp had died in, and past the twisted panels of light metal which had made up the bulkhead. He could see light, vaguely green-grey, forming a rectangle beneath him. Air trapped in his suit bubbled round him, along his legs, upwards to his feet. He was slowed for a moment, buoyed up by the air in his boots, and for a second he thought he wasn't going to make it, that he was going to hang there upside-down and drown. Then the air bubbled out through the holes in his boots punched there by Lamm's laser, and Horza sank.

He struggled down through the water to the rectangle of light, then swam through the open rear doors and into the shimmering green depths of the water under the shuttle; he kicked and went up, breaking out into the waves with a gasp, sucking warm, fresh air into his lungs. He felt his eyes adjust to the slanted but still bright sunlight of late afternoon.

He grabbed hold of the shuttle's dented, punctured nose – sticking above the water by about two metres – and looked around, trying to see the island, but without success. Still just treading water and letting his battered body and brain recover, Horza watched the up-tilted nose of the craft sink lower in the water and tip slowly forward so that the shuttle gradually floated almost level in the waves, its top surface just awash. The Changer, his arm muscles straining and hurting, eventually hauled himself onto the top of the shuttle, and lay there like a beached fish.

He started to shut off the pain signals, like a weary servant picking up the litter of breakables after an employer's destructive rage.

It was only lying there, with small waves washing over the top surface of the shuttle's fuselage, that he realised that all the water he had been coughing up and swallowing was fresh. It hadn't occurred to him that the Circlesea would be anything other than salt, like most planetary oceans, but in fact there was not even the slightest tang of it, and he congratulated himself that at least he would not die of thirst.

He stood up carefully, in the centre of the shuttle roof, waves breaking round his feet. He looked around, and could see the island – just. It looked very small and far away in the early evening light, and, while there was a faint warm breeze blowing more or less towards the island, he had no idea which way any currents might be taking him.

He sat down, then lay back, letting the waters of the Circlesea wash over the flat surface beneath him and break in small lines of surf against his much-damaged suit. After a while he just fell asleep, not really meaning to, but not stopping himself when he realised that he was, telling himself to sleep for only an hour or so.

He woke up to see the sun, though still high in the sky, looking dark red as it shone through the layers of dust above the distant Edgewall. He got to his feet again; the shuttle didn't seem to have sunk any lower in the water. The island was still far away, but it looked a little nearer than it had earlier; the currents, or the winds, such as they were, seemed to be carrying him in roughly the right direction. He sat down again.

The air was still warm. He thought of taking the suit off but decided against it; it was uncomfortable but perhaps he would get too cold without it. He lay back again.

He wondered where Yalson was now. Had she survived Lamm's

bomb, and the wreck? He hoped so. He thought she probably had; he couldn't imagine her dead, or dying. It was little enough to go on, and he refused to believe he was superstitious, but not being able to imagine her dead was somehow comforting. She'd survive. Take more than a tactical nuke and a billion-tonne ship impacting a berg the size of a small continent to polish that girl off. . . . He found himself smiling, remembering her.

He would have spent more time thinking about Yalson, but there was something else he had to think about as well.

Tonight he would Change.

It was all he could do. Probably by now it was irrelevant. Kraiklyn was either dead or – if surviving – unlikely ever to meet Horza again, but the Changer had prepared for the transformation; his body was waiting for it, and he could think of nothing better to do.

The situation, he told himself, was far from hopeless. He wasn't badly injured, he seemed to be heading for the island, where the shuttle might still be, and if he could make it in time there was always Evanauth, and that Damage game. Anyway, the Culture might be looking for him by now, so it wouldn't do to keep the same identity for too long. What the hell, he thought; he would Change. He would go to sleep as the Horza the others knew him as, and he would wake up as a copy of the captain of the *Clear Air Turbulence*.

He prepared his bruised and aching body for the alteration as best he could: relaxing muscles and readying glands and groups of cells; sending deliberate signals from brain to body and face through nerves that only Changers possessed.

He watched the sun, dimming through red stages somewhere low over the ocean.

Now he would sleep; sleep, and become Kraiklyn; take on yet another identity, another shape to add to the many he had assumed already during his life. . . .

Maybe there was no point, maybe he was only taking this new shape on to die in. *But*, he thought, *what have I got to lose?*

Horza watched the falling, darkening red eye of the sun until he entered the sleep of Changing, and in that Changing trance, though his eyes were closed, and beneath their lids also altering, he seemed to see that dying glare still. . . .

Animal eyes. Predator's eyes. Caged behind them, looking out. Never sleeping, being three people. Ownership; rifle and ship and Company. Not much yet maybe, but one day . . . with just a little, little luck, no more than everybody else had a right to . . . one day he would show them. *He* knew how good he was, *he* knew what he was fit for, and who was fit for him. The rest were just tokens; they were his because they were under his command; it was his ship, after all. The women especially – just game pieces. They could come and go and he didn't care. All you had to do with any of them was share their danger and they thought you were wonderful. They couldn't see that for him there was no danger; he had a lot left to do in life, he *knew* he wasn't going to die some stupid, squalid little combat death. The galaxy, one day, would know his name, and either mourn him or curse him, when eventually he did have to die. . . . He hadn't decided yet whether it would be mourn or curse . . . maybe it depended on how the galaxy treated him in the meantime. . . . All he needed was the tiniest break, just the sort of thing the others had had, the leaders of the bigger, more successful, better known, more feared and respected Free Companies. They must have had them. . . . They might seem greater than he was now, but one day they would look up to him; everybody would. All would know his name: *Kraiklyn*!

Horza woke in the dawn light, still lying on the wave-washed shuttle roof, like something washed up and spread upon a table. He was half awake, half asleep. It was colder, the light was thinner and more blue, but nothing else had changed. He started to drift back to sleep again, away from pain and lost hopes.

Nothing else had changed . . . only him. . . .

He had to swim for the island.

He had woken for the second time the same morning, feeling different, better, rested. The sun was angling up and out of the overhead haze.

The island was closer, but he was going past it. The currents were taking him and the shuttle away now, having swept no closer than two kilometres to the group of reefs and sandbanks round the isle. He cursed himself for sleeping so long. He got out of the suit – it was useless now and deserved to be ditched – and left it lying on the still just-awash shuttle roof. He was hungry, his stomach rumbled, but he felt fit and ready for the swim. He estimated it was about three kilometres. He dived in and struck out powerfully. His right leg hurt where he'd been hit by Lamm's laser and his body still ached in places, but he could do it; he knew he could.

He looked back once, after he'd swum for a few minutes. He could see the suit but not the shuttle. The empty suit was like the abandoned cocoon of some metamorphosed animal, riding opened and empty, seeming just above the surface of the waves behind. He turned away and kept swimming.

The island came closer, but very slowly. The water was warm at first, but it seemed to get colder, and the aches in his body increased. He ignored them, switching them off, but he could feel himself slowing, and he knew that he'd started off too fast. He paused, treading water for a moment; then, after drinking a little of the warm fresh water, set off again, stroking more deliberately and steadily for the grey tower of the distant island.

He told himself how lucky he'd been. The shuttle crash hadn't injured him badly – though the aches still plagued him, like noisy relatives locked in a distant room, disturbing his concentration. The warm water, though apparently getting colder, was fresh, so that he could drink from it and wouldn't dehydrate; yet it crossed his mind that he would have been more buoyant had it been salty.

He kept going. It ought to have been easy but it was getting more difficult all the time. He stopped thinking about it; he concentrated on moving; the slow, steady, rhythmic beat of arms and legs forcing him through the water; up waves, over, down; up, over, down.

Under my own power, he told himself, *under my own power*.

The mountain on the island grew larger very slowly. He felt as though he was building it, as though the effort required to make it appear larger in his sight was the same as if he was toiling to construct that peak; heap it up rock by rock, with his own hands . . .

Two kilometres. Then one.

The sun angled, rose.

Eventually, the outer reefs and shallows; he passed them in a daze, into shallower water.

A sea of aching. An ocean of exhaustion.

He swam towards the beach, through a fan of waves and surf radiating from the reef-gap he'd swum through . . .

. . . and felt as though he'd never taken the suit off, as though he wore it still, and it was stiff with rust or age, or filled with heavy water or wet sand; dragging, stiffening, pulling him back.

He could hear waves breaking on the beach, and when he looked up he could see people on it: thin dark people, dressed in rags, gathered round tents and fires or walking between them. Some were in the water ahead of him, carrying baskets, large open-work baskets which they held on their waists, gathering things from the sea as they waded through it, putting what they collected in their baskets.

144

They hadn't seen him, so he swam on, making a slow, crawling motion with his arms and kicking feebly with his legs.

The people harvesting the sea didn't appear to notice him; they kept on wading through the surf, stooping occasionally to pick from the sands underneath, their eyes sweeping and probing, scanning and searching, but too close in; not seeing him. His stroke slowed to a gasping, dying crawl. He could not lift his hands free of the water, and his legs stayed paralysed. . . .

Then through the surf noise, like something from a dream, he heard several people shouting nearby, and splashes coming close. He was still swimming weakly when another wave lifted him, and he saw several of the skinny people clad in loincloths and tattered tunics, wading through the water towards him.

They helped Horza in through the breaking waves, over sun-streaked shallows and onto the golden sands. He lay there while the thin and haggard people crowded round. They talked quietly to each other in a language he hadn't heard before. He tried to move but couldn't. His muscles felt like lengths of limp rag.

'Hello,' he croaked. He tried it in all the languages he knew, but none seemed to work. He looked into the faces of the people around him. They were human, but that word covered so many different species throughout the galaxy it was a continuing subject for debate who was and who wasn't human. As in all too many matters, the consensus of opinion was starting to resemble what the Culture had to say on the subject. The Culture would lay down the law (except, of course, that the Culture didn't have any real laws) about what being human was, or how intelligent a particular species was (while at the same time making clear that pure intelligence didn't really mean much on its own), or on how long people should live (though only as a rough guide, naturally), and people would accept these things without question, because everybody believed the Culture's own propaganda, that it was fair, unbiased, disinterested, concerned only with absolute truth . . . and so on.

So were these people around him really human? They were about Horza's height, they seemed to have roughly the same bone structure, bilateral symmetry and respiratory system; and their faces – though each was different – all had eyes, mouth, nose and ears.

But they all looked thinner than they ought to have been, and their skin, regardless of hue or shade, looked somehow diseased.

Horza lay still. He felt very heavy again, but at least he was on dry land. On the other hand, it didn't look as though there was much food on the island, judging by the state of the bodies around him. He

145

assumed that was why they were so thin. He raised his head weakly and tried to see through the clumps of thin legs towards the shuttle craft he had seen earlier. He could just see the top of the machine, sticking up above one of the large canoes beached on the sands. Its rear doors were open.

A smell wafted under Horza's nose and made him feel sick. He put his head down onto the sand again, exhausted.

The talking stopped and the people turned, their thin, tanned or anyway dark bodies shuffling round to face up the beach. A space opened in their ranks just above Horza's head, and try as he might he couldn't get up on one elbow or swivel his head to see what or who was coming. He lay and waited, then the people to his right all drew back and a line of eight men appeared on that side, holding a long pole together in their left hands, their other arms stuck out for balance. It was the litter he had seen being carried into the jungle the day before, when the shuttle had overflown the island. He watched to see what it held. Two lines of men turned the litter so that it faced Horza and set it down. Then all sixteen sat down, looking exhausted. Horza stared.

On the litter sat the most enormous, obscenely fat human Horza had ever seen.

He had mistaken the giant for a pyramid of golden sand the previous day, when he had seen the litter and its huge burden from the CAT's shuttle. Now he could see that his first impression had been close in shape if not in substance. Whether the vast cone of human flesh belonged to a male or a female Horza couldn't tell; great mammary-like folds of naked flesh spilled from the creature's upper and middle chest, but they drooped over even more enormous waves of nude, hairless torso-fat, which lay partly cradled in the vast beefs of the giant's akimboed legs and partly overflowing those to droop into the canvas surface of the litter. Horza could see no stitch of clothing on the monster, but no trace of genitals either; whatever they were, they were quite buried under rolls of golden-brown flesh.

Horza looked up to the head. Rising from a thick cone of neck, gazing out over concentric ramparts of chins, a bald dome of puffy flesh contained a limp and rambling length of pale lips, a small button nose, and slits where eyes must be. The head sat on its layers of neck, shoulder and chest fat like a great golden bell on top of a many-decked temple. The sweat-glistened giant suddenly moved its hands, rolling them round on the end of the bloated fat-bound balloons of its arms, until the merely chubby fingers met and clasped as tightly as their size would allow. As the mouth opened to speak, another one of the skinny humans, his rags slightly less tattered than those of the others, moved into Horza's field of vision, just behind and to the side of the giant.

The bell of head moved a few centimetres to one side and swivelled round, saying something to the man behind that Horza couldn't catch. Then the giant raised his or her arms with obvious effort and gazed round the skinny humans gathered around Horza. The voice sounded like congealing fat being poured into a jug; it was a drowning voice, Horza thought, like something from a nightmare. He listened, but couldn't understand the language being used. He looked round to see what effect the giant's words were having on the famished-looking crowd. His head spun for a moment, as though his brain had shifted while his skull stayed still; he was suddenly back in the hangar of the *Clear Air Turbulence*, when the Company had been looking at him, and he had felt as naked and vulnerable as he did now.

'Oh, not again,' he moaned in Marain.

'Oh-hoo!' said the golden rolls of flesh, the voice tumbling over the slopes of fat in a faltering series of tones. 'Gracious! Our bounty from the sea *speaks*!' The hairless dome of head turned further round to the man standing by its side. 'Mr First, isn't this wonderful?' the giant burbled.

'Fate is kind to us, Prophet,' the man said gruffly.

'Fate favours the beloved, yes, Mr First. It sends our enemies away and brings us bounty – bounty from the sea! Fate be praised!' The great pyramid of flesh shook as the arms went higher, trailing folds of paler flesh as the turret-like head went back, the mouth opening to expose a dark space where only a few small fangs glinted like steel. When the bubbling voice spoke again it was in the language Horza couldn't make out, but it was the same phrase repeated over and over again. The giant was quickly joined by the rest of the crowd, who shook their hands in the air and chanted hoarsely. Horza closed his eyes, trying to wake from what he knew was not a dream.

When he opened his eyes the skinny humans were still chanting, but they were crowded around him again, blocking out his view of the golden-brown monster. Their faces eager, their teeth bared, their hands stretched out like claws, the crowd of starving, chanting humans fell on him.

They stripped off his shorts. He tried to struggle, but they held him down. In his exhaustion he was probably no stronger than any one of them, and they had no difficulty pinning him; they rolled him over, pulled his hands behind him and tied them there. Then they tied his feet together and pulled his legs back until his feet were almost

147

touching his hands, and bound them to his wrists by a short length of rope. Naked, trussed like an animal ready for the slaughter, Horza was dragged across the hot sand, past a weakly burning fire, then hauled upright and lowered over a short pole stuck into the beach, so that it ran up between his back and his tied limbs. His knees sank into the sand, taking most of his weight. The fire burned in front of him, sending acrid wood-smoke into his eyes, and the awful smell returned; it seemed to come from various pots and bowls spread around the fire. Other fires and collections of pans were littered across the beach.

The huge pile of flesh the man named Mr First had called 'prophet' was set down near the fire. Mr First stood at the obese human's side, staring at Horza through deep-set eyes contained within a pale and grubby face. The golden giant on the litter clapped chubby hands together and said, 'Stranger, gift of the sea, welcome. I . . . am the great prophet Fwi-Song.'

The vast creature spoke a crude form of Marain. Horza opened his mouth to tell them his name, but Fwi-Song continued. 'You have been sent to us in our time of testing, a morsel of human flesh on the tide of nothingness, a harvest-thing plucked from the tasteless wash of life, a sweetmeat to share and be shared in our victory over the poisonous bile of disbelief! You are a sign from Fate, for which we give thanks!' Fwi-Song's huge arms lifted up; rolls of shoulder fat wobbled on either side of the turret-like head, nearly covering the ears. Fwi-Song shouted out in a language Horza didn't know, and the crowd echoed the phrase, chanting it several times.

The fat-smothered arms were lowered again. 'You are the salt of the sea, ocean-gift.' Fwi-Song's syrupy voice changed back into Marain once more. 'You are a sign, a blessing from Fate; you are the one to become many, the single to be shared; yours will be the gaining gift, the blessed beauty of transubstantiation!'

Horza stared, horrified, at the golden giant, unable to think of anything to say. What *could* you say to people like this? Horza cleared his throat, still hoping to say something, but Fwi-Song went on.

'Be told then, gift of the sea, that we are the Eaters; the Eaters of ashes, the Eaters of filth, the Eaters of sand and tree and grass; the most basic, the most loved, the most real. We have laboured to prepare ourselves for our day of testing, and now that day is gloriously near!' The golden-skinned prophet's voice grew shrill; folds of fat shook as Fwi-Song's arms opened out. 'Behold us then, as we await the time of our ascension from this mortal plane, with empty bellies and voided bowels and hungry minds!' Fwi-Song's pudgy hands met in a slap; the fingers interweaved like huge, fattened maggots.

'If I can—' croaked Horza, but the giant was talking to the crowd of grubby people again, the voice bubbling out over the golden sands and the cooking fires and the dull, malnourished people.

Horza shook his head a little and looked out over the expanse of beach to the open-doored shuttle in the distance. The more he looked at the craft, the more certain he became it was a Culture machine.

It was nothing he could pin down, but he grew more certain with every moment spent looking at the machine. He guessed it was a forty- or fifty-seater; just about big enough to take all the people he had seen on the island. It didn't look particularly new or fast, and it didn't look armed at all, but something about the whole way its simple, utilitarian form had been put together spoke of the Culture. If the Culture designed an animal-drawn cart or an automobile, they would still share something in common with the device at the far end of the beach, for all the gulf of time between the epochs each represented. It would have helped if the Culture had used some sort of emblem or logo; but, pointlessly unhelpful and unrealistic to the last, the Culture refused to place its trust in symbols. It maintained that it was what it was and had no need for such outward representation. The Culture was every single individual human and machine in it, not one thing. Just as it could not imprison itself with laws, impoverish itself with money or misguide itself with leaders, so it would not misrepresent itself with signs.

All the same, the Culture did have one set of symbols it was very proud of, and Horza didn't doubt that if the machine he was looking at was a Culture craft, it would have some Marain writing on or in it somewhere.

Was it in some way connected with the mass of flesh still talking to the scrawny humans around the fire? Horza doubted it. Fwi-Song's Marain was shaky and ill tutored. Horza's own grasp of the language was far from perfect, but he knew enough about the tongue to realise Fwi-Song did it some violence when he or she used it. Anyway, the Culture was not in the habit of loaning out its vehicles to religious nut-cases. Was it here to evacuate them, then? Lift them to safety when the Culture's high-technology shit hit the rotating fan that was the Vavatch Orbital? With a sinking feeling, Horza realised this was probably the answer. So there was no escape. Either these crazies sacrificed him or did whatever it was they were set on doing to him, or it was a ride into captivity, courtesy of the Culture.

149

He told himself not to assume the worst. After all, he now looked like Kraiklyn, and it wasn't *that* likely the Culture's Minds had made all the correct connections between him, the *CAT* and Kraiklyn. Even the Culture didn't think of everything. But . . . they probably did know he'd been on *The Hand of God 137*; they probably did know he'd escaped from it; they probably did know that the *CAT* was in that volume at the time. (He recalled the statistics Xoralundra had quoted to the *Hand*'s captain; yes, the GCU must have won the battle. . . . He remembered the *CAT*'s rough-running warp motors; probably producing a wake any self-respecting GCU could track from centuries away) . . . Damn it; he wouldn't put it past them. Maybe they were testing everybody they were picking up from Vavatch. They would know in seconds, from just a single sample cell; a skin flake, a hair; for all he knew he'd been sampled already, a micromissile sent from the nearby shuttle picking up some tiny piece of tissue. . . . He dropped his head, his neck muscles aching with all the others in his battered, bruised, exhausted body.

Stop it, he told himself. *Thinking like a failure. Too damn sorry for yourself. Get yourself out of this. Still got your teeth and your nails . . . and your brain. Just bide your time. . . .*

'For lo,' Fwi-Song warbled, 'the godless ones, the most hated, the despised-by-the-despised, the Atheists, the Anathematics, have sent us this instrument of the Nothingness, the Vacuum, to us. . . .' As the giant said those words Horza looked up and saw Fwi-Song point along the beach to the shuttle. 'But we shall not waver in our faith! We shall resist the lure of the Nothingness between the stars where the godless ones, the Anathematised of the Vacuum exist! We shall stay part of what is a part of us! We shall not treat with the great Blasphemy of the Material. We shall stand as the rocks and trees stand – firm, rooted, secure, staunch, unyielding!' Fwi-Song's arms went out again, and the voice bellowed out. The gruff-voiced man with the dirty pale skin shouted something at the seated crowd, and they shouted back. The prophet smiled at Horza from across the fire. Fwi-Song's mouth was a dark hole, with four small fangs protruding when the lips formed a smile. They shone in the sunlight.

'This the way you treat all your guests?' Horza said, trying not to cough until the end of his sentence. He cleared his throat. Fwi-Song's smile vanished.

'Guest you are not, sea-wanton, salt-gift. Prize: ours to keep, mine to use. Bounty from the sea and the sun and the wind, brought to us by Fate. Hee-hee.' Fwi-Song's smile returned with a girlish giggle, and

150

one of the huge hands went to cover the pale lips, 'Fate recognises its prophet, sends him tasty treats! Just when some of my flock were having second thoughts, too! Eh, Mr First?' The turret-head turned to the thin figure of the paler man, standing with arms folded, by the giant's side. Mr First nodded:

'Fate is our gardener, and our wolf. It weeds out the weak to honour the strong. So the prophet has spoken.'

'And the word which dies in the mouth lives in the ear,' Fwi-Song said, turning the huge head back to look at Horza. *At least*, Horza thought, *now I know it's a male. For whatever that's worth.*

'Mighty Prophet,' Mr First said. Fwi-Song smiled wider but continued looking at Horza. Mr First went on, 'The sea-gift should see the fate that awaits him. Perhaps the treacherous coward Twenty-seventh—'

'Oh, *yes*!' Fwi-Song clapped his huge hands together and a smile lit up his whole face. For a second Horza thought he saw small white eyes beyond the slits staring at him. 'Oh let's, yes! Bring the coward, let us do what must be done.'

Mr First spoke in ringing tones to the emaciated humans gathered around the fire. A few stood up and walked off behind Horza, towards the forest. The rest started singing and chanting.

After a few minutes Horza heard a scream, then a series of yells and screams, gradually coming closer. At last the people who had left came back, carrying a short, thick log, much like the one Horza was held by. Swinging on the pole was a young man, screaming, shouting in the language Horza didn't understand, and struggling. Horza saw drops of sweat and saliva fall from the young man's face and spot the sand. The log was sharpened at one end; that point was driven into the sand on the opposite side of the fire from Horza, so that the young man faced the Changer.

'This, my libation from the seas,' Fwi-Song said to Horza, pointing at the young man, who was quivering and moaning, his eyes rolling about in their sockets and his lips dribbling, 'this is my naughty boy; called Twenty-seventh, since his rebirth. This was one of our respect-ed, much loved sons, one of our anointed, one of our fellow morsels, one of our brotherly taste buds on the great tongue of life.' Fwi-Song's voice chortled with laughter as he spoke, as though he knew the absurdity of the part he was playing and couldn't resist hamming it up. 'This splinter from our tree, this grain from our beach, this reprobate dared to run towards the seven-times-cursed vehicle of the Vacuum. He spurned the gift of burden with which we honoured him;

151

he chose to abandon us and flee across the sands when the alien enemy passed over us yesterday. He did not trust our salving grace, but turned instead to an instrument of darkness and nothingness, towards the soaking shade of the soulless ones, the Anathematics.' Fwi-Song looked at the man, still shaking on the post across the fire from Horza. The prophet's face went stern with reproach. 'By the workings of Fate the traitor who ran from our side and put his prophet's life at risk was caught – so that he might learn his sad mistake, and make good his terrible crime.' Fwi-Song's arm dropped. The vast head shook.

Mr First shouted to the people round the fire. They faced the young man called Twenty-seventh and chanted. The ghastly smells Horza had sensed earlier came back, making his eyes mist and his nose tingle.

While the people chanted and Fwi-Song watched, Mr First and two of the women followers dug up small sacks from the sand. Out of them they brought some thin lengths of cloth which they proceeded to wrap round their bodies. As Mr First put his vestments on, Horza saw a large, cumbersome-looking projectile pistol, held in a string holster beneath the man's grubby tunic. Horza presumed that was the gun fired at the shuttle the day before, when he and Mipp had overflown the island.

The young man opened his eyes, saw the three people in their cloths and started screaming.

'Hear how the stricken soul cries out for its lesson, pleads for its bounty of regret, its solace of refreshing suffering,' Fwi-Song smiled, looking at Horza. 'Our child Twenty-seventh knows what awaits him, and while his body, already proved so weak, breaks before the storm, his soul cries out, "Yes! Yes! Mighty Prophet! Succour me! Make me part of you! Give me your strength! Come to me!" Is it not a sweet and uplifting sound?'

Horza looked into the prophet's eyes and said nothing. The young man went on screaming and trying to tear himself away from the stump. Mr First was crouched before him, on his knees, his head bowed, muttering to himself. The two women dressed in the dull cloth were preparing bowls of steaming liquid from the vats and pots around the fire, warming some over the flames. The smells came to Horza, turning his stomach.

Fwi-Song switched to the other language and spoke to the two women. They looked at Horza, then came up to him with the bowls. Horza drew his head away as they shoved the containers under his nose. He wrinkled his face up in disgust at what looked and smelled like fish entrails in a sauce of excrement. The women took the awful stuff away; it left a stink in his nose. He tried breathing through his mouth.

The young man's mouth had been wedged open with blocks of wood, and his choking screams altered in pitch. While Mr First held him, the women ladled the liquids from the bowls into his mouth. The young man spluttered and wailed, choked and tried to spit. He moaned, then threw up.

'Let me show you my armoury, my benefaction,' Fwi-Song said to Horza, and reached behind his vast body. He brought back a large bundle of rags, which he startled to unfold. Glittering in the sunlight, metal devices like tiny man-traps were revealed. Fwi-Song put one finger to his lips while he surveyed the collection, then picked up one of the small metal contraptions. He put it into his mouth, fitting both parts over the pins Horza had seen earlier. 'Zhare,' Fwi-Song said, raising his mouth in a broad smile towards the Changer. 'What 'oo you shink of zhat?' The artificial teeth sparkled in his mouth; rows of sharp, serrated points. 'Or zhese?' Fwi-Song swapped them for another set, full of tiny fangs like needles, then another, with angled teeth like hooks with barbs, then another, with holes set in them. 'Goo', eh?' He smiled at Horza, leaving the last pair in. He turned to Mr First. 'Wha' you shink, Nishtur Shursht? Ehs? Or . . .' Fwi-Song took out the set with the holes, put in another set, like long, blade-like spades. 'Zheze? A 'ink eeg a rar ah nishe. Esh, rert ush zhtart wish eez. Ret's punish zhoze naughty tootsiesh.'

Twenty-seventh's voice was becoming hoarse. One of his legs was lifted out in front of him and held by four kneeling men. Fwi-Song was lifted and carried on the litter to just in front of the young man; he bared the blade-teeth, then leaned forward and with a quick, nodding motion, bit off one of Twenty-seventh's toes.

Horza looked away.

In the next half-hour or so of leisurely paced eating, the enormous prophet nibbled at various bits of Twenty-seventh's body, attacking the extremities and the few remaining fat deposits with his various sets of teeth. The young man gained fresh breath with each new site of butchery.

Horza watched and didn't watch, sometimes trying to think himself into a kind of defiance that would let him work out a way to get back at this grotesque distortion of a human being, at other times just wanting the whole awful business to be over and done with. Fwi-Song left his ex-disciple's fingers until last, then used the teeth with the holes in like wire-strippers. "Ery 'asty,' he said, wiping his blood-stained face with one gigantic forearm.

Twenty-seventh was cut down, moaning, covered in streaks of blood, and only semi-conscious. He was gagged with a length of rag, then pinned down flat, face up, on the sand, wooden spikes through the palms of his mangled hands and a huge boulder crushing his feet. He started screaming weakly again through the gag when he saw the prophet Fwi-Song on his litter being carried over towards him. Fwi-Song was lowered almost on top of the moaning form, then he struggled with some cords at the side of his litter until a small flap under his great bulk flopped open, over the face of the gagged, blood-spattered human on the sand beneath. The prophet gave a sign, and he was lowered on top of the man, quieting the sound of moaning. The prophet smiled, and settled himself with little movements of his huge body, like a bird nestling down over its eggs. His vast bulk obliterating all trace or shape of the human under him, Fwi-Song hummed to himself while the emaciated crowd looked on, singing very slowly and quietly, swaying together as they stood. Fwi-Song started to rock backwards and forwards softly, very slowly at first, then faster as sweat appeared in beads on the golden dome of his face. He panted, and made a rough gesture towards the crowd; the two women dressed in the lengths of cloth came forward and started to lick at the trickles of blood which had spilled from the prophet's mouth, over the folds of his chins and down the expanse of his chest and breasts like red milk. Fwi-Song gasped, seemed to sag and stay still for a moment, and then, with a surprisingly fast and fierce motion, clouted both the lapping women across the head with his mighty arms. The women scurried off, rejoining the crowd. Mr First started a louder chant, which the others took up.

At last Fwi-Song ordered himself to be lifted again. The litter bearers hauled his massive frame into the air, to reveal the crushed body of Twenty-seventh, his moaning silenced for ever.

They lifted him out, beheaded the corpse and removed the top of the skull. They ate his brains, and it was only then that Horza threw up.

'And now we are become each other,' Fwi-Song intoned solemnly to the youth's hollow head, then threw its bloody bowl over his shoulder into the fire. The rest of the body was taken down to the sea and thrown in.

'Only ceremony and the love of Fate distinguish us from the beasts, o mark of Fate's devotion,' Fwi-Song warbled to Horza as the prophet's vast body was cleaned and perfumed by the attendant women. Tied to his post, stuck in the ground, his mouth fouled, Horza breathed carefully and deliberately, and did not try to reply.

Twenty-seventh's body floated slowly out to sea. Fwi-Song was towelled down. The skinny humans sat about listlessly, or tended the awful-smelling liquid in the bubbling vats. Mr First and his two women helpers took off their lengths of cloth, leaving the man in his grimy but whole tunic and the women in their tattered rags. Fwi-Song had his litter placed on the sand in front of Horza.

'See, bounty from the waves, harvest from the rolling ocean, my people prepare to break their fast.' The prophet swept one fat-wobbling arm about to indicate the people tending the fires and cauldrons. The smell of rotting food filled the air.

'They eat what others leave, what others will not touch, because they want to be closer to the fabric of Fate. They eat the bark from the trees and the grass from the ground and the moss from the rocks; they eat the sand and the leaves and the roots and the earth; they eat the shells and the entrails of sea-animals and the carrion of the land and the ocean; they eat their bodily products and share mine. I am the fount. I am the well-spring, the taste on their tongues.

'You, bubble of froth on the ocean of life, are a sign. Crop of the ocean, you will come to see, before the time of your unmaking, that you are all you have eaten, and that food is merely undigested excrement. This I have seen; this you will see.'

One of the attendant women came back from the sea with Fwi-Song's freshly cleaned sets of teeth. He took them from her and put them in the rags somewhere behind him. 'All shall fall but we, all go to their deaths, their unmakings. We alone will be made in our unmaking, brought into the glory of our ultimate consummation.'

The prophet sat smiling at Horza, while around him – as the long afternoon's shadows drew out across the sands – the emaciated, ill-looking people sat down to their foul meals. Horza watched them try to eat. Some did, encouraged by Mr First, but most could keep nothing down. They gasped for breath and gulped at the liquids, but often as not they vomited up what they had just forced down. Fwi-Song looked on them sadly, shaking his head.

'You see, even my closest children are not ready yet. We must pray and entreat that they are ready when the time comes, as it must, in a few days' time. We must hope that their bodies' lack of grasp, of sympathy with all things, will not make them despised in the eyes and mouth of God.'

You fast bastard. You're within range, if you only knew. I could blind you from here; spit in your little eyes and maybe . . .

But, Horza thought, maybe not. The giant's eyes were set so deep within the flabby skin of his brows and cheeks that even the venomous spittle with which Horza could have hit the golden monster might not find its way to the membranes of the eye. But it was all Horza could find to give him solace in his situation. He could spit at the prophet, and that was it. Perhaps there would come a point when it might make some difference, but to do it now would be stupid. A blind, enraged Fwi-Song struck Horza as something to try to avoid even more than a sighted, tittering one.

Fwi-Song talked on to Horza, never questioning, never really stopping, repeating himself more and more often. He told him about his revelations and his past life; as a circus freak, then as a palace pet for some alien satrap on a Megaship, then as a convert to a fashionable religion on another Megaship, his revelation occurring there, when he persuaded a few converts to join him on an island to await the End of All Things. More followers had arrived when the Culture announced what the fate of the Vavatch Orbital was going to be. Horza was only half listening, his mind racing as he tried to think of a way out.

'. . . We await the end of all things, the last day. We prepare ourselves for our final consummation by mixing the fruits of earth and sea and death with our fragile bodies of flesh and blood and bone. You are our sign, our aperitif, our scent. You must feel honoured.'

'Mighty Prophet,' Horza said, swallowing hard and doing his best to keep his voice calm. Fwi-Song stopped talking, the eyes narrowing still further and a frown forming. Horza went on, 'I am indeed your sign. I bring you myself; I am the follower . . . the disciple numbered Last. I come to rid you of the machine from the Vacuum.' Horza looked over at the Culture shuttle, sitting with its rear doors open at the far end of the beach. 'I know how to remove this source of temptation. Let me prove to you my devotion by performing this small service for your great and majestic self. Then you will know I am your last and most faithful servant: the one numbered Last, the one come before the unmaking, to . . . to steel your followers for the test to come and remove the Anathematics' temptation device. I have mixed with the stars and the air and ocean, and I bring you this message, this deliverance.' Horza stopped there, his throat and lips dry, his eyes running as the highly spiced stench of the Eaters' food drifted on a light breeze around him. Fwi-Song sat quite still on his litter, looking into Horza's face with his slit-eyes narrowed and his bulbous brows creased.

'Mr First!' Fwi-Song said, turning to where the pale-skinned man in the tunic was massaging one of the Eaters' bellies while the unfortunate follower lay moaning on the ground. Mr First rose and came over to the giant prophet, who nodded at Horza and spoke in the language the Changer couldn't understand. Mr First bowed slightly, then went behind Horza, taking something from under his tunic as he went out of the Changer's field of view. Horza's heart thudded. He looked desperately back at Fwi-Song. What had the prophet said? What was Mr First going to do? Hands appeared over Horza's head, gripping something. The Changer closed his eyes.

A rag was tied tightly over his mouth. It smelled of the foul food. His head was forced back against the stake. Then Mr First went back to the prone, groaning Eater. Horza stared at Fwi-Song, who said:

'There. Now, as I was saying . . .'

Horza didn't listen. The fat prophet's cruel faith was little different from a million others; only the degree of its barbarity made it unusual in these supposedly civilised times. Another side effect of the war, maybe; blame the Culture. Fwi-Song talked, but there was no point in listening.

Horza recalled that the Culture's attitude to somebody who believed in an omnipotent God was to pity them, and to take no more notice of the substance of their faith than one would take of the ramblings of somebody claiming to be Emperor of the Universe. The nature of the belief wasn't totally irrelevant – along with the person's background and upbringing, it might tell you something about what had gone wrong with them – but you didn't take their views *seriously*.

That was the way Horza felt about Fwi-Song. He had to treat him as the maniac he obviously was. The fact that his insanity was dressed in religious trappings meant nothing.

No doubt the Culture would disagree, claiming that there was ample common ground between insanity and religious belief, but then what else could you expect from the Culture? The Idirans knew better, and Horza, while not agreeing with everything the Idirans stood for, respected their beliefs. Their whole way of life, almost their every thought, was illuminated, guided and governed by their single religion/philosophy: a belief in order, place and a kind of holy rationality.

They believed in order because they had seen so much of its opposite, first in their own planetary background, taking part in the extraordinarily fierce evolutionary contest on Idir, and then – when they finally entered into the society of their local stellar cluster – around them, between and amongst other species. They had suffered because of that lack of order; they had died by the millions in stupid, greed-inspired wars in which they became involved through no fault of their own. They had been naïve and innocent, over-dependent on others thinking in the same calm, rational way they always did.

They believed in the destiny of *place*. Certain individuals would always belong in certain places – the high ground, the fertile lands, the temperate isles – whether they had been born there or not; and the same applied to tribes, clans and races (and even to species; most of the ancient holy texts had proved sufficiently flexible and vague to cope with the discovery that the Idirans were not alone in the universe. The texts which had claimed otherwise were promptly ditched, and their authors were first ritually cursed and then thoroughly forgotten). At its most mundane, the belief could be expressed as the certainty that there was a place for everything, and everything ought to be in its place. Once everything was in its place, God would be happy with the universe, and eternal peace and joy would replace the current chaos.

The Idirans saw themselves as agents in this great reordering. They were the chosen – at first allowed the peace to understand what God desired, and then goaded into action rather than contemplation by the very forces of disorder they gradually understood they had to fight. God had a purpose beyond study for them. They had to find their own place, in the whole galaxy at least; perhaps even outside that, as well. The more mature species could look to their own salvation; they had to make their own rules and find their own peace with God (and it was a sign of his generosity that he was happy with their achievements even when they denied Him). But the others – the swarming, chaotic, struggling peoples – they needed guidance.

The time had come to do away with the toys of self-interested striving. That the Idirans had realised this was the sign of it. In them, and in the Word that was their inheritance from the divine, the Spell within their genetic inheritance, a new message was abroad: *Grow up. Behave. Prepare.*

Horza didn't believe in the Idirans' religion any more than Balveda had, and indeed he could see in its over-deliberate, too-planned ideals exactly the sort of life-constricting forces he so despised in the Culture's initially more benign ethos. But the Idirans relied on themselves, not on their machines, and so they were still part of life. To him, that made all the difference.

Horza knew the Idirans would never subdue all the less-developed civilisations in the galaxy; their dreamed-of day of judgement would never come. But the very certainty of that ultimate defeat made the Idirans safe, made them normal, made them part of the general life of the galaxy; just one more species, which would grow and expand and then, finding the plateau phase all non-suicidal species eventually arrived at, settle down. In ten thousand years the Idirans would be just another civilisation, getting on with their own lives. The current era of conquests might be fondly remembered, but it would be irrelevant by then, explained away by some creative theology. They had been quiet and introspective before; so they would be again.

In the end, they were rational. They listened to common sense before their own emotions. The only thing they believed without proof was that there was a purpose to life, that there was something which was translated in most languages as 'God', and that that God wanted a better existence for His creations. At the moment they pursued this goal themselves, believed themselves to be the arms and hands and fingers of God. But when the time came they would be able to assimilate the realisation that they'd got it wrong, that it was not up to them to bring about the final order. They would themselves become calm; they would find their own place. The galaxy and its many and varied civilisations would assimilate them.

The Culture was different. Horza could see no end to its policy of continual and escalating interference. It could easily grow for ever, because it was not governed by natural limitations. Like a rogue cell, a cancer with no 'off' switch in its genetic composition, the Culture would go on expanding for as long as it was allowed to. It would not stop of its own accord, so it had to *be* stopped.

This was a cause he had long ago decided to devote himself to, Horza told himself, listening to Fwi-Song droning on. Also, a cause he would serve no more, if he didn't get away from the Eaters.

Fwi-Song talked for a little longer, then – after a word from Mr First – had his litter turned round so that he could address his followers. Most of them were either being very ill or looking it. Fwi-Song switched to the local language Horza didn't understand, and gave what was evidently a sermon. He ignored the occasional bout of vomiting from his flock.

The sun dipped lower over the ocean, and the day cooled.

The sermon over, Fwi-Song sat silently on his litter as, one by one, the Eaters came up to him, bowed and spoke earnestly to him. The prophet's dome-like head wore a large smile, and every now and again it would nod with what looked like agreement.

Later, the Eaters sang and chanted while Fwi-Song was washed and oiled by the two women who had helped officiate at Twenty-seventh's death. Then, his vast body gleaming in the rays of the falling sun, Fwi-Song was carried, waving cheerfully, off the beach and into the small forest beneath the island's single stunted mountain.

Fires were stoked and wood was brought. The Eaters dispersed to their tents and camp fires, or set off in small groups with crudely made baskets, apparently to gather fresh debris they would later try to eat.

At about sunset, Mr First joined the five quiet Eaters who sat around the fire Horza was by now tired of facing. The emaciated humans had taken little or no notice of the Changer, but Mr First came and sat near the man tied to the post. In one hand he held a small stone, in the other some of the artificial teeth Fwi-Song had used on Twenty-seventh earlier that day. Mr First sat grinding and polishing the teeth while he talked to the other Eaters. After a couple of them had gone to their tents, Mr First went behind Horza and undid the gag. Horza breathed through his mouth to get rid of the stale taste, and exercised his jaw. He shifted, trying to ease the accumulating aches in his arms and legs.

'Comfortable?' Mr First said, squatting down again. He continued to sharpen the metal fangs; they flickered in the firelight.

'I've felt better,' Horza said.

'You'll feel worse, too . . . friend.' Mr First made the last word sound like a curse.

'My name's Horza.'

'I don't care what your name is.' Mr First shook his head. 'Your name doesn't matter. *You* don't matter.'

'I had started to form that impression,' Horza admitted.

'Oh, had you?' Mr First said. He got up and came closer to the Changer. 'Had you *really*?' He lashed out with the steel teeth he held in his hand, catching Horza across the left cheek. 'Think you're clever, eh? Think you're going to get out of this, do you?' He kicked Horza in the belly. Horza gasped and choked. 'See – you don't matter. You're just a hunk of meat. That's all anybody is. Just meat. And anyway,' he kicked Horza again, 'pain isn't real. Just chemicals and electrics and that sort of thing, *right*?'

'Oh,' Horza croaked, his wounds aching briefly, 'yes. Right.'

'OK,' Mr First grinned. 'You remember this tomorrow, OK. You're just a piece of meat, and the prophet's a bigger one.'

'You . . . ah, don't believe in souls, then?' Horza said diffidently, hoping this wouldn't lead to another kick.

'Fuck your soul, stranger,' Mr First laughed. 'You'd better hope there's no such thing. There's people that are natural eaters and there's those that are always going to get eaten, and I can't see that their souls are going to be any different, so as you're obviously one of those that are always going to get eaten, you'd better hope there isn't any such thing. That's your best bet, believe me.' Mr First brought out the rag he had taken from Horza's mouth. He tied it back there, saying, 'No – no soul at all would be the best thing for you, friend. But if it turns out you have got one, you come back and tell me, so I can have a good laugh, right?' Mr First pulled the knotted rag tight, hauling Horza's head against the wooden stake.

Fwi-Song's lieutenant finished sharpening the sets of gleaming metal teeth, then rose and spoke to the other Eaters sitting around the fire. After a while they went to some of the small tents, and soon they were all off the beach, leaving only Horza to watch the few dying fires.

The waves crashed softly on the distant surf-line, stars arced slowly above, and the dayside of the Orbital was a bright line of light overhead. Shining in the starlight and the O-light, the silent, waiting bulk of the Culture shuttle sat, its rear doors open like a cave of safe darkness.

Horza had already tested the knots restraining his hands and feet. Shrinking his wrists wouldn't work; the rope, twine or whatever they had used was tightening very slightly all the time; it would just take up the slack as quickly as he could produce it. Perhaps it shrank when drying and they had wet it before tying him. He couldn't tell. He could intensify the acid content in his sweat glands where the rope touched his skin, and that was always worth a try, but even the long night of Vavatch probably wouldn't give enough time for the process to work.

Pain isn't real, he told himself. *Crap.*

He awoke at dawn, along with several of the Eaters, who walked slowly down to the water to wash in the surf. Horza was cold. He started shivering as soon as he woke, and he could tell that his body temperature had dropped a long way during the night in the light trance required for altering the skin cells on his wrists. He strained at the ropes, testing for some give, the slightest tearing of fibres or strands. There was nothing, just more pain from the palms of his hands where some sweat had run down onto skin unchanged and therefore unprotected from the acid his sweat glands had been producing. He worried about that for about a second, recalling that if he was ever to impersonate Kraiklyn properly he would need to lift the

161

man's finger and palm prints and so would need his skin in perfect Changing condition. Then he laughed at himself for worrying about that when he wasn't even likely to see the day out.

He vaguely considered killing himself. It was possible; with only a little internal preparation, he could use one of his own teeth to poison himself. But, while there was still any chance, he could not bring himself to think of it seriously. He wondered how Culture people faced the war; they were supposed to be able to *decide* to die, too, though it was said to be more complicated than simple poison. But how did they resist it, those soft, peace-pampered souls? He imagined them in combat, auto-euthenising almost the instant the first shots landed, the first wounds started to appear. The thought made him smile.

The Idirans had a death trance, but it was only for use in cases of extreme shame and disgrace, or when a life's work was completed, or a crippling disease threatened. And unlike the Culture – or the Changers – they felt their pain to the full, undampened by genofixed inhibitors. The Changers regarded pain as a semi-redundant hangover from their animal evolution; the Culture was simply frightened of it: but the Idirans treated it with a sort of proud contempt.

Horza looked across the beach, over the two big canoes towards the open rear doors of the shuttle. A pair of brightly coloured birds were strutting around on its top, making little ritualised movements. Horza watched them for a while, as the Eaters' camp gradually woke up and the morning sun brightened. Mist rose from the thin forest and there were a few clouds, high up in the sky. Mr First came yawning and stretching out of his tent, then took the heavy projectile pistol out from under his tunic and fired it in the air. This seemed to be a signal for all the Eaters to wake and set about their daily business if they hadn't already done so.

The noise of the crude weapon frightened the two birds on the roof of the Culture shuttle; they took to the air and flew away over the trees and shrubs, around the island. Horza watched them go, then let his eyes drop, staring at the golden sand and breathing slow and deep.

'Your big day, stranger,' Mr First said with a grin, coming up to the Changer. He put the pistol into the string holster under his tunic. Horza looked at the man, but said nothing. *Another feast in my honour*, he thought.

Mr First walked around Horza, looking down at him. Horza followed him with his eyes where he could and waited for the man to spot whatever damage the acid-sweat had succeeded in inflicting on the rope round his wrists, but Mr First didn't notice anything, and when he reappeared in Horza's view he was still smiling slightly, nodding his head a little, seemingly satisfied that the man tied to the stake was still well enough restrained. Horza did his best to stretch, straining at the bonds at his wrists. There was not even a hint of give. It hadn't worked. Mr First left, to supervise the launching of a fishing canoe.

Fwi-Song was brought out of the forest on his litter not long before noon, as the fishing canoe was returning.

'Gift of the seas and air! Tribute of the great Circlesea's vast wealth! See what a wondrous day awaits you now!' Fwi-Song had himself brought up to Horza, and was put down to one side of the fire. He smiled at the Changer. 'All the night you have had time to think of what the day now holds; for all the darkness you have been able to look into the fruits of the Vacuum. You have seen the spaces between the stars, seen how much there is of nothing, how little there is of anything. Now you can appreciate what an honour lies in store for you; how lucky you are to be my sign, my offering!' Fwi-Song clapped his hands with delight, and his enormous body shook up and down. The chubby hands went to his mouth as he spoke, and the folds of flesh over his eyes lifted momentarily to reveal the whites within. 'Ho-hoo! What fun we all shall have!' The prophet made a sign, and his litter carriers took him down to the sea to be washed and anointed.

Horza watched the Eaters prepare their food; they gutted the fish, throwing away the meat and keeping the offal and skins, heads and spikes. They removed the shells from the animals inside and threw the animals away. They ground up the shells with the weeds and some brightly coloured sea slugs. Horza watched all this happen in front of him, and saw just how run-down the Eaters really were; the scabs and sores, the deficiency diseases and general weakness. The colds and coughs, peeling skin and partly deformed limbs all spoke of a very gradually fatal diet. The dead meat and animals from the sea were returned to the waves via great blood-soaked baskets. Horza watched as closely as his gag and the distance would allow, but none of the Eaters seemed to take a surreptitious bite of the raw meat as they threw it from the baskets into the waves.

Fwi-Song, being dried on the sand just up the beach from the line of breakers, watched the food being thrown into the sea and nodded with approval, speaking quiet words of encouragement to his flock. Then he clapped his hands, and the litter was slowly carried along the beach to the fire and the Changer.

'Offertory thing! Benefaction! Prepare yourself!' Fwi-Song warbled, settling down in his litter with little movements which sent ripples all over the great folds and sweeps of his massive body. Horza started to breathe harder, felt his heart pound. He swallowed, and strained again at the rope holding his hands. Mr First and the two women were digging at the sand for the thin robes in their buried sacks.

All the Eaters gathered round the fire, facing Horza. Their eyes looked black or vaguely interested, nothing more. There was a listlessness about their actions and expressions which Horza found even more depressing than outright hatred or sadistic glee would have been.

The Eaters began to chant and sing. Mr First and the two women were twisting the dull lengths of cloth around their bodies. Mr First looked at Horza and grinned.

'Oh happy moment in the ending days!' Fwi-Song said, raising his voice and hands, his choked tones ringing out towards the centre of the island. The smells of the Eaters' foul cooking drifted past the Changer again. 'Let this one's unmaking and making be a symbol for us!' Fwi-Song continued, letting his arms drop back in enormous rolls of white flesh. The golden-brown surfaces gleamed in the sunlight as the prophet clasped his fat fingers together. 'Let his pain be our delight, as our unmaking shall be our joining; let his flaying and consummation be our satisfaction and delectation!' Fwi-Song raised his head and spoke loudly in the language the others understood. Their chanting altered and grew louder. Mr First and the two women approached Horza.

Horza felt Mr First take the gag from his mouth. The pale-skinned man spoke to the two women, who went to the bubbling vats of stinking liquid. Horza's head was feeling very light; there was a taste he knew too well at the back of his throat, as though some of the acid from his wrists had somehow found its way to his tongue. He strained again at his bonds behind him, feeling the muscles shake. The chanting went on; the women were ladling the foul broth into bowls. His empty stomach was churning already.

There are two main ways to escape bonds apart from those open to non-Changers [the Academy's lecture notes said]: by acid-sweat pulse on a sustained level where the binding material is susceptible to such an attack, and by malleable preferential tapering of the limb-point involved.

Horza tried to coax a little more strength from his tired muscles.

Excessive acid-sweating can damage not only the adjacent skin surfaces, but also the body as a whole through dangerously altered chemical imbalances. Over-much tapering poses the risk of the muscles being so wasted and the bone so weakened that their subsequent use may be severely restricted in the short- and long-term escape attempt.

Mr First was approaching with the wooden blocks he would fit into Horza's mouth. A couple of the larger Eaters had stood up near the front of the crowd and advanced slightly, ready to assist Mr First. Fwi-Song was reaching behind his back. The women started forward from the bubbling vats.

'Open wide, stranger,' Mr First said, holding out the two wooden blocks. 'Or do we use a crowbar?' Mr First smiled.

Horza's arms strained. His upper arm moved. Mr First saw the movement and halted momentarily. One of Horza's hands jerked free. It shot round in an instant, nails ready to rake Mr First's face. The pale-skinned man drew back, not quickly enough.

Horza's nails caught Mr First's robe and tunic as they flapped out from his dodging body. Already straining as far out from the stake as he could, Horza felt his clawed hand rip through the two layers of material without connecting with the flesh underneath. Mr First staggered back, bumping into one of the women carrying the bowls of stinking gruel, knocking it from her hands. One of the wooden wedges sailed from Mr First's hand and landed in the fire. Horza's arm completed its swing just as the two Eaters in the front of the crowd came forward quickly and caught the Changer by the head and arm.

'Sacrilege!' Fwi-Song screamed. Mr First looked at the woman he had bumped into, at the fire, at the prophet, then back with a furious look at the Changer. He lifted one arm to look at the tears in his robe and tunic. 'The gift-filth desecrates our vestments!' Fwi-Song shouted. The two Eaters held Horza, pinning his arm back where it had been and his head to the stake. Mr First started towards Horza, taking the gun out from under his tunic and holding it by the barrel, like a club. 'Mr First!' Fwi-Song snapped, stopping the pale-skinned man in his tracks. 'Shtand gack! Hold gat arn out; ee'll show gish naught goy how we geel wish hish short!'

Horza's free arm was straightened out in front of him. One of the Eaters holding him put his leg round the back of the post, bracing himself there and trapping Horza's other hand where it was. Fwi-Song had a set of gleaming steel teeth in his mouth, the holed ones. He glared at the Changer while Mr First stepped back, still holding the projectile pistol. The prophet nodded to another two Eaters in the crowd; they took Horza's hand and prised the fingers apart, tying that wrist to a pole. Horza felt his whole body shake. He cut off all feeling in that hand.

'Naughty, naughty gisht 'rom the shee!' Fwi-Song said. He leant forward, buried Horza's index finger in his mouth, closed the stripper teeth over them, cutting into the flesh, and then pulled quickly back.

The prophet chewed and swallowed, watching the Changer's face as he did so, and frowning. '*Not* gery tashty, genegiction 'rom the oceansh currentsh!' The prophet licked his lips. 'An' not shore enush 'or you, eisher, sho it wood sheen? Letch shee 'ot elsh nee can . . .' Fwi-Song was frowning again. Horza looked past the Eaters holding him to the hand stretched out over the pole, one finger stripped bare, the bones limp, blood dripping from the thin tip.

Beyond that, Fwi-Song sat frowning on his litter on the sand, Mr First near his side, still glaring at Horza and holding the gun barrel. As Fwi-Song's silence continued, Mr First looked at the prophet. Fwi-Song said, '. . . not elsh nee can . . . nee can . . .' Fwi-Song reached up and took the stripper teeth with some difficulty from his mouth. He laid them in front of him with the rest on their rag, and put one pudgy hand to his throat, the other onto the vast hemisphere of his belly. Mr First looked on, then back at Horza, who did his best to smile. The Changer opened his teeth glands and sucked poison.

'Mr First . . .' Fwi-Song began, then put out the hand on his belly towards the other man. Mr First seemed uncertain what to do. He transferred the gun from one hand to the other, and took the prophet's offered hand with his free one. 'I think I . . . I . . .' Fwi-Song said, as his eyes started to open from slits to small ovals. Horza could see his face changing colour already. *Soon the voice, as the vocal cords react.* 'Help me, Mr First!' Fwi-Song took hold of a lump of fat round his throat as though trying to undo a scarf tied too tightly; he stuck his fingers into his mouth, down his throat, but Horza knew that wouldn't work; the prophet's stomach muscles were already paralysed – he couldn't vomit the poison up. Fwi-Song's eyes were wide now, glaring white; his face was going grey-blue. Mr First was goggling at the prophet and still holding his huge hand; his own was buried somewhere inside the great golden fist of Fwi-Song's. 'He-ll-p!' squeaked the prophet. Then nothing but choking noises. The white eyes bulged, the vast frame shook, the dome-head went blue.

Somebody in the crowd started screaming. Mr First looked at Horza, and brought up the big pistol. Horza tensed, then spat with all his might.

The spittle splashed across Mr First's face, from mouth to one ear in a sickle shape which just took in one eye. Mr First staggered back. Horza breathed in, sucked more poison, then spat and blew at the same time, landing a second burst of spittle right across Mr First's eyes. Mr First clutched at his face, dropping the gun. His other hand was still caught in Fwi-Song's grip as the obese prophet shook and quivered, his eyes wide but seeing nothing. The people holding Horza wavered; he could feel it in them. More people in the crowd were crying out. Horza jerked his body and snarled, spitting again, at one of the men holding the pole his hand was tied to. The man screamed shrilly and fell back; the others let go of him or the pole and ran. Fwi-Song was going blue from the neck down, still quivering and clutching his throat with one hand and Mr First with the other. Mr First was on his knees, his face lowered, moaning as he tried to wipe the spittle from his face and remove the unbearable burning from his eyes.

Horza looked round quickly; the Eaters were watching either their prophet and his chief disciple, or him, but they weren't doing anything either to aid them or to stop him. Not all of them were crying or screaming; some were still chanting, quickly and fearfully as though something they could say would stop whatever terrible things were happening. Gradually, though, they were backing off, away both from the prophet and Mr First, and from the Changer. Horza pulled and jerked his hand tied to the pole; it started to come free.

'Aah!' Mr First suddenly raised his head, hand clutching at one eye, and screamed for all his worth; his hand, still caught in that of the prophet, jerked out straight as he tried to pull free. Fwi-Song still held him in his grip, though, even as he quaked and stared and turned blue. Horza's hand came free; he tugged at the bonds behind him and did his best with the crippled free hand to untie the knots. The Eaters were moaning now, some still chanting, but they were moving away. Horza roared – partly at them, partly at the stubborn knots behind him. Several in the crowd ran. One of the women dressed in the ragged vestment clothes screamed, threw her bowl of gruel at him, missing him, then fell sobbing to the sand.

Horza felt the ropes behind him give. He got the other arm free, then one foot. He stood shakily, watching Fwi-Song gargle and choke, while Mr First howled, shaking his head this way and that and pulling and swinging his gripped hand as though in some monstrous travesty of a handshake. Eaters were running for the canoes or the shuttle, or throwing themselves onto the sand. Horza struggled free at last, and staggered towards the grossly imbalanced duo of men linked by the hand. He plunged forward and grabbed the fallen pistol from the sands. As he knelt and then stood, Fwi-Song, as though suddenly seeing Horza again, gave one last gurgling, gagging splutter of noise, and tipped slowly towards the side Mr First was pulling and tugging from. Mr First fell to his knees again, still screaming as the venom seared the membranes of his eyes and attacked the nerves beyond. As Fwi-Song toppled and his arm and hand went slack, Mr First looked up and round, in time to see through his pain the vast bulk of the prophet falling towards him. He howled once, on an indrawn breath as he pulled his hand free at last from the now blue clump of chubby fingers; he started to rise to his feet, but Fwi-Song rolled over and crashed into him, knocking him to the sand. Before Mr First could utter another sound, the immense prophet had fallen over his disciple, flattening him into the sand from head to buttocks.

Fwi-Song's eyes closed slowly. The hand at his throat flopped across the sand and into the outer edge of the fire, where it started to sizzle.

Mr First's legs beat a tattoo on the sand just as the last of the Eaters ran away, jumping tents and fires and racing for the canoes or shuttle or forest. Then the two skinny legs sticking out from under the prophet's body were reduced to spasms, and after a while they stopped moving altogether. None of their movements had succeeded in shifting Fwi-Song's huge body a centimetre.

Horza blew some sand off the clumsy-feeling pistol and moved upwind from the smell of the prophet's hand burning in the fire. He checked the gun, looking round the deserted stretch of beach around the fires and tents. The canoes were being launched. Eaters were crowding into the Culture shuttle.

Horza stretched his aching limbs, loked at his bare-boned finger, then shrugged, put the gun under one armpit, put his good hand round the set of bones, pulled and twisted. His useless bones snapped from their sockets and he threw them onto the fire.

Pain isn't real anyway, he told himself shakily, and started for the Culture shuttle at a slow run.

The Eaters in the shuttle saw him coming straight towards them, and started screaming again. They piled out. Some of them ran down the beach to wade out after the escaping canoes; others scattered into the forest. Horza slowed down to let them go, then looked warily at the open doors of the Culture craft. He could see seats inside, up the short ramp, and lights and a far bulkhead. He took a deep breath and walked up the gentle slope of ramp, into the shuttle.

'Hello,' said a crudely synthesised voice. Horza looked around. The shuttle looked pretty well used and old. It was Culture, he was fairly certain of that, but it wasn't as neat and spanking-new as the Culture liked its products to look. 'Why were those people so frightened of you?'

Horza was still looking round, wondering where and what to address.

'I'm not sure,' he said shrugging. He was naked and still holding the gun, with only a couple of strips of flesh on one finger, though the bleeding had quickly stopped. He thought he must look a threatening figure anyway, but maybe the shuttle couldn't tell that. 'Where are you? What are you?' he said, deciding to feign ignorance. He looked around in a very obvious manner, hamming up a display of looking forward, through a door in the bulkhead, to a control area forward.

'I'm the shuttle. Its brain. How do you do?'

'Fine,' Horza said, 'just fine. How are you?'

'Very well, considering, thank you. I haven't been bored at all, but it is nice to have somebody to talk to at last. You speak very good Marain; where did you learn?'

'Ah . . . I did a course in it,' Horza said. He did some more looking around. 'Look, I don't know where to look when I talk to you. Where should I look, huh?'

'Ha ha,' the shuttle laughed. 'I suppose you'd best look up here; forward towards the bulkhead.' Horza did so. 'See that little round thing right in the middle, near the ceiling? That's one of my eyes.'

'Oh,' Horza said. He waved and smiled. 'Hi. My name's . . . Orab.'

'Hello, Orab. I'm called Tsealsir. Actually that's only part of my name designation, but you can call me that. What was happening out there? I haven't been watching the people I'm here to rescue; I was told not to, in case I got upset, but I did hear people screaming when they came near and they seemed frightened when they came inside me. Then they saw you and ran away. What is that you're holding? Is it a gun? I'll have to ask you to put that away for safe keeping. I'm here to rescue people who want to be rescued when the Orbital is destructed, and we can't have dangerous weapons on board, in case

169

somebody gets hurt, can we? Is that finger hurt? I have a very good medkit on board. Would you like to use it, Orab?'

'Yes, that might be an idea.'

'Good. It's on the inward side of the doorway through to my front compartment on the left.'

Horza started walking past the rows of seats towards the front of the shuttle. For all its age, the shuttle smelled of . . . he wasn't quite sure. All the synthetic materials it was made from, he supposed. After the natural but god-awful odours of the last day, Horza found the shuttle much more pleasant, even if it was Culture and therefore belonged to the enemy. Horza touched the gun he was carrying as though doing something to it.

'Just putting the safety catch on,' he told the eye in the ceiling. 'Don't want it to go off, but those people out there were trying to kill me earlier, and I feel safer with it in my hand, know what I mean?'

'Well, not exactly, Orab,' the shuttle said, 'but I think I can understand. But you'll have to give the gun to me before we take off.'

'Oh sure. As soon as you close those rear doors.' Horza was in the doorway between the main compartment and the smaller control area now. It was in fact a very short corridor, less than two metres long, with opened doors to each compartment. Horza looked round quickly, but he couldn't see another eye. He watched a large flap open at about hip level to reveal a comprehensive medical kit.

'Well, Orab, I'd close those doors to make you feel a bit safer if I could, but you see I'm here to rescue people who want to be rescued when the time comes to destruct the Orbital, and I can't close those doors until just before I leave, so that everybody who wants to can get on board. Actually I can't really understand why anybody wouldn't want to escape, but they told me not to get worried if some people stayed behind. But I must say I think that would be kind of silly, don't you, Orab?'

Horza was rummaging through the medkit but looking above it at other outlines of doors set in the wall of the short corridor. He said, 'Hmm? Oh, yeah, that would be. When is the place due to blow, anyway?' He poked his head round the corner, into the control compartment or flight deck, looking up at another eye set in the corresponding position to the one in the main compartment, but looking forward from the other side of the thick wall between the two. Horza grinned and gave a little wave, then ducked back.

'Hi,' the shuttle laughed. 'Well, Orab, I'm afraid that we're going to be forced to destruct the Orbital in forty-three standard hours.

170

Unless, of course, the Idirans see sense and are reasonable and withdraw their threat to use Vavatch as a war base.'

'Oh,' Horza said. He was looking at one of the door outlines above the opened one the medkit was protruding from. As far as he could guess, those two eyes were back to back, separated by the thickness of the wall between the two compartments. Unless there was a mirror he couldn't see, he was invisible to the shuttle while he remained in the short corridor.

He looked back, out through the open rear doors; the only movement came from the tops of some distant trees and the smoke from the fires. He checked the gun. The projectiles seemed to be hidden in some sort of magazine, but a little circular indicator with a sweep hand indicated either one bullet left or one expended out of twelve.

'Yes,' the shuttle said. 'It's very sad, of course, but these things are necessary in wartime I suppose. Not that I pretend to understand it all. I'm just a humble shuttle, after all. I'd actually been given away as a present to one of the Megaships because I was too old-fashioned and crude for the Culture, you know. I thought they could have upgraded me but they didn't; they just gave me away. Anyway, they need me now, I'm happy to say. We have quite a job on our hands, you know, getting everybody who wants to get off away from Vavatch. I'll be sorry to see it go; I've had some happy times here, believe me. . . . But that's just the way things go, I suppose. How's that finger going, by the way? Want me to have a look at it? Bring the medkit stuff round into one of the two compartments so I can take a look. I might be able to help, you know? Oh! Are you touching one of the other lockers in that corridor?'

Horza was trying to lever open the door nearest the roof by using the barrel of the gun. 'No,' he said, heaving away at it. 'I'm nowhere near it.'

'That's odd. I'm sure I can feel something. Are you sure?'

'Of course I'm sure,' Horza said, putting all his weight behind the gun. The door gave way, revealing tubes, fibre-runs, metal bottles and various other unrecognisable bits of machinery, electrics, optics and field units.

'Ouch!' said the shuttle.

'Hey!' Horza shouted. 'It just blew open! There's something on fire in there!' He raised the gun, holding it in both hands. He sighted carefully; about *there*.

'*Fire!*' yelped the shuttle. 'But that's not possible!'

'You think I can't tell *smoke* when I see it, you crazy goddamned machine?' Horza yelled. He pulled the trigger.

The gun exploded, throwing his hands up and him back. The noise of the shuttle's exclamation was covered by the crack and bang of the bullet hitting inside and exploding. Horza covered his face with his arm.

'I'm blind!' wailed the shuttle. Now smoke really was pouring from the compartment Horza had opened. He staggered into the control compartment.

'You're on fire in here, too!' he yelled. 'There's smoke coming out everywhere!'

'What? But that can't be—'

'You're on fire! I don't know how you can't feel it or smell it! You're burning!'

'I don't trust you!' the machine yelled. 'Put that gun away or— '

'You've got to trust me!' Horza yelled, looking all over the control area for where the shuttle's brain might be located. He could see screens and seats, readout screens and even the place where manual controls might be hidden; but no indication of where the brain was. 'Smoke's pouring out everywhere!' he repeated, trying to sound hysterical.

'Here! Here's an extinguisher! I'm turning mine on!' the machine shouted. A wall unit spun round, and Horza grabbed the bulky cylinder attached to the inside of the flap. He wrapped his four good fingers on his injured hand round the pistol grip. A hissing noise and a light vapour-like steam was appearing from various places in the compartment.

'Nothing's happening!' Horza screamed. 'There's loads of black smoke and its— arrch!' He pretended to cough. '. . . Aargh! It's getting thicker!'

'Where is it coming from? Quickly!'

'Everywhere!' Horza yelled, glancing all round the control area. 'From near your eye . . . under the seats, over the screens, under the screens . . . I can't see . . . !'

'Go on! I can smell smoke, too, now!'

Horza looked at the slight smudge of grey filtering into the control area from the spluttering fire in the short corridor where he had shot the craft. 'It's . . . coming from those places, and those info screens on either side of the end seats, and . . . just above the seats, on the side walls where that bit juts out—'

'What?' screamed the shuttle brain. 'On the left facing forward?'

172

'Yes!'

'Put that one out first!' the shuttle screeched.

Horza dropped the extinguisher and gripped the gun in both hands again, aiming it at the bulge in the wall over the left-hand seat. He pulled the trigger: once, twice, three times. The gun blasted, shaking his whole body; sparks and bits of flying debris flew from the holes the bullets were smashing in the casing of the machine.

'EEEeee . . .' said the shuttle, then there was silence.

Some smoke rose from the bulge and it joined with that coming from the corridor to form a thin layer under the ceiling. Horza let the gun down slowly, looking around and listening.

'Mug,' he said.

He used the hand-held extinguisher to put out the small fires in the wall of the corridor and where the shuttle's brain had been, then he went out into the passenger area to sit near the open doors while the smoke and the fumes cleared. He couldn't see any Eaters on the sand or in the forest, and the canoes were out of sight, too. He looked for some door controls and found them; the doors closed with a hiss, and Horza grinned.

He went back to the control area and started punching buttons and opening sections of panelling until he got some life from the screens. They all suddenly blinked on while he was fiddling with some buttons on the arm of one of the couch-like seats. The noise of surf in the flight deck made him think the doors had opened again, but it was only some external microphones relaying the noise from outside. Screens flickered and lit up with figures and lines, and flaps opened in front of the seats; control wheels and levers sighed out smoothly and clicked into place, just ready to be held and used. Feeling happier than he had been in many days, Horza started an eventually successful but longer and more frustrating search for some food; he was very hungry.

Some small insects were running in orderly lines over the huge body collapsed on the sands, one hand of which was sticking, charred and blackened, into the dying flames of a fire.

The little insects started by eating the deep-set eyes, which were open. They hardly noticed as the shuttle rose, wobbling, into the air, picked up speed and turned inelegantly above the mountain, then roared off, through the early evening air, away from the island.

Interlude in darkness

The Mind had an image to illustrate its information capacity. It liked to imagine the contents of its memory store written out on cards; little slips of paper with tiny writing on them, big enough for a human to read. If the characters were a couple of millimetres tall and the paper about ten centimetres square and written on both sides, then ten thousand characters could be squeezed onto each card. In a metre-long drawer of such cards maybe one thousand of them – ten million pieces of information – could be stored. In a small room a few metres square, with a corridor in the middle just wide enough to pull a tray out into, you could keep perhaps a thousand trays arranged in close-packed cabinets: ten billion characters in all.

A square kilometre of these cramped cells might contain as many as one hundred thousand rooms; a thousand such floors would produce a building two thousand metres tall with a hundred million rooms. If you kept building those squat towers, squeezed hard up against each other until they entirely covered the surface of a largish standard-G world – maybe a billion square kilometres – you would have a planet with one trillion square kilometres of floor space, one hundred quadrillion paper-stuffed rooms, thirty light-years of corridors and a number of potential stored characters sufficiently large to boggle just about anybody's mind.

In base 10 that number would be a 1 followed by twenty-seven zeros, and even that vast figure was only a fraction of the capacity of the Mind. To match it you would need a thousand such worlds; systems of them, a clusterful of information-packed globes . . . and that vast capacity was physically contained within a space smaller than a single one of those tiny rooms, inside the Mind. . . .

In darkness the Mind waited.

It had counted how long it had waited so far; it had tried to estimate how long it would have to wait in the future. It knew to the smallest imaginable fraction of a second how long it had been in the tunnels of the Command System, and more often than it needed to it thought about that number, watched it grow inside itself. It was a form of security, it supposed; a small fetish; something to cling to.

It. had explored the Command System tunnels, scanning and surveying. It was weak, damaged, almost totally helpless, but it had been worthwhile taking a look around the maze-like complex of tunnels and caverns just to take its attention off the fact that it was there as a refugee. The places it could not get to itself it sent its one remaining remote drone into, so that it could have a look, and see what there was to be seen.

And all of it was at once boring and frighteningly depressing. The level of technology possessed by the builders of the Command System was very limited indeed; everything in the tunnels worked either mechanically or electronically. Gears and wheels, electric wires, superconductors and light-fibres; very crude indeed, the Mind thought, and nothing it could possibly interest itself in. A glance through any of the machines and devices in the tunnel was sufficient to know them exactly – what they were made of, how they had been made, even what they were made for. No mystery, nothing to employ the mind.

There was something too about the inexactitude of it all that the Mind found almost frightening. It could look at some carefully machined piece of metal or some delicately moulded bit of plastic, and know that to the people who had built the Command System – to their eyes – these things were exact and precise, constructed to fine tolerances with dead straight lines, perfect edges, smooth surfaces, immaculate right angles . . . and so on. But the Mind, even with its damaged sensors, could see the rough edges, the crudity of the parts and the components involved. They had been good enough for the people at the time, and no doubt they had fulfilled the most important criterion of all; they worked. . . .

But they *were* crude, clumsy, imperfectly designed and manufactured. For some reason the Mind found this worrying.

And it would have to *use* this ancient, crude, shop-soiled technology. It would have to *connect* with it.

It had thought it through as best it could, and decided to formulate plans for what to do if the Idirans did get somebody through the Quiet Barrier and threatened it with discovery.

It would arm, and it would make a place to hide in. Both actions implied damage to the Command System, so it would not act until it

178

knew it was definitely threatened. Once it knew it was, it would be forced to risk the Dra'Azon's displeasure.

But it might not come to that. It hoped it wouldn't; planning was one thing, execution was another. It was unlikely to have very much time either to hide or to arm. Both plans might perforce be rather crudely implemented, especially as it had only one remote drone and its own badly crippled fields with which to manipulate the engineering facilities of the System.

Better than nothing, though. Better still to have problems than to let death eradicate them all. . . .

There was, however, another less immediately relevant, but more intrinsically worrying, problem it had discovered, and it was implied in the question: who was it?

Its higher functions had had to close down when it had transferred from four- to three-dimensional space. The Mind's information was held in binary form, in spirals composed of protons and neutrons; and neutrons – outside a nucleus, and also outside hyperspace – decayed (into protons, ha-ha; not too long after entering the Command System, the vast majority of its memory would have consisted of the stunningly illuminating message: '0000000 . . .'). So it had effectively frozen its primary memory and cognitive functions, wrapping them in fields which prevented both decay and use. It was working instead on back-up picocircuitry, in real space, and using real-space light to think with (how humiliating).

In fact, it could still access all that stored memory (though the process was complicated, and so *slow*), so all was not lost there. . . . But as for thinking, as for *being itself* – another matter entirely. It wasn't its real self. It was a crude, abstracted copy of itself, the mere ground plan for the full labyrinthine complexity of its true personality. It was the truest possible copy its limited scale was theoretically capable of providing, and it was still sentient; conscious by even the most rigorous of standards. Yet an index was not the text, a street plan was not the city, a map not the land.

So *who was it?*

Not the entity it thought it was, that was the answer, and it was a disconcerting one. Because it knew that the self it was now could never think of all the things its old self would have thought of. It felt unworthy. It felt fallible and limited and . . . dull.

But think positively. Patterns, images, the telling analogy . . . make the ill work to good. Just think. . . .

If it was not itself, then it *would* be not itself.

As it was now to what it had been before, so the remote drone was to it now (nice connection).

The remote drone would be more than just its eyes and ears on the surface, in or near the Changers' base, keeping look-out; more than just its assistant in the doubtless frantic preparations to equip and secrete which would ensue if the drone did raise the alarm; more. And less.

Look on the happy side, think of the good things. Hadn't it been *clever*? Yes, it had.

Its escape from the spare-parts warship had been, though it thought it itself, quite breathtakingly masterful and brilliant. Its courageous use of warp so deep into a gravity well would have been foolhardy in the extreme in anything else but the dire circumstances it had found itself in, but was anyway superbly skilled. . . . And its stunning cross-realm transfer, from hyper- to real space, was not simply even more brilliant and even braver than anything else it had done, it was almost certainly a first; there was nothing anywhere in its vast store of information to indicate that anybody had *ever* done that before. It was proud.

But after all that, here it was, trapped; an intellectual cripple, a philosophical shadow of its former self.

Now all it could do was wait, hoping that whoever came to find it would be friendly. The Culture must know; the Mind was certain its signal had worked and that it would be picked up somewhere. But the Idirans knew as well. It didn't think they would just try to storm in, because they knew as well as it did that antagonising the Dra'Azon was a bad idea. But what if the Idirans found a way in and the Culture couldn't? What if the whole region of space around the Sullen Gulf was now Idiran held? The Mind knew there was only one thing it could do if it fell into Idiran hands, but not only did it not want to destruct for purely personal reasons, it didn't want to destruct anywhere near Schar's World anyway, for the same reason that the Idirans wouldn't come charging in. But if it *was* captured in the planet, that might be the last time it would have a chance to destroy itself. By the time it was taken off the planet the Idirans might have found a way of stopping it from destructing.

Perhaps it had made a mistake in escaping at all. Perhaps it should have just destructed along with the rest of the ship and saved all this complication and worry. But it had seemed like an almost heaven-sent opportunity to escape – finding itself so close to a Planet of the Dead when it had been attacked. It wanted to live anyway, but it would have been . . . wasteful to throw away such a great chance even if it had been perfectly sanguine about its own survival or destruction.

Well, there was nothing to be done about it now. It was here and it just had to wait. Wait and think. Consider all the options (few) and possibilities (many). Rack those memories as best it could for anything that might be relevant, that might help. For example (and the one really interesting bit *would* be a bad one), it had discovered that the Idirans had probably employed one of the Changers who had actually served with the caretaker staff on Schar's World. Of course perhaps the man was dead, or busy on something else, or too far away, or the information had been incorrect in the first place and the intelligence-gathering section of the Culture had got it wrong. . . . But if not, then that man would be the one obvious person to send after something hiding in the Command System tunnels.

It was part of the Mind's very construction – at every level – to believe that there was no such thing as bad knowledge except in very relative terms, but it really did wish that it hadn't had that bit of information in its memory banks; it would just as soon not have known anything about this man, this Changer who knew Schar's World and probably worked for the Idirans. (Perversely, it found itself wishing it knew this man's *name*.)

But with any luck he would be irrelevant, or the Culture would get here first. Or the Dra'Azon being would recognise a fellow Mind in trouble and help, or . . . anything.

In darkness the Mind waited.

. . . Hundreds of those planets were empty; the hundred million room towers were there; the little rooms, the cabinets and the trays and the cards and the spaces for the numbers and letters were there; but nothing was written, nothing held, on any of the cards. . . . (Sometimes the Mind liked to imagine travelling down the narrow spaces between the cabinets, one of its remote drones floating between the banked files of memory in the thin corridors, from room to room, for floor after floor, kilometre after kilometre, over buried continents of rooms, filled-in oceans of rooms, levelled ranges, felled forests, covered deserts of rooms.) . . . These whole systems of dark planets, those trillions of square kilometres of blank paper, represented the Mind's future; the spaces it would fill in its life to come.

If it had one.

7.

A Game of Damage

'Damage – the game banned everywhere. Tonight, in that unprepossessing building across the square under the dome, they'll gather: the Players of the Eve of Destruction . . . the most select group of rich psychotics in the human galaxy, here to play the game that is to real life what soap opera is to high tragedy.

'This is the bi-port city of Evanauth, Vavatch Orbital, the very same Vavatch Orbital that in about eleven standard hours from now is due to be blasted into its component atoms as the Idiran–Culture war in this part of the galaxy, near the Glittercliff and Sullen Gulf, reaches a new high in standing-by-your-principles-regardless and a new low in common sense. It's that imminent destruction that's attracted these scatological vultures here, not the famous Megaships or the azure-blue technological miracles of the Circlesea. No, these people are here because the whole Orbital is doomed to be blown away shortly, and they think it's kind of amusing to play Damage – an ordinary card game with a few embellishments to make it attractive to the mentally disturbed – in places on the verge of annihilation.

'They've played on worlds about to suffer massive comet or meteorite strikes, in volcanic calderas about to blow, in cities due for nuclear bombardment in ritualistic wars, in asteroids heading for the centre of stars, in front of moving cliffs of ice or lava, inside mysterious alien spacecraft discovered empty and deserted and set on courses aiming them into black holes, in vast palaces about to be sacked by android mobs, and just about everywhere you can think of you'd rather *not* want to be immediately after the Players leave. It might seem like a strange sort of way to get your kicks, but it takes all sorts to make a galaxy, I guess.

'So here they've come, these hyper-rich dead-beats, in their rented ships or their own cruisers. Right now they're sobering up and coming down, going through plastic surgery or behaviour therapy – or both – to make them acceptable in what passes for normal society, even in

185

these rarefied circles, after months spent in whatever expensive and unlikely debauchery or perversion particularly appeals to them or happens to be in fashion at the moment. At the same time, they or their minions are scraping together their Aoish credits – all actual; no notes – and scouting hospitals, asylums and freeze-stores for new Lives.

'Here, too, have come the hangers-on – the Damage groupies, the fortune seekers, the past failures at the game desperate for another try if they can only raise the money and the Lives . . . and Damage's very own special sort of human debris: the moties, victims of the game's emotional fall-out; mind-junkies who only exist to lap at the crumbs of ecstasy and anguish falling from the lips of their heroes, the Players of the Game.

'Nobody knows exactly how all these different groups hear about the game or even how they all get here in time, but the word goes out to those who really need to or want to hear about it, and like ghouls they come, ready for the game and the destruction.

'Originally Damage was played on such occasions because only during the breakdown of law and morality, and the confusion and chaos normally surrounding Final Events, could the game be carried out in anything remotely resembling part of the civilised galaxy; which, believe it or not, the Players like to think they're part of. Now the subsequent nova, world-busting or other cataclysm is seen as some sort of metaphysical symbol for the mortality of all things, and as the Lives involved in a Full Game are all volunteers, a lot of places – like good old pleasure-oriented, permissive Vavatch – let the game take place with official blessing from the authorities. Some people say it's not the game it used to be, even that it's become something of a media event, but *I* say it's still a game for the mad and the bad; the rich and the uncaring, but not the careless; the unhinged . . . but well connected. People still die in Damage, and not just the Lives, either, or the Players.

'It's been called the most decadent game in history. About all you can say in the game's defence is that it, rather than reality, occupies the warped minds of some of the galaxy's more twisted people; gods know what they would get up to if it wasn't there. And if the game does any good apart from reminding us – as if we needed reminding – how crazy the bipedal, oxygen-breathing carboniform can become, it does occasionally remove one of the Players and frighten the rest for a while. In these arguably insane times, *any* lessening or attenuation of madness is maybe something to be grateful for.

'I'll be filing another report again some time during the course of the game, from within the auditorium if I can get in there. But in the meantime, goodbye and take care. This is Sarble the Eye, Evanauth City, Vavatch.'

The image on the wrist screen of a man standing in sunlight on a plaza faded; the half-masked, youngish face disappearing.

Horza put his terminal screen back onto his cuff. The time display winked slowly with the countdown to Vavatch's destruction.

Sarble the Eye, one of the most famous of the humanoid galaxy's freelance reporters, and also one of the most successful at getting into places he wasn't supposed to, would now probably be trying to enter the games hall – if he hadn't got in already; the broadcast Horza had just watched had been recorded that afternoon. Doubtless Sarble would be in disguise, so Horza was glad he'd bribed his way in before the reporter's broadcast went out and the security guards round the hall got even more wary; it had been hard enough as it was.

Horza, in his new guise as Kraiklyn, had posed as a motie – one of the emotional junkies who followed the erratic, secretive progress of the major game series round the more tawdry fringes of civilisation, having discovered that all but the most expensive reserved places had been sold out the day before. The five Aoish credit Tenths he had started out with that morning were now reduced to three; though he also had some money keyed into a couple of credit cards he'd bought. That currency would shrink in real value, though, as the destruction time drew nearer.

Horza took a deep, satisfying breath and looked around the big arena. He had climbed as high as he could up the banked steps, slopes and platforms, using the interval before the game began to get an overview of the whole thing.

The dome of the arena was transparent, showing stars and the bright shining line that was the Orbital's far side, now in daylight. The lights of shuttles coming and going – mostly going – traced lines across the still points. Beneath the dome cover hung a smoky haze, lit with the popping lights of a small firework display. The air was filled, too, with the chanting of massed voices; a choir of scalecones stood banked on the far side of the auditorium. The humanoids forming the choir appeared identical in all but stature and in the tones they produced from their puffed-out chests and long necks. They seemed to be making the ambient racket, but as he looked around the arena Horza could make out the faint purple edges in the air where other, more localised sound fields held command, over smaller stages where dancers danced, singers sang, strippers stripped, boxers boxed, or people just stood around talking.

Banked all around, the paraphernalia of the game seethed like a vast storm. Maybe ten or even twenty thousand people, mostly humanoid but some utterly different, including not a few machines and drones, they sat or lay or walked or stood, watching magicians, jugglers, fighters, immolators, hypnotics, couplers, actors, orators and a hundred other types of entertainers all doing their turns. Tents had been pitched on some of the larger terraces; rows of seats and couches remained on others. Many small stages frazzled with lights, smoke and glittering holograms and soligrams. Horza saw a 3-D maze spread out over several terraces, full of tubes and angles, some clear, some opaque, some moving, some staying still. Shadows and forms moved inside.

A slow-motion animal trapeze act arced gradually overhead. Horza recognised the beasts performing it; it would become a combat act later on.

Some people walked by Horza: tall humanoids in fabulous clothes, glittering like a gaudy night city seen from the air. They chattered in almost inaudibly high voices, and from a network of fine, golden coloured tubes branching all around their bright red and dark purple faces, tiny puffs of incandescent gas pulsed out, wreathing their semi-scaled necks and naked shoulders, and trailing and dimming behind them in a fiery orange glow. Horza watched them pass. Their cloaks, flowing out behind as though hardly heavier than the air through which they moved, flickered with the image of an alien face, each cloak showing part of one huge moving image, as though a projector overhead was focused on the capes of the moving group. The orange gas touched Horza's nostrils and his head swam for a second. He let his immune-glands deal with the narcotic, and continued to look around the arena.

The eye of the storm, the still, quiet spot, was so small it could easily have been missed in even a slow and attentive scan of the auditorium. It was not in the centre, but set at one end of the ellipsoid of level ground forming the lowest visible level of the arena. There, under a canopy of still dark lighting units, a round table stood, just about large enough to accommodate at its rim the sixteen large, differently styled chairs which each faced a wedge of colour fixed to the top of the table. A console set into the table itself faced each chair, on which straps and other restraining devices lay opened. Behind each of the seats lay an area of clear space on which small seats, twelve in all, were placed. A small fence separated them from the larger seats in front, and another fence cordoned off the set of twelve seats from a larger area behind where people, most of them moties, were already quietly waiting.

The game seemed to have been delayed. Horza sat down on what was either an over-designed seat or a rather unimaginative piece of sculpture. He was almost on the highest level of the terraces of the arena, with a good view over most of the rest. There was nobody near by. He reached deep inside his heavy blouse and peeled off some artificial skin from his abdomen. He rolled the skin into a ball and threw it into a large pot that held a small tree, just behind where he sat; then he checked the Aoish credit Tenths, the negotiable memory card, the pocket terminal and the light CRE pistol which had been hidden by the paunch of fake skin. Out of the corner of his eye he saw a small, darkly dressed man approach. The man looked at Horza with his head tilted, from about five metres off, then came closer.

'Hey, you want to be a Life?'

'No. Goodbye,' Horza said. The small man sniffed and walked off, stopping further along the walkway to prod a shape lying near the edge of a narrow terrace. Horza looked over and saw a woman there raise her head groggily, then shake it slowly, moving sinuous lengths of bedraggled white hair. Her faced showed briefly in the light of an overhead spot; she was beautiful but looked very tired. The small man spoke to her again, but she shook her head and made a motion with one hand. The small man walked off.

The flight in the ex-Culture shuttle had been relatively uneventful; after some confusion, Horza had succeeded in patching through to the Orbital's navigation system, discovered where he was in relation to the *Olmedreca*'s last known position, and set off to find whatever was left of the Megaship. He'd accessed a news service while gorging himself on Culture emergency rations, and found a report on the *Olmedreca* in the index. The pictures showed the ship, listing a little and fractionally bow-down, floating in a calm sea surrounded by ice, the first kilometre of its hull seemingly buried inside the huge tabular berg. Small aircraft and a few shuttles hovered and flew about the gigantic wreck, like flies above the carcass of a dinosaur. The commentary accompanying the visuals spoke of a mysterious second nuclear explosion aboard the craft. It also reported that when police craft had arrived, the Megaship had proved to be deserted.

Hearing that, Horza had immediately altered the shuttle's destination, swinging the craft round, to head for Evanauth.

Horza had had three Tenths of an Aoish credit. He had sold the shuttle for five Tenths. It was absurdly cheap, especially given the imminent destruction of the Orbital, but he had been in a hurry, and the dealer who accepted the craft was certainy taking a risk handling the machine; it was very obviously a Culture design, the brain had equally obviously been shot out of it, so there could be little doubt it had been stolen. The Culture would treat the destruction of the craft's consciousness as murder.

In three hours Horza had sold the shuttle, bought clothes, cards, a gun, a couple of terminals and some information. All except the information had been cheap.

Horza now knew that there was a craft answering the description of the *Clear Air Turbulence* on the Orbital, or rather underneath it, inside the ex-Culture General Systems Vehicle called *The Ends of Invention*. He found that hard to believe, but there was no other craft it could be. According to the information agency, a ship fitting the *CAT*'s description had been brought on board by one of the Evanauth Port shipbuilders to have repairs made to its warping units; it had arrived under tow two days previously, with only its fusion motors working. He could not, however, find out its name or exact location.

It sounded to Horza like the *CAT* had been used to rescue the survivors of Kraiklyn's band; it must have come over the O wall on remote control, using its warp units. It had picked the Free Company up, then hopped back over again, damaging its warp motors in the process.

He had also been unable to find out who the survivors might be, but assumed Kraiklyn must be one of them; nobody else could have brought the *CAT* over the Edgewall. He hoped he'd find Kraiklyn at the Damage game. Either way, Horza had decided to make for the *CAT* afterwards. He still intended to head for Schar's World, and the *Clear Air Turbulence* was the most likely way of getting there. He hoped Yalson was alive. He also hoped it was true about *The Ends of Invention* being totally demilitarised, and the volume around Vavatch being free of Culture ships. After all this time he wouldn't have put it past the Culture's Minds to have found out about the *CAT* being in the same volume of space as *The Hand of God 137* when it came under attack, and to have made a connection or two.

He sat back in the seat – or sculpture – and relaxed, letting the internal pattern of the motie drop from his mind and body. He had to start thinking like Kraiklyn again; he closed his eyes.

After a few minutes he could hear things starting to happen down in the lower reaches of the arena. He brought himself to and looked around. The white-haired woman who had been lying on the nearby terrace had got up; she was walking, a little unsteadily, down into the arena, her long, heavy dress sweeping over the steps. Horza got up, too, following quickly down the stairs in the wake of her perfume. She didn't look at him when he skipped past her. She was fiddling with an askew tiara.

The lights were on over the coloured table where the game would be played. Some of the stages in the auditorium were starting to close up or go dim. People were gradually gravitating towards the game table, to the seats and loungers and standing areas overlooking it. In the glare of the overhead lights, tall figures in black robes moved slowly, checking pieces of the game equipment. They were the adjudicators: Ishlorsinami. The species was renowned for being the most unimaginative, humourless, prissy, honest and incorruptible group in the galaxy and they always officiated at Damage games because hardly anybody else could be trusted.

Horza stopped by a food stall to stock up on food and drink; he watched the game table and the figures around it while his order was prepared. The woman with the heavy dress and long white hair passed him, still going down the steps. Her tiara was almost straight, though her long, loose gown was crumpled. She yawned as she went past.

Horza paid for his food with a card, then followed the woman again, going towards the growing crowd of people and machines starting to cluster all around the outer perimeter of the game area. The woman looked suspiciously at him when he half ran, half walked down the steps past her again.

Horza bribed his way into one of the better terraces. He pulled the hood of his heavy blouse out from the thick collar, stretching it over his forehead and out a little so that his face was in shadow. He didn't want the real Kraiklyn to see him now. The terrace jutted out over lower ones, slanting down with an excellent view of the table itself and the gantries above. Most of the fenced areas around the table were visible too. Horza settled onto a soft lounger near a noisy group of extravagantly dressed tripedals who hooted a lot and kept spitting into a large pot in the centre of their group of gently rocking couches.

The Ishlorsinami seemed to have satisfied themselves that everything was working and was set up fairly. They walked down a ramp set into the surface of the arena's ellipsoid floor. Some lights went off; a quietfield slowly cut off the sounds from the rest of the auditorium.

Horza took a quick look round. A few stages and sets still showed lights, but they were going out. The slow-motion animal trapeze act was still going on, though, high up in the darkness below the stars; the huge ponderous beasts were swinging through the air, field harnesses glittering. They somersaulted and twisted, but now as they did so, passing each other in mid-air, they reached out with their clawed paws, slashing slowly and silently at each other's fur. Nobody else seemed to be watching.

Horza was surprised to see the woman he had passed twice on the stairs walk past him again and drape herself over a vacant couch which had been reserved near the front of the terrace. Somehow he hadn't thought she would be rich enough to afford this area.

Without a fanfare or announcement, the Players of the Eve of Destruction appeared, coming up the ramp in the arena floor, led by a single Ishlorsinami. Horza checked his terminal; it was exactly seven hours standard to the Orbital's destruction. Applause, cheers and, near Horza at least, loud hooting greeted the contestants, though the quietfields muffled everything. As they appeared from the shadows on the ramp, some of the Players acknowledged the crowd who had come to see them play, while other Players totally ignored them.

Horza recognised few of them. The ones he did know, or had at least heard of, were Ghalssel, Tengayet Doy-Suut, Wilgre and Neeporlax. Ghalssel of Ghalssel's Raiders – probably the most successful of the Free Companies. Horza had heard the mercenary ship arrive from about eleven kilometres away, while he was making the deal with the shuttle saleswomen. She had frozen at the time; her eyes glazed. Horza didn't like to ask whether she thought the noise was the Culture coming to destroy the Orbital a few hours early or just coming to get her for buying a hot shuttle craft.

Ghalssel was an average-looking man, stocky enough to be obviously from a high-G planet, but without the look of compressed power that most such people possessed. He was simply dressed and his head was clean shaven. Supposedly only a Damage game, where such things were banned, could force Ghalssel out of the suit he always wore.

Tengayet Doy-Suut was tall, very dark and also simply dressed. The Suut was the champion Damage Player, on both game average, wins and maximum credits. He had come from a recently Contacted planet twenty years before, and had been a champion player of games of chance and bluff there, too. That was where he had had his face removed and a stainless-steel mask grafted on; only the eyes looked alive: expressionless soft jewels set in the sculpted metal. The mask had a matt finish, to prevent his opponents seeing his cards reflected in his face.

Wilgre had to be helped up the ramp by some slaves from his retinue. The blue giant from Ozhleh, clad in a mirror robe, looked almost as though he was being rolled up the slope by the small humans behind, although the hem of his robe kicked out now and again to show where his four stubby legs were scrabbling to propel his great body up the ramp. In one of his two hands he held a large mirror, in the other a whip lead on the end of which a blinded rogothuyr – its four paws encrusted with precious metals, its snout encased in a platinum muzzle and its eyes replaced by emeralds – padded like a lithe nightmare in pure white. The animal's giant head swept from side to side as it used its ultrasonic sense to map out its surroundings. On another terrace, almost opposite Horza's, all thirty-two of Wilgre's concubines threw aside their body veils and went down on their knees and elbows, worshipping their lord. He waved the mirror at them briefly. Virtually every magnifier and micro-camera smuggled into the auditorium also swivelled to focus on the thirty-two assorted females, reputedly the finest one-sex harem in the galaxy.

Neeporlax presented something of a contrast. The youth was a shambling, gaunt, shoddily clothed figure, blinking in the lights of the arena and clutching a soft toy. The boy was perhaps the second-best Damage Player in the galaxy, but he always gave his winnings away, and the average meterbed hotel would have thought twice about admitting him; he was diseased, half blind, incontinent and albino. His head was liable to shake out of control at an anxious moment in a game, but his hands held holocards as though the plastics had been set in rock. He, too, was assisted up the ramp, by a young girl who helped him to his seat, combed his hair and kissed his cheek, then went to stand in the area behind the twelve seats set immediately aft of the youth's chair.

Wilgre raised one of his chubby blue hands and threw a few Hundredths at the crowd beyond the fences; people scrabbled for the coins. Wilgre always mixed in a few higher denominations as well. Once, at a game a few years previously inside a moon heading for a black hole, he had thrown a Billion away with the small change, disposing of perhaps a tenth of a per cent of his fortune with just one flick of the wrist. A decrepit asteroid tramp, who had just been turned down as a Life because he had only one arm, ended up buying his own planet.

The rest of the Players were a pretty varied-looking bunch as well;

but with one exception, Horza didn't recognise them. Three or four of the others were greeted with shouts and some fireworks, so presumably they were well known; the rest were either disliked or unknown.

The last player to come up the ramp was Kraiklyn.

Horza settled back in his lounger, smiling. The Free Company leader had had a little temporary facial alteration done – probably pull-off – and his hair was dyed, but it was him all right. He wore a light-coloured one-piece fabric suit, he was clean shaven and his hair was brown. Perhaps the others on the *CAT* wouldn't have recognised him, but Horza had studied the man – to see how he carried himself, how he walked, how the muscles in his face were set – and to the Changer, Kraiklyn stood out like a boulder in a pebble-field.

When all the Players were seated, their Lives were led in to sit on the seats immediately behind each Player.

The Lives were all humans; most already looked half dead anyway, though they were all physically whole. One by one they were taken to their seats, strapped in and helmeted. The lightweight black helmets covered their faces except for the eyes. Most slumped forward once they were strapped in; a few sat more upright, but none raised their eyes or looked round. All the regular Players had the full complement of Lives allowed; some had them specially bred, while others had their agents supply all they wanted. The less rich, not so well known Players, like Kraiklyn, had the sweepings of prisons and asylums, and a few paid depressives who had willed their share of any proceeds to somebody else. Often members of the Despondent sect could be persuaded to become Lives, either for free or for a donation to their cause, but Horza couldn't see any of their distinctive tiered head-dresses or bleeding-eye symbols.

Kraiklyn had only managed to find three Lives; it didn't look as though he would be staying all that long in the game.

The white-haired woman in the reserved seat near the front of the terrace got up, stretched and walked up the terrace, between the couches and loungers, a bored expression on her face. Just as she drew level with Horza's couch, a commotion erupted on a terrace behind them. The woman stopped and looked. Horza turned round. Even through the quietfield he could hear a man shouting; what looked like a fight had broken out. A couple of security guards were trying to restrain two people rolling about on the floor. The crowd on the terrace had made a circle about the disturbance and were looking on, dividing their attention between the preparations for the Damage game and the fisticuffs on the terrace beside them. Eventually the two people on the floor were brought to their feet, but instead of both being restrained, only one was – a youngish man who looked vaguely familiar to Horza, though he appeared to have been disguising himself with a blond wig which was now slipping off his head.

The other person who had been fighting, another man, produced some sort of card from his clothes and showed it to the young man, who was still shouting. Then the two uniformed guards and the man who had brandished the card led the young man away. The man with the card took something small from behind one of the young man's ears as he was frog-marched off to an access tunnel. The young woman with the long white hair crossed her arms and walked on up the terrace. The circle of people on the terrace above closed again, like a hole in cloud.

Horza watched the woman weave her way through more couches until she left the terrace and he lost sight of her. He looked up. The duelling animals still spun and leapt; their white blood seemed to glow as it matted their shaggy hides. They snarled silently and scythed at each other with their long forelimbs, but their acrobatics and their aiming had deteriorated; they were starting to look tired and clumsy. Horza looked back to the game table; they were all ready, and the game was about to begin.

Damage was just a fancy card game: partly skill, partly luck and partly bluff. What made it interesting was not just the high sums involved, or even the fact that whenever a player lost a life he lost a Life – a living, breathing human being – but the use of complicated conscious-ness-altering two-way electronic fields around the game table.

With the cards in his or her hand, a player could alter the emotions of another player, or sometimes of several others. Fear, hate, despair, hope, love, camaraderie, doubt, elation, paranoia; virtually every emotional state the human brain was capable of experiencing could be beamed at another player or used for oneself. From far enough away, or in a field shield close in, the game could look like a pastime for the deranged or the simple-minded. A player with an obviously strong hand might suddenly throw it in; somebody with nothing at all might gamble all the credits they had; people broke down weeping or started laughing uncontrollably; they might moan with love at a player known to be their worst enemy or claw at their restraining straps to free themselves for a murdering attack on their best friend.

Or they could kill themselves. Damage players never did get free from their chairs (should they ever do so, an Ishlorsinami would shoot them with a heavy stun gun) but they could destroy themselves. Each game console, from which the emotor units radiated the relevant emotions, on which the cards were played and where the players could see the time and the number of Lives they each had left, contained a small hollow button, inside which a needle filled with poison lay ready to inject any stabbing finger which pushed it.

Damage was one of those games in which it was unwise to make too many enemies. Only the very strong-willed indeed could defeat the urge to suicide implanted in their brains by a concerted attack of half a table of players.

At the finish of each hand of cards, when the money which had been gambled was taken by the player with the most card points, all the other players who had stayed with the betting lost a Life. When they had none left they were out of the game, as they would be if they ran out of money. The rules said the game ended when only one player had any Lives left, though in practice it finished when the remaining contestants agreed that if they stayed any longer they were likely to lose their own Lives to whatever disaster was about to ensue. It could get very interesting at the end of a game when the moment of destruction was very close, the hand had gone on for some time, a great deal of money had been gambled on that one hand, and one or several players would not agree to call it a day; then the sophisticates really were separated from the simians, and it became even more a game of nerve. Quite a few of the best Damage players of the past had perished trying to out-dare and out-stay each other in such circumstances.

From a spectator's point of view, Damage's special attraction was that the closer you stood to the emotor unit of any particular player, the more of the emotions they were experiencing affected you directly, too. A whole subculture of people hooked on such third-hand feelings had grown up in the few hundred years since Damage had become such a select but popular game: the moties.

There were other groups playing Damage. The Players of the Eve of Destruction were simply the most famous and the richest. The moties could get their emotional fix in lots of places throughout the galaxy, but only in a full game, only on the edge of annihilation, only with the very best players (plus a few hopefuls) could the most intense experiences be obtained. It was one of these unfortunates Horza had impersonated when he had discovered that an access pass could not be had for less than twice the amount of money he had made on the shuttle. Bribing a door guard had been a lot cheaper.

The real moties were packed tightly behind the fence separating them from the Lives. Sixteen clumps of sweating, nervous-looking people – like the game players, mostly male – they jostled and pressed forward, trying to get near to the table, near to the Players.

Horza watched them as the cards were dealt by the chief Ishlor-sinami. Moties jumped up and down, trying to see what was happening, and security guards fitted with baffle helmets to keep out the emotor pulses patrolled the perimeter of the fence, tapping nerver prods on their thighs or palms and watching warily.

'. . . Sarble the Eye . . .' somebody near by said, and Horza turned to see. A cadaverous-looking human lying on a couch behind and to Horza's left was talking to another and pointing up to the terrace where the disturbance had occurred a few minutes earlier. Horza heard the words 'Sarble' and 'caught' a few more times from elsewhere around him as the news spread. He turned round to watch the game as the Players started to inspect their hands; the betting began. Horza thought it was a pity the reporter had been caught, but it might mean that the security guards relaxed a little, giving him a better chance of not being asked for his pass.

Horza was sitting a good fifty metres from the nearest player, a woman whose name he had heard mentioned but had forgotten. As the first hand progressed, only mild versions of what she was feeling and was being made to feel impinged upon his consciousness. Nevertheless, he didn't enjoy the sensation, and switched on the lounger's baffle field, using the small control set on one arm of the couch. Had he wanted, he could have cancelled the immediate effect of the player he just happened to be sitting behind and substituted the effects of any of the other emotor units on the table. The effect would have been nothing like as intense as what the moties or the Lives were experiencing, but it would certainly have given a good idea of what the Players were going through. Most of the other people around him were using their lounger's controls in that way, flicking from one player to another in an attempt to judge the overall state of the game. Horza would concentrate on Kraiklyn's broadcast emotions later, but for now he just wanted to settle in and get the general feel of the game.

Kraiklyn dropped out of the first hand early enough to be sure of avoiding losing a Life when it finished; with so few Lives of his own it was the wisest course unless he had a very strong hand. Horza watched the man carefully as he sat back in his seat and relaxed, his emotor unit dormant. Kraiklyn licked his lips and wiped his brow. Horza decided in the next hand he would eavesdrop on what Kraiklyn was going through, just to see what it was like.

The hand finished. Wilgre won. He waved, acknowledging the cheers of the crowd. Some moties had fainted already; at the other end of the ellipsoid, in its cage, the rogothuyr snarled. Five Players lost Lives; five seated humans, sitting hopeless and despairing as the effects of the emotor fields still resounded in them, went suddenly slack in their chairs as their helmets sent a neural blast through their skulls strong enough to stun the Lives sitting around them and to make the nearest moties, and the Player each Life belonged to, flinch.

Ishlorsinami undid the restrainers on the dead humans' seats and carried them away down the access ramp. The remaining Lives gradually recovered, but they sat as listless as before. The Ishlor-sinami claimed they always checked that each volunteering Life was genuine, and that the drugs they gave them simply stopped them from becoming hysterical, but it was rumoured that there were ways round the Ishlorsinami screening process, and that some people had suc-ceeded in disposing of their enemies by drugging or hypnotising them and 'volunteering' them for the game.

As the second hand began, and Horza switched on his couch monitor to experience Kraiklyn's emotions, the white-haired woman came back down the aisle and resumed her place in front of Horza, at the front of the terrace, draping herself tiredly over the piece of furniture as though she was bored.

Horza did not know enough about Damage as a card game to be able to follow exactly what was going on with the cards, either by reading the various emotions being passed round the table, or by analysing each hand after it was finished – as the first hand was already being analysed by the hooting tripeds near him – when the cards as they had been dealt and played were flashed up on the arena's internal broad-cast circuits. But he tuned in to Kraiklyn's feelings just to see what they were like.

The captain of the *Clear Air Turbulence* was being hit from various directions. Some of the emotions were contradictory, which Horza guessed meant that there was no concerted effort being made on Kraiklyn; he was just taking most people's secondary armament. There was a considerable urge to like Wilgre – that attractive blue colour . . . and with those four little comical feet, he couldn't really be much of a threat. . . . A bit of a clown, really, for all his money . . . The woman sitting on Kraiklyn's right, on the other hand, stripped to the waist, with no breasts, and a sheath for a ceremonial sword slung across her naked back: she was one to watch. . . . But it was a laugh really. . . . *Nothing really matters; everything is just a joke; life is, the game is . . . one card's pretty much like another when you come to think about it. . . . For all it matters might as well throw the lot in the air. . . .* It was nearly his turn to play. . . . First that flat-chested bitch . . . boy, did he have a card he was going to hit *her* with. . . .

Horza switched off again, unsure whether he was hearing Kraiklyn's own thoughts about the woman, or ones somebody else was trying to get him to think about her.

He picked up Kraiklyn's thoughts later on in the hand, when the woman was out and sitting back and relaxing, her eyes closed. (Horza looked briefly at the white-haired woman on the couch down in front of him; she was watching the game apparently, but one leg was slung over the side of her lounger, swinging to and fro, as though her mind was somewhere else.) Kraiklyn was feeling good. First of all that slut next to him was out, and he was sure it was because of some of the cards he had played, but also there was a sort of inner exhilaration. . . . Here he was, playing with the best players in the galaxy . . . the *Players*. Him. Him . . . (a sudden inhibitory thought blocked out a name he was about to think) . . . and he really wasn't doing that badly at all. . . . He was keeping up. . . . In fact this hand was looking pretty damn good. . . . At last things were going right. . . . He was going to win something. . . . Too many things had . . . well, there was that . . . *Think about the cards!* (suddenly) *Think about here and now! Yes, the cards . . . Let's see . . . I can hit that fat blue oaf with* . . . Horza switched off again.

He was sweating. He hadn't fully realised the degree of feedback from the Player's mind that was involved. He had thought it was just the emotions beamed at them; he hadn't dreamed he would be so much *in* Kraiklyn's mind. Yet this was only a taste of what Kraiklyn himself was getting full blast, and the moties and Lives behind him. Real feedback, only just under control, only just stopping from becoming the emotional equivalent of a loudspeaker howl, building to destruction. Now the Changer realised the attraction of the game, and why people had been known to go mad when playing it.

Much as he disliked the experience, Horza felt new respect for the man he intended at least to remove and replace, and most likely to kill.

Kraiklyn had a sort of advantage in as much as the thoughts and emotions being beamed back at him were at least partly emanating from his own mind, whereas the Lives and the moties had to put up with extremely powerful blasts of what was entirely somebody else's way of feeling something. All the same, it had to take a considerable strength of character, or a vast amount of hard training, to be able to handle what Kraiklyn was obviously coping with. Horza switched back in again and thought, *How do the moties stand it?* And, *Watch out; maybe this is how they started*.

Kraiklyn lost the hand, two rounds of betting later. The half-blind albino, Neeporlax, was defeated, too, and the Suut raked in his winnings, his steel face glowing in the light reflected from the Aoish credits in front of him. Kraiklyn was slumped in his seat, feeling, Horza knew, like death. A pulse of a sort of resigned, almost grateful agony swept through Kraiklyn from behind as his first Life died, and Horza felt it, too. He and Kraiklyn both winced.

Horza switched off and looked at the time. Less than an hour had passed since he had bluffed his way past the guards at the outer doors of the arena. He had some food, on a low table by his couch, but he got up all the same and walked away from the table, up the terrace towards the nearest walkway, where food stalls and bars waited.

Security guards were checking passes. Horza saw them moving from person to person on the terrace. He kept his face to the front but flicked his eyes from side to side, watching the guards as they moved. One was almost directly in his path, bending to ask an old-looking female, who was lying on an airbed which blew perfumed fumes round her thin, exposed legs. She was sitting watching the game with a big smile on her face, and she took a while to notice the guard. Horza walked a little faster so that, when the guard straightened, he would be past her.

The old lady flashed her pass and turned quickly back to the game. The guard put out an arm in front of Horza.

'May I see your pass, sir?'

Horza stopped and looked into the face of the young, burly woman. He looked back down to the couch he had been on.

'I'm sorry, I think I left it down there. I'll be back in a second; can I show it to you then? I'm in a bit of a hurry.' He shifted his weight from one foot to the other and bent a little at the waist. 'I got wrapped up in the last hand there. Too much to drink before the game started; always the same; never learn. All right?' He put out his hands, looked a little sheepish, and made as if to clap the guard on her shoulders. He shifted his weight again. The guard looked down to where Horza had indicated he had left his pass.

'For now, sir. I'll look at it later. But you really shouldn't go leaving it lying about. Don't do it again.'

'Right! Right! Thank you!' Horza laughed and went off at a quick walk, onto the circular walkway and then to a toilet, just in case he was being watched. He washed his face and hands, listened to a drunk woman singing somewhere in the echoing room, then left by another exit and walked round to another terrace, where he got something else to eat and had a drink. He bribed his way into a different terrace again, this one even more expensive than the one he had been on originally, because it was next to the one which held Wilgre's concubines. A soft wall of shining black material had been erected at the rear and sides of their terrace to keep out the nearer eyes, but their body scent wafted strongly over the terrace Horza now found himself on. Genofixed before conception not only to be stunningly attractive to a wide variety of humanoid males, the females in the harem also had highly accentuated aphrodisiac pheromones. Before Horza knew what was happening he had an erection and had started to sweat again. Most of the men and women around him were in a state of obvious sexual arousal, and those not plugged into the game on some sort of exotic double-fix were engaged in sexual foreplay or actual intercourse. Horza made his immune glands start up again, and walked stiffly to the front of the terrace, where five couches had been vacated by two males and three females, who were rolling around on the ground in front, just behind the restraining barrier. Clothes lay scattered on the terrace floor. Horza sat on one of the five free couches. A female head, beaded with sweat, appeared from the tangle of heaving bodies long enough to look at Horza and breathe, 'Feel free; and if you would like to . . .' Then her eyes rolled upwards and she moaned. Her head disappeared again.

Horza shook his head, swore and made his way out of the terrace. His attempt to recover the money he had spent bribing his way in was met with a pitying laugh.

Horza ended up sitting on a stool in front of a combined bar and betting stall. He ordered a drug bowl and made a small bet on Kraiklyn to win the next hand, while his body gradually freed itself of the effects of the concubines' doctored sweat glands. His pulse lowered and his breathing shallowed; perspiration stopped rolling down his brow. He sipped his drug bowl and sniffed the fumes, while watching Kraiklyn lose first one and then another hand, though in the first one he pulled out early enough not to lose a Life. Nevertheless, he was down to one Life now. It was possible for a Damage player to gamble his own life if he had no other remaining behind him, but it was a rare thing, and in games where the very best met hopefuls, as in this one, the Ishlorsinami tended to forbid it.

201

The captain of the *Clear Air Turbulence* was taking no chances. He dropped out of every game before he could lose a Life, obviously waiting for a hand that would be almost unbeatable before gambling for what might be the last time in the game. Horza ate. Horza drank. Horza sniffed. Sometimes he tried to look over at the terrace he had been on at first, where the bored-looking woman was, but he couldn't see for the lights. Now and again he looked up at the fighting animals on the trapezes. They were tired now, and injured. The elaborate choreography of their earlier movements was gone, and they were reduced to hanging grimly onto their trapeze with one limb and striking out at each other with the other clawed arm whenever they happened to come close enough. Drops of white blood fell like sparse snow and settled on an invisible force field twenty metres beneath them.

Gradually the Lives died. The game went on. Time, according to who you were, dragged or flashed by. The price of drinks and drugs and food went up slowly as the destruction time crept closer. Through the still transparent dome of the old arena the lights of departing shuttles blazed now and again. A fight broke out between two punters at the bar. Horza got up and moved away before the security guards came to break it up.

Horza counted his money. He had two Aoish credit Tenths left, plus some money credited to the negotiable cards, which were becoming harder and harder to use as the accepting computers in the Orbital's financial network were closed down.

He leant on a restraining bar on a circular walkway, watching the game progress on the table below. Wilgre was leading; the Suut was just behind. They had both lost the same number of Lives, but the blue giant had more money. Two of the hopefuls had left the game, one after trying unsuccessfully to persuade the officiating Ishlorsinami that he could afford to gamble with his own life. Kraiklyn was still in there; but, from the close-up of his face which Horza caught on a monitor screen in a drug bar he passed, the Man was finding the going hard.

Horza toyed with one of the Aoish credit Tenths, wishing the game would end, or at least that Kraiklyn would get put out. The coin stuck to his hand, and he looked down into it. It was like looking into a tiny, infinite tube, lit from the very bottom. By bringing it up to your eye, with the other closed, you could experience vertigo.

The Aoish were a banker species, and the credits were their greatest invention. They were just about the only universally acceptable

202

medium of exchange in existence, and each one entitled the holder to convert a coin into either a given weight of any stable element, an area on a free Orbital, or a computer of a given speed and capacity. The Aoish guaranteed the conversion and never defaulted, and although the rate of exchange could sometimes vary to a greater extent than was officially allowed for – as it had during the Idiran–Culture war – on the whole the real and theoretical value of the currency remained predictable enough for it to be a safe, secure hedge against uncertain times, rather than a speculator's dream. Rumour – as ever, contrary enough to be suspiciously believable – had it that the group in the galaxy which possessed the greatest hoard of the coins was the Culture; the most militantly unmoneyed society on the civilised scene. Horza didn't really believe that rumour either, though; in fact he thought that it was just the sort of rumour the Culture would spread about itself.

He pushed the coins away into a pocket inside his blouse as he saw Kraiklyn reaching to the centre of the game table and toss some coins into the large pile already there. Watching carefully now, the Changer made his way round to the nearest money-changer's bar, got eight Hundredths for his single Tenth (an exorbitant rate of commission, even by Vavatch standards) and used some of the change to bribe his way into a terrace with some unoccupied couches. There he plugged into Kraiklyn's thoughts.

Who are you? The question leapt out at him, into him.

The sensation was one of vertigo, a stunning dizziness, a vastly magnified equivalent of the disorientation which sometimes affects the eyes when they fasten on a simple and regular pattern, and the brain mistakes its distance from that pattern, the false focus seeming to pull at the eyes, muscles against nerves, reality against assumptions. His head did not swim; it seemed to sink, foundering, struggling.

Who are you? (Who am I?) Who are you?

Slam, slam, slam: the sound of the barrage falling, the sound of doors closing; attack and incarceration, explosion and collapse together.

Just a little accident. A slight mistake. One of those things. A game of Damage, and a high-tech impressionist . . . unfortunate combination. *Two harmless chemicals which, when mixed—* . . . Feedback, a howl like pain, and something breaking . . .

A mind between mirrors. He was drowning in his own reflection (something breaking), falling through. One fading part of him – the part which didn't sleep? Yes? No? – screamed from down the deep, dark pit, as it fell: *Changer . . . Changer . . . Change— . . . (eee) . . .*

. . . The sound faded, whisper-quieted, became the wind-moan of stale air through dead trees on a barren midnight solstice, the soul's midwinter in some calm, hard place.

He knew—

(*Start again. . . .*)

Somebody knew that somewhere a man sat in a seat, in a big hall in a city in . . . on a big place, a big threatened place; and the man was playing . . . playing a game (a game which killed). The man still there, living and breathing. . . . But his eyes did not see, his ears did not hear. He had one sense now: this one, inside here, fastened . . . inside here.

Whisper: *Who am I?*

There'd been a little accident (*life a succession of same; evolution dependent on garbling; all progress a function of getting things wrong*). . . .

He (*and forget who this 'he' is, just accept the nameless term while this equation works itself out*) . . . he is the man in the chair in the hall on the big place, fallen somewhere inside himself, somewhere inside . . . another one. A double, a copy, somebody pretending to be him.

. . . But something wrong with this theory . . .

(*Start again. . . .*)

Marshal forces.

Need clues, reference points, something to hold onto.

Memory of a cell dividing, seen in time lapse, the very start of independent life, though still dependent. *Hold that image.*

Words (names); need words.

Not yet, but . . . something about turning inside out; a place . . .

What am I looking for?'

Mind.

Whose?

(Silence)

Whose?

(Silence)

Whose? . . .

(Silence)

(*. . . Start again. . . .*)

Listen. This is shock. You were hit, hard. This is just some form of shock, and you'll recover.

You are the man playing the game (as are we all) . . . Still something wrong, though, something both missing and added. Think of those vital errors; think of that dividing cell, same and not-same, the place that's turned inside out, the cell cluster turning itself inside out, looking like a split brain (unsleeping, moving). Listen for somebody trying to talk to you. . . .

(Silence)

(This from that very pit of night, naked in the wasteland, the ice-wind moaning his only covering, alone in the freezing darkness under a sky of chill obsidian:)

Whoever tried to talk to me? When did I ever listen? When was I ever other than just myself, caring only for myself?

The individual is the fruit of mistake; therefore only the process has validity. . . . So who's to speak for him?

The wind howls, empty of meaning, a soak for warmth, a cess for hope, distributing his body's exhausted heat to the black skies, dissolving the salty flame of his life, chilling to the core, sapping and slowing. He feels himself falling again, and knows that this time it is a deeper plunge, to where the silence and the cold are absolute, and no voice cries out, not even this one.

(Howled like the wind:) *Whoever cared enough to talk to me?*

(Silence)

Whoever ever cared—

(Silence)

Who—?

(Whisper:) *Listen: 'The Jinmoti of—'*

. . . *Bozlen Two.*

Two. Somebody had spoken once. *He* was the Changer, he was the error, the imperfect copy.

He was playing a different game from the other one (but he still intended to take a life). He was watching, feeling what the other was feeling, but feeling more.

Horza. Kraiklyn.

Now he knew. The game was . . . Damage. The place was . . . a world where a ribbon of the original idea was turned inside out . . . an Orbital: Vavatch. The Mind in Schar's World. Xoralundra. Balveda. *The* (and finding his hate, he hammered it into the wall of the pit, like a peg for a rope) *Culture*!

A breach in the cell wall; waters breaking; light freeing; illumination . . . leading to

rebirth.

Weight and cold and bright, bright light . . .

. . . Shit. Bastards. Lost it all, thanks to a Pit of Self-Doubt treble . . .
A wave of despondent fury swept over him, and something died.

Horza tore the flimsy headset away. He lay quivering on the couch, his
eyes gummed and smarting, staring up at the auditorium lights and
the two white fighting animals hanging half-dead from the trapezes
overhead. He forced his eyes closed, then pulled them open again,
away from the darkness.

Pit of Self-Doubt. Kraiklyn had been hit by cards which made the
target player question their own identity. From the tenor of
Kraiklyn's thoughts before he'd pulled the headset off, Horza
thought Kraiklyn hadn't been too terrified by the effect, just disorientated. He'd been sufficiently distracted by the attack to lose the hand,
and that was all his opponents had been aiming for. Kraiklyn was out
of the game.

The effect on *him*, trying to be Kraiklyn but knowing he wasn't,
had been more severe. That was all it was. Any Changer would have
had the same problem; he was certain. . . .

The trembling began to fade. He sat up and swung his feet off the
couch. He had to leave. Kraiklyn would be going, so he had to.

Pull yourself together, man.

He looked down to the playing table. The breastless woman had
won. Kraiklyn glared at her as she raked in her winnings and his
straps were unfastened. On the way out of the arena, Kraiklyn passed
the limp, still warm body of his last Life as it was released from its
seat.

He kicked the corpse; the crowd booed.

Horza stood up, turned and bumped into a hard, unyielding body.

'May I see that pass now, sir?' said the guard he'd lied to earlier.

He smiled nervously, aware that he was still trembling a little; his
eyes were red, and his face was covered in sweat. The guard gazed
steadily at him, her face expressionless. Some of the people on the
terrace were watching them.

'I'm . . . sorry. . . .' the Changer said slowly, patting his pockets
with shaking hands. The guard put out her hand and took his left
elbow.

'Perhaps you'd better—'

'Look,' Horza said, bending closer to her. 'I . . . I haven't got one.
Would a bribe do?' He started to reach inside his blouse for the
credits. The guard kicked up with her knee and twisted Horza's left
arm behind his back. It was all done in the most expert fashion, and

Horza had to jump to ride the kick tolerably. He let his left shoulder disconnect and started to crumple, but not before his free hand had lightly scratched the guard's face (and that, he realised as he fell, had been an instinctive reaction, nothing reasoned; for some reason he found this amusing).

The guard caught Horza's other arm and pinned both his hands behind his back, using her lock-glove to secure them there. With her other hand she wiped blood from her cheek. Horza knelt on the terrace surface, moaning the way most people would have with an arm broken or dislocated.

'It's all right, everybody; just a little problem over a pass. Please continue with your enjoyment,' the guard said. Then she pulled her arm up; the locked glove hauled Horza up, too. He yelped with pretended pain, and then, head down, was pushed up the steps to the walkway. 'Seven three, seven three; male code green incoming walk seven spinwards,' the guard told her lapel mike.

Horza felt her start to weaken as soon as they got to the walkway. He couldn't see any other guards yet. The pace of the woman behind him faltered and slowed. He heard her gasp, and a couple of drunks leaning on an auto-bar looked at them quizzically; once turned on his bar stool to watch.

'Seven . . . thr—' the guard began. Then her legs buckled. Horza was dragged down with her, the locked glove staying tight while the muscles in the woman's body relaxed. He connected his shoulder again, twisted and heaved; the field filaments in the glove gave way, leaving him with livid bruises already starting to form on his wrists. The guard lay on her back on the walkway floor, her eyes closed, breathing lightly. Horza had scraped her with a non-lethal poison nail, he thought; anyway he had no time to wait and see. They were sure to come looking for the guard soon, and he couldn't afford to let Kraiklyn get too far ahead of him. Whether he was heading back to the ship, as Horza expected he would, or staying to observe more of the game, Horza wanted to stay close.

His hood had fallen back during the fall. He pulled it forward, then hoisted the woman up, dragged her to the bar where the two drunks sat and heaved her onto a bar stool, putting his arms crossed on the bar in front and letting her head rest on them.

The drunk who had watched what had happened grinned at the Changer. Horza tried to grin back. 'Look after her, now,' he said. He noticed a cloak at the foot of the other drunk's bar stool and lifted it up, smiling at its owner, who was too busy ordering another drink to notice. Horza put the cloak round the woman guard's shoulders, hiding her uniform. 'In case she gets cold,' he told the first drunk, who nodded.

Horza walked off quietly. The other drunk, who hadn't noticed the woman until then, got his drink from the flap in the counter in front of him, turned round to talk to his friend, noticed the woman draped across the bar, nudged her and said, 'Hey, you like the cloak, uh? How about I get you a drink?'

Before he left the auditorium, Horza looked up. The fighting animals would fight no more. Beneath the shining hoop that was Vavatch's far – and, at the moment, day – side, one beast lay, in a broad, shallow pool of milky blood, high in the air, its huge four-limbed frame an X poised over the proceedings beneath, the dark fur and heavy head gashed, white flecked. The other creature hung, swaying gently, from its trapeze; it dripped white blood and twisted slowly, hanging by one closed and locked set of talons, as dead as its fallen adversary.

Horza racked his brains, but could not recall the names of these strange beasts. He shook his head and hurried away.

He found the Players' area. An Ishlorsinami stood by some double doors in a corridor deep underneath the arena surface. A small crowd of people and machines stood or sat around. Some were asking the silent Ishlorsinami questions; most were talking amongst themselves. Horza took a deep breath, then, waving one of his now useless negotiable account cards, elbowed his way through the crowd, saying, 'Security; come on, out of the way there. Security!' People protested but moved. Horza planted himself in front of the tall Ishlorsinami. Steely eyes looked down at him from a thin, hard face. 'You,' Horza said, snapping his fingers. 'Where did that Player go? The one in the light one-piece suit, brown hair.' The tall humanoid hesitated. 'Come on, man,' Horza said. 'I've been chasing that card-sharp round half the galaxy. I don't want to lose him now!'

The Ishlorsinami jerked his head in the direction of the corridor leading to the main arena entrance. 'He just left.' The humanoid's voice sounded like two pieces of broken glass being rubbed together. Horza winced, but nodded quickly and, pushing his way back through the crowd, ran up the corridor.

In the vestibule of the arena complex there was an even bigger crowd. Guards, wheeled security drones, private bodyguards, car drivers, shuttle pilots, city police; people with desperate looks waving negotiable cards; others listing those who were buying space on shuttle buses and hovers running out to the port area; people just hanging around waiting to see what was going to happen or hoping that an ordered taxi was about to show up; people just wandering around with lost expressions on their faces, their clothes torn and dishevelled; others with smiles, all confidence, clutching bulky bags and pouches to themselves and frequently accompanied by a hired guard of their own: they all milled around in the vast expanse of noisy, bustling space which led from the auditorium proper to the plaza outside, in the open air, under the stars and the bright line of the Orbital's far side.

Pulling his hood further over his face, Horza pushed through a barricade of guards. They still seemed concerned with keeping people out, even at this late stage in the game and in the countdown to destruction, and he was not hindered. He looked over the swirling mass of heads, capes, helmets, casings and ornamentation, wondering how he was going to catch Kraiklyn in this lot, or even see him. A wedge of uniformed quadrupeds pushed past him, some tall dignitary carried on a litter in their midst. As Horza was still staggering, a soft pneumatic tyre rolled over his foot as a mobile bar touted its wares. 'Would you like a drug-bowl cocktail, sir?' said the machine.

'Fuck off,' Horza told it, and he turned to head after the wedge of four-legged creatures making for the doors.

'Certainly, sir; dry, medium or—?'

Horza elbowed his way through the crowd after the quadrupeds. He caught up with them, and in their wake had an easy passage to the doors.

Outside, it was surprisingly cold. Horza saw his breath in front of him as he looked quickly around, trying to spot Kraiklyn. The crowd outside the arena was hardly less thick and rowdy than that inside. People hawked wares, sold tickets, staggered about, paced to and fro, tried to beg money from strangers, picked pockets, scanned the skies or peered down the broad spaces between buildings. A constant bright stream of machines appeared, roaring out of the sky or sweeping up the boulevards, stopped, and after taking people on, raced off again.

Horza just couldn't see properly. He noticed a huge hire-guard: a three-metre-tall giant in a bulky suit, holding a large gun and looking about with a vacant expression on a broad, pale face. Wisps of bright red hair poked from underneath his helmet.

'You for hire?' Horza asked, doing a sort of breast stroke to get to the giant through a knot of people watching some fighting insects. The broad face nodded gravely, and the huge man came to attention.

'That I am,' the great voice rumbled.

'Here's a Hundredth,' Horza said quickly, shoving a coin into the man's glove, where it looked quite lost. 'Let me up on your shoulders. I'm looking for somebody.'

'All right,' the man said, after a second's thought. He bent down slowly on one knee, the rifle in his hand put out to steady him, butt first on the ground. Horza slung his legs over the giant's shoulders. Without being asked, the man straightened and stood again, and Horza was hoisted high above the heads of the people in the crowd. He pulled the hood of the blouse over his face again, and scanned the mass of people for a figure in a light one-piece suit, although he knew that Kraiklyn might have changed by now, or even have left. A tight, nervous feeling of desperation was building in Horza's belly. He tried to tell himself that it didn't matter that much if he lost Kraiklyn now, that he could still make his way alone to the port area and so to the GSV that the *Clear Air Turbulence* was on; but his guts refused to be calmed. It was as though the atmosphere of the game, the terminal excitement of the Orbital, the city, the arena in their last hours, had altered his own body chemistry. He could have concentrated on it and *made* himself relax, but he couldn't afford to do that now. He had to look for Kraiklyn.

He scanned the gaudy collection of individuals waiting in a cordoned area for shuttles, then recalled Kraiklyn's thought about having wasted a lot of money. He looked away and surveyed the rest of the crowd.

He saw him. The captain of the *Clear Air Turbulence* was standing, his suit partly covered by a grey cloak, his arms folded and his feet apart, in a queue of people waiting to get buses and taxis, thirty metres away. Horza dipped forward and leant over until he was looking at the hire-guard's upside-down face. 'Thanks. You can put me down now.'

'I have no change,' the man rumbled as he stooped; the vibration went up through Horza's body.

'That's OK. Keep it.' Horza jumped off the guard's shoulders. The giant shrugged as Horza ran, swerving and ducking to get past people, towards where he had seen Kraiklyn.

He had his terminal fastened to his left cuff; the time was minus two and a half hours. Horza squeezed and shoved and excused and apologised his way through the crowd, and on his way saw many people squinting at watches, terminals and screens, heard many little synthesised voices squawk the hour, and nervous humans repeat it.

There was the queue. It looked surprisingly orderly, Horza thought, then he noticed that it was being supervised by the same security guards who had been inside the areana. Kraiklyn was near the front of the queue now, and a bus had almost finished filling up. Road cars and hovers waited behind it. Kraiklyn pointed at one of them as a security guard with a notescreen talked to him.

Horza looked at the row of waiting people and guessed there must be several hundreds of them in it. If he were to join it he would lose Kraiklyn. He looked around quickly, wondering what other way there might be of following.

Somebody crashed into him from behind, and Horza turned round to the noise of shouting and voices and a press of brightly dressed people. A masked woman in a tight silver dress was shouting and screaming at a small, puzzled-looking man with long hair, clad only in intricate loops of dark green string. The woman shouted incoherently at the small man and struck out at him with her open hands; he backed off, shaking his head. People watched. Horza checked that he hadn't had anything stolen when he was bumped into, then looked round again for some transport, or a taxi tout.

An aircraft flew overhead noisily and dropped leaflets written in a language Horza didn't understand.

'. . . Sarble,' a transparent-skinned man said to a companion as they both squeezed out of the nearby crowd and went past Horza. The man was trying to look at a small terminal screen as he walked. Horza caught a glimpse of something which puzzled him. He turned his own terminal onto the appropriate channel.

He was watching what looked like the same incident he had seen for real in the auditorium a few hours earlier: the disturbance on the terrace above his own when he'd heard that Sarble the Eye had been caught by the security guards. Horza frowned and brought the screen on his cuff closer.

It *was* that same place, it *was* that incident, seen from almost exactly the same angle and apparent distance he'd watched it from. He grimaced at the screen, trying to imagine where the picture he was watching now could have been taken from. The scene ended and was replaced by candid shots of various eccentric-looking beings enjoying themselves in the auditorium, as the Damage game went on somewhere in the background.

. . . *If I'd stood up*, Horza thought, *and moved over just a—*
It was the woman.

The woman with the white hair he'd seen early on, standing in the highest part of the arena, fiddling with a tiara: she'd been on that same terrace, been standing by his lounger when the incident on the terrace above took place. She was Sarble the Eye. Probably the tiara was the camera and the person on the higher terrace was a decoy, a plant.

Horza snapped off the screen. He smiled, then shook his head as though to dislodge the small, useless revelation from the centre of his attention. He had to find some transport.

He started walking quickly through the crowd, threading his way through people in groups and lines and queues, looking for a free vehicle, an open door, a tout's eyes. He caught a glimpse of the queue Kraiklyn was in. The *CAT*'s commander was at the open door of a red road car, apparently arguing with its driver and two other people in the queue.

Horza felt sick. He started to sweat; he wanted to kick out, to throw all the people crowding around him out of his path, away from him. He doubled back. He would have to risk trying to bribe his way into Kraiklyn's queue at the front. He was five metres away from the queue when Kraiklyn and the two other people stopped arguing and got into the taxi, which drove off. As he turned his head to watch it go past, his stomach sinking, his fists clenching, Horza saw the white-haired woman again. She wore a hooded blue cloak, but the hood fell back as she squeezed out of the crowd to the edge of the road, where a tall man put his arm round her shoulders and waved into the plaza. She pulled the hood up again.

Horza put his hand into his pocket and onto the gun, then went forward towards the couple – just as a sleek, matt-black hover hissed out of the darkness and stopped beside them. Horza stepped forward quickly as the hover's side door winged open and the woman who was Sarble the Eye stooped to enter.

Horza reached out and tapped the woman on the shoulder. She whirled round to face him. The tall man started towards him, and Horza shoved his hand forward and up in his pocket, so that the gun pressed out. The man stopped, looking down, uncertain; the woman froze, one foot on the door's sill.

'I think you're going my way,' Horza said quickly. 'I know who you are.' He nodded at the woman. 'I know about that thing you had on your head. All I want is a lift to the port. That's all. No fuss.' He gestured with his head in the direction of the security guards at the head of the main queue.

The woman looked at the tall man, then at Horza. She stepped back slowly. 'OK. After you.'

'No, you first.' Horza motioned with the hand in his pocket. The woman smiled, shrugged and got in, followed by the tall man and Horza.

'What's *he*—?' began the driver, a fierce-looking bald woman.

'A guest,' Sarble told her. 'Just drive.'

The hover rose. 'Straight ahead,' Horza said. 'Fast as you like. I'm looking for a red-coloured wheeled car.' He took the gun out of his pocket and pivoted round so that he faced Sarble the Eye and the tall man. The hover accelerated.

'I *told* you they put that 'cast out too soon,' the tall man hissed in a hoarse high voice. Sarble shrugged. Horza smiled, glancing occasionally out of the window at the traffic around the cab, but watching the other two people from the corner of his eye.

'Just bad luck,' Sarble said. 'I kept bumping into this guy inside the place, too.'

'You really are Sarble, then?' Horza said to the woman. She didn't look round and didn't reply.

'Look,' the man said, turning to Horza, 'we'll take you to the port, if that's where this red car's going, but just don't try anything. We'll fight if we have to. I'm not afraid to die.' The tall man sounded frightened and angry at the same time; his yellow-white face looked like a child's, about to cry.

'You've convinced me.' Horza grinned. 'Now, why not watch out for the red car? Three wheels, four doors, driver, three people in the back. Can't miss it.'

The tall man bit his lip. Horza motioned him to look forward, with a small movement of the gun.

'That it?' the bald-headed driver said. Horza saw the car she meant. It looked right.

'Yes. Follow it; not too close.' The hover dropped back a little.

They entered the port area. Cranes and gantries were lit in the distance; parked road vehicles, hovers and even light shuttles lay scattered on either side of the road. The car was just ahead now, following a couple of struggling hover buses up a shallow ramp. Their own hover's engine laboured as they climbed.

The red car branched off the main route and followed a long curve of roadway, water glittering darkly on either side.

'*Are* you really Sarble?' Horza asked the white-haired woman, who still didn't turn to him. 'Was that you earlier, outside the hall? Or not? Is Sarble really lots of people?'

The people in the car said nothing. Horza just smiled, watching them carefully, but nodding and smiling to himself. There was silence in the hover, only the wind roaring.

The car left the roadway and angled down a fenced boulevard past huge gantries and the lit masses of towering machinery, then sped along a road lined on both sides with dark warehouses. It started to slow by the side of a small dock.

'Pull back,' Horza said. The bald-headed woman slowed the hover as the red car cruised by the dockside, under the square cages of crane legs.

The red car drew up by a brightly lit building. A pattern of lights revolving round the top of the construction spelt out 'SUB-BASE ACCESS 54' in several languages.

'Fine. Stop,' Horza said. The hover stopped, sinking on its skirts. 'Thanks.' Horza got out, still facing the man and the white-haired woman.

'You're just lucky you didn't try anything,' the man said angrily, nodding sharply, his eyes glistening.

'I know,' Horza said. 'Bye now,' he winked at the white-haired woman. She turned and made what he suspected was an obscene gesture with one finger. The hover rose, blasted forward, then skidded round and roared off the way it had come. Horza looked back at the sub-plate shaft entrance, where the three people who had got out of the car stood silhouetted against the light inside. One of them might have looked back down the dock towards Horza; he wasn't sure they did, but he shrank back into the shadows of the crane above him.

Two of the people at the access tube went into the building and disappeared. The third person, who might have been Kraiklyn, walked off towards the side of the dock.

Horza pocketed the gun again and hurried on, underneath another crane.

A roaring noise like the one that Sarble's hover had made when it drew away from him – but much louder and deeper – came from inside the dock.

Lights and spray filled the sea-end of the dock as a huge air-cushion vehicle, similar in principle to but vastly bigger than the hover Horza had commandeered, swept in from the expanse of black ocean. Lit by starlight, by the glow of the Orbital's daylight side arcing overhead and by the craft's own lights, the billows of spray kicked up into the air with a milky luminescence. The big machine lumbered between the walls of the dock, its engines shrieking. Beyond it, out to sea, Horza could see another couple of clouds, also lit from inside by flashing lights. Fireworks burst from the leading craft as it came slowly up the dock. Horza could make out an expanse of windows, and what appeared to be people dancing inside. He looked back down the dockside; the man he was following was mounting the steps to a footbridge which crossed high over the dock. Horza ran quietly, ducking behind the legs of cranes and leaping over lengths of thick hawsers. The lights of the hover flashed on the dark superstructure of the cranes; the scream of the jets and impellers echoed between concrete walls.

As though pointing out the comparative crudity of the scene, a small craft – dark, and silent but for the tearing noise its passage made through the atmosphere – rushed overhead, zooming and disappearing into the night sky, specking once against the loop of the Orbital's daytime surface. Horza gave it a glance, then watched the figure on the small bridge, lit by the flashing lights of the hover still making its lumbering way up the dock underneath. The second craft was just swinging into position outside the dock to follow it.

Horza came to the steps leading to the walkway of the narrow suspension bridge. The man, who walked like Kraiklyn and wore a grey cloak, was about halfway across. Horza couldn't see much of what the terrain was like on the other side of the dock, but guessed he stood a good chance of losing his quarry if he let him get to the other side before he started after him. Probably the man – Kraiklyn, if it was him – had worked this out; Horza guessed he knew he was being followed. He set off across the bridge. It swayed slightly underneath him. The noise and lights of the giant hovercraft were almost underneath; the air filled with the smell of brine, kicked up from the shallow water in the dock. The man didn't look round at Horza, though he must have felt Horza's footsteps swinging the bridge with his own.

The figure left the bridge at the far end. Horza lost sight of him and started running, the gun out in front of him, the air-cushion vehicle beneath blasting gusts of spray-soaked air about him, soaking him. Loud music blared from the craft, audible even through the scream of the engines. Horza skidded along the bridge at its end and ran quickly down the spiral steps to the dockside.

Something sailed out of the darkness under the spiral of steps and crashed into his face. Immediately afterwards something slammed into his back and the rear of his skull. He lay on something hard, groggily wondering what had happened, while lights swept over him, the air in his ears roared and roared, and music played somewhere. A bright light shone straight into his eyes, and the hood over his face was thrown back.

He heard a gasp: the gasp of a man tearing a hood away from a face only to see his own face staring back at him. (*Who are you?*) If that was what it was, then that man was vulnerable now, shocked for just a few seconds (*Who am I?*). . . . He had enough strength to kick up hard with one leg, forcing his arms up at the same time and grabbing some material, his shin connecting with a groin. The man started to go over Horza's shoulders, heading for the dock; then Horza felt his own shoulders grasped, and as the man he held thumped to the ground to one side and behind him, he was pulled over—

Over the side of the dock; the man had landed right on the edge and had gone over, taking Horza with him. They were falling.

He was aware of lights, than shadow, the grip he had on the man's cloak or suit and one hand still on his shoulder. Falling: how deep was the dock? The noise of wind. Listen for the sound of—

It was a double impact. He hit water, then something harder, in a crumpling collision of fluid and body. It was cold, and his neck ached. He was thrashing about, unsure which way was up, and groggy from the blows to his head; then something pulled at him. He punched out, hit something soft, then pulled upright and found himself standing in a little over a metre of water, staggering forward. It was bedlam – light and sound and spray everywhere, and somebody hanging onto him.

Horza flailed out again. Spray cleared momentarily, and he saw the wall of the dock a couple of metres to his right and, directly in front of him, the rear of the giant hovercraft, receding slowly five or six metres ahead. A powerful gust of oily, fiery air knocked him over, splashing into the water again. The spray closed over him. The hand let go, and he fell back through the water once more, going under.

Horza struggled upright in time to see his adversary heading off through the spray, following the slowly moving hovercraft up the dock. He tried to run, but the water was too deep; he had to force his legs forward in a slow-motion, nightmarish version of a run, angling his torso so that his weight carried him forward. With exaggerated twistings of his body from side to side he strode after the man in the grey cloak, using his hands like paddles in an attempt to gain speed. His head was reeling; his back, face and neck all hurt terribly, and his vision was blurred, but at least he was still chasing. The man in front seemed more anxious to get away than to stay and fight.

The blattering exhaust of the still moving hover blew another hole in the spray towards the two men, revealing the slab of stern rising above the bulbous wall of the machine's skirt, bowing out from fully three metres above the surface of the water in the dock. First the man in front of him, and then Horza, was blown back by the pulse of hot, choking fumes. The water was getting shallower. Horza found that he could bring his legs out of the water far enough to wade faster. The noise and spray swept over them again, and for a moment Horza lost sight of his quarry; then the view ahead was clear, and he could see the big air-cushion vehicle on a dry area of concrete. The walls of the dock extended high on either side, but the water and the clouds of spray were almost gone. The man in front staggered to the brief ramp leading from the now only ankle-deep water onto the concrete, staggered and almost fell, then started running weakly after the hovercraft, now powering faster along the level concrete down the canyon of the dock.

Horza finally splashed out of the water and ran after the man, following the wetly flapping grey cloak.

The man stumbled, fell and rolled. As he started to rise Horza slammed into him, bowling them both over. He lashed out at the man's face, shadowed in the light coming from behind him, but missed. The man kicked out at Horza, then tried to get away again. Horza threw himself at the man's legs, bringing him down once more, the wet cloak flopping over his head. Horza scrambled over on all fours and rolled him over face up. It *was* Kraiklyn. He drew his hand back for a punch. The pale, shaved face underneath him was twisted in terror, put in shadow by some lights coming from behind Horza, where another great roaring noise was. . . . Kraiklyn screamed, looking not at the man wearing his own real face, but behind him, above him. Horza whirled round.

A black mass blowing spray rushed towards him; lights blazed high above. A siren sounded, then the crushing black bulk was over him, hitting him, knocking him flat, pounding at his eardrums with noise and pressure, pressing, pressing, pressing. . . . Horza heard a gurgling sound; he was being rammed into Kraiklyn's chest; they were both being rubbed into the concrete as though by an immense thumb.

Another hovercraft; the second one in the line he'd seen.

Abruptly, with a single sweeping stroke of pain bruising him from feet to head, as if a giant was trying to sweep him up off the floor with a huge hard brush, the weight was lifted off. In its place was utter darkness, noise fit to burst skulls, and violent, turbulent, crushing air pressure.

They were under the skirts of the big vehicle. It was right above them, moving slowly forward or maybe – it was too dark to see anything – stationary over the concrete apron, perhaps about to settle on the concrete, crushing them.

As though it was just another part of the maelstrom of battering pain, a blow thudded into Horza's ear, knocking him sideways in the darkness. He rolled on the rough concrete, pivoting on one elbow as soon as he could and bracing one leg while he struck out with the other in the direction the punch had come from; he felt his foot hit something yielding.

He got to his feet, ducking as he thought of whirling impeller blades just overhead. The eddies and vortices of hot oil-filled air rocked him like a small boat bobbing in a chopping sea. He felt like a puppet controlled by a drunk. He staggered forward, his arms out, and hit Kraiklyn. They started to fall again, and Horza let go, punching with all his might at the place he guessed the man's head was. His fist crashed into bone, but he didn't know where. He skipped back, in case there was a retaliatory kick or punch on its way. His ears were popping; his head felt tight. He could feel his eyes vibrating in their sockets; he thought he was deaf but he could feel a thudding in his chest and throat, making him breathless, making him choke and gasp. He could make out just a hint of a border of light all around them, as though they were under the middle of the hovercraft. He saw something, just an area of darkness, on that border, and lunged at it, swinging his foot from low down. Again he connected, and the dark part of the border disappeared.

He was blown off his feet by a crushing down-draught of air and tumbled bodily along the concrete, thumping into Kraiklyn where he lay on the ground after Horza's last kick. Another punch hit Horza on the head, but it was weak and hardly hurt. Horza felt for and found Kraiklyn's head. He lifted it and banged it off the concrete, then did it again. Kraiklyn struggled, but his hands beat uselessly off Horza's shoulders and chest. The area of lightness beyond the dim shape on the ground was enlarging, coming closer. Horza banged Kraiklyn's head against the concrete one more time, then threw himself flat. The rear edge of the skirt scrubbed over him; his ribs ached and his skull felt as though somebody was standing on it. Then it was over, and they were in the open air.

The big craft thundered on, trailing remnants of spray. There was another one fifty metres down the dock and heading towards him.

Kraiklyn was lying still, a couple of metres away.

Horza got up onto all fours and crawled over to the other man. He looked down into his eyes, which moved a little.

'I'm Horza! *Horza!*' he screamed, but couldn't even hear anything himself.

He shook his head, and with a grimace of frustration on the face that was not really his own and which was the last thing the real Kraiklyn ever saw, he gripped the head of the man lying on the concrete and twisted it sharply, breaking the neck, just as he had broken Zallin's.

He managed to drag the body to the side of the dock just in time to get out of the way of the third and last hovercraft. Its towering skirt bulged past two metres away from where he half lay, half sat, panting and sweating, his back against the cold wet concrete of the dock, his mouth open and his heart thudding.

He undressed Kraiklyn, took off the cloak and the light-coloured one-piece day suit he wore, then climbed out of his own torn blouse and bloody pantaloons and put on what Kraiklyn had been wearing. He took the ring Kraiklyn wore on the small finger of his right hand. He picked at his own hands, at the skin where palm became wrist. It came away cleanly, a layer of skin sloughing off his right hand from wrist to fingertips. He wiped Kraiklyn's limp, pale right palm on a damp bit of clothing, then put the skin over it, pressing it down hard. He lifted the skin off carefully and positioned it back on his own hand. Then he repeated the operation using his left hand.

It was cold and it seemed to take a very long time and a lot of effort. Eventually, while the three big air-cushion vehicles were stopping and letting passengers off half a kilometre down the dock, Horza finally staggered to a ladder of metal rungs set into the concrete wall of the dock, and with shaking hands and quivering feet hauled himself to the top.

He lay for a while, then got up, climbed the spiral stairs to the small footbridge, staggered across it and down the other side, and entered the circular access building. Brightly dressed and excited people, just off the big hovers and still in a party mood, quietened when they saw him wait near the elevator doors for the capsule which would take them down to the spaceport area half a kilometre under their feet. Horza couldn't hear very much, but he could see their anxious looks, sense the awkwardness he was causing with his battered, bloody face and his ripped, soaking clothes.

At last the elevator appeared. The party goers piled in, and Horza, supporting himself on the wall, stumbled in too. Somebody held his arm, helping him, and he nodded thanks. They said something which he heard as a distant rumble; he tried to smile and nod again. The elevator dropped.

219

The underside greeted them with an expanse of what looked like stars. Gradually, Horza realised it was the light-speckled top of a spacecraft larger than anything he'd ever seen or even heard about before; it had to be the demilitarised Culture ship, *The Ends of Invention*. He didn't care what it was called, as long as he could get aboard and find the *CAT*.

The elevator had come to a halt in a transparent tube above a spherical reception area hanging in hard vacuum a hundred metres under the base of the Orbital. From the sphere, walkways and tube tunnels spread out in all directions, heading for the access gantries and open and closed docks of the port area itself. The doors to the closed docks, where ships could be worked on in pressurised conditions, were all open. The open docks themselves, where ships simply moored and airlocks were required, were empty. Replacing them all, directly underneath the spherical reception area, just as it was directly underneath almost the entire port area, was the ex-Culture General Systems Vehicle *The Ends of Invention*. Its broad, flat top stretched for kilometre after kilometre in all directions, almost totally blocking out the view of space and stars beyond. Instead its top surface glittered with its own lights where various connections had been made with the access tubes and tunnels of the port.

He felt dizzy again, registering the sheer scale of the vast craft. He hadn't seen a GSV before, far less been inside one. He knew of them and what they were for, but only now did he appreciate what an achievement they represented. This one was theoretically no longer part of the Culture; he knew it was demilitarised, stripped bare of most equipment, and without the Mind or Minds which would normally run it; but just the structure alone was enough to impress.

General Systems Vehicles were like encapsulated worlds. They were more than just very big spaceships; they were habitats, universities, factories, museums, dockyards, libraries, even mobile exhibition centres. They represented the Culture – they were the Culture. Almost anything that could be done anywhere in the Culture could be done on a GSV. They could make anything the Culture was capable of making, contained all the knowledge the Culture had ever accumulated, carried or could construct specialised equipment of every imaginable type for every conceivable eventuality, and continually manufactured smaller ships: General Contact Units usually, warcraft now. Their complements were measured in millions at least. They crewed their offspring ships out of the gradual increase in their own population. Self-contained, self-sufficient, productive and, in peacetime at least, continually exchanging information, they were the Culture's ambassadors, its most visible citizens and its technological and intellectual big guns. There was no need to travel from the galactic backwoods to some distant Culture home-planet to be amazed and impressed by the stunning scale and awesome power of the Culture; a GSV could bring the whole lot right up to your front door. . . .

Horza followed the brightly dressed crowds through the bustling reception area. There were a few people in uniform, but they weren't stopping anybody. Horza felt in a daze, as though he was only a passenger in his own body, and the drunken puppeteer he had felt in the control of earlier was now sobered up a little and guiding him through the crowds of people towards the doors of another elevator. He tried to clear his head by shaking it, but it hurt when he did that. His hearing was coming back very slowly.

He looked at his hands, then sloughed the imprinter-skin from his palms, rubbing it on each of the lapels of the daysuit until it rolled off and fell to the floor of the corridor.

When they got off the second elevator they were in the starship. The people dispersed through broad, pastel-shaded corridors with high ceilings. Horza looked one way then another, as the elevator capsule swished back up towards the reception sphere. A small drone floated towards him. It was the size and shape of a standard suit backpack, and Horza eyed it warily, uncertain whether it was a Culture device or not.

'Excuse me, are you all right?' the machine said. Its voice was robust but not unfriendly. Horza could just hear it.

'I'm lost,' Horza said, too loudly. 'Lost,' he repeated, more quietly, so that he could hardly hear himself. He was aware that he was swaying a little as he stood there, and he could feel water trickling into his boots and dripping off the sodden cloak onto the soft, absorbent surface under his feet.

'Where do you want to go?' the drone asked.

'To a ship called . . .' Horza closed his eyes in weary desperation. He didn't dare give the real name. '. . . *The Beggar's Bluff*.'

The drone was silent for a second, then said, 'I'm afraid there is no such craft aboard. Perhaps it is in the port area by itself, not on the *Ends*.'

'It's an old Hronish assault ship,' Horza said tiredly, looking for somewhere to sit down. He spotted some seats set into the wall a few metres away and made his way over there. The drone followed him, lowering itself as he sat so that it was still at his eye level. 'About a hundred metres long,' the Changer went on, no longer caring if he was giving some sort of game away. 'It was being repaired by some port shipbuilders; had some damage to its warping units.'

'Ah. I *think* I have the one you want. It's more or less straight down from here. I have no record of its name, but it sounds like the one you want. Can you manage to get there yourself, or shall I take you?'

'I don't know if I can manage,' Horza said truthfully.

'Wait a moment.' The drone stayed floating silently in front of Horza for a moment or two; then it said, 'Follow me, then. There is a traveltube just over here and down a deck.' The machine backed off and indicated the direction they should head in by extending a hazy field from its casing. Horza got up and followed it.

They went down a small open AG lift shaft, then crossed a large open area where some of the wheeled and skirted vehicles used on the Orbital had been stored; just a few examples, the drone explained, for posterity. The *Ends* already had a Megaship aboard, stored in one of its two General bays, thirteen kilometres below, in the bottom of the craft. Horza didn't know whether to believe the drone or not.

On the far side of the hangar they came to another corridor, and there they entered a cylinder, about three metres in diameter and six long, which rolled its door closed, flicked to one side and was instantly sucked into a dark tunnel. Soft lights lit the interior. The drone explained that the windows were blanked out because, unless you were used to it, a capsule's journey through a GSV could be unsettling, due both to its speed and to the suddenness of the changes of direction, which the eye saw but the body didn't feel. Horza sat down heavily in one of the folding seats in the middle of the capsule, but only for a few seconds.

'Here we are. Smallbay 27492, in case you need it again. Innerlevel S-10-right. Goodye.' The capsule door rolled down. Horza nodded to the drone and stepped out into a corridor with straight, transparent walls. The capsule door closed, and the machine vanished. He had a brief impression of it flickering past him, but it happened so fast he could have been wrong. Anyway, his vision was still blurred.

He looked to his right. Through the walls of the corridor he looked into clear air. Kilometres of it. There was some sort of roof high above, with just a suggestion of wispy clouds. A few tiny craft moved. Level with him, far enough away for the view to be both hazy and vast, were hangars: level after level after level of them. Bays, docks, hangars – call them what you wanted; they filled Horza's sight for square kilometres, making him dizzy with the sheer scale of it all. His brain did a sort of double take, and he blinked and shook himself, but the view did not go away. Craft moved, lights went on or off, a layer of cloud far below made the view further down still more hazy, and something whizzed by the corridor Horza stood in: a ship, fully three hundred metres long. The ship passed along the level he was on, swooped, and far far away did a left turn, banking gracefully in the air to disappear into another bright and vast corridor which seemed to pass by at right angles to the one Horza stood staring at. In the other direction, the one that the ship had appeared from, was a wall, seemingly blank. Horza looked closer and rubbed his eyes; he saw that the wall had an orderly speckle of lights in a grid across it: thousands and thousands of windows and lights and balconies. Smaller craft flitted about its face, and the dots of traveltube capsules flashed across and up and down.

Horza couldn't take much more. He looked to his left and saw a smooth ramp leading down underneath the tube the capsule travelled in. He stumbled down it, into the welcomingly small space of a two-hundred-metre-long Smallbay.

Horza wanted to cry. The old ship sat on three short legs, square in the centre of the bay, a few bits and pieces of equipment scattered around it. There was nobody else in the bay that Horza could see, just machinery. The *CAT* looked old and battered, but intact and whole. It appeared that repairs were either finished or not yet started. The main hold lift was down, resting on the smooth white deck of the bay. Horza went over to it and saw a light ladder leading up into the brightness of the hold itself. A small insect landed briefly on his wrist. He flapped a hand at it as it flew off. How very *untidy* of the Culture, he thought absently, to allow an insect on board one of their sparkling vessels. Still, officially at least, the *Ends* was no longer the Culture's. Wearily he climbed the ladder, hampered by the damp cloak and accompanied by the squelching noises coming from his boots.

The hold smelled familiar, though it looked oddly spacious with no shuttle in it. There was nobody about. He went up the stairs from the hold to the accommodation section. He walked along the corridor towards the mess, wondering who was alive, who was dead, what changes had been made, if any. It had only been three days, but he felt as though he had been away for years. He was almost at Yalson's cabin when the door was quickly pulled open.

Yalson's fair-haired head came out, an expression of surprise, even

223

joy, starting to form on it. 'Haw—' she said, then stopped, frowned at him, shook her head and muttered something, ducking back into her cabin. Horza had stopped.

He stood there, thinking he was glad she was alive, realising he hadn't been walking properly – not like Kraiklyn. His tread had sounded like his own instead. A hand appeared from Yalson's door as she pulled on a light robe, then she came out and stood in the corridor, looking at the man she thought was Kraiklyn, her hands on her hips. Her lean, hard face looked slightly concerned, but mostly wary. Horza hid his hand with the missing finger behind his back.

'What the hell happened to you?' she said.

'I got in a fight. What does it look like?' He got the voice right. They stood looking at each other.

'If you want any help—' she began. Horza shook his head.

'I'll manage.'

Yalson nodded, half smiling, looking him up and down. 'Yeah, all right. You manage, then.' She jerked a thumb over her shoulder, in the direction of the mess. 'Your new recruit just brought her gear aboard. She's waiting in the mess, though if you look in now she might not think it's such a wonderful idea to join up.'

Horza nodded. Yalson shrugged, then turned and walked up the corridor, through the mess towards the bridge. Horza followed her. 'Our glorious captain,' she said to somebody in the room as she went through. Horza hesitated at Kraiklyn's cabin door, then went forward to stick his head round the door of the mess.

A woman was sitting at the far end of the mess table, her legs crossed over a chair in front of her. The screen was switched on above her as though she had been watching it; it showed a view of a Megaship being lifted bodily out of the water by hundreds of small lifter tugs clustered under and around it. They were recognisably antique Culture machines. The woman had turned from the sight, though, and was gazing towards Horza when he looked round the side of the door.

She was slim and tall and pale. She looked fit, and her black-coloured eyes were set in a face just starting to show worried surprise at the battered face looking at her from the doorway. She had on a light suit, the helmet of which lay on the table in front of her. A red bandanna was tied round her head, below the level of her close-cropped red hair. 'Oh, Captain Kraiklyn,' she said, swinging her feet off the seat and leaning forward, her face showing shock and pity. 'What happened?'

224

Horza tried to speak, but his throat was dry. He couldn't believe what he saw. His lips worked and he licked them with a dry tongue. The woman started to rise from the table, but he put out one hand and gestured her to stay where she was. She sat slowly back down, and he managed to say, 'I'm all right. See you later. Just . . . just stay . . . there.' Then he pushed himself away from the door and stumbled down the corridor to Kraiklyn's cabin. The ring fitted into the door, and it swung open. He almost fell inside.

In something like a trance he closed the door, stood there looking at the far bulkhead for a while, then slowly sat down, on the floor.

He knew he was still stunned, he knew his vision was still blurred and he wasn't hearing perfectly. He knew it was unlikely – or, if it wasn't, then it was very bad news indeed, but he was sure; absolutely certain. As certain as he had been about Kraiklyn when he first walked up that ramp to the Damage table, into the arena.

As though he hadn't had enough shocks for one evening, the sight of the woman sitting at the mess-room table had all but silenced him and stopped his mind from working. What was he going to do? He couldn't think. The shock was still resounding through his mind; the image seemed stuck behind his eyes.

The woman in the mess room was Perosteck Balveda.

8.

The Ends of Invention

Maybe she's a clone, Horza thought. *Maybe it's coincidence.* He sat on the floor of Kraiklyn's cabin – his cabin now – staring at the locker doors in the far wall; aware that he needed to do something, but not sure what it ought to be. His brain wasn't able to take all the knocks and shocks it had had. He needed to sit and think for a moment.

He tried telling himself he was mistaken, that it wasn't really her, that he was tired and confused and getting paranoid, seeing things. But he knew it was Balveda, though sufficiently altered so that probably only a close friend or a Changer could possibly recognise her, but definitely *her*, alive and well and probably armed to the teeth. . . .

He got up, mechanically, still staring straight ahead. He took off the wet clothes and went out of the cabin, down to the wash area, where he left the clothes to dry and cleaned himself up. Back in the cabin he found a robe and put it on. He started inspecting the small, packed space and finally came across a small voice recorder. He flicked it back and listened.

'. . . ahhh . . . including, ahh, Yalson,' Kraiklyn's voice said from the small speaker in the machine, 'who I guess was, umm . . . in her relationship, with ahh . . . Horza Gobuchul. She's . . . been pretty abrupt, and I don't think I've had the support from her . . . which she . . . which I ought to get. . . . I'll have a word with her if it goes on, but, ahhh . . . for now, during the repairs and such . . . there doesn't seem much point . . . I'm not putting off . . . ah . . . I just think we'll see how she shapes up after the Orbital's blown and we're on our way.

'Ahh . . . now this new woman . . . Gravant . . . she's all right. I get the impression she might . . . ah, need . . . need a bit of ordering around . . . seems to need discipline. . . . I don't think she'll have, ah, too much conflict with anybody. Yalson, especially, I was worried about, but I don't think . . . ah, I think it'll be fine. But you can never tell with women, ah . . . of course, so . . . but I like her. . . . I think she's got class and maybe . . . I don't know . . . maybe she could make a good number two if she shapes up.

'I really need more people. . . . Umm . . . things haven't gone all that well recently, but I think I've been . . . they've let me down. Jandraligeli, obviously . . . and I don't know; I'll see if maybe I can do something about him because . . . he's really sort of just been . . . ahh . . . he's betrayed me; that's the way . . . that's what it is I think; anybody would agree. So maybe I'll have a word with Gahlssel, at the game, assuming he arrives. . . . I don't think the guy's really up to standard and I'll tell Ghalssel as much because we're both . . . in the same, ah . . . business, and I'm . . . I know that he'll have heard . . . well, he'll listen to what I have to say, because he knows about the responsibilities of leadership and . . . just, ah . . . the way I do.

'Anyway . . . I'll do some more recruiting after the game, and after the GSV takes off there'll be some time . . . we have enough time still to run in this bay and I'll put the word out. There's bound to be . . . a lot of people ready to sign on. . . . Ah, oh yeah; mustn't forget about the shuttle tomorrow. I'm sure I can get the price down. Ah, I could just win at the game, of course—' The small voice from the speaker laughed: a tinny echo. '. . . and just be incredibly rich and—' The laughter came again, distorted. '. . . and not give a fuck about any of this crap any more . . . shit, just . . . ha . . . give the *CAT* away . . . well, sell it . . . and retire. . . . But we'll see. . . .'

The voice faded. Horza switched off the machine in the silence. He put it down where he had found it, and rubbed the ring on the small finger of his right hand. Then he took off the robe and put his – *his* – suit on. It started talking to him; he told it to turn its voice off.

He looked at himself in the reverser field on the locker doors, drew himself up, made sure the plasma pistol strapped to his thigh was switched on, pushed the pains and tiredness to the back of his mind, then went out of the cabin and up the corridor to the mess.

Yalson and the woman who was Balveda were sitting talking in the long room, at the far end of the table under the screen, which had been turned off. They looked up when he came in. He went over and sat a couple of seats down from Yalson, who looked at his suit and said, 'We going somewhere?'

'Maybe,' Horza said, looking briefly at her, then switching his gaze to the Balveda woman, smiling and saying, 'I'm sorry, Ms Gravant; but I'm afraid, having reconsidered your application, I have to turn you down. I'm sorry, but there's no place for you on the *CAT*. I hope you understand.' He clasped his hands on the table and grinned again.

Balveda – the more he looked the surer he was that it was her – looked crestfallen. Her mouth opened slightly; she looked from Horza to Yalson then back again. Yalson was frowning deeply.

'But—' Balveda began.

'What the hell are you talking about?' Yalson said angrily. 'You can't just—'

'You see,' Horza smiled, 'I've decided that we need to cut down on the numbers on board, and—'

'What?' Yalson exploded, slapping the table with the palm of her hand. 'That's six of us left! What the hell are six of us meant to do . . . ?' Her voice trailed off, then came back lower and slower, her head twisting to one side, her eyes narrowing as she looked at him. '. . . Or have we just struck lucky in . . . oh, a game of *chance* perhaps, and don't want to cut in more directions than absolutely necessary?'

Horza looked briefly at Yalson again, smiled and said, 'No, but you see I've just re-hired one of our ex-members, and that does alter the plans a bit. . . . The place I had intended to slot Ms Gravant into in the ship's company is now filled.'

'You got Jandraligeli to come back, after what you called him?' laughed Yalson, stretching back in her seat.

Horza shook his head.

'No, my dear,' he said. 'As I would have been able to tell you if you hadn't kept interrupting, I just met our friend Mr Gobuchul in Evanauth, and he's keen to rejoin.'

'Horza?' Yalson seemed to shake a little, her voice on an edge of tension, and he could see her trying to control herself. *Oh gods*, a small voice inside him said, *why does this hurt so much?* Yalson said, 'Is he alive? Are you sure it was him? Kraiklyn, are you?'

Horza switched his gaze rapidly from one woman to the other. Yalson was leaning forward over the table, her eyes glittering in the mess-room light, her fists clenched. Her lean body seemed tensed, the golden down on her dark skin shining. Balveda looked uncertain and confused. Horza saw her start to bite her lip, then stop.

'I wouldn't kid you about it, Yalson', Horza assured her. 'Horza is alive and well, and not very far away.' Horza looked at the repeater screen on his suit cuff, where the time showed. 'As a matter of fact, I'm meeting him at one of the port reception spheres in . . . well, just before the GSV takes off. He said he had one or two things to work out in the city first. He said to say . . . ahhh . . . he hoped you were still betting on him. . . .' He shrugged. 'Something like that.'

'You're not kidding!' Yalson said, her face creasing with a smile.

231

She shook her head, put a hand through her hair, slapped the table softly a couple of times. 'Oh . . .' she said, then sat back again in her seat. She looked from the woman to the man and shrugged, silent.

'So you see, Gravant, you just aren't needed right now,' Horza told Balveda. The Culture agent opened her mouth, but it was Yalson who spoke first, coughing quickly and then saying.

'Oh, let her stay, Kraiklyn. What difference does it make?'

'The difference, Yalson,' Horza said carefully, thinking hard about Kraiklyn, 'is that I am captain of this ship.'

Yalson seemed about to say something, but instead she turned to Balveda and spread her hands. She sat back, one hand picking at the edge of the table, her eyes lowered. She was trying not to smile too much.

'Well, Captain,' Balveda said, rising from her seat, 'you do know best. I'll get my gear.' She walked quickly from the mess. Her footsteps merged with others, and Horza and Yalson both heard some muffled words. In a moment, Dorolow, Wubslin and Aviger, gaily dressed and looking flushed and happy, piled into the mess, the older man with his arm around the small, plump woman.

'Our captain!' Aviger shouted. Dorolow held one of his hands at her shoulder. She smiled. Wubslin waved dreamily; the stocky engineer looked drunk. 'Been at the wars, I see,' Aviger went on, staring at Horza's face, which still showed signs of being in a fight, despite his internal attempts to minimise the damage.

'What has Gravant done, Kraiklyn?' Dorolow squeaked. She seemed merry, too, and her voice was even higher than he remembered it.

'Nothing,' Horza said, smiling at the three mercenaries. 'But we're getting Horza Gobuchul back from the dead, so I decided we didn't need her.'

'*Horza*?' Wubslin said, his large mouth opening wide in an almost exaggerated expression of surprise. Dorolow looked past Horza at Yalson, the look on her face saying, 'Is this true?' through her grin. Yalson shrugged and looked happily, hopefully, still slightly suspiciously, at the man she thought was Kraiklyn.

'He'll be coming aboard shortly before the *Ends* leaves,' Horza said. 'He had some sort of business in the city. Maybe something shady.' Horza smiled in the condescending way Kraiklyn sometimes had. 'Who knows?'

'There,' Wubslin said, looking unsteadily at Aviger over Dorolow's stooped frame. 'Maybe that guy was looking for Horza. Maybe we should warn him.'

'What guy? Where?' Horza asked.

'He's seeing things,' Aviger said, waving one hand. 'Too much liverwine.'

'*Rubbish*!' Wubslin said loudly, looking from Aviger to Horza, and nodding. 'And a drone.' He held both hands out in front of his face, palms together, then separated them by about a quarter-metre. 'Little bugger. No bigger'n that.'

'Where?' Horza shook his head. 'Why do you think somebody might be after Horza?'

'Out there, under the traveltube,' Aviger said, while Wubslin was saying:

'Way he came out of that capsule, like he expected to be in a fight any second, and . . . aww, I can just *tell* . . . that guy was . . . police . . . or *something*. . . .'

'What about Mipp?' asked Dorolow. Horza was silent for a second, frowning at nothing and nobody in particular. 'Did Horza mention Mipp?' Dorolow asked him.

'Mipp?' he said, looking at Dorolow. 'No.' He shook his head. 'No, Mipp didn't make it.'

'Oh, I'm sorry,' Dorolow said.

'Look,' Horza said, staring at Aviger and Wubslin, 'you think there's somebody out there looking for one of us?'

'A man,' Wubslin nodded slowly, 'and a little, tiny, really *mean*-looking drone.'

With a chill, Horza recalled the insect which had settled momentarily on his wrist in the smallbay outside, just before he had boarded the *CAT*. The Culture, he knew, had machines – artificial bugs – that size.

'Hmm,' Horza said, pursing his lips. He nodded to himself, then looked at Yalson. 'Go and make sure Gravant gets off the ship, quickly, all right?' He stood up and got out of the way while Yalson moved. She went down the corridor to the cabins. Horza looked at Wubslin and motioned the engineer forward towards the bridge, with his eyes. 'You two stay here,' he said quietly to Aviger and Dorolow. Slowly they let go of each other and sat down in a couple of seats. Horza went through to the bridge.

He pointed Wubslin to the engineer's seat and sat down in the pilot's. Wubslin sighed heavily. Horza closed the door, then quickly reeled through all he had learned about the procedures on the bridge during the first weeks he had been aboard the *CAT*. He was reaching forward to open the communicator channels when something moved under the console, near his feet. He froze.

Wubslin peered down, then bent with an audible effort and stuck his big head down between his legs. Horza smelled drink.

'Haven't you finished *yet*?' Wubslin's muffled voice said.

'They took me off to another job; I only just got back,' wailed a small, thin, artificial voice. Horza sat back in his seat and looked under the console. A drone, about two thirds the size of the one which had escorted him from the elevator to the *CAT*'s bay, was disentangling itself from a jumble of fine cables protruding from an open inspection hatch.

'What', Horza said, 'is *that*?'

'Oh,' Wubslin said wearily, belching, 'same one that's been here . . . you remember. Come on, you,' he said to the machine. 'The captain wants to do a communication test.'

'Look,' the little machine said, its synthesised voice full of exasperation, 'I have *finished*. I'm just tidying everything *away*.'

'Well get a move on,' Wubslin said. He withdrew his head from underneath the console and looked apologetically at Horza. 'Sorry, Kraiklyn.'

'Never mind, never mind.' Horza waved his hand. He powered up the communicator. 'Ah . . .' He looked at Wubslin. 'Who's controlling traffic movements around here? I've forgotten who to ask for. What if I want the bay doors opened?'

'Traffic? Doors opened?' Wubslin looked at Horza with a puzzled expression. He shrugged and said, 'Well, just traffic control, I suppose, like when we came in.'

'Right,' Horza said; he flicked the switch on the console and said, 'Traffic control, this is . . .' His voice trailed off.

He'd no idea what Kraiklyn had called the *CAT* instead of its real name. He hadn't got that as part of the information he'd bought, and it was one of the many things he had meant to learn once he'd accomplished the most immediate task of getting Balveda off the ship, and with luck following a false trail. But the news that there might be somebody looking for him in this bay – or anybody, for that matter – had rattled him. He said, '. . . This is the craft in Smallbay 27492. I want immediate clearance to leave the bay and the GSV; we'll quit the Orbital independently.'

Wubslin stared at Horza.

'This is Evanauth Port traffic control, GSV temporary section. One moment, Smallbay 27492,' said the speakers set in Horza and Wubslin's seat headrests. Horza turned to Wubslin, switching off the communicator send button.

'This thing *is* ready to fly, isn't it?'

'Wha—? Fly?' Wubslin looked perplexed. He scratched his chest, looked down at the drone still working to stuff the wires back under the console. 'I suppose so, but— '

'Great.' Horza started switching everything on, motors included. He noticed the bank of screens carrying information about the bow laser flickering on along with everything else. At least Kraiklyn had had that repaired.

'Fly?' Wubslin repeated. He scratched his chest again and turned towards Horza. 'Did you say "fly"?'

'Yes. We're leaving.' Horza's hands flicked over the buttons and sensor switches, adjusting the systems of the waking ship as though he really had been doing it for years.

'We'll need a tug. . . .' Wubslin said. Horza knew the engineer was right. The *CAT*'s anti-gravity was only strong enough to produce an internal field; the warp units would blow so close to (in fact, inside) a mass as great as the *Ends*, and you couldn't reasonably use the fusion motors in an enclosed space.

'We'll get one. I'll tell them it's an emergency. I'll say we've got a bomb aboard, or something.' Horza watched the main screen come on, filling the previously blank bulkhead in front of him and Wubslin with a view of the rear of the Smallbay.

Wubslin got his own monitor screen to display a complicated plan which Horza eventually identified as a map of their level of the GSV's vast interior. He only glanced at it at first, then ignored the view on the main screen and looked more carefully at the plan, and finally put a holo of the GSV's whole internal layout onto the main screen, quickly memorising all he could.

'What . . .' Wubslin, paused, belched again, rubbed his belly through his tunic and said, 'What about Horza?'

'We'll pick him up later,' Horza said, still studying the layout of the GSV. 'I made other arrangements in case I couldn't meet him when I said.' Horza punched the transmit button again. 'Traffic control, traffic control, this is Smallbay 27492. I need emergency clearance. Repeat, I need emergency clearance and a tug straight away. I have a malfunctioning fusion generator I can't close down. Repeat, nuclear fusion generator breakdown, going critical.'

'What!' a small voice screeched. Something banged into Horza's knee, and the drone working under the console wobbled quickly into view, festooned with cables like a streamer-draped party goer. '*What* did you say?'

'Shut up and get off the ship. '*Now*,' Horza told it, turning up the gain on the receiver circuits. A hissing noise filled the bridge.

'With pleasure!' the drone said, and shook itself to get rid of the cables looped round its casing. 'As usual I'm the last to be told what's going on, but I know I don't want to stick around this—' it was muttering when the hangar lights went out.

At first Horza thought the screen had blown, but he slid the wavelength control up, and a dim outline of the bay reappeared, showing its appearance on infra-red. 'Oh-oh,' said the drone, turning first to the screen, then looking back at Horza. 'You lot did pay your *rent*, didn't you?'

'Dead,' Wubslin announced. The drone got rid of the last of its cables. Horza looked sharply at the engineer.

'What?'

Wubslin pointed at the transceiver controls in front of him. 'Dead. Somebody's cut us off from traffic control.'

A shudder ran through the ship. A light blinked, indicating that the main hold lift had just slammed up automatically.

A draught briefly stirred the air in the flight deck, then died. More lights started flashing on the console. 'Shit,' Horza said. 'Now what?'

'Well, goodbye chaps,' the drone said hurriedly. It shot past them, sucked the door open and whooshed down the corridor, heading for the hangar stairwell.

'Pressure drop?' Wubslin said to himself, scratching his head for a change and knotting his brows as he looked at the screens in front of him.

'Kraiklyn!' Yalson's voice shouted from the seat headrest speakers. A light on the console showed that she was calling from the hangar.

'What?' Horza snapped.

'What the hell's going on?' Yalson shouted. 'We were nearly crushed! The air's going from the Smallbay and the hangar lift just emergencied on us! What's *happening*?'

'I'll explain,' Horza said. His mouth was dry, and he felt as though there was a lump of ice in his guts. 'Is Ms Gravant still with you?'

'Of course she's still fucking with me!'

'Right. Come back up to the mess room right away. Both of you.'

'Kraiklyn—' Yalson began, then another voice cut in, starting from a distance but quickly coming closer to the mike.

'Closed? Closed? Why is this lift door closed? *What* is going on on this vessel? Hello, bridge? Captain?' A sharp *tap-tap* noise came from the headrest speakers, and the synthesised voice went on, 'Why am I being obstructed? Let me off this ship at—'

236

'Get out of the way, you idiot!' Yalson said, then: 'It's that goddam drone again.'

'You and Gravant get up here,' Horza repeated. 'Now.' Horza closed down the hangar com circuit. He wheeled out of the seat and patted Wubslin on the shoulder. 'Strap in. Get us ready to roll. Everything.' Then he swung through the open door. Aviger was in the corridor, coming from the mess to the bridge. He opened his mouth to speak but Horza squeezed quickly past him. 'Not now, Aviger.' He put his right glove to the lock on the armoury door. It clicked open. Horza looked inside.

'I was only going to ask—'

'. . . what the hell's going on?' Horza completed the old man's sentence for him as he lifted the biggest neural stun pistol he could see, slammed the armoury doors shut and paced quickly down the corridor, through the mess room where Dorolow was sitting asleep in a chair, and into the corridor through the accommodation section. He switched the gun on, turned its power control to maximum, then held it behind his back.

The drone appeared first, flying up the steps and darting along the corridor at eye level. 'Captain! I really must prot—'

Horza kicked a door open, caught the bevelled front of the drone as it came towards him and threw the machine into the cabin. He slammed the door shut. Voices were coming up the steps from the hangar. He held onto the handle of the cabin door. It was pulled hard, then thumped. 'This is out*rageous*!' a distant, tinny voice wailed.

'Kraiklyn,' Yalson said as her head appeared at the top of the steps. Horza smiled, readying the gun he held behind his back. The door resounded again, shaking his hand.

'Let me *out*!'

'Kraiklyn, what *is* going on?' Yalson said, coming along the corridor. Balveda was almost up the stairs, carrying a large kitbag over her shoulder.

'I'm going to lose my *temper*!' The door shook again.

A whine, high and urgent, came from behind Yalson, from Balveda's kitbag; then a static-like crackle. Yalson didn't hear the high-pitched whine – which was an alarm. Horza, though, was distantly aware of Dorolow stirring somewhere behind him in the mess room. At the burst of static, which was a highly compressed message or signal of some sort, Yalson started to turn back to Balveda. At the same moment Horza leapt forward, taking his hand off the cabin door handle and bringing the heavy stun gun round to bear on Balveda. The Culture woman was already dropping the kitbag, one

237

hand flashing – so fast even Horza could hardly follow the movement –
down to her side. Horza threw himself into the space between Yalson
and the corridor bulkhead, knocking the woman mercenary to one
side. At the same time, with the big stun gun pointing straight at
Balveda's face, he pulled the trigger. The weapon hummed in his
hand as he continued forward, dropping. He tried to keep the gun
pointing at Balveda's head all the way down. He hit the deck just
before the sagging Culture agent did.

Yalson was still staggering back after being thumped against the far
bulkhead. Horza lay on the deck watching Balveda's feet and legs for a
second, then he quickly scrambled up, saw Balveda move groggily,
her red-haired head scraping on the deck surface, her dark eyes
opening briefly. He pulled the stun-gun trigger again, keeping it
depressed and pointing the gun at the woman's head. She shook
spastically for a second, saliva drooling from one corner of her mouth,
then went limp. The red bandanna rolled off her head.

'Are you crazy?' Yalson screamed. Horza turned to her.

'Her name isn't Gravant; it's Perosteck Balveda, and she's an agent
in the Culture's Special Circumstances section. That's their euphemism for Military Intelligence, in case you didn't know,' he said. Yalson
was backed up almost to the mess-room entrance, her eyes full of fear,
her hands clutching at the surface of the bulkhead on either side of
her. Horza went up to her. She shrank from him, and he sensed her
getting ready to strike out. He stopped short of her, turned the stun
gun round and handed it to her, grip first. 'If you don't believe me
we'll probably all end up dead,' he said, edging the gun forward
towards her hands. She took it eventually. 'I'm serious,' he told her.
'Search her for weapons. Then get her into the mess and strap her into
a seat. Tie her hands down, tight. And her legs. Then strap in
yourself. We've leaving; I'll explain later.' He started to go past her,
then he turned and looked into her eyes.

'Oh, and keep stunning her every now and again, on maximum
power. Special Circumstancers are *very* tough.' He turned and went
towards the mess room. He heard the stun gun click.

'Kraiklyn,' Yalson said.

He stopped and turned round again. She was pointing the gun
straight at him, holding it in both hands and level with his eyes. Horza
sighed and shook his head.

'Don't,' he said.

'What about Horza?'

'He's safe. I swear it. But he'll be dead if we don't get out of here

238

now. *And* if she wakes up.' He nodded past Yalson at the long, inert form of Balveda. He turned again, then walked into the mess, the back of his head and the nape of his neck tingling with anticipation.

Nothing happened. Dorolow looked up from the table and said, 'What was that noise?' as Horza went past.

'What noise?' Horza said as he went through to the bridge.

Yalson watched Kraiklyn's back as he walked through the mess room. He said something to Dorolow, then he was through to the bridge. She let the stun gun down slowly; it hung in one hand. She looked at the gun thoughtfully and said to herself, quietly, 'Yalson, my girl, there are times when I think you're a little too loyal.' She raised the gun again as the cabin door opened just a crack and a small voice said, 'Is it *safe* out there yet?'

Yalson grimaced, pushed the door open and looked at the drone, which was retreating further into the cabin. She nodded her head to the side and said, 'Get out here and give me a hand with this bod, you liverless piece of clockwork.'

'Wake up!' Horza kicked Wubslin's leg as he swung back into his chair. Aviger was sitting in the third seat in the flight deck, looking anxiously at the screens and controls. Wubslin jumped, then looked round with bleary eyes.

'Eh?' he said, then: 'I was just resting my eyes.'

Horza pulled out the *CAT*'s manual controls from their recess in the edge of the console. Aviger looked at them with apprehension.

'Just how hard did you knock your head?' he said to Horza.

Horza smiled coldly at him. He scanned the screens as fast as he could and threw the safety switches on the ship's fusion motors. He tried traffic control once more. The Smallbay was still dark. The outside pressure gauge registered zero. Wubslin was talking to himself as he checked over the craft's monitoring systems.

'Aviger,' Horza said, not looking at the older man, 'I think you'd better strap in.'

'What for?' Aviger asked quietly, measuredly. 'We can't go anywhere. We can't move. We're stuck here until a tug arrives to take us out, aren't we?'

'Of course we are,' Horza said, adjusting the readying controls of the fusion motors and putting the ship leg controls on automatic. He turned and looked at Aviger. 'Tell you what; why don't you go and get that new recruit's kitbag? Take it down to the hangar and shove it into a vactube.'

'What?' Aviger said, his already creased face becoming more lined as he frowned. 'I thought she was leaving.'

'She was, but whoever is trying to keep us in here started evacuating the air from the Smallbay before she could get off. Now I want you to take her kitbag and all the other gear she may have left lying around and stow it in a vactube, *all right*?'

Aviger got up from the seat slowly, looking at Horza with a tense, worried expression on his face. 'All right.' He started to leave the bridge, then hesitated, looking back at Horza. 'Kraiklyn, why am I putting her kitbag in the vactube?'

'Because there's almost certainly a very powerful bomb in it; that's why. Now get down there and *do it*.'

Aviger nodded and left, looking even less happy. Horza turned back to the controls. They were almost ready. Wubslin was still talking to himself and hadn't strapped in properly, but he seemed to be doing his part competently enough, despite frequent belches and pauses to scratch his chest and head. Horza knew he was putting the next bit off, but it had to be done. He pressed the ident button.

'This is Kraiklyn,' he said, and coughed.

'Identification complete,' the console said immediately. Horza wanted to shout, or at least to sag in his seat with relief, but he hadn't the time to do either, and Wubslin would have thought it a little strange. So might the ship's computer, for that matter: some machines were programmed to watch for signs of joy or relief after the formal identification was over. So he did nothing to celebrate, just brought the fusion motor primers up to operating temperature.

'Captain!' The small drone dashed back into the bridge, coming to a halt between Wubslin and Horza. 'You will let me off this ship at once and report the irregularities taking place aboard immediately, or—'

'Or what?' Horza said, watching the temperature in the *CAT*'s fusion motors soar. 'If you think you can get off this ship you're welcome to try; probably Culture agents would blow you to dust even if you did get out.'

'Culture agents?' the small machine said with a sneer in its voice. 'Captain, for your information this GSV is a demilitarised civilian vessel under the control of the Vavatch Hub authorities and within the terms laid down in the Idiran–Culture War Conduct Treaty drawn up shortly after the commencement of hostilities. How—'

'So who turned the lights off and let the air out, idiot?' Horza said, turning to the machine briefly. He looked back to the console, turning the bow radar up as high as it would go and taking readings through the blank wall of the rear of the Smallbay.

'*I* don't know,' the drone said, 'but I rather doubt it would be Culture agents. Who or what do you think these supposed agents are after? You?'

'What if they were?' Horza took another look at the holo display of the GSV's internal layout. He briefly magnified the volume around Smallbay 27492 before switching the repeater screen off. The drone was silent for a second, then backed off through the doorway.

'Great. I'm locked in an antique with a paranoid lunatic. I think I'll go and look for somewhere safer than this.'

'You do that!' Horza yelled down the corridor after it. He turned the hangar circuit back on. 'Aviger?' he said.

'I've done it,' said the old man's voice.

'Right. Get to the mess fast and strap in.' Horza killed the circuit again.

'Well,' Wubslin said, sitting back in his seat and scratching his head, looking at the bank of screens in front of him with their arrays of figures and graphs, 'I don't know what it is you're intending to do, Kraiklyn, but whatever it is, we're as ready as we'll ever be to do it.' The stout engineer looked across at Horza, lifted himself slightly from his seat and pulled the restraining straps over his body. Horza grinned at him, trying to look confident. His own seat's restrainers were a little more sophisticated, and he just had to throw a switch for cushioned arms to swing over and inertia fields to come on. He pulled his helmet over his head from the hinged position and heard it hiss shut.

'Oh my God,' Wubslin said, looking slowly away from Horza to stare at the almost featureless rear wall of the Smallbay shown on the main screen. 'I sure as hell hope you're not going to do what I think you are.'

Horza didn't reply. He hit the button to talk to the mess. 'All right?'

'Just about, Kraiklyn, but—' Yalson said. Horza killed that circuit, too. He licked his lips, took the controls in his gloved hands, sucked in a deep breath, then flicked the thumb buttons on the *CAT*'s three fusion motors. Just before the noise started he heard Wubslin say:

'Oh, my God, you are—'

The screen flashed, went dark, then flashed again. The view of the Smallbay's rear wall was lit by three jets of plasma bursting from underneath the ship. A noise like thunder filled the bridge and reverberated through the whole craft. The two outboard motors were the main thrust, vectored down for the moment; they blasted fire onto the deck of the Smallbay, scattering the machinery and equipment from underneath and around the craft, slamming it into walls and off the roof as the blinding jets of flame steadied under the vessel. The inboard, lift-only nose motor fired raggedly at first, then settled quickly, starting to burn its own hole through the thin layer of ultradense material which covered the Smallbay floor. The *Clear Air Turbulence* stirred like a waking animal, groaning and creaking and shifting its weight. On the screen, a huge shadow veered across the wall and the roof in front as the infernal light from the nose fusion motor burned under the ship; rolling clouds of gas from burning machinery were starting to haze over the view. Horza was amazed that the walls of the Smallbay had held out. He flicked the bow laser at the same time as increasing the fusion motor power.

The screen detonated with light. The wall ahead burst open like a flower seen in time lapse, huge petals throwing themselves towards the ship and a million pieces of wreckage and debris flashing past the vessel's nose on the shock wave of air bursting in from the far side of the lasered wall. At the same time, the *Clear Air Turbulence* lifted off. The leg-weight readouts stopped at zero, then blanked out as the legs, glowing red with heat, stowed themselves inside the hull. Emergency undercarriage cooling circuits whined into action. The craft started to slew to one side, shaking with its own power and with the impact of debris swirling about it. The view ahead cleared.

Horza steadied the ship, then gunned the rear motors, flinging some of their power backwards, towards the Smallbay doors. A rear screen showed them glowing white hot. Horza would dearly have liked to head that way, but reversing and ramming the doors with the *CAT* would have probably been suicidal, and turning the craft in such a confined space impossible. Just going forward was going to be hard enough. . . .

The hole wasn't big enough. Horza saw it coming towards him and knew straight away. He used one shaking finger on the laser beam-spread control set in the semi-wheel of the controls, turning the spread up to maximum then firing once more. The screen washed out with light again, all around the perimeter of the hole. The *CAT* stuck its nose and then its body into another Smallbay. Horza waited for something to hit the sides or roof of the white-hot gap, but nothing happened; they sailed through on their three pillars of fire, throwing light and wreckage and waves of smoke and gas before them. The dark waves blasted out over shuttles; the whole Smallbay they were now moving slowly through was full of shuttles of every shape and description. They were floating over them, battering them and melting them with their fire.

Horza was aware of Wubslin sitting on the seat beside him, his eyes

242

locked onto the view ahead, his legs drawn up as far as possible so that his knees stuck up above the edge of the console, and his arms locked in a sort of square over his head, each hand grasping the bicep of the other arm. His face was a mask of fear and incredulity when Horza turned round to glance at him, and grinned. Wubslin pointed frenziedly at the main screen. 'Watch!' he shrieked over the racket.

The *CAT* was shaking and bouncing, rocked by the stream of superheated matter pouring from under its hull. It would be using the atmosphere around it to produce plasma, now that there was air available, and in the relatively confined space of the Smallbays the turbulence created was enough to shake the vessel bodily.

There was another wall ahead, coming up faster than Horza would have liked. They were slewing slightly again as well; he narrowed the laser angle again and fired, pulling the ship round at the same time. The wall flashed once around its edges; the roof and floor of the Smallbay flashed in loops of flame where the laser caught them, and dozens of parked shuttles ahead of them pulsed with light and heat.

The wall ahead started to fall slowly back, but the *CAT* was coming up on it faster than it was crumpling. Horza gasped and tried to pull back; he heard Wubslin howl, as the vessel's nose hit the undamaged centre of the wall. The view on the main screen tilted as the ship rammed into the wall material. Then the nose came down, the *Clear Air Turbulence* quivered like an animal shaking water from its fur, and they were rocking and yawing into yet another Smallbay. It was totally empty. Horza gunned the engines a little more, took a couple of bursts with the laser at the next wall, then watched in amazement as this wall, instead of falling back like the last one, crashed down towards them like a vast castle drawbridge, slamming in one fiery piece onto the deck of the empty Smallbay. In a fury of steam and gas, a mountain of water appeared over the top of the collapsing wall and poured out in a huge wave towards the approaching ship.

Horza heard himself shouting. He rammed the motor controls full on and kept the laser fire button hard down.

The *CAT* leapt forward. It flashed over the surface of the cascading water, enough of the plasma heat smashing into its liquid surface to instantly fill all the space of Smallbays its passage had created with a boiling fog of steam. As the tide of water continued to pour from the flooded Smallbay and the *CAT* screeched above it, the air about the ship filled with superheated steam. The external pressure gauge went up too quickly for the eye to follow; the laser blasted even more vapour off the water in front, and with an explosion like the end of the world the next wall blew out ahead of the vessel – weakened by the laser and finally blasted away by the sheer pressure of steam. The *Clear Air Turbulence* shot out from the tunnel of linked Smallbays like a bullet from a gun.

Motors flaming, in the middle of a cloud of gas and steam which it quickly outdistanced, it roared into a canyon of air-filled space between towering walls of bay doors and opened accommodation sections, lighting up kilometres of wall and cloud, screaming with its three flame-filled throats, and seemingly pulling after it a tidal wave of water and a volcano-like cloud of steam, gas and smoke. The water fell, turning from a solid wave into something like heavy surf, then spray, then just rain and water vapour, following the huge flapping card of the bay door tumbling through the air. The *CAT* wrenched itself round, twisting and slewing through the air in an attempt to check its headlong rush towards the far wall of Smallbay doors facing it across that vast internal canyon. Then its motors flickered and went out. The *Clear Air Turbulence* started to fall.

Horza gunned the controls, but the fusion motors were dead. The screen showed the wall of doors to other bays on one side, then air and clouds, then the wall of bay doors on the other side. They were in a spin. Horza looked over at Wubslin as he fought with the controls. The engineer was staring at the main screen with a glazed expression on his face. 'Wubslin!' Horza screamed. The fusion motors stayed dead.

'Aaah!' Wubslin seemed to have woken up to the fact that they were falling out of control; he leapt at the controls in front of him. 'Just fly it!' he shouted. 'I'll try the primers! Must have over-pressured the motors!'

Horza wrestled with the controls while Wubslin tried to restart the engines. On the screen, walls spun crazily about them and clouds beneath them were coming up fast – beneath them; really beneath them; a dead flat layer of clouds. Horza shook the controls again.

The nose motor burst into life, guttering wildly, sending the spinning craft careering off towards one side of the artificial cliff of bay doors and walls. Horza cut the motor out. He steered into the spin, using the craft's control surfaces rather than the motors, then he aimed the whole ship straight down and put his fingers on the laser buttons again. The clouds flashed up to meet the vessel. He closed his eyes and squeezed the laser controls.

The Ends of Invention was so huge it was built on three almost totally separate levels, each over three kilometres deep. They were pressure

244

levels, there because otherwise the differential between the very bottom and the very top of the giant ship would have been the difference between standard sea level and a mountain top somewhere in the tropopause. As it was, there existed a three-and-a-half-thousand-metre difference between the base and roof of each pressure level, making sudden journeys by traveltube from one to the other inadvisable. In the immense open cave that was the hollow centre of the GSV the pressure levels were marked by force fields, not anything material, so that craft could pass from one level to another without having to go outside the vessel, and it was towards one of those boundaries, marked by cloud, that the *Clear Air Turbulence* was falling.

Firing the laser did no good whatsoever, though Horza didn't know that at the time. It was a Vavatch computer, which had taken over the internal monitoring and control from the Culture's own Minds, which opened a hole in the force field to let the falling vessel through. It did so in the mistaken assumption that less damage would be caused to *The Ends of Invention* by letting the rogue vessel fall through than having it impact.

In the centre of a sudden maelstrom of air and cloud, in its own small hurricane, the *CAT* burst through from the thick air at the bottom of one pressure level and into the thin atmosphere at the top of the one below. A vortex of rag-clouded air blew out after it like an inverted explosion. Horza opened his eyes again and saw with relief the distant floor of the GSV's cavernous interior, and the climbing figures on the main fusion motors' monitor screens. He hit the engine throttles again, this time leaving the nose motor alone. The two main engines caught, shoving Horza back in his seat against the cloying hold of the restrainer fields. He pulled the nose of the diving craft up, watching the floor far below gradually disappear from view as it was replaced by the sight of another wall of opened bay doors. The doors were much larger than those of the Smallbays in the level they had just left, and the few craft Horza could see either nosing into or appearing out of the lit lengths of the huge hangars were full-size starships.

Horza watched the screen, piloting the *Clear Air Turbulence* exactly like an aircraft. They were travelling quickly along a vast corridor over a kilometre across, with the layer of clouds about fifteen hundred metres above them. Starships were moving slowly through the same space, a few on their own AG fields, most towed by light lifter tugs. Everything else was moving slowly and without a fuss; only the *CAT* disturbed the calm of the giant ship's interior, screaming through the air on twin swords of brilliant flame pulsing from white-hot plasma chambers. Another cliff-face of huge hangar doors faced them. Horza looked about him at the curve of main screen and pulled the *CAT* over on a long banking left turn, diving a little at the same time to head down an even broader canyon of space. They flashed over a slow-moving clipper being towed towards a distant open Mainbay, rocking the starship in their wake of superheated air. The wall of doors and opened entrances slanted towards them as Horza tightened the turn. Ahead, Horza could see what looked like a cloud of insects: hundreds of tiny black specks floating in the air.

Far beyond them, maybe five or six kilometres away, a thousand-metre square of blackness, bordered with a slowly flashing strip of subdued white light, was the exit from *The Ends of Invention*. It was a straight run.

Horza sighed and felt his whole body relax. Unless they were intercepted, they had done it. With a little luck now, they might even get away from the Orbital itself. He gunned the engines, heading for the inky square in the distance.

Wubslin suddenly sat forward, against the pull of acceleration, and punched some buttons. His repeater screen set in the console magnified the centre section of the main screen, showing the view ahead. 'They're people!' he shouted.

Horza frowned over at the man. 'What?'

'People! Those are people! They must be in AG harnesses! We're going to go right through them!'

Horza looked briefly over at Wubslin's repeater screen. It was true; the black cloud which almost filled the screen was made up of humans, flying slowly about in suits or ordinary clothes. There were thousands of them, Horza saw, less than a kilometre ahead, and closing quickly. Wubslin was staring at the screen, waving his hand at the people. 'Get out the way! Get out the way!' he was shouting.

Horza couldn't see a way round, over or beneath the mass of flying people. Whether they were playing some curious mass aerial game or were just enjoying themselves, they were too many, too close, too widespread. 'Shit!' Horza said. He got ready to cut the rear plasma motors before the *Clear Air Turbulence* went into the cloud of humans. With luck they might make it through before they had to relight them, and so not incinerate too many people.

'No!' Wubslin screamed. He threw the restraining straps off, leapt across towards Horza and dived at the controls. Horza tried to fend the bulky engineer off, but failed. The controls were wrenched from

246

his hands, and the view on the main screen tipped and swirled, pointing the nose of the speeding ship away from the black square of the GSV exit, away from the huge cloud of airborne people, and towards the cliff of brightly lit Mainbay entrances. Horza clouted Wubslin across the head with his arm, sending the man falling to the floor, stunned. He grabbed the controls back from the relaxing fingers of the engineer, but it was too late to turn away. Horza steadied and aimed. The *Clear Air Turbulence* darted for an open Mainbay; it flashed through the open entrance and swept over the skeleton of a starship being rebuilt in the bay, the light from the *CAT*'s motors starting fires, singeing hair, smouldering clothes and blinding unprotected eyes.

Horza saw Wubslin lying unconscious on the floor out of the corner of his eye, rocking gently as the *CAT* careered through the half-kilometre length of Mainbay. The doors to the next bay were open, and the next and the next. They were flying through a two-kilometre tunnel, racing over the repair and docking facilities of one of Evanauth's displaced shipbuilders. Horza didn't know what was at the far end, but he could see that before they got there they would have to fly over the top of a large spaceship which almost filled the third bay along. Horza vectored the fusion fire ahead so that they started to slow. Twin beams of fire flashed on either side of the main screen as the fusion power kicked forward. Wubslin's unrestrained body slid forward on the floor of the bridge, wedging under the console and his own seat. Horza lifted the *CAT*'s nose as the blunt snout of the parked spacecraft sitting in the bay ahead approached.

The *Clear Air Turbulence* zoomed towards the ceiling of the Mainbay, flashed between it and the top surface of the ship, then fell on the other side and, although still slowing, shot through the final Mainbay and into another corridor of free air space. It was too narrow. Horza dived the craft again, saw the floor coming up and fired the lasers. The *CAT* burst through a rising cloud of glowing wreckage, bumping and shaking, Wubslin's squat frame sliding out from under the console and floating back up towards the rear door of the bridge.

At first Horza thought they were out at last, but they weren't; they were in what the Culture called a General bay.

The *CAT* fell once more, then levelled out again. It was in a space which seemed even larger than the main interior of the GSV. It was flying through the bay they had stored the Megaship in: the same Megaship Horza had seen on the screen earlier being lifted out of the water by a hundred or so ancient Culture lifter craft.

Horza had time to look around. There was plenty of space, lots of room and time. The Megaship lay on the floor of the giant bay, looking for all the world like a small city sitting on a great slab of metal. The *Clear Air Turbulence* flew past the stern of the Megaship, past tunnels full of propeller blades tens of metres across, round the side of its rearmost outrigger, where beached pleasure craft waited for a return to water, over the towers and spires of its superstructure, then out over its bows. Horza looked forward. The doors, if they were doors, of the General bay faced him, two kilometres away. They were that same distance from top to bottom, and twice that across. Horza shrugged and checked the laser again. He was becoming, he realised, almost blasé about the whole thing. *What the hell?* he thought.

The lasers picked a hole in the wall of material ahead, punching a slowly widening gap which Horza aimed straight for. A vortex of swirling air was starting to form around the hole; as the *CAT* rushed closer, it was caught in a small horizontal cyclone of air and started to twist. Then it was through, and in space.

In a quickly dispersing bubble of air and crystals of ice, the craft burst from the body of the General Systems Vehicle, swooping into vacuum and star-washed darkness at last. Behind it, a force field slammed across the hole its passage had created in the doors of the General bay. Horza felt the plasma motors stutter as their supply of outside air disappeared, then the internal tanks took up the slack. He was about to cut them and slide gently into the start-up procedure for the craft's warp engines when the speakers in his headrest crackled.

'This is Evanauth port police. All right, you son of a bitch, just keep on that heading and slow right down. Evanauth port police to rogue craft: halt on that heading. A—'

Horza pulled on the controls, taking the *CAT* on a huge accelerating arc up over the stern of the GSV, flashing past the outside of the kilometre-square exit he had been heading for earlier. Wubslin, moaning now, bumped around the inside of the bridge as the *CAT* lifted its nose to head straight up, towards the maze of abandoned docks and gantries that was Evanauth port. As it went it turned, still twisting slightly from the spin it had picked up from the vortex of air bursting from the General bay. Horza let it twist, steadying it only as they approached the top of the loop, the port facilities coming up fast then sliding underneath as the craft levelled out.

'Rogue ship! This is your last warning!' the speakers blared. 'Stop now or we'll blow you out of the sky! God, he's heading for—' The transmission cut off. Horza grinned to himself. He was indeed heading for the gap between the underside of the port and the top of the GSV. The *Clear Air Turbulence* flashed through spaces between traveltube connections, elevator shafts, graving dock gantries, transit areas, arriving shuttle craft and crane towers. Horza guided the ship through the maze with the fusion motors still blazing at maximum boost, throwing the small craft through the few hundred metres of crowded space between the Orbital and the General Systems Vehicle. The rear radar *ping*ed, picking up following echoes.

Two towers, hanging under the Orbital like upside-down sky-scrapers, between which Horza was aiming the *CAT*, suddenly blossomed with light, scattering wreckage. Horza cringed in his seat as he corkscrewed the ship into the space between the two clouds of debris.

'Those were across the bows,' crackled the speakers again. 'The next ones will be straight up your ass, boy racer.' The *CAT* shot out over the dull grey plain of slanting material that was the start of the *Ends'* nose. Horza turned the *CAT* over and dived down, following the slope of the vast craft's bows. The rear radar signal stopped briefly, then reappeared.

He flipped the ship over again. Wubslin, his arms and legs waving weakly, was dumped onto the *CAT*'s bridge ceiling and stuck there like a fly while Horza did a section of an outside loop.

The ship was racing, powering away from the Orbital port area and the big GSV, heading for space. Horza remembered about Balveda's gear, and quickly reached over to the console, closing the vactube circuit from there. A screen showed that all the vactubes had been rotated. The rear screen showed something flame inside the twin plumes of plasma fire. The rear radar pinged insistently.

'Goodbye, *stupid*!' the voice in the headrest speakers said. Horza threw the ship to one side.

The rear screen went white, then black. The main screen pulsated with colours and broken lines. The speakers in Horza's helmet, as well as the speakers set into the seat, howled. Every instrument on the console flashed and wavered.

Horza thought for a second they had been hit, but the motors were still blasting, the main screen was starting to clear, and the other instruments were recovering, too. The radiation meters were bleeping and flashing. The rear screen stayed blank. A damage monitor indicated that the sensors had been knocked out by a very strong pulse of radiation.

Horza started to realise what had happened when the rear radar didn't start pinging again after it recovered. He threw back his head and laughed.

There had indeed been a bomb in Balveda's kitbag. Whether it had gone off because it was caught in the *CAT*'s plasma exhaust or because somebody – whoever had been trying to keep the ship on board the GSV in the first place – had detonated it remotely the instant the fleeing craft was far enough away from the *Ends* not to cause too much damage, Horza didn't know. Whatever; the explosion seemed to have caught the pursuing police vessels.

Laughing uproariously, Horza angled the *CAT* further away from the great circle of brilliantly lit Orbital, heading straight out towards the stars and readying the warp engines to take over from the plasma motors. Wubslin, back on the deck, one leg caught on the arm of his own chair, moaned distantly.

'Mother,' he said. 'Mother, say it's only a dream. . . .'

Horza laughed louder.

'You lunatic,' breathed Yalson, shaking her head. Her eyes were wide. 'That was the craziest thing I've ever seen you do. You're mad, Kraiklyn. I'm leaving. I resign as of now . . . Shit! I wish I'd gone with Jandraligeli, to Ghalssel. . . . You can just drop me off first place we get to.'

Horza sat down wearily in the seat at the head of the mess-room table. Yalson was at the far end, under the screen, which was switched into the bridge main screen. The *CAT* was proceeding under full warp, two hours out on its journey from Vavatch. There had been no further pursuit following the destruction of the police craft, and now the *CAT* was gradually coming round to the course Horza had set, into the war zone, towards the edge of the Glittercliff, towards Schar's World.

Dorolow and Aviger were sitting, plainly still shaken, to one side of Yalson. The woman and the elderly man were both staring at Horza as though he was pointing a gun at them. Their mouths were open, their eyes were glazed. On the other side of Yalson the slack form of Perosteck Balveda was leaning forward, head down, her body pulling against the restraining straps of the seat.

The mess room was chaotic. The *CAT* hadn't been readied for violent manoeuvring, and nothing had been stowed away. Plates and containers, a couple of shoes, a glove, some half-unravelled tapes and spools and various other bits and pieces now lay strewn about the floor of the mess. Yalson had been hit by something, and a small trickle of blood had dried on her forehead. Horza hadn't let anybody move, apart from brief visits to the heads, for the last two hours; he'd told everybody to stay where they were over the ship PA while the *CAT* headed away from Vavatch on a twisting, erratic course. He had kept the plasma motors and laser warm and ready, but no further pursuit came. Now he reckoned they were safe and far enough away to warp straight.

He had left Wubslin on the bridge, nursing the battered and abused systems of the *Clear Air Turbulence* as best he could. The engineer had apologised for grabbing at the controls and had become very subdued, not meeting Horza's eyes but tidying up one or two bits of loose debris on the bridge and stuffing some of the loose wires back under the console. Horza told Wubslin he had nearly killed them all, but on the other hand so had he, so they would forget it this time; they'd escaped intact. Wubslin nodded and said he didn't know how; he couldn't believe the ship was virtually undamaged. Wubslin wasn't undamaged; he had bruises everywhere.

'I'm afraid,' Horza said to Yalson once he had sat down and put his feet up, 'our first port of call is rather bleak and underpopulated. I'm not sure you'll want to be dropped off there.'

Yalson put the heavy stun pistol down onto the table surface. 'And just where the hell are we going? What's going *on*, Kraiklyn? What was all that craziness back on the GSV? What's she doing here? Why is the Culture involved?' Yalson nodded at Balveda during this speech, and Horza kept looking at the unconscious Culture agent when Yalson stopped, waiting for an answer. Aviger and Dorolow were looking at him expectantly, too.

Before Horza could answer, the small drone appeared from the corridor leading from the accommodation section. It floated in, looked round the mess room, then sat itself bodily on the table in the middle. 'Did I hear something about it being explanation time?' it said. It was facing Horza.

Horza looked away from Balveda, to Aviger and Dorolow, then to Yalson and the drone. 'Well, you might as well all know that we are now heading for a place called Schar's World. It's a Planet of the Dead.'

Yalson looked puzzled. Aviger said, 'I've heard of those. But we won't be allowed in.'

'This is getting worse,' the drone said. 'If I were you, Captain Kraiklyn, I would turn back to *The Ends of Invention* and surrender yourself there. I'm sure you'd get a fair trial.'

Horza ignored the machine. He sighed, looking round at the mess, stretched his legs and yawned. 'I'm sorry you're all being taken, perhaps against your will, but I've got to get there, and I can't afford to stop anywhere to let you off. You've all got to come.'

'Oh we do, do we?' said the small drone.

'Yes,' Horza said, looking at it, 'I'm afraid so.'

'But we won't be able to get anywhere near this place,' Aviger protested. 'They don't let anybody in. There's some sort of zone around them they don't let people into.'

'We'll see about that when we get there.' Horza smiled.

'You're not answering my questions,' Yalson said. She looked at Balveda again, then down at the gun lying on the table. 'I've been zapping this poor bitch every time she flicks an eyelid, and I want to know why I've been doing it.'

'It'll take a while to explain it all, but what it boils down to is there's something on Schar's World which both the Culture and the Idirans want. I have . . . a contract, a commission from the Idirans, to get there and find this thing.'

'You really are a paranoid,' the drone said incredulously. It rose off the table and turned round to look at the others. 'He really is a lunatic!'

'The Idirans are hiring *us* – *you* – to go after something?' Yalson's voice was full of disbelief. Horza looked at her and smiled.

'You mean this woman', Dorolow said, pointing at Balveda, 'was sent by the Culture to join us, infiltrate. . . . Are you serious?'

'I'm serious. Balveda was looking for me. Also for Horza Gobuchul. She wanted to get to Schar's World, or to stop us from getting there.' Horza looked at Aviger. 'There *was* a bomb in amongst her gear, by the way; it went off just after I rotated it out the tubes. It blew the police ships away. We all got a blast of radiation, but nothing lethal.'

'And what about Horza?' Yalson said, looking grimly at him. 'Was that just some trick, or did you really meet him?'

'He is alive, Yalson, and as safe as any of us.'

Wubslin appeared through the door from the bridge, still with an apologetic look on his face. He nodded at Horza and sat down near by. 'All looking fine, Kraiklyn.'

'Good,' Horza said. 'I was just explaining to everybody else about our journey to Schar's World.'

'Oh,' Wubslin said. 'Yeah.' He shrugged at the others.

252

'Kraiklyn,' Yalson said, leaning forward on the table and looking intently at Horza, 'you just about got us all killed fuck knows how many times back there. You probably *did* kill quite a few people during those . . . in-door aerobatics. You've saddled us with some secret agent from the Culture. You're practically kidnapping us to take us towards a planet in the middle of a war zone where nobody's even allowed in, to look for *something* both sides want enough to . . . Well, if the Idirans are hiring a decimated bunch of second-rate mercenaries, they must be pretty desperate; and if the Culture really was behind the attempt to keep us in that bay, they must be scared stiff to risk violating the neutrality of the *Ends* and breaking some of their precious rules of war.

'You may think you know what's going on and think the risk is worth it, but I don't, and I don't like this feeling of being kept in the dark at all, either. Your track record recently's been crap; let's face it. Risk your own life if you want to, but you don't have any right to risk ours, too. Not any more. Maybe we don't all want to side with the Idirans, but even if we did prefer them to the Culture, none of us signed up to start fighting in the middle of the war. Shit, Kraiklyn, we're neither . . . equipped nor *trained* well enough to go up against those guys.'

'I know all that,' Horza said. 'But we shouldn't be encountering any battle forces. The Quiet Barrier round Schar's World extends far enough out so that it's impossible to watch it all. We go in from a randomly picked direction, and by the time we're spotted, there's nothing anybody could do about it, no matter what sort of ship they have. A Main Battle Fleet couldn't keep us out. When we leave it'll be the same.'

'What you're trying to say is,' Yalson said, sitting back in her seat, '"Easy in, easy out".'

'Maybe I am,' laughed Horza.

'Hey,' Wubslin said suddenly, looking at his terminal screen, which he had just taken from his pocket. 'It's nearly time!' He got up and disappeared through the doors leading to the bridge. In a few seconds the screen in the mess changed, the view swivelling round until it showed Vavatch. The great Orbital hung in space, dark and brilliant, full of night and day, blue and white and black. They all looked up at the screen.

Wubslin came back in and sat in his seat again. Horza felt tired. His body wanted rest, and lots of it. His brain was still buzzing from the concentration and the amount of adrenalin it had required to pilot the

CAT through and out of *The Ends of Invention*, but he couldn't rest yet. He couldn't decide what was the best thing to do. Should he tell them who he was, tell them the truth, that he was a Changer, that he had killed Kraiklyn? How loyal were any of them to the leader they didn't yet know was dead? Yalson the most, perhaps; but surely she would be glad to know that *he* was alive. . . . Yet she was the one who had said that perhaps they weren't all on the Idirans' side. . . . She had never shown any sympathy for the Culture before when he had known her, but perhaps she had changed her mind.

He could even Change back; there was a fairly long journey now during which it shouldn't be beyond him, perhaps with the help of Wubslin, to change the fidelities in the *CAT*'s computer. But should he tell them – should he let them know? And Balveda: what was he going to do with her? He had had some idea of using her to bargain with the Culture, but it looked as though they had escaped now, and next stop was Schar's World, where she would at best be a liability. He ought to kill her now, but he knew, first of all, that that might not go down well with the others, especially Yalson. He also knew, although he didn't like to admit it, that he would find it personally painful to kill the Culture agent. They were enemies, they had both been very close to death and the other had done little or nothing to intervene, but actually to kill her would be very difficult.

Or maybe he only wanted to pretend that he would find it very difficult; maybe it would be no bother at all, and the sort of bogus camaraderie of doing the same job, though on different sides, was just that: a fake. He opened his mouth to ask Yalson to stun the Culture agent again.

'Now,' Wubslin said.

With that, Vavatch Orbital started to disintegrate.

The view of it on the mess-room screen was a compensated hyperspace version, so that, although they were already outside the Vavatch system, they were watching it virtually in real time. Right at the appointed hour the unseen, unnamed, very much still militarised General Systems Vehicle which was somewhere in the vicinity of the Vavatch planetary system started its bombardment. It was almost certainly an Ocean class GSV, the same one which had sent the message that they had all watched some days ago on the mess screen, heading in towards Vavatch. That would make the warcraft very much smaller than the behemoth of *The Ends of Invention*, which was – for war purposes – obsolete. One Ocean class could fit inside either of the *Ends'* General bays, but while the larger craft – by that time an hour out from the Orbital – was full of people, the Ocean class would be packed with other warships, and weaponry.

Gridfire struck the Orbital. Horza paused and watched the screen as it lit up suddenly, flashing once over its whole surface until the sensors coped with the sudden increase in brilliance and compensated. For some reason Horza had thought the Culture would just splash the gridfire all over the massive Orbital and then spatter the remains with CAM, but they didn't do that; instead a single narrow line of blinding white light appeared right across the breadth of the day side of the Orbital, a thin fiery blade of silent destruction which was instantly surrounded by the duller but still perfectly white cover of clouds. That line of light was part of the grid itself, the fabric of pure energy which lay underneath the entire universe, separating this one from the slightly younger, slightly smaller antimatter universe beneath. The Culture, like the Idirans, could now partially control that awesome power, at least sufficiently to use it for the purposes of destruction. A line of that energy, plucked from nowhere and sliced across the face of the three-dimensional universe, was down there: on and inside the Orbital, boiling the Circlesea, melting the two thousand kilometres of transparent wall, annihilating the base material itself, straight across its thirty-five-thousand-kilometre breadth.

Vavatch, that fourteen-million-kilometre hoop, was starting to uncoil. A chain, it had been cut.

There was nothing left now to hold it together; its own spin, the source of both its day–night cycle and its artificial gravity, was now the very force tearing it all apart. At about one hundred and thirty kilometres per second, Vavatch was throwing itself into outer space, unwinding like a released spring.

The livid line of fire appeared again, and again, and again, working its way methodically round the Orbital from where the original burst had struck, neatly parcelling the entire Orbital into squares, thirty-five thousand kilometres to a side, each containing a sandwich of trillions upon trillions of tonnes of ultradense base material, water, land and air.

Vavatch was turning white. First the gridfire seared the water into a border of clouds; then the outrushing air, spilling from each immense flat square like heavy fumes off a table, turned its load of water vapour to ice. The ocean itself, no longer held by the spin force, was shifting, spilling with infinite slowness over one edge of every plate of ruptured base material, becoming ice and swirling away into space.

255

The precise, brilliant line of fire marched on, going back in reverse-spin direction, neatly dissecting the still curved, still spinning sections of the Orbital with its sudden, lethal flashes of light – light from outside the normal fabric of reality.

Horza remembered what Jandraligeli had called it, back when Lenipobra had been enthusing about the destruction.

'The weaponry of the end of the universe,' the Mondlidician had said. Horza watched the screen and knew what the man had meant.

It was all going. All of it. The wreck of the *Olmedreca*, the tabular berg it had collided with, the wreck of the *CAT*'s shuttle, Mipp's body, Lenipobra's, whatever was left of Fwi-Song's corpse, Mr First's . . . the living bodies of the other Eaters – if they hadn't been rescued, or had still refused . . . the Damage game arena, the docks and Kraiklyn's dead body, the hovercraft . . . animals and fishes, birds, germs, all of it: everything flash-burned or flash-frozen, suddenly weightless, spinning into space, going, dying.

The relentless line of fire completed its circuit of the Orbital, back almost to where it had started. The Orbital was now a rosette of white flat squares backing slowly away from each other towards the stars: four hundred separate slabs of quickly freezing water, silt, land and base material, angling out above or underneath the plane of the system's planets like flat square worlds themselves.

There was a moment of grace then, as Vavatch died in solitary, blazing splendour. Then at its dark centre, another blazing star patch rose, bursting white as the Hub was struck with the same terrible energy which had smashed the world itself.

Like a target, then, Vavatch blazed.

Just as Horza thought that the Culture would be content with that, the screen lit up once more. Every one of those flat cards, and the Hub, of the exploded Orbital blazed once with an icy, sparkling brilliance as though a million tiny white stars were shining through each shattered piece.

The light faded, and those four hundred expanses of flat worlds with their centre Hub were gone, replaced by a grid of diced shapes, each exploding away from the others as well as from the rest of the disintegrating Orbital.

Those pieces flashed, too, bursting slowly with a billion pinpricks of light which, when they faded, left debris almost too small to make out.

Vavatch was now a swollen and spiralled disc of flashing, glittering splinters, expanding very slowly against the distant stars like a ring of bright dust. The glinting, sparkling centre made it look like some huge, lidless and unblinking eye.

The screen flashed one final time. No single points of light could be made out this time. It was as though the whole now vague but bloated image of the shattered circular world glowed with some internal heat, making a torus-shaped cloud out of it, a halo of white light with a fading iris at its centre. Then the show was over, and only the sun lit up the slowly blooming nimbus of the annihilated world.

On other wavelengths there would probably be a lot still to see, but the mess-room screen was on normal light. Only the Minds, only the starships, would see the whole destruction perfectly; only they would be able to appreciate it for all that it had to offer. Of the entire range of the electromagnetic spectrum, the unaided human eye could see little more than one per cent: a single octave of radiation out of an immense long keyboard of tones. The sensors on a starship would see everything, right across that spectrum, in far greater detail and at a much slower apparent speed. The whole display that was the Orbital's destruction was, for all its humanly perceivable grandeur, quite wasted on the animal eye. A spectacle for the machines, thought Horza; that was all it was. A sideshow for the damn machines.

'Chicel . . .' Dorolow said. Wubslin exhaled loudly and shook his head. Yalson turned and looked at Horza. Aviger stayed with his head turned to the screen.

'Amazing what one can accomplish when one puts one's mind to it, eh . . . Horza?'

At first, stupidly, he thought that Yalson had said it, but of course it was Balveda.

She brought her head up slowly. Her deep, dark eyes were open; she looked groggy, and her body still sagged against the webbing of the seat straps. The voice had been clear and steady, though.

Horza saw Yalson reaching for the stun gun on the table. She reached out and brought the gun closer to her but left it lying on the table. She was looking suspiciously at the Culture agent. Aviger and Dorolow and Wubslin were staring at her, too.

'Are the batteries on that stun gun running down?' Wubslin said. Yalson was still looking at Balveda, her eyes narrowed.

'You're a little confused, Gravant, or whoever you are,' Yalson said. 'That's Kraiklyn.'

Balveda smiled at Horza. He left his face blank. He didn't know what to do. He was exhausted, worn out. It was too much of an effort. Let what was going to happen, happen. He'd had enough of deciding.

'Well,' Balveda said to him, 'are you going to tell them, or shall I?'

He said nothing. He watched Balveda's face. The woman drew a deep breath and said, 'Oh all right, I'll tell them.' She turned to Yalson. 'His name is Bora Horza Gobuchul, and he's impersonating Kraiklyn. Horza's a Changer from Heibohre and he works for the Idirans. Has done for the last six years. He's Changed to *become* Kraiklyn. I imagine your real leader is dead. Horza probably killed him, or at least left him somewhere in or around Evanauth.

'I'm very sorry.' She looked around the others, including the small drone. 'But unless I'm much mistaken we're all taking a little trip to a place called Schar's World. Well, you are, anyway. I have a feeling my own journey might be a little shorter – and infinitely longer.' Balveda smiled ironically at Horza.

'Two?' the drone on the table said to nobody in particular. 'I'm stuck in a leaky museum-piece with *two* paranoid lunatics?'

'You're not,' Yalson was saying, ignoring the machine and gazing at Horza. 'You're not, are you? She's lying.'

Wubslin turned and looked at him. Aviger and Dorolow exchanged glances. Horza sighed and took his feet off the table, sitting a little straighter in his seat. He leaned forward and put his elbows on the table, his chin in his hands. He was watching, feeling, trying to gauge the mood of the various people in the room. He was aware of their distances, the tension in their bodies, and how much time he would need to get to the plasma pistol on his right hip. He raised his head and looked at all of them, settling his gaze on Yalson. 'Yes,' he said, 'I am.'

Silence filled the mess room. Horza waited for a reaction. Instead the sound of a door opening came from down the corridor through the accommodation section. They all looked at the doorway.

Neisin appeared, wearing only a pair of grubby, stained shorts. His hair was sticking out in every direction, his eyes were slits, his skin was patchy with dry and moist areas, and his face was very pale. A smell of drink gradually worked its way through the mess. He looked round the room, yawned, nodded at them, pointed vaguely at some of the still uncleared debris lying around and said, 'This place is nearly in as big a mess as my cabin. You'd think we'd been manoeuvring or something. Sorry. Thought it was time to eat. Think I'll go back to bed.' He yawned again and left. The door closed.

Balveda was laughing quietly. Horza could see some tears in her eyes. The others just looked confused. The drone said:

'Well, Mr Observant there is probably the only person on this mobile asylum with an untroubled mind at the moment.' The machine turned on the table, scratching the surface as it faced Horza. 'Are you really claiming to be one of these fabled human impersonators?' it asked with a sneer in its voice.

Horza looked down the table, then into Yalson's wary, frowning eyes. 'That's what I am.'

'They're extinct,' Aviger said, shaking his head.

'They're not extinct,' Balveda told him, her thin, finely moulded head turning briefly to the old man. 'But they're part of the Idiran sphere now; absorbed. Some of them always did support the Idirans, the rest either left or decided they might as well throw in their lot with them. Horza's one of the first lot. Can't stand the Culture. He's taking you all to Schar's World to kidnap a shipwrecked Mind for his Idiran masters. A Culture Mind. So that the galaxy will be free from human interference and the Idirans can have a free run at—'

'All right, Balveda,' Horza said. She shrugged.

'*You're* Horza,' Yalson said, pointing at him. He nodded. She shook her head. 'I don't believe it. I'm starting to come round to the drone's way of thinking; you're both crazy. You took a nasty blow to the head, Kraiklyn, and you, lady' – she looked at Balveda – 'have had your brains scrambled by this thing.' Yalson picked up the stun gun and then put it down again.

'I don't know,' Wubslin said, scratching his head and looking at Horza as though he was some sort of exhibit. 'I thought the captain seemed a bit strange. I couldn't imagine him doing what he just did in the GSV.'

'What did you do, Horza?' Balveda said. 'I seem to have missed something. How *did* you get away?'

'I flew out, Balveda. Used the fusion motors and the laser and blasted out.'

'Really?' Balveda laughed again, throwing her head back. She went on laughing, but her laughter was a little too loud, and the tears were coming too quickly to her eyes. 'Ho ho. Well, I am impressed. I thought we had you.'

'When did you find out?' he asked her quietly. She sniffed and tried to wipe her nose on her shoulder.

'What? That you weren't Kraiklyn?' She played her tongue along her top lip. 'Oh, just before you came aboard. We had a microdrone pretending to be a fly. It was programmed to land on anybody approaching the ship while it was in the Smallbay and take a skin cell or hair or something away with it. We identified you from your own chromosomes. There was another agent outside; he must have used his effector on the bay controls when he monitored you starting to get ready to leave. I was supposed to . . . do whatever I could if you appeared. Kill you, capture you, disable the ship: anything. But they didn't tell me until too late. They knew somebody might overhear if they warned me, but they must have started to get worried.'

'That was the noise you heard from her kitbag,' Horza told Yalson, 'just before I zapped her.' He looked back at Balveda. 'I got rid of the gear, by the way, Balveda. Dumped it all through the vactubes. Your bomb went off.'

Balveda seemed to sag a little further in her seat. He guessed that she had been hoping her gear was on board. At the very least she might have been hoping the bomb had still to be triggered and that, while she would die, she would not die in vain, or alone.

'Oh yes,' she said, looking down at the table, 'the vactubes.'

'What about Kraiklyn?' Yalson asked.

'He's dead,' Horza said. 'I killed him.'

'Oh well,' Yalson tutted, and rapped her fingers on the table surface. 'That's that. I don't know if you two really are mad or if you're telling the truth; both possibilities are pretty awful.' She looked from Balveda to Horza, raising her eyebrows at the man and saying, 'By the way, if you really are Horza, it's a lot less pleasant to see you back than I thought it was going to be.'

'I'm sorry,' he told her. She turned her head away from him.

'I still think the best thing to do is to head back for *The Ends of Invention* and lay the whole thing before the authorities.' The drone rose fractionally above the surface of the table and looked round at them all. Horza leant forward and tapped its casing. It faced him.

'Machine,' he said, 'we're going to Schar's World. If you want to go back to the GSV I'll gladly put you in a vactube and let you make your own way back. But you mention returning and getting a fair trial one more time and I'm going to blast your synthetic fucking brains out, understand?'

'How *dare* you speak to me like that!' the drone bellowed. 'I'll have you know I am an Accredited Free Construct, certified sentient under the Free Will Acts by the Greater Vavatch United Moral Standards Administration and with full citizenship of the Vavatch Heterocracy. I am near to paying off my Incurred Generation Debt, when I'll be free to do *exactly* what I like, and have already been accepted for a degree course in applied paratheology at the University of—'

'Will you shut your goddamn . . . speaker and *listen?*' Horza shouted, breaking into the machine's breathless monologue. 'We're

260

not on Vavatch, and I don't care how god-damn smart you are, or how many qualifications you've got. You're on this ship and you do as I say. You want to get off? Get off now and float back to whatever's left of your precious fucking Orbital. Stay, and you obey orders. Or get junked.'

'Those are my choices?'

'Yes. Use some of your accredited free will and decide right now.'

'I . . .' The drone rose from the table, then sank again. 'Hmm,' it said. 'Very well. I shall stay.'

'And obey all orders.'

'And obey all orders . . .'

'Good, at—'

'. . . within reason.'

'Machine,' Horza said, reaching for the plasma pistol.

'Oh good grief, man!' the drone exclaimed. 'What do you want? A *robot*?' Its voice sneered. 'I don't have an Off button on my reasoning functions; I can't choose *not* to have free will. I could quite easily swear to obey all orders regardless of the consequences; I could vow to sacrifice my life for you if you asked me to; but I'd be lying, so that I could live.

'I swear to be as obedient and faithful as any of your human crew . . . in fact as the *most* obedient and faithful of them. For pity's sake, man, in the name of all reason, what more can you ask?'

Sneaky bastard. Horza thought. 'Well,' he said, 'I suppose that will just have to do. Now, can—'

'But I am obliged to serve immediate notice on you that under the terms of my Retrospective Construction Agreement, my Incurred Generation Debt Loan Agreement and my Employment Contract, your forcible removal of myself from my place of work makes you liable for the servicing of said debt until my return, as well as risking civil and criminal proceedings—'

'Fucking hell, drone,' Yalson interrupted. 'Sure it wasn't law you were going to study?'

'I take full responsibility, machine,' Horza told it. 'Now, *shut*—'

'Well, I hope you're properly insured,' the drone muttered.

'—*up*!'

'Horza?' Balveda said.

'Yes, Perosteck?' He turned to her with a sense of relief. Her eyes were glittering. She licked her top lip again, then looked back at the surface of the table, her head down. 'What about me?'

'Well,' he said slowly, 'it did cross my mind to blow you out a

261

vactube. . . .' He saw her tense. Yalson, too: she turned in her seat to face him, clenching her fists and opening her mouth. Horza went on, '. . . But you may be of some use yet, and . . . oh, call it sentiment.' He smiled. 'You'll have to behave, of course.'

Balveda looked up at him. There was hope in her eyes, but also the piteousness of those who don't want to hope too soon. 'You mean that, I hope,' she said quietly. Horza nodded.

'I mean it. I couldn't possibly get rid of you anyway, before I find out how the hell you got off *The Hand of God.*'

Balveda relaxed, breathing deeply. When she laughed it was softly. Yalson was looking with a jaundiced expression at Horza and still rapping her fingers on the table. 'Yalson,' Horza said, 'I'd like you and Dorolow to take Balveda and . . . strip her. Take her suit and everything else off.' He was aware of them all looking at him. Balveda was arching her eyebrows with faked shock. He went on, 'I want you to take the surgery equipment and run every sort of test you can on her once she's naked to make sure she hasn't got any skin pouches, implants or prosthetics; use the ultrasound and the X-ray gear and the NMR and anything else we've got. Once you've done that you can find something for her to wear. Put her suit in a vactube and dump it. Also any jewellery or other personal possessions of any sort or size, regardless of how innocent they may look.'

'You want her washed and anointed, put in a white robe and placed on a stone altar, too?' Yalson said acidly. Horza shook his head.

'I want her clean of anything, anything at all that could be used as a weapon or that could turn into one. The Culture's latest gadgetry for the Special Circumstancers includes things called memoryforms; they might looked like a badge, or a medallion . . .' He smiled at Balveda, who nodded back wryly, '. . . or anything else. But do a certain something to them – touch them in the right place, make them wet, speak a certain word – and they become a communicator, a gun or a bomb. I don't want to risk there being anything more dangerous than Ms Balveda herself on board.'

'What about when we get to Schar's World?' Balveda said.

'We'll give you some warm clothes. If you wrap up well, you'll be all right. No suit, no weapons.'

'And the rest of us?' asked Aviger. 'What are we supposed to do when you get to this place? Assuming they'll let you in, which I doubt.'

'I'm not sure yet,' Horza said truthfully. 'Maybe you'll have to come with me. I'll have to see what I can do about the ship's fidelities.

Possibly you'll all be able to stay on board; perhaps you'll all have to hit dirt with me. However, there are some other Changers there, people like myself but not working for the Idirans. They should be able to look after you if I'm to be gone for any amount of time. Of course,' he said, looking at Yalson, 'if any of you want to come along with me, I'm sure that we can treat this as a normal operation in terms of share-outs and so forth. Once I'm finished with the *CAT*, those of you who so desire may want to take it over for yourselves, run it any way you like; sell it if you want; it's up to you. At any rate, you'll all be free to do as you wish, once I've accomplished my mission on Schar's World – or done my best to, at least.'

Yalson had been looking at him, but now she turned away, shaking her head. Wubslin was looking at the deck. Aviger and Dorolow stared at each other. The drone was silent.

'Now,' Horza said, rising stiffly, 'Yalson and Dorolow, if you wouldn't mind seeing to Ms Balveda . . .' With a show of some reluctance, Yalson sighed and got up. Dorolow started to undo some of the restraining straps around the Culture agent's body. 'And do be *very* careful with her,' Horza continued. 'Keep one person well away from her with the gun pointed in her direction the whole time, while the other does the work.'

Yalson muttered something under her breath and leaned to pick up the stun gun from the table. Horza turned to Aviger. 'I think somebody should tell Neisin about all the excitement he's missed, don't you?' Aviger hesitated, then nodded.

'Yes, Kraik—' He stopped, spluttered, then said no more. He got up from his seat and went quickly down the corridor towards the cabins.

'I think I'll open up the forward compartments and have a look at the laser, Kraiklyn, if that's all right with you,' Wubslin said. 'Oh, I mean Horza.' The engineer stood, frowning and scratching his head. Horza nodded. Wubslin found a clean undamaged beaker and took a cold drink from the dispenser, then went down the corridor through the accommodation section.

Dorolow and Yalson had freed Balveda. The tall, pale-skinned Culture woman stretched, closing her eyes and arching her neck. She ran a hand through her short red hair. Dorolow watched warily. Yalson held the stun gun. Balveda flexed her shoulders, then indicated she was ready.

'Right,' Yalson said, waving Balveda forward with the gun. 'We'll do this in my cabin.'

Horza stood up to let the three women by. As Balveda passed, her long, easy stride unencumbered by the light suit, he said, 'How *did* you get off *The Hand of God*, Balveda?'

She stopped and said, 'I killed the guard and then sat and waited, Horza. The GCU managed to take the cruiser intact. Eventually some nice soldier drones came and rescued me.' She shrugged.

'Unarmed, you killed an Idiran in full battle armour and toting a laser?' Horza said sceptically. Balveda shrugged again.

'Horza, I didn't say it was easy.'

'What about Xoralundra?' Horza asked through a grin.

'Your old Idiran friend? Must have escaped. A few of them did. At any rate, he wasn't among the dead or captured.'

Horza nodded and waved her by. Followed by Yalson and Dorolow, Perosteck Balveda went down the corridor to Yalson's cabin. Horza looked at the drone sitting on the table.

'Think you can make yourself useful, machine?'

'I suppose, as you obviously intend to keep us all here and take us to this unattractive-sounding rockball on the edge of nowhere, I might as well do what I can to make the journey as safe as possible. I'll help with the vessel's maintenance, if you like. I would prefer, though, if you called me by my name, and not just by that word you manage to make sound like an expletive: "machine". I am *called* Unaha-Closp. Is it asking too much for you to address me as such?'

'Why, certainly not, Unaha-Closp,' Horza said, trying to look and sound sufficiently bogus in his abjection. 'I shall most assuredly ensure that I call you that in future.'

'It might,' the drone said, rising from the table to the level of Horza's eyes, 'seem amusing to you, but it matters to me. I am not just a computer, I am a drone. I am conscious and I have an individual identity. Therefore I have a name.'

'I told you I'd use it,' Horza said.

'Thank you. I shall go and see if your engineer needs any help inspecting the laser housing.' It floated to the door. Horza watched it go.

He was alone. He sat down and looked at the screen, down at the far end of the mess. The debris that had been Vavatch glowed with a barren glare; that vast cloud of matter was still visible. But it was cooling, dead and spinning away; becoming less real, more ghostly, less substantial all the time.

He sat back and closed his eyes. He would wait a while before going to sleep. He wanted to give the others time to think about what they

264

had found out. They would be easier to read then; he would know if he was safe for the moment or whether he would have to watch them all. He also wanted to wait until Yalson and Dorolow had finished with Balveda. The Culture agent might be biding her time, now she thought she had longer to live, but she might still try something. He wanted to be awake in case she did. He still hadn't decided whether to kill her now or not, but at least he, too, now had time to think.

The *Clear Air Turbulence* completed its last programmed course correction, swinging its nose towards the Glittercliff face; not in the precise direction of the Schar's World star, but onto the general bearing.

Behind it, still expanding, still radiating, still slowly dissolving in the system to which it had given its name, the unnumbered twinkling fragments of the Orbital called Vavatch blew out towards the stars, drifting on a stellar wind that rang and swirled with the fury of the world's destruction.

Horza sat alone in the mess room a little longer, watching the remnants dissipate.

Light against the darkness, a fat torus of nothing, just debris. An entire world just wiped out. Not merely destroyed – the very first cut of the Grid energies would have been enough to do that – but obliterated, taken carefully, precisely, artistically apart; annihilation made into an aesthetic experience. The arrogant grace of it, the absolute-zero coldness of that sophisticated viciousness . . . it impressed almost as much as it appalled. Even he would admit to a certain reluctant admiration.

The Culture had not wasted its lesson to the Idirans and the rest of the galactic community. It had turned even that ghastly waste of effort and skill into a thing of beauty. . . . But it was a message it would regret, Horza thought, as the hyper-light sped and the ordinary light crawled through the galaxy.

This was what the Culture offered, this was its signal, its advertisement, its legacy: chaos from order, destruction from construction, death from life.

Vavatch would be more than its own monument; it would commemorate, too, the final, grisly manifestation of the Culture's lethal idealism, the overdue acknowledgement that not only was it no better than any other society, it was much, much worse.

They sought to take the unfairness out of existence, to remove the mistakes in the transmitted message of life which gave it any point or advancement (a memory of darkness swept through him, and he shivered). . . . But theirs was the ultimate mistake, the final error, and it would be their undoing.

Horza considered going to the bridge to switch the view on the screen to real space, and so see the Orbital intact again, as it had been a few weeks before when the real light the *CAT* was now travelling through had left the place. But he shook his head slowly, though there was nobody there to see, and watched the quiet screen at the far end of the disordered and deserted room instead.

State of play: two

The yacht dropped anchor within a wooded bay. The water was clear, and ten metres beneath the sparkling waves the sandy floor of the anchorage was visible. Tall everblues were spread in a rough crescent around the small inlet, their dusty-looking roots sometimes visible on the ochre sandstone they clung to. There were some small cliffs of the same rock, sprinkled with bright flowers and overlooking golden beaches. The white yacht, its long reflection flickering on the water like a silent flame, feathered its tall sails and swung slowly into the faint breeze coming through one arm of the woods and over the cupped bay.

People took small canoes or dinghies to the shore, or jumped into the warm water and swam. Some of the ceerevells, which had escorted the yacht on its voyage from its home port, stayed to play in the bay; their long red bodies slipped through the water under and around the vessel's hull, and their snorting breath echoed from the low cliffs facing the water. Sometimes they nudged the boats heading for the shore, and a few of the swimmers played with the sleek animals, diving to swim with them, touch them, hold onto them.

The shouts of the people in the boats drew gradually further away. They beached the small craft and disappeared into the woods, going to explore the uninhabited island. The small waves of the inland sea lapped at the disturbed sand.

Fal 'Ngeestra sighed and, after walking once around the yacht, sat down near the stern on a padded seat. She played absently with one of the ropes tied between the stanchions, rubbing it with her hand. The boy who had been talking to her during the morning, when the yacht was sailing slowly out from the mainland towards the islands, saw her sitting there, and came to talk to her.

'Aren't you going to look at the island?' he said. He was very thin and light looking. His skin was a deep, almost golden yellow. There was a sheen about it which made Fal think of a hologram because it looked somehow deeper than his skinny arms and legs were thick.

269

'I don't feel like it,' Fal said. She hadn't wanted the boy to talk to her earlier and she didn't want to talk to him now. She was sorry she'd agreed to come on the cruise.

'Why not?' the boy said. She couldn't remember his name. She hadn't been paying attention when he started talking to her, and she wasn't even sure he had told her his name, though she assumed he had.

'I just don't.' She shrugged. She wasn't looking at him.

'Oh,' he said. He was silent for a while. She was aware of the sunlight reflecting from his body, but she still didn't turn to look at him. She watched the distant trees, the waves, the ruddy bodies of the ceerevells hump-backing on the surface of the water as they rose to vent and then dive again. The boy said, 'I know how you feel.'

'Do you?' she said, and turned to look at him. He looked a little surprised. He nodded.

'You're fed up, aren't you?'

'Maybe,' she said, looking away again. 'A little bit.'

'Why does that old drone follow you about everywhere?'

She darted a glance at the boy. Jase was below decks just then, getting a drink for her. It had come aboard at the port with her and had stayed not too far away all the time – the hovering, protective way it usually did. She shrugged again and watched a flock of birds rise from the interior of the island. They called and dipped and wheeled in the air. 'It looks after me,' she said. She stared at her hands, watching the sunlight reflect from her nails.

'Do you need looking after?'

'No.'

'Then why does it look after you?'

'I don't know.'

'You're very mysterious, you know,' he said. She wasn't looking, but she thought she heard a smile in his voice. She shrugged soundlessly. 'You're like that island,' he said. 'You're strange and mysterious like it is.'

Fal snorted and tried to look scathing; then she saw Jase appearing from a doorway, carrying a glass. She got up quickly, followed by the boy, walked down the deck, and met the old drone, taking the glass from it and smiling at it gratefully. She buried her face in the container and sipped at the drink, looking out through the glass at the boy.

'Well, hello, young man,' Jase said. 'Aren't you going to have a look at the island?' Fal wanted to kick the machine because of its hearty voice and the way it had said almost what the boy had said to her.

270

'I might,' the boy said, looking at her.

'You should,' Jase said, starting to float towards the stern. The old machine extended a curved field, like a shadow without something to cast it, out from its casing and round the boy's shoulders. 'By the way, I couldn't help overhearing you when you were talking earlier,' it said, gently guiding the boy down the deck. His golden head turned over his shoulder to look at Fal, who was still drinking her drink very slowly, and just starting to follow Jase and the boy, a couple of paces behind. The boy looked away from her and towards the drone at his side, which was saying, 'You were talking about not getting into Contact. . . .'

'That's right.' The boy's voice was suddenly defensive. 'I was talking about that, so?' Fal continued to walk behind the drone and the boy. She smacked her lips. Ice in the glass clinked.

'You sounded bitter,' Jase said.

'I'm *not* bitter,' the boy said quickly. 'I just think it isn't fair, that's all.'

'That you weren't picked?' Jase asked. They were approaching the seats round the stern where Fal had sat a few minutes earlier.

'Well, yes. It's all I've ever wanted, and I think they made a mistake. I know I'd be good. I thought with the war and all that they would need more people.'

'Well, yes. But Contact has far more applicants than it can use.'

'But I thought one of the things that they considered was how much you wanted to get in, and I know nobody could have wanted to get in as much as I do. Ever since I can remember I've wanted . . .' The boy's voice trailed off as they came to the seats. Fal sat down; so did the boy. Fal was looking at him now but not listening. She was thinking.

'Perhaps they don't think you're mature enough yet.'

'I *am* mature!'

'Hmm. They very rarely take people so young, you know. For all I know they're looking for a special sort of immaturity when they do take people your age.'

'Well, that's silly. I mean, how do you know what to do if they don't tell you what they want? How can you prepare? I think it's all really unfair.'

'In a way I think it's meant to be,' Jase replied. 'They get so many people applying, they can't take them all or even just take the best because there are so many of *them*, so they choose at random from them. You can always reapply.'

'I don't know,' the boy said, sitting forward and putting his elbows on his knees and his head into his hands, staring at the polished wood of the deck. 'Sometimes I think they just tell you that so you won't feel bad when they reject you. I think they do maybe take the very best. But I think they've made a *mistake*. But because they won't tell you why you've failed, what can you *do* about it?'

. . . She was thinking about failure too.

Jase had congratulated her on her idea about finding the Changer. Only that morning, when they were on the ancient steam funicular down from the lodge, they had heard about the events at Vavatch, when the Changer called Bora Horza Gobuchul had appeared and escaped on the pirate ship, taking their agent Perosteck Balveda with him. Her hunch had been right, and Jase was effusive in its praise, making the point that it wasn't her fault the man had got away. But she was depressed. Sometimes being right, thinking the correct thing, predicting accurately, depressed her.

It had all seemed so obvious to her. It hadn't been a supernatural omen or anything silly like that when Perosteck Balveda suddenly turned up (on the battle-damaged but victorious GCU *Nervous Energy*, which was towing most of a captured Idiran cruiser), but it had seemed so . . . so *natural* that Balveda ought to be the one to go in search of the missing Changer. By that time they'd had more information about what had been going on in that volume of space when that particular duel had been going on; and the reported, possible and probable movements of various ships had pointed (again, she thought, fairly obviously) to the privateer craft called the *Clear Air Turbulence*. There were other possibilities, and they were followed up, too, as far as the already stretched resources of Contact's Special Circumstances section would allow, but she was always certain that if any of the branching possibilities was going to bear fruit it would be the Vavatch connection. The captain of the *Clear Air Turbulence* was called Kraiklyn; he played Damage. Vavatch was the most obvious site for a full Damage game in years. Therefore the most likely place to intercept the vessel – apart from Schar's World if the Changer already had control – was Vavatch. She had stuck her neck out by insisting that Vavatch was the most likely place, and that the woman agent Balveda should be one of those to go there, and now it had all come true and she realised it wasn't really her neck she had stuck out at all. It was Balveda's.

But what else could be done? The war was accelerating throughout an immense volume; there were many other urgent missions for the few Special Circumstances agents, and anyway Balveda was the only really good one within range. There was one young man they'd sent in with her, but he was only promising, not experienced. Fal had known all along that if it came to it, Balveda would risk her own life, not the man's, if infiltrating the mercenaries was the only chance of getting to the Changer and through him to the Mind. It was brave but, Fal suspected, it was mistaken. The Changer knew Balveda; he might well recognise her, no matter how much she'd altered her own appearance (and there's hadn't been time for Balveda to undergo radical physical change). If the Changer realised who she was (and Fal suspected he had), Balveda had far less chance of completing her mission than even the most callow and nervous but unsuspected rookie agent. *Forgive me, lady*, Fal thought to herself. *I'd have done better by you if I could. . . .*

She had tried to hate the Changer all that day, tried to imagine him and hate him because he had probably killed Balveda, but apart from the fact that she found it hard to imagine somebody when she had no idea what he might look like (the ship's captain, Kraiklyn?), for some reason the hatred would not materialise. The Changer did not seem real.

She liked the sound of Balveda; she was brave and daring, and Fal hoped against hope that Balveda would live, that somehow she would survive it all and that one day, maybe, they would meet, perhaps after the war. . . .

But that didn't seem real, either.

She couldn't believe in it; she couldn't imagine it the way she had imagined, say, Balveda finding the Changer. She had seen that in her mind, and had willed it to happen. . . . In her version, of course, it was Balveda who won, not the Changer. But she couldn't imagine meeting Balveda, and somehow that was frightening, as though she had started to believe in her own prescience so much that the inability to imagine something clearly enough meant that it would never happen. Either way, it was depressing.

What chance had the agent of living through the war? Not a good one at the moment, Fal knew that, but even supposing Balveda did somehow save herself this time, what were the chances she'd wind up dead anyway, later on? The longer the war went on, the more likely it was. Fal felt, and the general concensus of opinion among the more clued-up Minds was, that the war would last decades rather than years.

Plus or minus a few months, of course. Fal frowned and bit her lip.

She couldn't see them getting the Mind; the Changer was winning, and she had all but run out of ideas. All she had thought of recently was a way – perhaps, just maybe – of putting Gobuchul off: probably not a way of stopping him completely, but possibly a way of making his job harder. But she wasn't optimistic, even if Contact's War Command agreed to such a dangerous, equivocal and potentially expensive plan. . . .

'Fal?' Jase said. She realised she was looking at the island without seeing it. The glass was growing warm in her hand, and Jase and the boy were both looking at her.

'What?' she said, and drank.

'I was asking what you thought about the war,' the boy said. He was frowning, looking at her with narrowed eyes, the sunlight sharp on his face. She looked at his broad, open face and wondered how old he was. Older than her? Younger? Did he feel like she did – wanting to be older, yearning to be treated as responsible?

'I don't understand. What do you mean? Think about it in what way?'

'Well,' the boy said, 'who's going to win?' He looked annoyed. She suspected it had been very obvious that she hadn't been listening. She looked at Jase, but the old machine didn't say anything, and with no aura field there was no way of telling what it was thinking or how it was feeling. Was it amused? Worried? She drank, gulping down the last of the cool drink.

'*We* are, of course,' she said quickly, glancing from the boy to Jase. The boy shook his head.

'I'm not so sure,' he said, rubbing his chin. 'I'm not sure we have the will.'

'The *will*?' Fal said.

'Yes. The desire to fight. I think the Idirans are natural fighters. We aren't. I mean, look at us. . . .' He smiled, as though he was much older and thought himself much wiser than she, and he turned his head and waved his hand lazily towards the island, where the boats lay tilted against the sand.

Fifty or sixty metres away Fal saw what looked like a man and woman coupling, in the shallows under a small cliff; they were bobbing up and down, the woman's dark hands clasped round the man's lighter neck. Was that what the boy was being so urbane about?

Good grief, the fascination of sex.

No doubt it was great fun, but then how could people take it so *seriously*? Sometimes she felt a sneaking envy for the Idirans; they got over it; after a while it no longer mattered. They were dual hermaphrodites, each half of the couple impregnating the other, and each usually bearing twins. After one or occasionally two pregnancies – and weanings – they changed from their fertile breeder stage to become warriors. Opinion was divided on whether they increased in intelligence or just underwent a personality alteration. Certainly they became more cunning but less open-minded, more logical but less imaginative, more ruthless, less compassionate. They grew by another metre; their weight almost doubled; their keratinous covering became thicker and harder; their muscles increased in bulk and density; and their internal organs altered to accommodate these power-increasing changes. At the same time, their bodies absorbed their reproductive organs, and they became sexless. All very linear, symmetrical and tidy, compared to the Culture's pick-your-own approach.

Yes, she could see why this gangly idiot sitting in front of her with his nervously superior smile would find the Idirans impressive. Young fool.

'This is—' Fal was annoyed, enough to be a little stuck for words. 'This is just us now. We haven't evolved . . . we've changed a lot, changed *ourselves* a lot, but we haven't evolved at all since we were running around killing ourselves. I mean each other.' She sucked her breath in, annoyed with herself now. The boy was smiling tolerantly at her. She felt herself blushing. 'We *are* still animals,' she insisted. 'We're natural fighters just as much as the Idirans.'

'Then how come they're winning?' the boy smirked.

'They had a head start. We didn't begin properly preparing for war until the last moment. Warfare has become a way of life for them; we're not all that good at it yet because it's been hundreds of generations since we had to do it. Don't worry,' she told him, looking down at her empty glass and lowering her voice slightly, 'we're learning quite fast enough.'

'Well, you wait and see,' the boy said, nodding at her. 'I think we'll pull out of the war and let the Idirans get on with their expansion – or whatever you want to call it. The war's been sort of exciting, and it's made a change, but it's been nearly four years now, and . . .' He waved one hand again. '. . . we haven't even *won* anything much yet.' He laughed. 'All we keep doing is running away!'

Fal stood up quickly, turning away in case she started to cry.

'Oh shit,' the boy was saying to Jase. 'I suppose I've gone and said something now. . . . Did she have a friend or a relation . . .?'

She walked down the deck, limping a little as the newly healed leg started to hurt again with a distant, nagging ache.

'Don't worry,' Jase was saying to the boy. 'Leave her alone and she'll be all right. . . .'

She put her glass inside one of the dark, empty cabins of the yacht, then kept going, heading for the forward superstructure.

She climbed up a ladder to the wheelhouse, then up another ladder to its roof, and sat there with her legs crossed (the recently broken leg hurt, but she ignored it) and looked out to sea.

Far away, almost on the haze-limit, a ridge of whiteness shimmered in the near-still air. Fal 'Ngeestra let out a long, sad breath and wondered if the white shapes – probably only visible because they were high up, in clearer air – were snowy mountain tops. Maybe they were just clouds. She couldn't remember the geography of the place well enough to work it out.

She sat there, thinking of those peaks. She remembered when once, high in the foothills where a small mountain stream levelled out onto a marshy plateau for a kilometre or so, arcing and swerving and bowing over the sodden, reed-covered land like an athlete stretching and flexing between games, she had found something which had made that winter day's walk memorable.

Ice had been forming in clear, brittle sheets at the side of the flowing stream. She had spent some time happily marching through the shallows of the water, crunching the thin ice with her boots and watching it drift downstream. She wasn't climbing that day, just walking; she had waterproofs on and carried little gear. Somehow the fact she wasn't doing anything dangerous or physically demanding had made her feel like a young child again.

She came to a place where the stream flowed over a terrace of rock, from one level of moor down to another, and there a small pool had carved itself into the rock just beneath the rapids. The water fell less than a metre, and the stream was narrow enough to jump: but she remembered that stream and that pool because there in the circling water, caught beneath the splashing rapids, floated a frozen circle of foam.

The water was naturally soft and peaty, and a yellow-white foam sometimes formed in the mountain streams of that area, blown by the winds and caught in the reeds, but she had never seen it collected into a circle like that and frozen. She laughed when she saw it. She waded in and carefully picked it up. It was only a little greater in diameter than the distance between her outstretched thumb and little finger and a few centimetres thick, not as fragile as she had at first feared.

The frothy bubbles had frozen in the cold air and almost freezing water, making what looked like a tiny model of a galaxy: a fairly common spiral galaxy, like this one, like hers. She held the light confection of air and water and suspended chemicals and turned it over in her hands, sniffing it, sticking her tongue out and licking it, looking at the dim winter sun through it, flicking her finger to see if it would ring.

She watched her little rime galaxy start to melt, very slowly, and saw her own breath blow across it, a brief image of her warmth in the air.

Finally she put it back where she had found it, slowly revolving in the pool of water at the base of the small rapids.

The galaxy image had occurred to her then, and she thought at the time about the similarity of the forces which shaped both the little and the vast. She had thought, *And which is really the most important?* but then felt embarrassed to have thought such a thing.

Every now and again, though, she went back to that thought, and knew that each was exactly as important as the other. Then later she would go back to her second thoughts on the matter and feel embarrassed again.

Fal 'Ngeestra took a deep breath and felt a little better. She smiled and raised her head, closing her eyes for a moment and watching the red sun-haze behind her eyelids. Then she ran a hand through her curly blonde hair and wondered again if the distant, wavering, unsure shapes over the shimmering water were clouds, or mountains.

9.

Schar's World

Imagine a vast and glittering ocean seen from a great height. It stretches to the clear curved limit of every angle of horizon, the sun burning on a billion tiny wavelets. Now imagine a smooth blanket of cloud above the ocean, a shell of black velvet suspended high above the water and also extending to the horizon, but keep the sparkle of the sea despite the lack of sun. Add to the cloud many sharp and tiny lights, scattered on the base of the inky overcast like glinting eyes: singly, in pairs, or in larger groups, each positioned far, far away from any other set.

That is the view a ship has in hyperspace as it flies like a microscopic insect, free between the energy grid and real space.

The small, sharp lights on the undersurface of the cloud cover are stars; the waves on the sea are the irregularities of the Grid on which a ship travelling in hyperspace finds traction with its engine fields, while that sparkle is its source of energy. The Grid and the plain of real space are curved, rather like the ocean and the cloud would be round a planet, but less so. Black holes show as thin and twisting waterspouts from clouds to sea; supernovae as long lightning flashes in the overcast. Rocks, moons, planets, Orbitals, even Rings and Spheres, hardly show at all. . . .

The two 'Killer' class Rapid Offensive Units *Trade Surplus* and *Revisionist* raced through the hyperspace, flashing underneath the web of real space like slim and glittering fish in a deep, still pond. They wove past systems and stars, keeping deep beneath the empty spaces where they were least likely to be traced.

Their engines were each a focus of energy almost beyond imagining, packing sufficient power within their two hundred metres to equal perhaps one per cent of the energy produced by a small sun, flinging the two vessels across the four-dimensional void at an equivalent speed in real space of rather less than ten light-years per hour. At the time, this was considered particularly fast.

They sensed the Glittercliff and Sullen Gulf ahead. They twisted their headlong rush to angle them deep inside the war zone, aiming themselves at the system which contained Schar's World.

Far in the distance, they could see the group of black holes which had created the Gulf. Those flutes of plunging energy had passed through the area millennia before, clearing a space of consumed stars behind them, creating an artificial galactic arm as they headed in a long spiral closer towards the centre of the slowly spinning island of stars and nebulae that was the galaxy.

The group of black holes was commonly known as the Forest, so closely were they grouped, and the two speeding Culture craft had instructions to try to force their way between those twisted, lethal trunks, if they were seen and pursued. The Culture's field management was considered superior to the Idirans', so it was thought they would have a better chance of getting through, and any chasing craft might even break off rather than risk tangling with the Forest. It was a terrible risk even to contemplate, but the two ROUs were precious; the Culture had not yet built many, and everything possible had to be done to make sure that the craft got back safely or, if the worst came to the worst, were destroyed utterly.

They encountered no hostile ships. They flashed across the inward face of the Quiet Barrier in seconds and delivered their prescribed loads in two short bursts, then twisted once and tore away at maximum speed, out through the thinning stars and past the Glittercliff, into the empty skies of the Sullen Gulf.

They registered hostile craft stationed near the Schar's World system starting off in pursuit, but they had been seen too late, and they quickly outdistanced the probing beams of track lasers. They set course for the far side of the Gulf, their strange mission completed. The Minds on board, and the small crew of humans each vessel carried (who were there more because they wanted to be than for their utility), hadn't been told why they were blasting empty space with expensive warheads, shooting off CREWSs at each other's target drones, dumping clouds of CAM and ordinary gas and releasing odd little unpowered signalling ships which were little more than unmanned shuttles packed with broadcasting equipment. The entire effect of this operation would be to produce a few spectacular flashes and flares and a scattering of radiation shells and wide-band signals before the Idirans cleared up the debris and blasted or captured the signal craft.

They had been asked to risk their lives on some damn-fool panic mission which seemed designed to convince nobody in particular that there had been a space battle in the middle of nowhere when there hadn't. And they had done it!

What was the Culture coming to? The Idirans seemed to relish suicide missions. You could easily form the impression that they considered being asked to carry out any other sort something of an insult. But the *Culture*? Where even in the war forces 'discipline' was regarded as a taboo word, where people always wanted to know *why* this and *why* that?

Things had come to a pretty pass indeed.

The two ships raced across the Gulf, arguing. On board, heated discussions were taking place between members of their crews.

It took twenty-one days for the *Clear Air Turbulence* to make the journey from Vavatch to Schar's World.

Wubslin had spent the time carrying out what repairs he could to the craft, but what the ship needed was another thorough overhaul. While structurally it was still sound, and life support functioned nearly normally, it had suffered a general degradation of its systems, though no catastrophic failures. The warp units ran a little more raggedly than before, the fusion motors were not up to sustained use in an atmosphere – they would get them down to and up from Schar's World, but not provide much more in-air flying time – and the vessel's sensors had been reduced in numbers and efficiency to a level not far above operational minimum.

They had still escaped lightly, Horza thought.

With the *CAT* under his control, Horza was able to switch off the computer's identity circuits. He didn't have to fool the Free Company, either; so, as the days passed, he Changed slowly to resemble his old self a little more. That was for Yalson and the other members of the Free Company. He was really striking two thirds of a compromise between Kraiklyn and the self he had been on the *CAT* before it had reached Vavatch. There was another third in there which he let grow and show itself on his face for nobody on board, but for a red-haired Changer girl called Kierachell. He hoped she would recognise that part of his appearance when they met again, on Schar's World.

'Why did you think we'd be angry?' Yalson asked him in the *CAT*'s hangar one day. They had set up a target screen at one end and put their lasers onto practice. The screen's built-in projector flashed images for them to shoot at. Horza looked at the woman.

'He was your leader.'

Yalson laughed. 'He was a manager; how many of them are liked by their staff? This is a business, Horza, and not even a successful one. Kraiklyn managed to get most of us retired prematurely. Shit! The only person you needed to fool was the ship.'

'There was that,' Horza said, aiming at a human figure darting across the distant screen. The laser spot was invisible, but the screen sensed it and flashed white light where it hit. The human figure, hit in the leg, stumbled but did not fall: half marks. 'I did need to fool the ship. But I didn't want to risk somebody being loyal to Kraiklyn.'

It was Yalson's turn, but she was looking at Horza, not the screen.

The ship's fidelities had been bypassed, and now all that was needed to command it was a numeric code, which only Horza knew, and the small ring he wore, which had been Kraiklyn's. He had promised that when they got to Schar's World, if there was no other way off the planet, he would set the *CAT*'s computer to free itself of all fidelity limitations after a given time, so that if he didn't come back out of the tunnels of the Command System the Free Company would not be stranded. 'You would have told us,' Yalson said, 'wouldn't you, Horza? I mean you would have let us know eventually.'

Horza knew she meant, would he have told *her*? He put his gun down and looked her in the eyes. 'Once I was sure,' he said, 'sure about the people, sure about the ship.'

It was the honest answer, but he wasn't certain it was the best one. He wanted Yalson, wanted not just her warmth in the ship's red night, but her trust, her care. But she was still distant.

Balveda lived; perhaps she wouldn't still be alive if Horza hadn't wanted Yalson's regard. He knew that, and it was a bitter thought, making him feel cheap and cruel. Even knowing that it was a definite thing would have been better than being uncertain. He couldn't say for sure whether the cold logic of this game dictated that the Culture woman should die or be left alive, or even if, the former being comfortably obvious, he could have killed her in cold blood. He had thought it through and still he didn't know. He only hoped that neither woman had guessed that any of this had gone through his mind.

Kierachell was another worry. It was absurd, he knew, to be concerned about his own affairs at such a time, but he couldn't stop thinking about the Changer woman; the closer they came to Schar's World, the more he remembered of her, the more real his memories became. He tried not to build it up too much, tried to recall the

284

boredom of the Changers' lonely outpost on the planet and the restlessness he had felt there even with Kierachell's company, but he dreamt about her slow smile and recalled her low voice in all its fluid grace with some of the heartache of a youth's first love. Occasionally he thought Yalson might sense that, too, and something inside him seemed to shrink with shame.

Yalson shrugged, hoisted her gun to her shoulder and fired at a four-legged shadow on the practice screen. It stopped in its tracks and dropped, seeming to dissolve into the line of shady ground at the bottom of the screen.

Horza gave talks.

It made him feel like some visiting lecturer at a college, but that's what he did. He felt he had to explain to the others why he was doing what he was, why the Changers supported the Idirans, why he believed in what they were fighting for. He called them briefings, and ostensibly they were about Schar's World and the Command System, its history, geography and so on, but he always (quite intentionally) ended up talking about the war in general, or about totally different aspects of it unrelated to the planet they were approaching.

The briefing cover gave him a good excuse to keep Balveda confined to her cabin while he paced up and down on the deck of the mess talking to the members of the Free Company; he didn't want his talks turning into a debate.

Perosteck Balveda had been no trouble. Her suit and a few items of harmless-looking jewellery and other bits and pieces had been jettisoned from a vactube. She had been scanned with every item the *CAT*'s limited sick-bay equipment could provide and had come up clean, and she seemed quite happy to be a well-behaved prisoner, confined to the ship as they all were and, apart from at night, locked in her cabin only occasionally. Horza didn't let her near the bridge, just in case, but Balveda showed no signs of trying to get to know the ship especially well – the way he had done when he came on board. She didn't even try to argue any of the mercenaries round to her way of thinking about the war and the Culture.

Horza wondered how secure she felt. Balveda was pleasant and seemed unworried; but he looked at her sometimes and thought he saw, briefly, a glimpse of inner tension, even despair. It relieved him in one way, but in another it gave him that same bad, cruel feeling he experienced when he thought about exactly why the Culture agent was still alive. Sometimes he was simply afraid of getting to Schar's

285

World, but increasingly as the voyage dragged on he came to relish the prospect of some action and an end to thought.

He called Balveda to his cabin one day, after they had all eaten in the mess. The woman came in and sat down on the same small seat he had sat in when Kraiklyn had summoned him just after he had joined the ship.

Balveda's face was calm. She sat elegantly in the small seat, her long frame at once relaxed and poised. Her deep dark eyes gazed out at Horza from the thin, smoothly shaped head, and her red hair – now turning black – shone in the lights of the cabin.

'Captain Horza?' she smiled, crossing her long-fingered hands on her lap. She wore a long blue gown, the plainest thing she had been able to find on the ship: something that had once belonged to the woman Gow.

'Hello, Balveda,' Horza said. He sat back on the bed. He wore a loose gown. For the first couple of days he had stayed in his suit, but while it stayed commendably comfortable, it was bulky and awkward in the confines of the *Clear Air Turbulence*, so he had discarded it for the voyage.

He was about to offer Balveda something to drink, but somehow, because that was what Kraiklyn had done with him, it didn't seem the right thing to do.

'What was it,' Horza?' Balveda said.

'I just wanted to . . . see how you were,' he said. He had tried to rehearse what he would say; assure her she was in no danger, that he liked her and that he was sure that this time the worst that would happen to her really would be internment somewhere, and maybe a swap, but the words would not come.

'I'm fine,' she said, smoothing her hand over her hair, her eyes glancing around the cabin briefly. 'I'm trying to be a model captive so you won't have an excuse for ditching me.' She smiled, but again he thought he sensed an edge to the gesture. Yet he was relieved.

'No,' he laughed, letting his head rock back on his shoulders with the laugh. 'I've no intention of doing that. You're safe.'

'Until we get to Schar's World?' she said calmly.

'After that, too,' he said.

Balveda blinked slowly, looking down. 'Hmm, good.' She looked into his eyes.

He shrugged. 'I'm sure you'd do the same for me.'

'I think I . . . probably would,' she said, and he couldn't tell

286

whether she was lying or not. 'I just think it's a pity we're on different sides.'

'It's a pity we're *all* on different sides, Balveda.'

'Well,' she said, clasping her hands on her lap again, 'there is a theory that the side we each think we're on is the one that will triumph eventually anyway.'

'What's that?' he grinned. 'Truth and justice?'

'Not either, really,' she smiled, not looking at him. 'Just . . .' She shrugged. 'Just life. The evolution you talked about. You said the Culture was in a backwater, a dead end. If we are . . . maybe we'll lose after all.'

'Damn, I'll get you on the good guys' side yet, Perosteck,' he said, with just a little too much heartiness. She smiled thinly.

She opened her mouth to say something, then thought the better of it and closed it again. She looked at her hands. Horza wondered what to say next.

One night, six days out from their destination – the system's star was fairly bright in the sky ahead of the ship, even on normal sight – Yalson came to his cabin.

He hadn't expected it, and the tap at the door brought him from a state between waking and sleep with a jarring coldness which left him disorientated for a few moments. He saw her on the door-screen and let her in. She came in quickly, closing the door after her and hugging him, holding him tight, soundless. He stood there, trying to wake up and work out how this had happened. There seemed to be no reason for it, no build-up of tension of any sort between them, no signs, no hints: nothing.

Yalson had spent that day in the hangar, wired up with small sensors and exercising. He had seen her there, working away, sweating, exhausting herself, peering at readouts and screens with her critical eyes, as though her body was a machine like the ship and she was testing it almost to destruction.

They slept together. But as though to confirm the exertions she had put herself through during the day, Yalson fell asleep almost as soon as they lay down; in his arms, while he was kissing and nuzzling her, breathing in the scent of her body again after what seemed like months. He lay awake and listened to her breathe, felt her move very slightly in his arms, and sensed her blood beat slower and slower as she fell into a deep sleep.

In the morning they made love, and afterwards he asked her, while

287

he held her and their sweat dried, 'Why?' as their hearts slowed. 'What changed your mind?' The ship hummed distantly around them.

She gripped him, hugging tighter still, and shook her head. 'Nothing,' she said, 'nothing in particular, nothing important.' He felt her shrug, and she turned her head away from his face, into his arm, towards the humming bulkhead. In a small voice she said, 'Everything; Schar's World.'

Three days out, in the hangar, he watched the members of the Free Company work out and practise firing their guns at the screen. Neisin couldn't practise because he still refused to use lasers after what had happened in the Temple of Light. He had stocked up on magazines of micro projectiles during his few sober moments in Evanauth.

After firing practice, Horza had each of the mercenaries test their AG harnesses. Kraiklyn had purchased a cheap batch of them and insisted that the Free Company members who didn't already have an anti-gravity unit in their suit buy a harness from him, at what he claimed was cost price. Horza had been dubious at first, but the AG units seemed serviceable enough, and certainly might be useful for searching the Command System's deeper shafts.

Horza was satisfied that the mercenaries would follow him in if they had to, down into the Command System. The long delay since the excitement of Vavatch, and the boring routine of the life on the *Clear Air Turbulence*, had made them hanker after something more interesting. As Horza had – honestly – described it, Schar's World didn't sound too bad. At least it was unlikely they would find themselves in a fire-fight, and nobody, including the Mind they might end up helping Horza search for, was going to start blowing things up, not with a Dra'Azon to reckon with.

The sun of the Schar's World system shone brightly ahead of them now, the brightest thing in the sky. The Glittercliff was not a visible feature of the sky ahead, because they were still inside the spiral limb and looking out, but it was noticeable that all the stars ahead were either quite close or very far away, with none in the gap between.

Horza had changed the *CAT*'s course several times, but kept it on a general heading which, unless they turned, wouldn't take it closer than two light-years from the planet. He would turn the craft and head in the following day. So far the journey had been uneventful. They had flown through the scattered stars without encountering anything out of the ordinary: no messages or signals, no distant flashes from battles, no warp wakes. The area around them seemed calm and undisturbed, as though all that was happening was what always happened: just the stars being born and dying, the galaxy revolving, the holes twisting, the gases swirling. The war, in that hurried silence, in their false rhythm of day and night, seemed like something they had all imagined, an inexplicable nightmare they had somehow shared, even escaped.

Horza had the ship watching, though, ready to alarm at the first hint of trouble. They were unlikely to find out anything before they got to the Quiet Barrier, but if everything was as peaceful and serene as that name implied, he thought he might not go arrowing straight in. Ideally he would like to rendezvous with the Idiran fleet units which were supposed to be waiting near by. That would solve most of his problems. He would hand Balveda over, make sure Yalson and the rest of the mercenaries were safe – let them have the *CAT* – and pick up the specialised equipment Xoralundra had promised him.

That scenario would also let him meet Kierachell alone, without the distraction of the others being there. He would be able to be his old self without making any concessions to the self the Free Company and Yalson knew.

Two days out, the ship's alarm went off. Horza was dozing in his bed; he raced out of the cabin and forward to the bridge.

In the volume of space before them, all hell seemed to have been let loose. Annihiliation light washed over them; it was the radiation from weapon explosions, registering pure and mixed on the vessel's sensors, indicating where warheads had gone off totally by themselves or in contact with something else. The fabric of three-dimensional space bucked and juddered with the blast from warp charges, forcing the *CAT*'s automatics to disengage its engines every few seconds to prevent them being damaged on the shock waves. Horza strapped in and brought all the subsidiary systems up. Wubslin came through the door from the mess.

'What is it?'

'Battle of some sort,' Horza said, watching the screens. The volume of affected space was more or less directly on the inward side of Schar's World; the direct route from Vavatch passed that way. The *CAT* was one and a half light-years away from the disturbance, too far away to be spotted on anything except the narrow beam of a track scanner and therefore almost certainly safe; but Horza watched the distant blasts of radiation, and felt the *CAT* ride the ripples of disturbed space with a sensation of nausea, even defeat.

'Message shell,' Wubslin said, nodding at a screen. There, sorting itself out from the noise of radiation, a signal gradually appeared, the words forming a few letters at a time like a field of plants growing and flowering. After a few repetitions of the signal – and it was being jammed, not simple interfered with by the battle's background noise – it was complete enough to read.

VESSEL CLEAR AIR TURBULENCE. MEET UNITS
NINETY-THIRD FLEET
DESTINATION/S.591134.45 MID. ALL SAFE.

'Damn,' breathed Horza.

'What's that mean?' Wubslin said. He punched the figures on the screen into the *CAT*'s navigational computer. 'Oh,' the engineer said, sitting back, 'it's one of the stars near by. I guess they mean to rendezvous halfway between it and . . .' He looked at the main screen.

'Yes,' Horza said, looking unhappily at the signal. It had to be a fake. There was nothing to prove it was from the Idirans: no message number, code class, ship originator, signatory; nothing genuine at all.

'That from the guys with three legs?' Wubslin said. He brought a holo display onto another screen, showing stars surrounded by spherical grids of thin green lines. 'Hey, we're not all that far away from there.'

'Is that right?' Horza said. He watched the continuing blasts of battle-light. He entered some figures into the *CAT*'s control systems. The vessel brought its nose round, angling it further over towards the Schar's World system. Wubslin looked at Horza.

'You don't think it is from them?'

'I don't,' Horza said. The radiation was fading. The engagement appeared to be over, or the action broken off. 'I think we might turn up there and find a GCU waiting for us. Or a cloud of CAM.'

'CAM? What – that stuff they dusted Vavatch with?' Wubslin said, and whistled. 'No thanks.'

Horza switched the screen with the message off.

Less than an hour later it all happened again: shells of radiation, warp disturbance, and this time two messages, one telling the *CAT* to ignore the first message, the other giving a new rendezvous point. Both seemed genuine; both were affixed with the word 'Xoralundra'. Horza, still chewing the mouthful of food he'd been eating when the

290

alarm went off for the second time, swore. A third message appeared, telling him personally to ignore those two signals and directing the *CAT* to yet another rendezvous area.

Horza shouted with anger, sending bits of soggy food arcing out to hit the message screen. He turned the wide-band communicator off completely, then went back to the mess.

'When do we reach the Quiet Barrier?'

'A few more hours. Half a day perhaps.'

'Are you nervous?'

'I'm not nervous. I've been there before. How about you?'

'If you say it'll be all right, I believe you.'

'It should be.'

'Will you know any of the people there?'

'I don't know. It's been a few years. They don't rotate personnel often, but people do leave. I don't know. I'll just have to wait and see.'

'You haven't seen any of your own people for a long time, have you?'

'No. Not since I left there.'

'Aren't you looking forward to it?'

'Maybe.'

'Horza . . . look, I know I told you we didn't ask each other about . . . about everything before we came aboard the *CAT*, but that was . . . before a lot of things changed—'

'But it's the way we've been, isn't it?'

'You mean you don't want to talk about it now?'

'Maybe. I don't know. You want to ask me about—'

'No.' She put her hand to his lips. He felt them there in the darkness. 'No, it's OK. It's all right; never mind.'

He sat in the centre seat. Wubslin was in the engineer's chair to Horza's right, Yalson to his left. The rest had crowded in behind them. He had let Balveda watch; there was little that could happen which she could affect now. The drone floated near the ceiling.

The Quiet Barrier was coming up. It showed as a mirrorfield directly in front of them, about a light-day in diameter. It had suddenly appeared on the screen when they were an hour out from the barrier. Wubslin had worried it was giving their position away, but Horza knew that the mirrorfield existed only in the *CAT*'s sensors. There was nothing there for anybody else to see.

Five minutes out, every screen went black. Horza had warned the rest about it, but even he felt anxious and blind when it happened.

'You're sure this is meant to happen?' Aviger said.

'I'd be worried if it didn't,' Horza told him. The old man moved somewhere behind him.

'I think this is incredible,' Dorolow said. 'This creature is virtually a god. I'm sure it can sense our moods and thoughts. I can feel it already.'

'Actually, it's just a collection of self-referencing—'

'Balveda,' Horza said, looking round at the Culture woman. She stopped talking and clapped a hand over her mouth, flashing her eyes. He turned back to the blank screen.

'When's this thing—' Yalson began.

APPROACHING CRAFT, the screen said, in a variety of languages.

'Here we go,' Neisin said. He was shushed by Dorolow.

'I respond,' Horza said, in Marain, into the tight-beam communicator. The other languages disappeared from the screen.

YOU ARE APPROACHING THE PLANET CALLED SCHAR'S WORLD, DRA'AZON PLANET OF THE DEAD. PROGRESS BEYOND THIS POINT IS RESTRICTED.

'I know. My name is Bora Horza Gobuchul. I wish to return to Schar's World for a short while. I ask this with all respect.'

'Smooth talker,' Balveda said. Horza glared briefly at her. The communicator would only transmit what he said, but he didn't want the woman to forget she was a prisoner.

YOU HAVE BEEN HERE BEFORE.

Horza couldn't tell if this was a question or not. 'I have been to Schar's World before,' he confirmed. 'I was one of the Changer sentinels.' There seemed little point in telling the creature when; the Dra'Azon called every time 'now' even though their language used tenses. The screen went blank, then repeated:

YOU HAVE BEEN HERE BEFORE.

Horza frowned and wondered what to say. Balveda muttered, 'Obviously hopelessly senile.'

'I have been here before,' Horza said. Did the Dra'Azon mean that because he had already been there he could not return?

'I can feel it, I can feel its presence,' Dorolow whispered.

THERE ARE OTHER HUMANS WITH YOU.

'Thanks a lot,' said the drone, Unaha-Closp, from somewhere near the ceiling.

'You see?' Dorolow said, her voice almost whimpering. Horza heard Balveda snort. Dorolow staggered slightly; Aviger and Neisin had to hold onto her to stop her from falling.

'I have not been able to set them down elsewhere,' Horza said. 'I ask your indulgence. If need be, they will stay on board this vessel.'

THEY ARE NOT SENTINELS. THEY ARE OTHER HUMANOID SPECIES.

'I alone need alight on Schar's World.'

ENTRY IS RESTRICTED.

Horza sighed. 'I alone request permission to land.'

WHY HAVE YOU COME HERE?

Horza hesitated. He heard Balveda snort quietly. He said, 'I seek one who is here.'

WHAT DO THE OTHERS SEEK?

'They seek nothing. They are with me.'

THEY ARE HERE.

'They . . .' Horza licked his lips. All his rehearsing, all his thoughts about what to say at this moment, seemed to be useless. 'They are not all here by choice. But I had no alternative. I had to bring them. If you wish, they will stay on board this craft in orbit around Schar's World, or further away inside the Quiet Barrier. I have a suit, I can—'

THEY ARE HERE AGAINST THEIR WILL.

Horza hadn't known Dra'Azon to interrupt before. He couldn't imagine it was a good sign. 'The . . . circumstances are . . . complicated. Certain species in the galaxy are at war. Choices become limited. One does things one would not normally do.'

THERE IS DEATH HERE.

Horza looked at the words written on the screen. He felt transfixed by them. There was silence on the bridge for a moment. Then he heard a couple of people moving awkwardly.

'What does that mean?' the drone Unaha-Closp said.

'There . . . there is?' Horza said. The words stayed on the screen,

C.P.—16

293

written in Marain. Wubslin tapped at a few buttons on his side of the console, buttons which would normally control the display on the screens in front of him, all of which now repeated the words on the main screen. The engineer was sitting in his seat, looking cramped and tense. Horza cleared his throat, then said, 'There was a battle, a conflict near by. Just before we got here. It might still be going on. There may be death.'

THERE IS DEATH HERE.

'Oh . . .' Dorolow said, and slumped into Neisin and Aviger's arms.

'We'd better get her to the mess,' Aviger said, looking at Neisin. 'Let her lie down.'

'Oh, all right,' Neisin said, glancing quickly at the woman's face. Dorolow appeared to be unconscious.

'I may be able to . . .' Horza began, then gave a deep breath. 'If there is death here I may be able to stop it. I may be able to prevent more death.'

BORA HORZA GOBUCHUL.

'Yes?' Horza said, gulping. Aviger and Neisin manhandled Dorolow's limp body out through the doorway into the corridor leading into the mess. The screen changed:

YOU ARE LOOKING FOR THE REFUGEE MACHINE.

'Ho-ho,' said Balveda, turning away with a smile on her face and putting one hand to her mouth.

'Shit!' said Yalson.

'Looks like our god isn't so stupid,' Unaha-Closp observed.

'Yes,' Horza said sharply. There seemed little point in trying to pretend now. 'Yes, I am. But I think—'

YOU MAY ENTER.

'What?' the drone said.

'Well, ya-hoo!' Yalson said, crossing her arms and leaning back against the bulkhead. Neisin came back through the door. He stopped when he saw the screen.

'That was quick,' he said to Yalson. 'What did he say?' Yalson just shook her head. Horza felt a wave of relief sweep through him. He looked at each word on the screen in turn, as though frightened that the short message could somehow conceal a hidden negation. He smiled and said:

'Thank you. Shall I go down alone to the planet?'

YOU MAY ENTER.
THERE IS DEATH HERE.
BE WARNED.

'What death?' Horza said. The relief waned; the Dra'Azon's words about death chilled him. 'Where is there death? Whose?'

The screen changed again, the first two lines disappearing. Now it simply said:

BE WARNED.

'I do not,' Unaha-Closp said slowly, 'like the sound of that at all.'

Then the screens were clear. Wubslin sighed and relaxed. The sun of the Schar's World system shone brightly ahead of them, less than a standard light-year away. Horza checked the figures on the navigation computer as its screen flickered back to normality along with the rest, displaying numbers and graphs and holographics. Then the Changer sat back in his seat. 'We're through all right,' he said. 'We're through the Quiet Barrier.'

'So nothing can touch us now, huh?' Neisin said.

Horza gazed at the screen, the single yellow dwarf star showing as a bright unwavering spot of light in the centre, planets still invisible. He nodded. 'Nothing. Nothing outside, anyway.'

'Great. Think I'll have a drink to celebrate.' Neisin nodded at Yalson, then swung his thin body out through the doorway.

'Do you think it meant only you can go down, or all of us?' Yalson asked. Still staring at the screen, Horza shook his head.

'I don't know. We'll go into orbit, then broadcast to the Changer base shortly before we try taking the *CAT* in. If Mr Adequate doesn't like it, he'll let us know.'

'You've decided it's male, then,' said Balveda, just as Yalson said:

'Why not contact them now?'

'I didn't like that bit about there being death here.' Horza turned towards Yalson. Balveda was at her side; the drone had floated down a little to eye level. Horza looked at Yalson. 'Just as a precaution. I don't want to give anything away too soon.' He turned his gaze to the Culture woman. 'Last I heard, the regular transmission was due from the base on Schar's World a few days ago. I don't suppose you heard

295

whether it had been received?' Horza grinned at Balveda in a way that was meant to show he didn't expect an answer, or at least not a truthful one. The tall Culture agent looked at the floor, seemed to shrug, then met Horza's eyes.

'I heard,' she said. 'It was overdue.'

Horza stayed looking at her. Balveda didn't take her eyes away. Yalson glanced from one to another. Eventually the drone Unaha-Closp said, 'Frankly, none of this inspires confidence. My advice would be to—' It stopped as Horza glared at it. 'Hmm,' it said, 'well, never mind that for now.' It floated sideways to the door and went out.

'Seems to be OK,' Wubslin said, not apparently addressing anybody in particular. He sat back from the console, nodding to himself. 'Yes, ship's back to normal now.' He turned round and smiled at the other three.

They came for him. He was in a gamehall playing floatball. He thought he was safe there, surrounded by friends in every direction (they seemed to float like a cloud of flies in front of him for a second, but he laughed that off, caught the ball, threw it and scored a point). But they came for him there. He saw them coming, two of them, from a door set in a narrow chimney of the spherical, ribbed gamehall. They wore cloaks of no colour, and came straight towards him. He tried to float away, but his power harness was dead. He was stuck in mid-air, unable to make progress in any direction. He was trying to swim through the air and struggle out of his harness so that he could throw it at them – perhaps to hit, certainly to send himself off in the other direction – when they caught him.

None of the people around him seemed to notice, and he realised suddenly they were not his friends, that in fact he didn't know any of them. They took his arms and, in an instant, without travelling past or through anything yet somehow making him feel they had turned an invisible corner to a place that was always there but out of sight, they were in an area of darkness. Their no-colour cloaks showed up in the darkness when he looked away. He was powerless, locked in stone, but he could see and breathe.

'Help me!'

'That is not what we are here for.'

'Who are you?'

'You know.'

'I don't.'

'Then we can't tell you.'

'What do you want?'

'We want you.'

'Why?'

'Why not?'
'But why me?'
'You have no one.'
'What?'
'You have no one.'
'What do you mean?'
'No family. No friends . . .'
'. . . no religion. No belief.'
'That's not true!'
'How would you know?'
'I believe in . . .'
'What?'
'Me!'
'That is not enough.'
'Anyway, you'll never find it.'
'What? Find what?'
'Enough. Let's do it now.'
'Do what?'
'Take your name.'
'I—'
And they reached together into his skull and took his name.
So he screamed.

'Horza!' Yalson shook his head, bouncing it off the bulkhead at the top of the small bed. He spluttered awake, the whimper dying on his lips, his body tense for an instant, then soft.

He put his hands out and touched the woman's furred skin. She put her hands behind his head and hugged him to her breast. He said nothing, but his heart slowed to the pace of hers. She rocked his body gently with her own, then pushed his head away, bent and kissed his lips.

'I'm all right now,' he told her. 'Just a nightmare.'

'What was it?'

'Nothing,' he said. He put his head back to her chest, nestling it between her breasts like a huge, delicate egg.

Horza had his suit on. Wubslin was in his usual seat. Yalson occupied the co-pilot's chair. They were all suited up. Schar's World filled the screen in front of them, the belly sensors of the *CAT* staring straight down at the sphere of white and grey beneath and magnifying it.

'One more time,' Horza said. Wubslin transmitted the recorded message for the third time.

'Maybe they don't use that code any more,' Yalson said. She

watched the screen with her sharp-browed eyes. She had cropped her hair back to about a centimetre over her skull, hardly thicker than the down which covered her body. The menacing effect jarred with the smallness of her head sticking out from the large neck of the suit.

'It's traditional; more of a ceremonial language than a code,' Horza said. 'They'll know it if they hear it.'

'You're sure we're beaming it at the right place?'

'Yes,' Horza said, trying to remain calm. They had been in orbit for less than half an hour, stationary above the continent which held the buried tunnels of the Command System. Almost the whole of the planet was covered in snow. Ice locked the thousand-kilometre peninsula where the tunnel system lay fast into the sea itself. Schar's World had entered another of its periodic ice ages seven thousand years previously, and only in a relatively thin band around the equator – between the slightly wobbling planet's tropics – was there open ocean. It showed as a steely grey belt around the world, occasionally visible through whorls of storm clouds.

They were twenty-five thousand kilometres out from the planet's snow-crusted surface, their communicator beaming down onto a circular area a few tens of kilometres in diameter at a point midway between the two frozen arms of sea which gave the peninsula a slight waist. That was where the entrance to the tunnels lay; that was where the Changers lived. Horza knew he hadn't made a mistake, but there was no answer.

There is death here, he kept thinking. A little of the planet's chill seemed to creep along his bones.

'Nothing,' Wubslin said.

'Right,' Horza said, taking the manual controls into his gloved hands. 'We're going in.'

The *Clear Air Turbulence* teased its warp fields out along the slight curve of the planet's gravity well, carefully edging itself down the slope. Horza cut the motors and let them return to their emergency-ready-only mode. They shouldn't need them now, and would soon be unable to use them as the gravity gradient increased.

The *CAT* fell with gradually increasing speed towards the planet, fusion motors at the ready. Horza watched displays on the screens until he was satisfied they were on course; then, with the planet seeming to turn a little beneath the craft, he unstrapped and went back to the mess.

Aviger, Neisin and Dorolow sat in their suits, strapped into the mess-room seats. Perosteck Balveda was also strapped in; she wore a thick jacket and matching trousers. Her head was exposed above the

298

soft ruff of a white shirt. The bulky fabric jacket was fastened up to her throat. She had warm boots on, and a pair of hide gloves lay on the table in front of her. The jacket even had a little hood, which hung down her back. Horza wasn't sure whether Balveda had chosen this soft, useless image of a space suit to make a point to him, or unconsciously, out of fear and a need for security.

Unaha-Closp sat in a chair, strapped against its back, pointing straight up at the ceiling. 'I trust', it said, 'we're not going to have the same sort of flying-circus job we had to endure the last time you flew this heap of debris.' Horza ignored it.

'We haven't had any word from Mr Adequate, so it looks like we're all going down,' he said. 'When we get there, I'll go in by myself to check things out. When I come back, we'll decide what we're going to do.'

'That is, *you'll* decide—' began the drone.

'What if you don't come back?' Aviger said. The drone made a hissing noise but went quiet. Horza looked at the toy-like figure of the old man in his suit.

'I'll come back, Aviger,' he said. 'I'm sure everybody at the base will be fine. I'll get them to heat up some food for us.' He smiled, but knew it wasn't especially convincing. 'Anyway,' he went on, 'in the unlikely event there is anything wrong, I'll come straight back.'

"Well, this ship's our only way off the planet; remember that, Horza,' Aviger said. His eyes looked frightened. Dorolow touched him on the arm of his suit.

'Trust in God,' Dorolow said. 'We'll be all right.' She looked at Horza. 'Won't we, Horza?'

Horza nodded. 'Yes. We'll be all right. We'll all be just fine.' He turned and went back to the bridge.

They stood in the high mountain snows, watching the midsummer sun sink in its own red seas of air and cloud. A cold wind blew her hair across her face, auburn over white, and he raised a hand, without thinking, to sweep it away again. She turned to him, her head nestling into his cupped hand, a small smile on her face.

'So much for midsummer's day,' she said. The day had been fair, still well below freezing, but mild enough for them to take their gloves off and push their hoods back. The nape of her neck was warm against his palm, and the lustrous, heavy hair brushed over the back of his hand as she looked up at him, skin white as snow, white as bone. 'That look, again,' she said softly.

'What look?' he said, defensively, knowing.

'The far-away one,' she said, taking his hand and bringing it to her mouth, kissing it, stroking it as though it was a small, defenceless animal.

'Well, that's just what you call it.'

She looked away from him, towards the livid red ball of the sun, lowering behind the distant range. 'That's what I see,' she told him. 'I know your looks by now. I know them all, and what they mean.'

He felt a twinge of anger at being thought so obvious, but knew that she was right, at least partly. What she did not know about him was only what he did not know about himself (but that, he told himself, was quite a lot still). Perhaps she even knew him better than he did himself.

'I'm not responsible for my looks,' he said after a moment, to make a joke of it. 'They surprise me, too, sometimes.'

'And what you do?' she said, the sunset's glow rubbing false colour into her pale, thin face. 'Will you surprise yourself when you leave here?'

'Why do you always assume I'm going to leave?' he said, annoyed, stuffing his hands into the thick jacket's pockets and staring at the hemisphere of disappearing star. 'I keep telling you, I'm happy here.'

'Yes,' she said. 'You keep telling me.'

'Why should I want to leave?'

She shrugged, slipped one arm through his, put her head to his shoulder. 'Bright lights, big crowds, interesting times; other people.'

'I'm happy here with you,' he told her, and put his arm round her shoulders. Even in the bulky quilting of the jacket, she seemed slim, almost fragile.

She said nothing for a moment, then, in quite a different tone: '. . . And so you should be.' She turned to face him, smiling. 'Now kiss me.'

He kissed her, hugged her. Looking down over her shoulder, he saw something small and red move on the trampled snow near her feet.

'Look!' he said, breaking away, stooping. She squatted beside him, and together they watched the tiny, stick-like insect crawl slowly, laboriously, over the surface of the snow: one more living, moving thing on the blank face of the world. 'That's the first one I've seen,' he told her.

She shook her head, smiling. 'You just don't look,' she chided.

He put out one hand and scooped the insect into his palm, before she could stop him. 'Oh, *Horza* . . .' she said, her breath catching on a tiny hook of despair.

He looked, uncomprehending, at her stricken expression, while the snow-creature died from the warmth of his hand.

The *Clear Air Turbulence* dropped towards the planet, circling its ice-bright layers of atmosphere from day to night and back again, tipping over the equator and tropics as it spiralled in.

Gradually it encountered that atmosphere – ions and gases, ozone and air. It swooped through the world's thin wrapping with a voice of fire, flashing like a large, steady meteorite across the night sky, then across the dawn terminator, over steel-grey seas, tabular bergs, ice tables, floes and shelves, frozen coasts, glaciers, mountain ranges, permafrost tundra, more crushed pack ice and, finally, as it bellied down on its pillars of flame, land again: land on a thousand-kilometre peninsula sticking out into a frozen sea like some monstrous fractured limb set in plaster.

'There it is,' Wubslin said, watching the mass-sensor screen. A bright, winking light tracked slowly across the display. Horza looked over.

'The Mind?' he asked. Wubslin nodded.

'Right density. Five kilometres deep . . .' He punched some buttons and squinted at figures scrolling across the screen. 'On the far side of the system from the entrance . . . and moving.' The pinpoint of light on the screen disappeared. Wubslin adjusted the controls, then sat back, shaking his head. 'Sensor needs an overhaul; its range is right down.' The engineer scratched his chest and sighed. 'Sorry about the engines, too, Horza.' The Changer shrugged. Had the motors been working properly, or had the mass sensor's range been adequate, somebody could have remained on the *CAT*, flying it if necessary, and relaying the Mind's position to the others in the tunnels. Wubslin seemed to feel guilty that none of the repairs he'd tried to effect had significantly improved the performance of either motors or sensor.

'Never mind,' Horza said, watching the waste of ice and snow passing beneath them. 'At least now we know the thing's in there.'

The ship guided them to the right area, though Horza recognised it anyway from the times he had flown the single small flyer the base was allowed. He looked for the flyer as they made their final approach, in case somebody happened to be using it.

The snow-covered plain was ringed by mountains; the *Clear Air Turbulence* swept over a pass between two peaks, shattering the silence, tearing dusty snow from the jagged ridges and crags of the barren rocks on either side. It slowed further, coming in nose-up on its tripod of fusion fire. The snow on the plain beneath picked itself up and stirred as though uneasy at first. Then as the craft dropped lower and lower the snow was blown, then ripped, from the frozen ground beneath and thrown away in vast swirling rolls of heated air mixing snow and water, steam and plasma particles, in a howling blizzard which swept across the plain, gathering strength as the vessel dropped.

Horza had the *CAT* on manual. He watched the screen ahead, saw the false, created wind of stormy snow and steam in front, and beyond it, the entrance to the Command System.

It was a black hole set in a rugged promontory of rock which fluted down from the higher cliffs behind like a piece of solidified scree. The snowstorm broiled round the dark entrance like mist. The storm was turning brown as the fusion flame heated the frozen ground of the plain itself, melting it and plucking it out in an earthy spray.

With hardly a bump, and only a little settling as the legs sank into the now soggy surface of the swept plain, the *CAT* touched the surface of Schar's World.

Horza looked straight ahead at the tunnel entrance. It was like a deep dark eye, staring back.

The motors died; the steam drifted. Disturbed snow fell back, and some new flakes formed as the suspended water in the air froze once more. The *CAT* clicked and creaked as it cooled from the heat produced by both the friction of re-entry and its own plasma jets. Water gurgled, turning to slush, over the scoured surface of the plain.

Horza switched the *CAT*'s bow laser to standby. There was no movement or sign from the tunnel. The view was clear now, the snow and steam gone. It was a bright, sunny, windless day.

'Well, here we are,' Horza said, and immediately felt foolish. Yalson nodded, still staring at the screen.

'Yup,' Wubslin said, checking screens, nodding. 'Feet have sunk in half a metre or so. We'll have to remember to run the motors for a while before we try to lift off, when we leave. They'll freeze solid in half an hour.'

'Hmm,' Horza said. He watched the screen. Nothing moved. There were no clouds in the light blue sky, no wind to move the snows. The sun wasn't warm enough to melt the ice and snow so there was no running water, not even any avalanches in the distant mountains.

With the exception of the seas – which still contained fish, but no longer any mammals – the only things which moved on Schar's World were a few hundred species of small insects, slow spreading lichen on rocks near the equator, and the glaciers. The humanoids' war, or the ice age, had wiped everything else out.

Horza tried the coded message once more. There was no reply.

'Right,' he said, getting up from his seat. 'I'll step out and take a look.' Wubslin nodded. Horza turned to Yalson. 'You're very quiet,' he said.

Yalson didn't look at him. She was staring at the screen and the unblinking eye of the tunnel entrance. 'Be careful,' she said. She looked at him. 'Just be careful, all right?'

Horza smiled at her, picked up Kraiklyn's laser rifle from the floor, then went through to the mess.

'We're down,' he said as he went through.

'See?' Dorolow said to Aviger. Neisin drank from his hip flask. Balveda gave the Changer a thin smile as he went from one door to the other. Unaha-Closp resisted the temptation to say anything, and wriggled out of the seat straps.

Horza descended to the hangar. He felt light as he walked; they had switched to ambient gravity on their way over the mountains, and Schar's World produced less pull than the standard-G used on the *CAT*. Horza rode the hangar's descending floor to the now refreezing marsh, where the breeze was fresh and sharp and clean.

'Hope everything's all right,' Wubslin said as he and Yalson watched the small figure wade through the snow towards the rocky promontory ahead. Yalson said nothing but watched the screen with unblinking eyes. The figure stopped, touched its wrist, then rose in the air and floated slowly across the snows.

'Ha,' Wubslin said, laughing a little. 'I'd forgotten we could use AG here. Too long on that damn O.'

'Won't be much use in those fucking tunnels,' Yalson muttered.

Horza landed just to the side of the tunnel entrance. From the readings he had already taken while flying over the snow, he knew the tunnel door field was off. Normally it kept the tunnel within shielded from the snow and the cold air outside, but there was no field there, and he could see that a little snow had blown into the tunnel and now lay in a fan shape on its floor. The tunnel was cold inside, not warm as it should be, and its black, deep eye seemed more like a huge mouth, now that he was close to it.

He looked back at the *CAT*, facing him from two hundred metres away, a shining metal interruption on the white expanse, squatting in a blast-mark of brown.

'I'm going inside,' he told the ship, aiming a tight beam at it rather than broadcasting the signal.

'OK,' Wubslin said in his ear.

'You don't want somebody there to cover you?' Yalson said.

'No,' Horza replied.

He walked down the tunnel, keeping close to the wall. In the first equipment bay were some ice sleds and rescue gear, tracking apparatus and signalling beacons. It was all much as he recalled it.

In the second bay, where the flyer should have been, there was nothing. He went on to the next one: more equipment. He was about forty metres inside the tunnel now, ten metres shy of the right-angled turn which led into the larger, segmented gallery where the living accommodation of the base lay.

The mouth of the tunnel was a white hole when he turned back to face it. He set the tight beam on wide aperture. 'Nothing yet. I'm about to look into the accommodation section. Bleep but don't reply otherwise.' The helmet speakers bleeped.

Before going round the corner he detached the suit's remote sensor from the side of the helmet and edged its small lens round the corner of sculpted rock. On an internal screen he saw the short length of tunnel, the flyer lying on the ground, and a few metres beyond it the wall of plastic planking which filled the tunnel and showed where the human accommodation section of the Changer base began.

By the side of the small flyer lay four bodies.

There was no movement.

Horza felt his throat closing up. He swallowed hard, then put the remote sensor back on the side of the helmet. He walked along the floor of fused rock to the bodies.

Two were dressed in light, unarmoured suits. They were both men, and he didn't recognise them. One of them had been lasered, the suit flash-burned open so that the melted metals and plastics had mingled with the guts and flesh inside; the hole was half a metre in diameter. The other suited man had no head. His arms were stuck out stiffly in front of him as though to embrace something.

There was another man, dressed in light, loose clothes. His skull had been smashed in from behind, and at least one arm was broken. He lay on his side, as frozen and dead as the other two. Horza was aware that he knew the man's name but he couldn't think of it just then.

Kierachell must have been asleep. Her slim body was lying straight, inside a blue nightgown; her eyes were closed, her face peaceful.

Her neck had been broken.

Horza looked down at her for a while, then took one of his gloves off and bent down. There was frost on her eyelashes. He was aware of the wrist seal inside the suit gripping his forearm tightly, and of the thin cold air his hand was exposed to.

Her skin was hard. Her hair was still soft, and he let it run through his fingers. It was more red than he remembered, but that might just have been the effect of the helmet visor as it intensified the poor light of the darkened tunnel. Perhaps he should take his helmet off, too, to see her better, and use the helmet lights. . . .

He shook his head, turning away.

He opened the door to the accommodation section – carefully, after listening for any noise coming through the wall.

In the open, vaulted area where the Changers had kept their outdoor clothes and suits and some smaller pieces of equipment, there was little to show that the place had been taken over. Further through the accommodation unit, he found traces of a fight: dried blood; laser burns; in the control room, where the base's systems were monitored, there had been an explosion. It looked like a small grenade had gone off under the control panel. That accounted for the lack of heating, and the emergency light. It looked as though somebody had been trying to repair the damage, judging by some tools, spare pieces of equipment and wiring lying around.

In a couple of the cabins he found traces of Idiran occupation. The rooms had been stripped bare; religious symbols were burned onto the walls. In another room the floor had been covered with some sort of soft, deep covering like dry gelatin. There were six long indentations in the material, and the room smelt of medjel. In Kierachell's room, only the bed was untidy. It had changed little otherwise.

He left it and went to the far end of the accommodation unit, where another wall of plastic boards marked the beginning of the tunnels.

He opened the door cautiously.

A dead medjel lay just outside, its long body seemingly pointing the way down the tunnel to the waiting shafts. Horza looked at it for a while, monitored its body for a moment (dead still, frozen), then

305

prodded it and finally shot it once through the head, just to be sure.

It was in standard fleet-ground-force uniform, and it had been wounded some time ago, badly. It looked like it had suffered from frostbite earlier, too, before it had died of its wounds and frozen. It was a male, grizzled, its green-brown skin leathery with age, its long muzzle-face and small delicate-looking hands deeply lined.

He looked down the dark tunnel.

Smooth fused floor, smooth arched walls, the tunnel went on into the mountain side. Blast doors made ribs along the tunnel sides, their tracks and slots carved across the floor and roof. He could see the elevator-shaft doors, and the boarding point for the service-tube capsules. He walked along, past the sets of ancient blast doors, until he came to the access shafts. The elevators were all at the bottom; the transit tube was locked shut. No power seemed to be running through any of the systems. He turned and walked back to the accommodation section, through it and past the bodies and the flyer without giving them a glance, and eventually out into the open air.

He sat down at the side of the tunnel entrance, in the snow, his back to the rock. They saw him from the *CAT*, and Yalson said, 'Horza! Are you all right?'

'No,' he said, turning the laser rifle off. 'No, I'm not.'

'What's wrong?' Yalson said quickly. Horza took the suit helmet off, putting it down on the snow beside him. The cold air sucked heat from his face, and he had to breathe hard in the thin atmosphere.

'There is death here,' he said to the cloudless sky.

10.

The Command System: Batholith

'It's called a batholith: a granitic intrusion which rose up like a molten bubble into the sedimentary and metamorphic rocks already here a hundred million years ago.

'Eleven thousand years ago the locals built the Command System in it, hoping to use the rock cover as protection from fusion warheads.

'They built nine stations and eight trains. The idea was that the politicos and military chiefs sat in one train, their seconds-in-command and deputies in another, and during a war all eight trains would be shuffled around the tunnels, halting in a station to be linked via hardened communication channels to the transceiver sites on the immediate surface and throughout the state, so they could run the war. The enemy would have a hard time cracking the granite that deep anyway, but hitting something as relatively small as a station would be even more difficult, and they never could be sure there would be a train in it, or that it would be manned, and on top of that they had to knock out the back-up train as well as the main one.

'Germ warfare killed them all off, and some time between then and ten thousand years ago the Dra'Azon moved in, pumping the air out of the tunnels and replacing it with inert gas. Seven thousand years ago a new ice age started, and about four thousand years after that the place got so cold Mr Adequate pumped the argon out and let the planet's own atmosphere back in; it's so desiccated, nothing's rusted in the tunnels for three millennia.

'About three and a half thousand years ago the Dra'Azon came to an agreement with most of the rival Galactic Federations which allowed ships in distress to cross the Quiet Barriers. Politically neutral, relatively powerless species were permitted to set up small bases on most of the Planets of the Dead to provide help for those in distress and – I suppose – to provide a sop to the people who had always wanted to know what the planets were like; certainly on Schar's World, Mr Adequate let us take a good look at the System every year, and turned a blind eye when we went down unofficially. However, nobody's ever taken unscrambled recordings of any sort out of the tunnels.

'The entrance we're at is here: at the base of the peninsula, above station four, one of the three main stations – the others are one and seven – where repair and maintenance facilities exist. There are no trains parked in four, three or five. There are two trains in station one, two in seven, one train each in the rest. At least that's where they ought to be; the Idirans may have moved them, though I doubt it.

'The stations are twenty-five to thirty-five kilometres apart, linked by twin sets of tunnels which only join up at each of the stations. The whole System is buried about five kilometres down.

'We'll take lasers . . . and a neural stunner, plus chaff grenades for protection – nothing heavier. Neisin can take his projectile rifle; the bullets he has are only light explosive. . . . But no plasma cannons or micronukes. They'd be dangerous enough in the tunnels anyway, God knows, but they might also bring down Mr Adequate's wrath, and we *don't* want that.

'Wubslin's rigged up our ship mass anomaly sensor into a portable set, so we can spot the Mind. In addition, I've got a mass sensor in my suit, so we shouldn't have any problem actually finding what we're after, even if it's hidden itself.

'Assuming the Idirans don't have their own communicators, they'll be using the Changers'. Our transceivers cover their frequencies and more, so we can listen in on them, but they can't hear us.

'So those are the tunnels. That Mind is in there somewhere, and so, presumably, are some Idirans and medjel.'

Horza stood in the mess room at the head of the table, under the screen. On the screen a diagram of the tunnels was superimposed over a map of the peninsula. The others looked at him. The empty semi-suit of the medjel he had found lay in the centre of the table.

'You want to take us *all* in?' the drone Unaha-Closp said.

'Yes.'

'What about the ship?' Neisin said.

'It can take care of itself. I'll programme its automatics so that it'll recognise us and defend itself against anybody else.'

'And you're going to take her?' Yalson asked, nodding at Balveda, who was sitting opposite her.

Horza looked at the Culture woman. 'I'd prefer to have Balveda where I can see her,' he said. 'I wouldn't feel safe leaving her here with any of you.'

'I still don't see why *I* have to go,' Unaha-Closp said.

'Because,' Horza told it, 'I don't trust you on board here, either. Besides, I want you to carry stuff.'

'What?' The drone sounded angry.

'I don't know that you're being completely honest here, Horza,' Aviger said, shaking his head ruefully. 'You say that the Idirans and medjel . . . well, that you're on their side. But here they are, and they've killed four of your own people already, and you think that they're somewhere inside these tunnels, wandering about. . . . And they're supposed to be about the best ground-troops in the galaxy. You want to send *us* up against them?'

'First of all,' Horza sighed, 'I am on their side. We're after the same thing. Secondly, it looks to me as though they don't have many weapons of their own, otherwise that medjel would certainly have been armed. All they probably have here are the Changers' weapons. Also it looks, from this medjel suit we've got' – he gestured at the webbed apparatus in the middle of the table, which he and Wubslin had been studying since they had brought it on board – 'like a lot of their equipment is blown. Only the lights and the heaters on this thing were working. Everything else had fused. My guess is all that happened when they came through the Quiet Barrier. They were all zapped *inside* the chuy-hirtsi, and their battle gear was fucked up. If the same thing happened to their weapons as happened to their suits, they're virtually unarmed, and with a lot of problems. With all these fancy new AG harnesses and lasers, we're much better equipped, even in the unlikely event that it does come to a fight.'

'Which is very likely, considering they won't have any communicators left,' Balveda said. 'You'll never get close enough to tell them. And even if you did, how are they supposed to know you're who you say you are? If they're the same lot you think they are, they came in here just after the Mind did; they won't even have heard of you. They certainly won't believe you.' The Culture agent looked round the others. 'Your surrogate captain is leading you to your deaths.'

'Balveda,' Horza said, 'I'm doing you a courtesy letting you in on all this; don't annoy me.'

Balveda arched her eyebrows, staying silent.

'How do we know these *are* the same lot who got here inside this weird animal anyway?' Neisin said. He looked suspiciously at Horza.

'They can't be anybody else,' Horza said. 'They were damn lucky to survive what the Dra'Azon did to them, and even the Idirans wouldn't risk sending any other forces in after they saw what had happened to this lot.'

'But that means they've been here for months,' Dorolow said. 'How are we supposed to find something if they've been here all this time and haven't found anything?'

'Perhaps they have,' Horza said, spreading his arms wide and smiling at the woman, a trace of sarcasm in his voice; 'but if they haven't, it's very possibly because they won't have any working gear with them. They'd have to search the whole Command System.

'Besides, if that warp animal was as badly damaged as I heard it was, they won't have had much control over it. Very likely they crash-landed hundreds of kilometres away and had to slog here through the snow. In that case they might have only been here for a few days.'

'I can't believe the god would let this happen,' Dorolow said, shaking her head and looking at the surface of the table in front of her. 'There must be something else to all this. I could feel its power and . . . and *goodness* when we came through the Barrier. It wouldn't let those poor people just be shot down like that.'

Horza rolled his eyes. 'Dorolow,' he said to her, leaning forward and planting his knuckles on the table top, 'the Dra'Azon are barely aware there's a war going on. They don't really give a damn about individuals. They recognise death and decay, but not hope and faith. As long as the Idirans, or we, don't wreck the Command System or blow the planet away, they won't give a damn who lives or dies.'

Dorolow sat back, silent but unconvinced. Horza straightened. His words sounded fine; he had the impression the mercenaries would follow him, but inside, deeper than where the words were coming from, he felt no more caring, no more alive than the snow-covered plain outside.

He, Wubslin and Neisin had gone back into the tunnels. They had investigated the accommodation section, and found more evidence of Idiran habitation. It looked as though a very small force – one or two Idirans and maybe half a dozen medjel – had stayed for a while at the Changer base after they had taken it over.

They had apparently taken a lot of freeze-dried emergency food supplies with them, the two laser rifles and the few small pistols the Changer base was allowed, and the four portable communication sets from the store room.

Horza had covered the dead Changers up with the reflector foil they had found in the base, and removed the semi-suit from the dead medjel. They had looked at the flyer, to see if it was serviceable. It wasn't; its micropile had been partially removed and badly damaged

312

in the process. Like almost everything else in the base, it was without power. Back on board the *Clear Air Turbulence*, Horza and Wubslin had dissected the medjel's suit and discovered the subtle but irreparable damage which had been inflicted on it.

All the time, whenever Horza wasn't worrying about what their chances and their choices were, each moment he stopped concentrating on what he was looking at or supposed to be thinking about, he saw a hard and frozen face, at right angles to the body it was attached to, with frost on the eyelashes.

He tried not to think about her. There was no point; nothing he could do. He had to go on, he had to see this through, even more so now.

He had thought for a long time about what he could do with the rest of the people on the *Clear Air Turbulence*, and decided he had no real choice but to take them all into the Command System with him.

Balveda was one problem; he wouldn't feel safe even leaving the whole crew to guard her, and he wanted the best fighters along with him, not stuck on the ship. He could have got round this problem just by killing the Culture agent, but the others had got too used to her, had come to like her just a little too much. If he killed her, he would lose them.

'Well, I think it's insanity to go down into those tunnels,' Unaha-Closp said. 'Why not just wait up here until the Idirans reappear, with or without this precious Mind?'

'First of all,' Horza said, watching the expressions on the others' faces for any sign of agreement with the drone, 'if they don't find it they probably won't reappear; these are Idirans, and a carefully chosen crack squad of them at that. They'll stay down there for ever.' He looked at the tunnel system drawn on the screen, then back at the people and the machine around the table. 'They could search for a thousand years in there, especially if the power's off and they don't know how to bring it back up, which I'm assuming they don't.'

'And you do, of course,' the machine said.

'Yes,' Horza said, 'I do. We can turn the power on at one of three stations: this one, number seven or number one.'

'It still works?' Wubslin looked sceptical.

'Well, it was working when I left. Deep geothermal, producing electricity. The power shafts are sunk about a hundred kilometres through the crust.

'Anyway, as I say, there's too much space down there for those Idirans and medjel to have a hope of searching properly without some sort of detection device. A mass anomaly sensor is the only one that'll work, and they can't have one. We have two. That's why we have to go in.'

'And fight,' Dorolow said.

'Probably not. They've taken communicators; I'll get in touch with them and explain who I am. Naturally I can't tell you the details, but I know enough about the Idiran military system, about their ships, even some of their personnel, to be able to convince them I am who I say I am. They won't know me personally, but they were told a Changer would be sent later.'

'Liar,' Balveda said. Her voice was cold. Horza felt the atmosphere in the mess change, become tense. The Culture woman was looking at him, her features set, determined, even resigned.

'Balveda,' he said softly, 'I don't know what you were told, but I was briefed on *The Hand of God*, and Xoralundra told me the Idiran ground force in the chuy-hirtsi knew I'd been sent for.' He said it calmly. 'OK?'

'That wasn't what I heard,' Balveda said, but he sensed she was not totally sure of herself. She had risked a lot to say that, probably hoping that he would at least threaten her or do something which would turn the others against him. It hadn't worked.

Horza shrugged. 'I can't help it if the Special Circumstances section can't brief you accurately, Perosteck,' he said, smiling thinly. The Culture agent's eyes looked away from the Changer's face, at the table, then at each of the other people sitting around it, as though testing them to see who they each believed. 'Look,' Horza said in his most honest-sounding and reasonable voice, spreading his hands out, 'I don't want to die for the Idirans, and God knows why, but I have come to *like* you lot. I wouldn't take you in there on a suicide mission. We'll be all right. If the worst comes to the worst we can always pull out. We'll take the *CAT* back through the Quiet Barrier and head for somewhere neutral. You can have the ship; I'll have a captured Culture agent.' He looked at Balveda, who was sitting in her seat with her legs crossed, her arms folded and her head down. 'But I don't think it'll come to that. I think we'll catch this glorified computer and be well rewarded for it.'

'What if the Culture's won the battle outside the Barrier and they're waiting for us when we come out, with or without the Mind?' Yalson asked. She didn't sound hostile, just interested. She was the only one he felt he could rely on, though he thought Wubslin would follow, too. Horza nodded.

'That's unlikely. I can't see the Culture falling back all over this volume but holding out here; but even if they did they'd have to be very lucky indeed to catch us. They can only see into the Barrier in real space, don't forget, so they'd have no warning of where we'd be coming out. No problem there.'

Yalson sat back, apparently convinced. Horza knew he looked calm, but inside he was tensed up, waiting for the mood of the rest to make itself clear. His last answer had been truthful, but the rest were either not the whole truth, or lies.

He had to convince them. He had to have them on his side. There was no other way he could carry out his mission, and he had come too far, done too much, killed too many people, sunk too much of his own purpose and determination into the task, to back out now. He *had* to track the Mind down, he *had* to go down into the Command System, Idirans or no Idirans, and he *had* to have the rest of what had been Kraiklyn's Free Company with him. He looked at them: at Yalson, severe and impatient, wanting the talking to stop and the job just to be got on with, her shadow of hair making her look both very young, almost child-like, and hard at the same time; Dorolow, her eyes uncertain, looking at the others, scratching one of her convoluted ears nervously; Wubslin, slumped comfortably in his seat, compressed, his stocky frame radiating relaxation. Wubslin's face had shown signs of interest when Horza described the Command System, and the Changer guessed the engineer found the whole idea of this gigantic train-set fascinating.

Aviger looked very dubious about the whole venture, but Horza thought that now he had made it clear nobody was going to be allowed to stay on the ship, the old man would accept this rather than go to the trouble of arguing about it. Neisin he wasn't sure about. He had been drinking as much as ever, been quieter than Horza remembered him, but while he didn't like being bossed around and told what he could and couldn't do, he was obviously fed up being stuck on the *Clear Air Turbulence*, and had already been out for a walk in the snow while Wubslin and Horza were looking at the medjel suit. Boredom would make him follow, if nothing else.

Horza wasn't worried about the machine Unaha-Closp; it would do as it was told, like machines always did. Only the Culture let them get so fancy they really did seem to have wills of their own.

As for Perosteck Balveda, she was his prisoner; it was as simple as that.

'Easy in, easy out . . .' Yalson said. She smiled, shrugged and, looking round at the others, said, 'What the fuck; it's something to do, isn't it?'

Nobody disagreed.

Horza was reprogramming the *CAT*'s fidelities once more, entering the computer's new instructions through a worn but still serviceable touchboard, when Yalson came onto the flight deck. She slipped into the co-pilot's seat and watched the man as he worked; the touchboard's illuminated display threw the shadows of Marain characters over his face.

After a while she said, looking at the markings on the illuminated board, 'Marain, eh?'

Horza shrugged. 'It's the only accurate language I and this antique share.' He tapped some more instructions in. 'Hey.' He turned to her. 'You shouldn't be in here when I'm doing this.' He smiled, to show her he wasn't serious.

'Don't you trust me?' Yalson said, smiling back.

'You're the only one I do,' Horza said, turning to the board again. 'It doesn't matter anyway, for these instructions.'

Yalson watched him for a little longer. 'Did she mean a lot to you, Horza?'

He didn't look up, but his hands paused over the touchboard. He stared at the illuminated characters.

'Who?'

'Horza . . .' Yalson said, gently.

He still didn't look at her. 'We were friends,' he said, as though talking to the touchboard.

'Yeah, well,' she said, after a pause, 'I suppose it must be pretty hard anyway, when it's your own people. . . .'

Horza nodded, still not looking up.

Yalson studied him for a little longer. 'Did you love her?'

He didn't reply immediately; his eyes seemed to inspect each of the precise, compact shapes in front of him, as though one of them concealed the answer. He shrugged. 'Maybe,' he said, 'once.' He cleared his throat, looked briefly round at Yalson, then leant back to the touchboard. 'That was a long time ago.'

Yalson got up then, as he went back to his task, and put her hands on his shoulders. 'I'm sorry, Horza.' He nodded again, and placed one hand over hers. 'We'll get them,' she said. 'If that's what you want. You and—'

He shook his head, looked round at her. 'No. We go for the Mind, that's all. If the Idirans do get in the way, I won't care, but . . . no, there's no point in risking more than we have to. Thanks, though.'

She nodded slowly. 'That's all right.' She bent, kissed him briefly, then went out. The man gazed at the closed door for a few moments, then turned back to the board full of alien symbols.

He programmed the ship's computer to fire warning, then lethal laser shots at anybody or anything approaching it unless they could be identified by the distinctive electromagnetic emission signature of their suit as one of the Free Company. In addition, it required Horza's – Kraiklyn's – identity ring to make the *CAT*'s elevator work and, once on board, to take control of the ship itself. Horza felt safe enough doing this; only the ring would let them take over the ship, and he was confident nobody could take that from him, not without a greater risk to themselves than even a squad of mean and hungry Idirans could provide.

But it was possible that he might be killed, and the others might survive. Especially for Yalson, he wanted them to have some sort of escape route that didn't depend totally on him.

They took down some of the plastic boarding in the Changer base so that if they did find the Mind they would be able to get it through. Dorolow wanted to bury the dead Changers, but Horza refused. He carried each of them to the tunnel entrance and left them there. He would take them with him when they left; return them to Heibohre. The natural freezer of Schar's World's atmosphere would preserve them until then. He looked down at Kierachell's face for a moment, in the waning light of late afternoon, while a bank of clouds coming in from the frozen sea built over the distant mountains, and the wind freshened.

He would get the Mind. He was determined to, and he felt it in his bones. But if it came to a fire-fight with the ones who had done this, he wouldn't shrink from it. He might even enjoy it. Perhaps Balveda wouldn't have understood, but there were Idirans and Idirans. Xoralundra was a friend, and a kind and humane officer – he supposed the old Querl would be considered a moderate – and Horza knew others in the military and diplomatic missions whom he liked. But there were Idirans who were real fanatics, who despised all other species.

Xoralundra would not have murdered the Changers; it would have been unnecessary and inelegant . . . but then you didn't send moderates on missions like this. You sent fanatics. Or a Changer.

Horza returned to the others. He got as far as the crippled flyer, now surrounded with the plastic boarding they had removed and facing the hole in the accommodation section as though it was about to enter a garage, when he heard firing.

He ran through the corridor leading to the rear of the section, readying his gun. 'What is it?' he said into his helmet mike.

'Laser. Down the tunnel, from the shafts,' Yalson's voice said. He ran into the open store-room area where the others were. The hole they had opened in the plastic boarding was four or five metres wide. As soon as Horza came through from the corridor, flame splashed from the wall alongside him, and he saw the brief airglows of lasertracks just to one side of his suit, leading back through the gap in the wall and down the tunnel. Obviously whoever was doing the shooting could see him. He rolled to one side and came up by Dorolow and Balveda, who were sheltering by a large portable winch. Holes burst through the wall of plastic boards, burning brightly, then going out. The whoop of laser-fire echoed down the tunnels.

'What happened?' Horza said, looking at Dorolow. He looked around the storage area. The rest were all there, taking cover where they could, apart from Yalson.

'Yalson went—' Dorolow began; then Yalson's voice cut in:

'I came through the hole in the wall and got shot at. I'm lying on the ground. I'm OK, but I'd like to know if it's all right to fire back. I won't damage anything, will I?'

'Fire!' Horza yelled, as another fan of glowing tracks spattered a line of burning craters over the inside wall of the store room. 'Fire back!'

'Thanks,' Yalson said. Horza heard the woman's gun snap, then the dopplered echo of sound produced by superheated air. Explosions crashed from down the tunnel. 'Hmm,' Yalson said.

'Think that's got—' Neisin said from the far side of the storage area. His voice cut off as more fire slammed into the wall behind him. The wall was pockmarked with dark, bubbling holes.

'Bastard!' Yalson said. She fired back, in short, rapid bursts.

'Keep his head down,' Horza told her. 'I'm coming forward to the wall. Dorolow, stay here with Balveda.' He got up and ran to the edge of the hole in the plastic boards. Smoking holes in the material showed how little protection it afforded, but he knelt there in its cover anyway. He could see Yalson's feet a few metres out into the tunnel, spread on the smooth fused floor. He listened to her gun firing, then said, 'Right. Stop long enough to let me see where it's coming from, then hit it again.'

'OK.' Yalson stopped firing. Horza stuck his head out, feeling incredibly vulnerable, saw a couple of tiny sparks far down the tunnel and off to one side. He brought the gun up and fired continually; Yalson's started again as well. His suit chirped; a screen lit up by his cheek, showing he'd been hit on the thigh. He couldn't feel anything. The side of the tunnel, far down at the elevator shafts, pulsated with a thousand sparks of light.

Neisin appeared at the other side of the gap in the boards, kneeling like Horza and firing his projectile rifle. The side of the tunnel detonated with flashes and smoke; shock waves blew up the tunnel, shaking the plastic boarding and ringing in Horza's ears.

'Enough!' he shouted. He stopped firing. Yalson stopped. Neisin put in one final burst, then stopped, too. Horza ran out through the gap, across the dark rock floor of the tunnel outside and over to the side wall. He flattened himself there, getting some cover from the slight protrusion of a blast door's edge further down the tunnel.

Where their target had been, there was a scatter of dull red shards lying on the tunnel floor, cooling from the yellow heat of the laser fire which had torn them from the wall. On the helmet nightsight, Horza could see a series of rippling waves of warm smoke and gas flowing silently under the roof of the tunnel from the damaged area.

'Yalson, get over here,' he said. Yalson rolled over and over until she bumped into the wall just behind him. She got quickly to her feet and flattened out beside him. 'I think we got it,' Horza broadcasted. Neisin, still kneeling at the gap in the boarding, looked out, the rapidfire micro-projectile rifle waving to and fro as though its owner expected a further attack from out of the tunnel walls.

Horza started forward, keeping his back to the wall. He got to the edge of the blast door. Most of its metre-thick bulk was stowed in its recess in the wall, but about half a metre protruded. Horza looked down the tunnel again. The wreckage was still glowing, like hot coals scattered on the tunnel floor. The wave of hot black smoke passed overhead, wafting slowly up the tunnel. Horza looked to his other side. Yalson had followed him. 'Stay here,' he said.

He walked down the side of the wall to the first of the elevator shafts. They had been firing at the third and last one, judging by the grouping of the craters and scars all around its open, buckled doors. Horza saw a half-melted laser carbine lying in the middle of the tunnel floor. He poked his head out from the wall, frowning.

Right on the very lip of the elevator shaft, between the scarred and holed doors, surrounded by a sea of dull, red-glowing wreckage, he was sure he could see a pair of hands – gloved, stubby-fingered,

319

injured (one finger was missing from the glove nearer him), but hands without a doubt. It looked like somebody was hanging inside the shaft by the tips of their fingers. He focused the tight beam of his communicator, aiming in the direction he was looking at. 'Hello?' he said in Idiran. 'Medjel? Medjel in the elevator shaft? Do you hear me? Report at once.'

The hands didn't move. He edged closer.

'What was it?' Wubslin's voice came through the speakers.

'Just a moment,' Horza said. He went closer, rifle ready. One of the hands moved slightly, as though trying to get a better grip on the lip of the tunnel floor. Horza's heart thudded. He went towards the tall open doors, his feet crunching on the warm debris. He saw semi-suited arms as he went closer, then the top of a long, laser-scarred helmet—

With a rasping noise he had heard medjel make when they charged during a battle, another third hand – he knew it was a foot, but it looked like a hand and it was holding a small pistol – flashed up from the elevator shaft at the same time as the medjel's head looked up and out, straight at him. He started to duck. The pistol cracked, its plasma bolt missing him by only a few centimetres.

Horza shot quickly, ducking and going to one side. Fire blew out all around the lip of the elevator, smashing into the gloves. With a scream the gloved hands vanished. Light flickered briefly in the circular shaft. Horza ran foward, stuck his head between the doors and looked down.

The dim shape of the falling medjel was lit by the guttering fire still burning on its suit gloves. Somehow it still held the plasma pistol; as it fell, screaming, it fired the small weapon, the cracks of its shots and the flashes from the bolts drawing further away as the creature holding it, firing it, whirled, its six limbs flailing, down into the darkness.

'Horza!' Yalson shouted. 'Are you all right? What the fuck was that?'

'I'm fine,' he said. The medjel was a tiny, wriggling shape, deep in the shaft's tunnel of vertical night. Its screams still echoed, the microscopic sparks of its burning hands and the firing plasma pistol still flaring. Horza looked away. A few small thuds recorded the hapless creature's contact with the sides of the shaft as it dropped.

'What's that *noise*?' Dorolow said.

'The medjel was still alive. It shot at me, but I got it,' Horza told them, walking away from the open elevator doors. 'It fell – it's still falling – down the elevator shaft.'

320

'Shit!' breathed Neisin, still listening to the faint, fading, echoing screams. 'How deep is that?'

'Ten kilometres, if none of the blast doors are shut,' Horza said. He looked at the external controls for the other two lifts and the transit capsule entrance. They had escaped more or less undamaged. The doors leading to the transit tubes were open. They had been closed when Horza inspected the area earlier.

Yalson shouldered her gun and walked down the tunnel towards Horza. 'Well,' she said, 'let's get this op on the road.'

'Yeah,' Neisin said. 'What the hell! These guys aren't so tough after all. That's one down already.'

'Yeah, deep down,' Yalson said.

Horza inspected the damage to his suit while the others came down the tunnel. There was a burn on the right thigh, a millimetre deep and a couple of finger-breadths wide. Save for the unlikely chance of another shot falling on the same place, it hadn't harmed the suit.

'A fine start, if you ask me,' the drone muttered as it started down the tunnels with the others.

Horza went back to the tall, buckled, pitted doors of the lift shaft and looked down. With the magnifier up full he could just make out a tiny sparkling, deep, deep below. The helmet's external mikes picked up a noise, but from so far away and so full of echoes, it sounded like nothing more than the wind starting to moan through a fence.

They clustered in front of the opened doors of an elevator shaft, not the one the medjel had fallen down. The doors were twice the height of any one of them, dwarfing them all, as though they were children. Horza had opened those doors, taken a good look, floated down on the suit's AG a little way, then come back up. It all looked safe.

'I'll go first,' he told the assembled group. 'If we hit any trouble, let off a couple of chaff grenades and get back up here. We're going to the main system level, about five kilometres down. Once we get through the doors that's us more or less in station four. From there we'll be able to turn on the power, something the Idirans haven't been able to do. After that we'll have transport in the form of transit-tube capsules.'

'What about the trains?' Wubslin asked.

'The transit tubes are faster,' Horza said. 'We might have to start a train up if we capture the Mind; depends exactly how big it is. Besides, unless they've moved them since I was here, the nearest trains will be at station two or station six, not here. But there is a spiral

321

tunnel at station one we could bring a System train up.'

'What about the transit tube up here?' Yalson said. 'If that's the way that medjel suddenly appeared, what's to stop another one hiking up the tunnel?'

Horza shrugged. 'Nothing. I don't want to fuse the doors closed in case we want to come back that way once we have the Mind, but if one of them does come up that way, so what? It'll be one less down there for us to worry about. Anyway, somebody can stay up here until we're all safely down the lift shaft, then follow us. But I don't think there will be another one so close behind that one.'

'Yes, that one you didn't manage to talk into believing you were both on the same side,' the drone said testily.

Horza squatted down on his haunches to look at the drone; it was invisible from above because of the pellet of equipment it was carrying.

'That one,' he said, 'didn't have a communicator, did it? Whereas any Idirans down there certainly will have the ones they took from the base, won't they? And medjel do as Idirans tell them to, right?' He waited for the machine to reply and when it didn't he repeated, 'Right?'

Horza had the impression that, had the drone been human, it would have spat.

'Whatever you say, *sir*,' the drone said.

'And what do I do, Horza?' Balveda said, standing in her fabric jumpsuit, wearing a fur jacket on top. 'Do you intend to throw me down the shaft and say you forgot I didn't have any AG, or do I have to walk down the transit tunnel?'

'You'll come with me.'

'And if we hit trouble, you'll . . . what?' Balveda asked.

'I don't think we'll hit any trouble,' Horza said.

'You're sure there were no AG harnesses in the base?' Aviger said.

Horza nodded. 'If there had been, don't you think one of the medjel we've encountered so far would have had them on?'

'Maybe the Idirans are using them.'

'They're too heavy.'

'They could use two,' Aviger insisted.

'There were no harnesses,' Horza said through his teeth. 'We were never allowed any. We weren't supposed to go into the Command System apart from yearly inspections, when we could power everything up. We did go in; we walked down the spiral to station four, like that medjel must have slogged up, but we weren't supposed to, and we

322

weren't allowed gravity harnesses. They'd have made getting down there too easy.'

'Dammit, let's *get* down there,' Yalson said impatiently, looking at the others. Aviger shrugged.

'If my AG fails with all this rubbish I'm carrying—' the drone began, its voice muffled by the pallet over its top surface.

'You drop any of that stuff down that shaft and you'd be as well to follow it, machine,' Horza said. 'Now just save your energy for floating, not talking. You'll follow me; keep five or six hundred metres up. Yalson, will you stay up here till we get the doors open?' Yalson nodded. 'The rest of you,' he looked round them, 'come after the drone. Don't bunch up too much but don't get separated. Wubslin, stay at the same level as the machine, and have chaff grenades ready.' Horza held his hand out to Balveda. 'Madam?'

He held Balveda to him; she rested her feet on his boots, facing away from him; then Horza stepped into the shaft, and they descended together into the night-dark depths.

'See you at the bottom,' Neisin said in the helmet speakers.

'We're not going to the bottom, Neisin,' Horza sighed, shifting his arm slightly round Balveda's waist. 'We're going to the main system level. I'll see you there.'

'Yeah, OK; wherever.'

They fell on AG without incident, and Horza forced open the doors at the system level five kilometres below in the rock.

There had been only one exchange with Balveda on the way down, a minute or so after they had started out:

'Horza?'

'What?'

'If any shooting starts . . . from down there, or anything happens and you have to let go . . . I mean, drop me . . .'

'*What*, Balveda?'

'Kill me. I'm serious. Shoot me; I'd rather that than fall all that way.'

'Nothing,' Horza said after a moment's thought, 'would give me greater pleasure.'

They dropped into the chill stone silence of the tunnel's black throat, clasped like lovers.

'God*damn* it,' Horza said softly.

He and Wubslin stood in a room just off the dark, echoing vault that was station four. The others were waiting outside. The lights on

323

Horza and Wubslin's suits illuminated a space packed with electric switching gear; the walls were covered with screens and controls. Thick cables snaked over the ceiling and along the walls, and metal floor-plates covered conduits filled with more electrical equipment.

There was a smell of burning in the room. A long black sooty scar had printed itself onto one wall, above charred and melted cabling.

They had noticed the smell on their walk through the connecting tunnels from the shaft to the station. Horza had smelt it and felt gall rise in his throat; the odour was faint and could not have turned the most sensitive of stomachs, but Horza had known what it meant.

'Think we can mend it?' Wubslin asked. Horza shook his head.

'Probably not. This happened once on a yearly test when I was here before. We powered up in the wrong sequence and blew that same cable-run; if they've done what we did there'll be worse damage further down, in the deeper levels. Took us weeks to repair it.' Horza shook his head. 'Damn,' he said.

'I guess it was pretty smart of those Idirans to figure out as much as they did,' Wubslin said, opening his visor to reach in and scratch his head awkwardly. 'I mean, to get this far.'

'Yes,' Horza said, kicking a large transformer. 'Too goddamn smart.'

They made a brief search of the station complex, then gathered again in the main cavern and crowded round the jury-rigged mass sensor Wubslin had removed from the *Clear Air Turbulence*. Wires and light-fibres were tangled about it, and attached to the top of the machine was a cannibalised screen from the ship's bridge, now plugged directly into the sensor.

The screen lit up. Wubslin fiddled with its controls. The screen hologram showed a diagrammatic representation of a sphere, with three axes shown in perspective.

'That's about four kilometres,' Wubslin said. He seemed to be talking to the mass sensor, not the people around it. 'Let's try eight. . . .' He touched the controls again. The number of lines on the axes doubled. One very faint smudge of light blinked near the edge of the display.

'Is that it?' Dorolow said. 'Is that where it is?'

'No,' Wubslin said, fiddling with the controls again, trying to get the little patch of light to become clearer. 'Not dense enough.' Wubslin doubled the range twice more, but only the single trace remained, submerged in clutter.

Horza looked round, orienting himself with the grid pattern shown on the screen. 'Would that thing be fooled by a pile of uranium?'

'Oh yeah,' Wubslin said, nodding. 'The power we're putting through it, any radiation will upset it a bit. That's why we're down to roughly thirty kilometres maximum anyway, see? Just because of all this granite. Yeah, if there's a reactor, even an old one, it'll show up when the sensor's reader waves get to it. But just like this, as a patch. If this Mind's only fifteen metres long and weighs ten thousand tonnes, it'll be really bright. Like a star on the screen.'

'OK,' Horza said. 'That's probably just the reactor down at the deepest service level.'

'Oh,' Wubslin said. 'They had reactors, too?'

'Back-up,' Horza said. 'That one was for ventilation fans if the natural circulation couldn't cope with smoke or gas. The trains have reactors, too, in case the geothermal failed.' Horza checked the reading on the screen with the built-in mass sensor in his suit, but the faint trace of the back-up reactor was out of its range.

'Should we investigate this one?' Wubslin asked, his face lit by the glowing screen.

Horza straightened up, shaking his head. 'No,' he said wearily. 'Not for now.'

They sat in the station and had something to eat. The station was over three hundred metres long and twice the width of the main tunnels. The metal rails the Command System trains ran on stretched across the level floor of fused rock in double tracks, appearing from one wall through an inverted U and disappearing through another, towards the repair and maintenance area. At either end of the station there were sets of gantries and ramps which rose almost to the roof. Those provided access to the two upper floors of the trains when they were in the station, Horza explained when Neisin asked about them.

'I can't wait to see these trains,' Wubslin mumbled, mouth full.

'You won't *be* able to see them if there's no light,' Aviger told him.

'I think it's intolerable that I have to go on carrying all that junk,' the drone said. It had set the equipment-loaded pallet down. 'And now I'm told I have to carry even more weight!'

'I'm not that heavy, Unaha-Closp,' said Balveda.

'You'll manage,' Horza told the machine. With no power the only thing they could do was use their suits' AG to float along to the next station; it would be slower than the transit tube, but quicker than walking. Balveda would have to be carried by the drone.

'Horza . . . I was wondering,' Yalson said.

'What?'

'How much radiation have we all soaked up recently?'

'Not much.' Horza checked the small screen inside his helmet. The radiation level wasn't dangerous; the granite around them gave off a little; but even if they hadn't been suited up, they'd have been in no real danger. 'Why?'

'Nothing.' Yalson shrugged. 'Just with all these reactors, and this granite, and that blast when the bomb went off in the gear you vac'd from the *CAT* . . . well, I thought we might have taken a dose. Being on the Megaship when Lamm tried to blow it apart didn't help, either. But if you say we're OK, we're OK.'

'Unless somebody's particularly sensitive to it, we haven't got much to worry about.'

Yalson nodded.

Horza was wondering whether they should split up. Should they all go together, or should they go in two groups, one down each of the foot tunnels which accompanied the main line and the transit tube? They could even split up further and have somebody go down each of the six tunnels which led from station to station; that was going too far, but it showed how many possibilities there were. Split up, they might be better placed for a flanking attack if one group encountered the Idirans, though they wouldn't initially have the same firepower. They wouldn't be increasing their chances of finding the Mind, not if the mass sensor was working properly, but they would be increasing their chances of stumbling into the Idirans in the first place. Staying together, though, in the one tunnel, gave Horza a feeling of claustrophobic foreboding. One grenade would wipe them out; a single fan of heavy laser-fire would kill or disable all of them.

It was like being set a cunning but unlikely problem in one of the Heibohre Military Academy's term exams.

He couldn't even decide which way to head. When they'd searched the station, Yalson had seen marks in the thin layer of dust on the foot-tunnel floor leading to station five, which suggested the Idirans had gone that way. But ought they to follow, or should they go in the opposite direction? If they followed, and he couldn't convince the Idirans he was on their side, they'd have to fight.

But if they went in the other direction and turned the electricity on at station one, they'd be giving power to the Idirans as well. There was no way of restricting the energy to one part of the Command System. Each station could isolate its section of track from the supply loop, but the circuitry had been designed so that no single traitor – or incompetent – could cut off the whole System. So the Idirans, too, would have use of the transit tubes, the trains themselves and the engineering workshops. . . . Better to find them and try to parley; settle the issue one way or the other.

Horza shook his head. This whole thing was too complicated. The Command System, with its tunnels and caverns, its levels and shafts, its sidings and loops and cross-overs and points, seemed like some infernal closed-circuit flow chart for his thoughts.

He would sleep on it. He needed sleep now, like the rest of them. He could sense it in them. The machine might get run down but it didn't need sleep, and Balveda still seemed alert enough, but all the rest were showing signs of needing a deeper rest than just sitting down. According to their body clocks it was time to sleep; he would be foolish to try to push them further.

He had a restrainer harness on the pallet. That should keep Balveda secure. The machine could stand guard, and he would use the remote sensor on his suit to watch for movement in the immediate area where they slept; they ought to be safe enough.

They finished their meal. Nobody disagreed with the idea of turning in. Balveda was trussed in the restrainer harness and barricaded in one of the empty store rooms off the platform. Unaha-Closp was told to sit itself up on one of the tall gantries and stay still unless it heard or saw anything untoward. Horza set his remote sensor near where he would sleep, on one of the lower girders of a hoist mechanism. He had wanted a word with Yalson, but by the time he had finished making all these arrangements several of the others, including Yalson, had fallen asleep already, lying back against the wall or laid out on the ground, their visors blanked or their heads turned away from the weak lights of the others' suits.

Horza watched Wubslin wander around the station for a bit, then the engineer, too, lay down, and everything was still. Horza switched the remote sensor on, primed to alarm if it sensed anything above a certain low level of movement.

He slept fitfully; his dreams woke him.

Ghosts chased him in echoing docks and silent, deserted ships, and when he turned to face them, their eyes were always waiting, like targets, like mouths; and the mouths swallowed him, so that he fell into the eye's black mouth, past ice rimming it, dead ice rimming the cold, swallowing eye; and then he wasn't falling but running, running with a leaden, pitch-like slowness, through the bone cavities in his own skull, which was slowly disintegrating; a cold planet riddled with tunnels, crashing and crumpling against a never-ending wall of ice, until the wreckage caught him and he fell, burning, into the cold eye-tunnel again, and as he fell, a noise came, from the throat of the cold ice-eye and from his own mouth and chilled him more than ice, and the noise said:

'EEEeee . . .'

State of play: three

Fal 'Ngeestra was where she liked being most: on top of a mountain. She had just made her first real climb since she'd broken her leg. It was a relatively unforbidding peak, and she had taken the easiest route, but now, here at the summit, drinking in the view, she was dismayed at how unfit she had become. The healed leg hurt a little deep inside, of course, but so did the muscles in both legs, as though she'd just climbed a mountain twice the height, and with a full pack. Just out of condition, she guessed.

She sat on the summit of the ridge, looking out over smaller white summits to the sharp, forested creases of the higher foothills and the rolling downs beyond, where grassland and trees combined. In the distance was the plain, rivers sparkling in the sunlight and – marking its far side – the hills where the lodge was, her home. Birds wheeled far away, in the high valleys beneath her, and sometimes light glinted from the plain, as some reflective surface moved.

A part of her listened to the distant bone-ache, assessing it, then switched the nagging sensation off. She wanted no distractions; she hadn't climbed all this way *just* to enjoy the view. She'd come up here for a purpose.

It meant something to climb, to haul this sack of bones and flesh all this way, and then look, then think, then be. She could have taken a flyer here any time when she'd been recovering, but she hadn't, even though Jase had suggested it. That was too easy. Being here wouldn't have meant anything.

She concentrated, her eyelids drooping, going through the quiet internal chant, the unmagical spell that called up the spirits buried in her genofixed glands.

The trance came on with an initial rush of dizzying force that made her put her hands out to each side, steadying herself when she didn't need steadying. The sounds in her ears, of her own blood coursing, of her breath's slow tide, loudened, took on strange harmonies. The light beyond her eyelids pulsed in time to the blood-beat. She felt herself frown, imagining her brow creasing like the folding hills, and one part of her, still distant, watching, thought, *Still not very good at this . . .*

She opened her eyes, and the world had changed. The far hills were forever rolling brown and green waves with a crest of breaking white foam. The plain fumed with light; the pattern of pastureland and copses in the foothills looked like camouflage, moving but not moving, like a tall building seen against quick clouds. The forested ridges were buckled divisions in some huge busy tree-brain, and the snow- and ice-covered peaks about her had become vibrating sources of a light that was sound and smell as well. She experienced a dizzying sense of concentricity, as though she was the nucleus of the landscape.

Here in an inside-out world, an inverted hollowness.

Part of it. Born here.

All she was, each bone and organ, cell and chemical and molecule and atom and electron, proton and nucleus, every elementary particle, each wave-front of energy, from here . . . not just the Orbital (dizzy again, touching snow with gloved hands), but the Culture, the galaxy, the universe . . .

This is our place and our time and our life, and we should be enjoying it. But are we? Look in from outside; ask yourself. . . . Just what are we doing?

Killing the immortal, changing to preserve, warring for peace . . . and so embracing utterly what we claimed to have renounced completely, for our own good reasons.

Well, it was done. Those people in the Culture who had really objected to the war were gone; they were no longer Culture, they were not part of the effort. They had become neutrals, formed their own groupings and taken new names (or claimed to be the real true Culture; yet another shading of confusion along the Culture's inchoate boundaries). But for once the names did not matter; what did matter was the disagreement, and the illfeeling produced by the split.

Ah, the contempt of it. The glut of contempt we seem to have achieved. Our own disguised contempt for 'primitives', the contempt of those who left the Culture when war was declared for those who chose to fight the Idirans; the contempt so many of our own people feel for Special Circumstances . . . the contempt we all guess the Minds must feel for us . . . and elsewhere; the Idirans' contempt for us, all of us humans; and human contempt for Changers. A federated disgust, a galaxy of scorn. Us with our busy, busy little lives, finding no better way to pass our years than in competitive disdain.

And what the Idirans must feel towards us. Consider: near-immortal, singular and unchanged. Forty-five thousand years of history, on one planet, with one all-embracing religion/philosophy; whole steady aeons of contented study, a calm age of devotion on that one worshipped place, uninterested in anything outside. Then, millennia ago in another ancient war, invasion; suddenly finding themselves pawns in somebody else's squalid imperialism. From introverted peacefulness, through ages of torment and repression – a forging force indeed – to extroverted militancy, determined zeal.

Who could blame them? They had tried to keep themselves apart, and been shattered, almost made extinct, by forces greater than those they could muster. No surprise that they decided the only way to protect themselves was to attack first, expand, become stronger and stronger, push their boundaries as far from the treasured planet of Idir as possible.

And there is even a genetic template for that catastrophe change from meek to fierce, in the step from breeder to warrior. . . . Oh, a savage and noble species, justifiably proud of themselves, and refusing to alter their genetic code, not far wrong in claiming perfection already. What they must feel for the swarming biped tribes of humankind!

Repetition. Matter and life, and the materials that could take change – that could evolve – forever repeating: life's food talking back to it.

And us? Just another belch in the darkness. Sound but not a word, noise without meaning.

We are nothing to them: mere biotomatons, and the most terrible example of the type. The Culture must seem like some fiendish amalgam of everything the Idirans have ever found repugnant.

We are a mongrel race, our past a history of tangles, our sources obscure, our rowdy upbringing full of greedy, short-sighted empires and cruel, wasteful diasporas. Our ancestors were the lost-and-found of the galaxy, continually breeding and breeding and milling and killing, their societies and civilisations forever falling apart and reforming. . . . There had to be something wrong with us, something mutant in the system, something too quick and nervous and frantic for our own good or anybody else's. We are such pathetic, fleshy things, so short lived, swarming and confused. And dull, just so stupid, to an Idiran.

Physical repugnance, then, but worse to come. We are self-altering, we meddle with the code of life itself, re-spelling the Word which is the Way, the incantation of being. Interfering with our own inheritance, and interfering in the development of other peoples (ha! an interest we share) . . . And worse still, worst of all, not just producing, but embracing and giving ourselves over totally to the ultimate anathema: the Minds, the sentient machines; the very image and essence of life itself, desecrated. Idolatry incarnate.

No wonder that they despise us. Poor sick mutations that we are, petty and obscene, servants of the machine-devils that we worship. Not even sure of our own identity: just who is Culture? Where exactly does it begin and end? Who is and who isn't? The Idirans know exactly who they are: purebred, the one race, or nothing. Do we? Contact is Contact, the core, but after that? The level of genofixing varies; despite the ideal, not everybody can mate successfully with everybody else. The Minds? No real standards; individuals, too, and not fully predictable – precocious, independent. Living on a Culture-made Orbital, or in a Rock, another sort of hollowed world, small wanderer? No; too many claiming some kind of independence. No clear boundaries to the Culture, then; it just fades away at the edges, both fraying and spreading. So who are we?

The buzz of meaning and matter about her, the mountains' song of light, seemed to rise around her like a cauldron tide, drenching and engulfing. She felt herself as the speck she was: a mote, a tiny struggling imperfect chip of life, lost in the surrounding waste of light and space.

She sensed the frozen force of the ice and snow around her, and felt consumed by the skin-burning chill of it. She felt the sun beat, and knew the crystals' fracturing and melting, knew the water as it dripped and slithered and became dark bubbles under ice and dewdrops on the icicles. She saw the fronded trickles, the tumbling streams and the cataracted rivers; she sensed the winding and unwinding loops as the river slowed and ox-bowed, calm, esturial . . . into lake, and sea, where vapour rose once more.

And she felt lost within it, dissolved within it, and for the first time in her young life was truly afraid, more frightened there and then than she had been when she'd fallen and broken her leg, during either the brief moments of falling, the stunning instant of impact and pain, or the long cold hours afterwards, crumpled in the snow and rocks, sheltering and shivering and trying not to cry. That was something she had long before prepared herself for; she knew what was happening, she had worked out the effects it might have and the ways she might react. It was a risk you took, something you understood. This was not, because now there was nothing to understand, and maybe nothing – including her – to understand it.

Help! Something wailed inside her. She listened, and could do nothing.

We are ice and snow, we are that trapped state.

We are water falling, itinerant and vague, ever seeking the lowest level, trying to collect and connect.

We are vapour, raised against our own devices, made nebulous, blown on whatever wind arises. To start again, glacial or not.

(She could come out, she felt the sweat bead on her brow, sensed her hands create their own moulds in the crisp crunching snow, and knew there was a way out, knew she could come down . . . but with nothing, having found nothing, done nothing, understood nothing. She would stay, then, she would fight it out.)

The cycle began again, her thoughts looping, and she saw the water as it flowed down gorges and valleys, or collected lower in trees, or fell straight back to lakes and the sea. She saw it fall on meadowland and on the high marshes and the moors, and she fell with it, terrace to terrace, over small lips of rock, foaming and circling (she felt the moisture on her forehead start to freeze, chilling her, and knew the danger, wondered again whether to come out of the trance, wondered how long she had sat here, whether they were watching over her or not). She felt dizzy again, and grabbed deeper at the snow around her, her gloves pressuring the frozen flakes; and as she did that, she remembered.

She saw the pattern of frozen foam once more; she stood again beside that ledge on the moor's cold surface, by the tiny waterfall and the pool where she had found the lens of frothed ice. She remembered holding it in her hands, and recalled that it did not ring when she flicked it with her finger, that it tasted of water, no more, when she touched it with her tongue . . . and that her breath blew across it in a cloud, another swirling image in the air. And that was her.

That was what it meant. Something to hold onto.

Who are we?

Who we are. Just what we're taken as being. What we know and what we do. No less or more.

Information being passed on. Patterns, galaxies, stellar systems, planets, all evolve; matter in the raw changes, progresses in a way. Life is a faster force, reordering, finding new niches, starting to shape; intelligence – consciousness – an order quicker, another new plane. Beyond was unknown, too vague to be understood (ask a Dra'Azon, perhaps, and wait for the answer) . . . all just refining, a process of getting it more right (if right itself was right). . . .

And if we tamper with our inheritance, so what? What is more ours to tamper with? What makes nature more right than us? If we get it wrong that's because we are stupid, not because the idea was bad. And if we are no longer on the breaking edge of the wave, well, too bad. Hand on the baton; best wishes; have fun.

Everything about us, everything around us, everything we know and can know of is composed ultimately of patterns of nothing; that's the bottom line, the final truth. So where we find we have any control over those patterns, why not make the most elegant ones, the most enjoyable and good ones, in our own terms? Yes, we're hedonists, Mr Bora Horza Gobuchul. We seek pleasure and have fashioned ourselves so that we can take more of it; admitted. We are what we are. But what about you? What does that make you?

Who are you?

What are you?

A weapon. A thing made to deceive and kill, by the long-dead. The whole subspecies that is the Changers is the remnant of some ancient war, a war so long gone that no one willing to tell recalls who fought it, or when, or over what. Nobody even knows whether the Changers were on the winning side or not.

But in any event, you were fashioned, Horza. You did not evolve in a way you would call 'natural'; you are the product of careful thought and genetic tinkering and military planning and deliberate design . . . and war; your very creation depended on it, you are the child of it, you are its legacy.

Changer change yourself . . . but you cannot, you will not. All you can do is try not to think about it. And yet the knowledge is there, the information implanted, somewhere deep inside. You could – you should – live easy with it, all the same, but I don't think you do. . . .

And I'm sorry for you, because I think I know now who you really hate.

She came out of it quickly, as the supply of chemicals from glands in her neck and brain stem shut off. The compounds already in the girl's brain cells began to break down, releasing her.

Reality blew around her, the breeze freshening cold against her skin. She wiped the sweat from her brow. There were tears in her eyes, and she wiped them, too, sniffing, and rubbing her reddened nose.

Another failure, she thought bitterly. But it was a young, unstable sort of bitterness, a kind of fake, something she assumed for a while, like a child trying on adult clothes. She luxuriated in the feeling of being old and disillusioned for a moment, then let it drop. The mood did not fit. Time enough for the genuine version when she was old, she thought wryly, smiling at the line of hills on the far side of the plain.

But it was a failure nevertheless. She had hoped for something to occur to her, something about the Idirans or Balveda or the Changer or the war or . . . anything. . . .

Instead, old territory mostly, accepted facts, the already known.

A certain self-disgust at being human, an understanding of the Idirans' proud disdain for her kind, a reaffirmation that at least one thing was its own meaning, and a probably wrong, probably over-sympathetic glimpse into the character of a man she had never met and never would meet, who was separated from her by most of a galaxy and all of a morality.

Little enough to bring down from the frozen peak.

She sighed. The wind blew, and she watched clouds mass far along the high range. She would have to start down now if she was going to beat the storm. It would seem like cheating not to get back down under her own steam, and Jase would scold her if conditions got so bad she had to send for a flyer to pick her up.

Fal 'Ngeestra stood. The pain in her leg came back, signals from her weak point. She paused for a moment, reassessing the state of that mending bone, and then – deciding it would hold up – started the descent towards the unfrozen world below.

11.

The Command System: Stations

He was being shaken gently.

'Wake up, now. Come on, wake up. Come on, now, up you get. . . .'

He recognised the voice as Xoralundra's. The old Idiran was trying to get him to wake up. He pretended to stay asleep.

'I know you're awake. Come on, now, it's time to get up.'

He opened his eyes with a false weariness. Xoralundra was there, in a bright blue circular room with lots of large couches set into alcoves in the blue material. Above hung a white sky with black clouds. It was very bright in the room. He shielded his eyes and looked at the Idiran.

'What happened to the Command System?' he said, looking around the circular blue room.

'That dream is over now. You did well, passed with flying colours. The Academy and I are very pleased with you.'

He couldn't help but feel pleased. A warm glow seemed to envelop him, and he couldn't stop a smile appearing on his face.

'Thanks,' he said. The Querl nodded.

'You did very well as Bora Horza Gobuchul,' Xoralundra said in his rumbling great voice. 'Now you should take some time off; go and play with Gierashell.'

He was swinging his feet off the bed, getting ready to jump down to the floor, when Xoralundra said that. He smiled at the old Querl.

'Who?' he laughed.

'Your friend; Gierashell,' the Idiran said.

'You mean Kierachell,' he laughed, shaking his head; Xoralundra must be getting old!

'I mean Gierashell,' the Idiran insisted coldly, stepping back and looking at him strangely. 'Who is Kierachell?'

'You mean you don't know? But how could you get her name wrong?' he said, shaking his head again at the Querl's foolishness. Or was this still part of some test?

'Just a moment,' Xoralundra said. He looked at something in his hand

341

which threw coloured lights across his broad, gleaming face. Then he slapped his other hand to his mouth, an expression of astonished surprise on his face as he turned to him and said, 'Oh! Sorry!' and suddenly reached over and shoved him back into the—

He sat upright. Something whined in his ear.

He sat back down again slowly, looking round in the grainy darkness to see if any of the others had noticed, but they were all still. He told the remote sensor alarm to switch off. The whine in his ear faded. Unaha-Closp's casing could be seen high on the far gantry.

Horza opened his visor and wiped some sweat from his nose and brows. The drone had no doubt seen him each time he woke up. He wondered what it was thinking now, what it thought of him. Could it see well enough to know that he was having nightmares? Could it see through his visor to his face, or sense the small twitches his body made while his brain constructed its own images from the debris of all his days? He could blank the visor out; he could set the suit to expand and lock rigid.

He thought about how he must look to it: a small, soft naked thing writhing in a hard cocoon, convulsed with illusions in its coma.

He decided to stay awake until the others started to rise.

The night passed, and the Free Company awoke to darkness and the labyrinth. The drone said nothing about seeing him wake up during the night, and he didn't ask it. He was falsely jolly and hearty, going round the others, laughing and slapping backs, telling them they'd get to station seven today and there they could turn on the lights and get the transit tubes working.

'Tell you what, Wubslin,' he said, grinning at the engineer as he rubbed his eyes, 'we'll see if we can't get one of those big trains working, just for the hell of it.'

'Well,' Wubslin yawned, 'if that's all right. . . .'

'Why not?' Horza said, spreading his arms out. 'I think Mr Adequate's leaving us to it; he's turning a blind eye to this whole thing. We'll get one of those super-trains running, eh?'

Wubslin stretched, smiling and nodding. 'Well, yeah, sounds like a good idea to me.' Horza smiled widely, winked at Wubslin and went to release Balveda. It was like going to release a wild animal, he thought, as he shifted the empty cable drum he had used to block the door. He half expected to find Balveda gone, miraculously escaped from her bonds and disappeared from the room without opening the door; but when he looked in, there she was, lying calmly in her warm

342

clothes, the harness making troughs in the fur of the jacket and still attached to the wall Horza had fixed it to.

'Good morning, Perosteck!' he said breezily.

'Horza,' the woman said grumpily, sitting slowly upright, flexing her shoulders and arching her neck, 'twenty years at my mother's side, more than I care to think of as a gay and dashing young blade indulging in all the pleasures the Culture has *ever* produced, one or two of maturity, seventeen in Contact and four in Special Circumstances have not made me pleasant to know or quick to wake in the mornings. You wouldn't have some water to drink, would you? I've slept too long, I wasn't comfortable, it's cold and dark, I had nightmares I thought were really horrible until I woke up and remembered what reality was like at the moment, and . . . I mentioned water a moment or two ago; did you hear? Or aren't I allowed any?'

'I'll get you some,' he said, going back to the door. He stopped there. 'You're right, by the way. You are pretty off-putting in the morning.'

Balveda shook her head in the darkness. She put one finger in her mouth and rubbed it around on one side, as though massaging her gums or cleaning her teeth, then she just sat with her head between her knees, staring at the jet-black nothing of the cold rock floor beneath her, wondering if this was the day she died.

They stood in a huge semi-circular alcove carved out of the rock and looking out over the dark space of station four's repair and maintenance area. The cavern was three hundred metres or more square, and from the bottom of the scooped gallery they stood on to the floor of the vast cave – littered with machinery and equipment – was a thirty-metre drop.

Great cradle-arms capable of lifting and holding an entire Command System train were suspended from the roof above, another thirty metres up in the gloom. In the mid-distance a suspended gantry lanced out over the cave, from a gallery on one side to the other, bisecting the cavern's dark bulk.

They were ready to move; Horza gave the order.

Wubslin and Neisin each headed down small side tubes towards the main Command System tunnel and the transit tubeway respectively, using AG. Once in the tunnels they would keep level with the main group. Horza switched on his own AG, rose about a metre from the floor and floated down a branch tunnel of the foot gallery, then started slowly forward, down into the darkness, towards station five, thirty kilometres away. The rest would follow him, also floating. Balveda shared the pallet with the equipment.

He smiled when Balveda sat down on the pallet; she suddenly reminded him of Fwi-Song sitting on his heavy-duty litter, in the space and sunlight of a place now gone. The comparison struck him as wonderfully absurd.

Horza floated along the foot tunnel, stopping to check the side tubes as they appeared and contacting the others whenever he did so. His suit senses were turned as high as they would go; any light, the slightest noise, an alteration in the air flow, even vibrations in the rock around him: all were catered for. Unusual smells would register, too, as would power flowing through the cables buried in the tunnel walls and any sort of broadcast communication.

He'd thought about signalling the Idirans as they went along, but decided not to. He had sent one short signal from station four, without receiving a reply, but to send more on the way would be to give too much away if (as he suspected) the Idirans were not in a mood to listen.

He moved through the darkness as though sitting on an invisible seat, the CREWS cradled in his arms. He heard his heartbeat, his breathing and the quiet slipstreaming of the cold, half-stale air around his suit. The suit registered vague background radiation from the surrounding granite, punctuated by intermittent cosmic rays. On the faceplate of the suit's helmet, he watched a ghostly radar image of the tunnels as they unwound through the rock.

In places the tunnel ran straight. If he turned he could see the main group following half a kilometre behind him. In other places the tunnel described a series of shallow curves, cutting down the view provided by the scanning radar to a couple of hundred metres or less, so that he seemed to float alone in the chill blackness.

At station five they found a battleground.

His suit had picked up odd scents; that had been the first sign, organic molecules in the air, carbonised and burnt. He'd told the others to stop, gone on ahead cautiously.

Four dead medjel were laid out near one wall of the dark, deserted cavern, their burned and dismembered bodies echoing the formation of frozen Changer corpses at the surface base. Idiran religious symbols had been burned onto the wall over the fallen.

There had been a fire-fight. The station walls were pocked with small craters and long laser scars. Horza found the remains of one laser rifle, smashed, a small piece of metal embedded in it. The medjel bodies had been torn apart by hundreds more of the same tiny projectiles.

At the far end of the station, behind the half-demolished remains of one set of access ramps, he found the scattered components of some crudely manufactured machine, a kind of gun on wheels, like a miniature armoured car. Its mangled turret still contained some of the projectile ammunition, and more bullets were scattered like windseeds about the flame-seared wreck. Horza smiled slightly at the debris, weighing a handful of the unused projectiles in his hand.

'The Mind?' Wubslin said, looking down at what was left of the small vehicle. 'It made this thing?' He scratched his head.

'Must have,' Horza said, watching Yalson poke warily at the torn metal of the wreck's hull with one booted foot, gun ready. 'There was nothing like this down here, but you could manufacture it, in one of the workshops; a few of the old machines still work. It'd be difficult, but if the Mind still had some of its fields working, and maybe a drone or two, it could do it. It had the time.'

'Pretty crude,' Wubslin said, turning over a piece of the gun mechanism in his hand. He turned and looked back at the distant corpses of the medjel and added, 'Worked well enough, though.'

'No more medjel, by my count,' Horza said.

'Still two Idirans left,' Yalson said sourly, kicking at a small rubber wheel. It rolled a couple of metres across the debris and flopped over again, near Neisin, who was celebrating the discovery of the demised medjel with a drink from his flask.

'You sure these Idirans aren't still here?' Aviger asked, looking round anxiously. Dorolow peered into the darkness, too, and made the sign of the Circle of Flame.

'Positive,' Horza said. 'I checked.' Station five hadn't been difficult to search; it was an ordinary station, just a set of points, a chicane in the Command System's double loop and a place for the trains to stop and connect themselves with the communication links to the planet's surface. There were a few rooms and storage areas off the main cavern, but no power-switching gear, no barracks or control rooms, and no vast repair and maintenance area. Marks in the dust showed where the Idirans had walked away from the station after the battle with the Mind's crude automaton, heading for station six.

'You think there'll be a train at the next station?' Wubslin said.

Horza nodded. 'Should be.' The engineer nodded, too, staring vacantly at the double sets of steel rails gleaming on the station floor.

Balveda swung herself off the pallet, stretching her legs. Horza still had the suit's infra-red sensor on, and saw the warmth of the Culture agent's breath waft from her mouth in a dimly glowing cloud. She clapped her hands and stamped her feet.

'Still not too warm, is it?' she said.

'Don't worry,' grumbled the drone from underneath the pallet. 'I may start to overheat soon; that ought to keep you cosy until I seize up completely.'

Balveda smiled a little and sat back on the pallet, looking at Horza. 'Still thinking of trying to convince your tripedal pals you're all on the same side?' she said.

'Huh!' said the drone.

'We'll see,' was all Horza would say.

Again his breathing, his heartbeat, the slow wash of stale air.

The tunnels led on into the deep night of the ancient rock like an insidious, circular maze.

'The war won't end,' Aviger said. 'It'll just die away.' Horza floated along the tunnel, half listening to the others talk over the open channel as they followed behind him. He'd switched his suit's external mikes from the helmet speakers to a small screen near his cheek; the trace showed silence. Aviger continued, 'I don't think the Culture will give in like everybody thinks it will. I think they'll keep fighting because they believe in it. The Idirans won't give in, either; they'll keep fighting to the last, and they and the Culture will just keep going at each other all the time, all over the galaxy eventually, and their weapons and bombs and rays and things will just keep getting better and better, and in the end the whole galaxy will become a battle-ground until they've blown up all the stars and planets and Orbitals and everything else big enough to stand on, and then they'll destroy all of each other's big ships and then the little ships, too, until everybody'll be living in single suits, blowing each other up with weapons that could destroy a planet . . . and that's how it'll end; probably they'll invent guns or drones that are even smaller, and there'll only be a few smaller and smaller machines fighting over whatever's left of the galaxy, and there'll be nobody left to know how it all started in the first place.'

'Well,' said Unaha-Closp's voice, 'that sounds like a lot of fun. And what if things go badly?'

'That's too negative an attitude to battle, Aviger.' Dorolow's high-pitched voice broke in, 'You have to be positive. Contest is formative; battle is a testing, war a part of life and the evolutionary process. In its extremity, we find ourselves.'

'. . . Usually in the shit,' Yalson said. Horza grinned.

'Yalson,' Dorolow began, 'even if you don't be—'

'Hold it,' Horza said suddenly. The screen near his cheek had flickered. 'Wait there. I'm picking up some sound from ahead.' He stopped, sat still in mid-air and put the sound from outside through the helmet speakers.

A low noise, deep and boomy, like heavy surf from a long way off, or a thunderstorm in distant mountains.

'Well, there's something making a noise up there,' Horza said.

'How far to the next station?' Yalson said.

'About two kilometres.'

'Think it's them?' Neisin sounded nervous.

'Probably,' Horza said. 'OK. I'm going ahead. Yalson, put Balveda in the restrainer harness. Everybody check weapons. No noise. Wubslin, Neisin, go forward slowly. Stop as soon as you can see the station. I'm going to try talking to these guys.'

The noise boomed vaguely on, making him think of a rockslide, heard from a mine deep inside a mountain.

He approached the station. A blast door came into view round a corner. The station would be only another hundred metres beyond. He heard some heavy clunking noises; they came down the dark tunnel, deep and resonant, hardly muffled by the distance, sounding like huge switches being closed, massive chains being fastened. The suit registered organic molecules in the air – Idiran scent. He passed the edge of the blast door and saw the station.

There was light in station six, dim and yellow, as though from a weak torch. He waited for Wubslin and Neisin to tell him they could see the station from their tunnels, then he went closer.

A Command System train stood in station six, its rotund bulk three storeys tall and three hundred metres long, half filling the cylindrical cavern. The light came from the train's far end, high at the front, where the control deck was. The sounds came from the train, too. He moved across the foot tunnel so he could see the rest of the station.

At the far end of the platform floated the Mind.

He stared at it for a moment, then magnified the image to make sure. It looked genuine; an ellipsoid, maybe fifteen metres long and three in diameter, silvery yellow in the weak light spilling from the train's control cabin, and floating in the stale air like a dead fish on the surface of a still pond. He checked the suit's mass sensor. It registered the fuzzy signal of the train's reactor, but nothing else.

'Yalson,' he said, whispering even though he knew it was unnecessary, 'anything on that mass sensor?'

'Just a weak trace; a reactor, I guess.'

'Wubslin,' Horza said, 'I can see what looks like the Mind in the station, floating at the far end. But it's not showing on either sensor. Would its AG make it invisible to the sensors?'

'Shouldn't,' Wubslin's puzzled voice came back. 'Might fool a passive gravity sensor, but not—'

A loud, metallic breaking noise came from the train. Horza's suit registered an abrupt increase in local radiation. 'Holy shit!' he said.

'What's happening?' Yalson said. More clicking, snapping noises echoed through the station, and another weak, yellow light appeared, from beneath the reactor car in the middle of the train.

'They're fucking about with the reactor carriage, that's what's happening,' Horza said.

'God,' Wubslin said. 'Don't they know how old all this stuff is?'

'What are they doing that for?' Aviger said.

'Could be trying to get the train to run under its own power,' Horza said. 'Crazy bastards.'

'Maybe they're too lazy to push their prize back to the surface,' the drone suggested.

'These . . . nuclear reactors, they can't explode, can they?' Aviger said, just as a blinding blue light burst from under the centre of the train. Horza flinched, his eyes closed. He heard Wubslin shout something. He waited for the blast, the noise, death.

He looked up. The light still flashed and sparkled, under the reactor car. He heard an erratic hissing noise, like static.

'Horza!' Yalson shouted.

'God's balls!' Wubslin said. 'I nearly filled my pants.'

'Its OK,' Horza said. 'I thought they'd blown the damn thing up. What *is* that, Wubslin?'

'Welding, I think,' Wubslin said. 'Electric arc.'

'Right,' Horza said. 'Let's stop these crazies before they blow us all away. Yalson, join me. Dorolow, meet up with Wubslin. Aviger, stay with Balveda.'

It took a few minutes for the others to arrange themselves. Horza watched the bright, flickering blue light as it sizzled away under the centre of the train. Then it stopped. The station was lit only by the two weak lights from the control deck and reactor car. Yalson floated down the foot tunnel and landed gently at Horza's side.

'Ready,' Dorolow said over the intercom. Then a screen in Horza's helmet flashed; a speaker beeped in his ear. Something had transmitted a signal near by; not one of their suits, or the drone.

'What was that?' Wubslin said. Then: 'Look, there. On the ground. Looks like a communicator.' Horza and Yalson looked at each other. 'Horza,' Wubslin said, 'there's a communicator on the floor of the tunnel here; I think it's on. It must have picked up the noise of Dorolow setting down beside me. That was what transmitted; they're using it as a bug.'

'Sorry,' Dorolow said.

'Well, don't touch the thing,' Yalson said quickly. 'Could be boobied.'

'So. Now they know we're here,' Aviger said.

'They were going to know soon anyway,' Horza said. 'I'll try hailing them; everybody ready, in case they don't want to talk.'

Horza cut his AG and walked to the end of the tunnel, almost onto the level platform of the station. Another communicator lying there transmitted its single pulse. Horza looked at the great, dark train and switched on his suit PA. He drew a breath, ready to speak in Idiran.

Something flashed from a slit-like window near the rear of the train. His head was knocked back inside the helmet, and he fell, stunned, his ears ringing. The noise of the shot echoed through the station. The suit alarm beeped frantically at him. Horza rolled over against the tunnel wall; more shots slammed down on him, flaring against the suit helmet and body.

Yalson ducked and ran. She skidded to the lip of the tunnel and raked fire over the window the shots were coming from, then swivelled, grabbed Horza by one arm and pulled him further into the tunnel. Plasma bolts crashed into the wall he'd been lying against. 'Horza?' she shouted, shaking him.

'Command override, level zero,' a small voice chirped in Horza's buzzing ears. 'This suit has sustained system-fatal damage automatically voiding all warranties from this point; immediate total overhaul required. Further use at wearer's risk. Powering down.'

Horza tried to tell Yalson he was all right, but the communicator was dead. He pointed to his head, to make her understand this. Then more shots, from the nose of the train, came bursting into the foot tunnel. Yalson dived to the floor and started firing back. 'Fire!' she yelled to the others. 'Get those bastards!'

Horza watched Yalson shooting at the far end of the train. Laser trails flicked out from the left side of their tunnel, tracer shells from the right, as the others joined in. The station filled with a spastic, blazing light; shadows leapt and danced across the walls and ceiling. He lay there, stunned, dull-headed, listening to the muffled cacophony of sound breaking against his suit like surf. He fumbled with his laser rifle, trying to remember how to fire it. He really had to help the others fight the Idirans. His head hurt.

Yalson stopped shooting. The front of the train glowed red where she'd been firing at it. The explosive shells from Neisin's gun crackled round the window the first shots had come from; short bursts of fire. Wubslin and Dorolow had come out of the main tunnel, past the slab of the train's rear. The crouched near the wall, firing at the same window as Neisin.

The plasma fire had stopped. The humans stopped shooting, too. The station went dark; the gunfire echoed, faded. Horza tried to stand up, but somebody seemed to have removed the bones from his legs.

'Anybody—' Yalson began.

Fire cascaded around Wubslin and Dorolow, lancing out from the lower deck of the last carriage. Dorolow screamed and fell. Hand spasming, her gun blasted wildly over the cavern roof. Wubslin rolled along the ground, shooting back at the Idirans. Yalson and Neisin joined in. The carriage's skin buckled and burst under the fusilade. Dorolow lay on the platform, moving spasmodically, moaning.

More shots came from the front of the train, bursting around the tunnel entrances. Then something moved midway up the rear carriage, near the rear access gantry; an Idiran ran from a carriage door and along the middle ramp. He levelled a gun and fired down, first at Dorolow where she lay on the ground, then at Wubslin, lying near the side of the train.

Dorolow's suit was blown tumbling and burning across the black floor of the station. Wubslin's gun arm was hit. Then Yalson's shots found the Idiran, scattering fire across his suit, the structure of the gantry and the side of the train. The ramp supports gave way before the Idiran's armoured suit; softening and disintegrating under the stream of fire, the gantry tubing sagged and collapsed, sending the top platform of the ramp crashing down, trapping the Idiran warrior underneath the smoking wreckage. Wubslin cursed and shot one-handed at the nose of the train, where the second Idiran was still firing.

Horza lay against the wall, his ears roaring, his skin cold and sweat-slicked. He felt numb, dissociated. He wanted to take his helmet off and gasp at some fresh air but knew he shouldn't. Even though the helmet was damaged it would still protect him if he was shot again. He compromised by opening the visor. Sound assaulted his ears. Shockwaves thrummed at his chest. Yalson looked back at him, motioned him further back down the tunnel as shots smacked into the floor near him. He stood, but fell, blacking out briefly.

The Idiran at the front of the train stopped firing for a moment, Yalson took the opportunity to look back at Horza again. He lay on the tunnel floor behind her, moving weakly. She looked out to where Dorolow lay, her suit ripped and smouldering. Neisin was almost out of his tunnel, firing long bursts down the station, scattering explosions all over the nose of the train. The air boomed with the rasping noise of his gun, ebbing and flowing through the cavern and accompanied by a pulsing wave of light that seemed to reach back from where the bullets struck and detonated.

Yalson was aware of somebody shouting – a woman's voice, yelling – but she could hardly hear over the noise of Neisin's gun. Plasma bolts came singing down the platform from the front of the train again, from high up, near the forward access ramps. She returned fire. Neisin poured shots in the same direction, paused.

'—in! Stop!' the voice shouted in Yalson's ears. It was Balveda, 'There's something wrong with your gun; it'll—' The Culture agent's voice was drowned by the noise of Neisin firing again. '—crash!' Yalson heard Balveda scream despairingly; then a line of light and sound seemed to fill the station from one end to the other, ending at Neisin. The bright stalk of noise and flame blossomed into an explosion Yalson felt through her suit. Bits of Neisin's gun were scattered across the platform; the man was thrown back against the wall. He fell to the ground and lay still.

'Mother*fucker*,' Yalson heard herself say, and she started running up the platform, enfilading the front of the train, trying to widen the angle of fire. Shots dipped to meet her, then cut out. There was a pause, while she still ran and fired, then the second Idiran appeared on the top level of the distant access ramp, holding a pistol in both hands. He ignored both her and Wubslin's fire and shot straight across the breadth of the cavern, at the Mind.

The silvery ellipsoid started to move, heading for the far foot tunnel. The first shot seemed to go right through it, as did a second; a third bolt made it vanish completely, leaving only a tiny puff of smoke where it had been.

The Idiran's suit glittered as Yalson and Wubslin's shots struck home. The warrior staggered; he turned as though to start firing down at them again, just as the armoured suit gave way; he was blown back and across the gantry, one arm disappearing in a cloud of flame and smoke; he fell over the edge of the ramp and crashed down to the middle level, the suit burning brightly, one leg snagging over the guard rails on the middle ramp. The plasma pistol was blown from his hand. Other shots tore at the wide helm, fracturing the blackened visor. He hung, limp and burning and pummelled with laser fire, for a few more seconds; then the leg caught on the guard rail gave way, snapping cleanly off and falling to the station floor. The Idiran slid, crumpling, to the deck of the ramp.

Horza listened, his ears still ringing.

After a while it was quiet. Acrid smoke stung his nose: fumes of burned plastic, molten metal, roasted meat.

He had been unconscious, then woken to see Yalson running up the platform. He had tried to give her covering fire, but his hands shook too much, and he hadn't been able to get the gun to work. Now everybody had stopped firing, and it was very quiet. He got up and walked unsteadily into the station, where smoke rose from the battered train.

Wubslin knelt by Dorolow's side, trying with one hand to undo one of the woman's gloves. Her suit still smouldered. The helmet visor was smeared red, covered with blood on the inside, hiding her face.

Horza watched Yalson come back down the station, gun still at the ready. Her suit had taken a couple of plasma bolts to the body; the roughly spiralled marks showed as black scars on the grey surface. She looked up suspiciously at the rear access ramps, where one Idiran lay trapped and unmoving; then she opened her visor. 'You all right?' she asked Horza.

'Yes. Bit groggy. Sore head,' he said. Yalson nodded; they went over to where Neisin lay.

Neisin was still just alive. His gun had exploded, riddling his chest, arms and face with shrapnel. Moans bubbled from the crimson ruin of his face. 'Fucking hell,' Yalson said. She took a small medipack from her suit and reached through what was left of Neisin's visor to inject the semi-conscious man's neck with painkiller.

'What's happened?' Aviger's tiny voice came from Yalson's helmet. 'Is it safe yet?' Yalson looked at Horza, who shrugged, then nodded.

'Yeah, it's safe, Aviger,' Yalson said. 'You can come in.'

'I let Balveda use my suit mike; she said she—'

352

'We heard,' Yalson said.

'Something about a . . . "barrelcrash"? That right . . .?' Horza heard Balveda's muffled voice affirming this. '. . . She thought Neisin's gun might blow up, or something.'

'Well, it did,' Yalson said. 'He looks pretty bad.' She glanced over at Wubslin, who was putting Dorolow's hand back down. Wubslin shook his head when he saw Yalson looking at him. '. . . Dorolow got blown away, Aviger,' Yalson said. The old man was silent for a moment, then said:

'And Horza?'

'Took a plasma round on the head-box. Suit damage; no communication. He'll live,' Yalson paused, sighed. 'Looks like we lost the Mind, though; it disappeared.'

Aviger waited another few moments before saying, his voice shaking, 'Well, a fine little mess. Easy in, easy out. Another triumph. Our Changer friend taking over where Kraiklyn left off!' His voice finished on a high pitch of anger; he switched his transceiver off.

Yalson looked at Horza, shook her head and said, 'Old asshole.'

Wubslin still knelt over Dorolow's body. They heard him sob a couple of times, before he, too, cut out of the open channel. Neisin's slowing breath spluttered through a mask of blood and flesh.

Yalson made the Circle of Flame sign over the red haze masking Dorolow's face, then covered the body with a sheet from the pallet. Horza's ears stopped ringing, the grogginess cleared. Balveda, freed from the restrainer harness, watched the Changer tend to Neisin. Aviger stood near by with Wubslin, whose arm wound had already been treated. 'I heard the noise,' Balveda explained. '. . . It has a distinctive noise.'

Wubslin had asked why Neisin's gun had exploded, and how Balveda had known it was going to happen.

'I'd have recognised it, too, if I hadn't been smacked on the head,' Horza said. He was teasing fragments of visor out of the unconscious man's face, spraying skin-gel onto the places where blood oozed. Neisin was in shock, probably dying, but they couldn't even take him out of his suit; too much blood had clotted between the man's body and the materials of the device he wore. It would plug the many small punctures effectively enough until the suit was removed, but then Neisin would start to bleed in too many places for them to cope with. So they had to leave him in the thing, as though in that mutual wreckage the human and machine had become one fragile organism.

'But what *happened*?' Wubslin said.

'His gun barrelcrashed,' Horza said. 'The projectiles must have been set to explode on too soft an impact, so the shells started to detonate when they hit the blast wave from the bullets in front, not the target. He didn't stop firing, so the blast front retarded right back into the muzzle of the gun.'

'The guns have sensors to stop it happening,' Balveda added, wincing with vicarious pain as Horza drew a long sliver of visor from an eye socket. 'I guess his wasn't working.'

'Told him that gun was too damn cheap when he bought it,' Yalson said, coming over to stand by Horza.

'Poor little bugger,' Wubslin said.

'Two more dead,' Aviger announced. 'I hope you're happy, Mr Horza. I hope you're so pleased about what your "allies" have—'

'Aviger,' Yalson said calmly, 'shut up.' The old man glared at her for a second, then stamped off. He stood looking down at Dorolow.

Unaha-Closp floated down from the rear access ramp. 'That Idiran up there,' it said, its voice pitched to betray mild surprise; 'he's alive. Couple of tons of junk on top of him, but he's still breathing.'

'What about the other one?' Horza said.

'No idea. I didn't like to go too close; it's terribly *messy* up there.'

Horza left Yalson to look after Neisin. He walked over the debris-strewn platform to the wreckage of the rear access gantry.

He was bare-headed. The suit's helmet was ruined, and the suit itself had lost its AG and motor power, as well as most of its senses. On back-up energy, the lights still worked, as did the small repeater screen set into one wrist. The suit's mass sensor was damaged; the wrist screen filled with clutter when linked to the sensor, barely registering the train's reactor at all.

His rifle was still working, for whatever that was worth now.

He stood at the bottom of the ramps and felt the dregs of heat seeping from the metal support legs, where laser fire had struck. He took a deep breath and climbed up the ramp to where the Idiran lay, his massive head sticking out of the wreckage, sandwiched between the two levels of ramp. The Idiran turned slowly to look at him, and one arm tensed against the wreckage, which creaked and moved. Then the warrior brought his arm out from beneath the press of metal and unfastened the scarred battle-helm; he let it fall to the floor. The great saddle-face looked up at the Changer.

'The greetings of the battle-day,' Horza said in careful Idiran.

'Ho,' boomed the Idiran, 'the little one speaks our tongue.'

'I'm even on your side, though I don't expect you to believe it. I belong to the intelligence section of the First Marine Dominate under the Querl Xoralundra.' Horza sat down on the ramp, almost level with the Idiran's face. 'I was sent in here to try to get the Mind,' he continued.

'Really?' the Idiran said. 'Pity; I believe my comrade just destroyed it.'

'So I hear,' Horza said, levelling the laser rifle at the big face viced between the twisted metal planking. 'You also "destroyed" the Changers back up at the base. *I* am a Changer; that's why our mutual masters sent me in here. Why did you have to kill my people?'

'What else could we do, human?' the Idiran said impatiently. 'They were an obstacle. We needed their weaponry. They would have tried to stop us. We were too few to guard them.' The creature's voice was laboured as it fought the weight of ramp crushing its torso and rib cylinder. Horza aimed the rifle straight at the Idiran's face.

'You vicious bastard, I ought to blow your fucking head off right now.'

'By all means, midget,' the Idiran smiled, the double set of hard lips spreading. 'My comrade has already fallen bravely; Quayanorl has started his long journey through the Upper World. I am captured and victorious at once, and you offer me the solace of the gun. I shall not close my eyes, human.'

'You don't have to,' Horza said, letting the gun down. He looked over, through the darkness of the station, at Dorolow's body, then into the dim, smoke-hazed light in the distance, where the nose and control deck of the train glowed faintly, illuminating an empty patch of floor where the Mind had been. He turned back to the Idiran. 'I'm taking you back. I believe there are still units of the Ninety-Third Fleet out beyond the Quiet Barrier; I have to report my failure and deliver a female Culture agent to the Fleet Inquisitor. I'm going to report you for exceeding your orders in killing those Changers; not that I expect it'll do any good.'

'Your story bores me, little one.' The Idiran looked away and strained once more at the press of twisted metal covering him, but to no avail. 'Kill me now; you do smell so, and your speech grates. Ours is not a tongue for animals.'

'What's your name?' Horza said. The saddle-head turned to him again; the eyes blinked slowly.

'Xoxarle, human. Now you'll sully it by trying to pronounce it, no doubt.'

'Well, you just rest there, Xoxarle. Like I said, we'll take you with us. First I want to check on the Mind you destroyed. A thought has just occurred to me.' Horza got to his feet. His head hurt abominably where the helmet had slammed into it, but he ignored the pounding in his skull and started back down the ramp, limping a little.

'Your soul is shit,' the Idiran called Xoxarle boomed after him. 'Your mother should have been strangled the moment she came on heat. We were going to eat the Changers we killed; but they smelled like filth!'

'Save your breath, Xoxarle,' Horza said, not looking at the Idiran. 'I'm not going to shoot you.'

Horza met Yalson at the bottom of the ramp. The drone had agreed to look after Neisin. Horza looked to the far end of the station. 'I want to see where the Mind was.'

'What do you think happened to it?' Yalson asked, falling into step beside him. He shrugged. Yalson went on, 'Maybe it did the trick it did earlier; went into hyperspace again. Maybe it reappeared somewhere else in the tunnels.'

'Maybe,' Horza said. He stopped by Wubslin, taking the man's elbow and turning him round from Dorolow's body. The engineer had been crying. 'Wubslin,' Horza said, 'guard that bastard. He might try and get you to shoot him, but don't. That's what he wants. I'm going to take the son of a bitch back to the fleet so they can court-martial him. Dirtying his name is a punishment; killing him would be doing him a favour; understand?'

Wubslin nodded. Still rubbing the bruised side of his head, Horza went off down the platform with Yalson.

They came to where the Mind had been. Horza turned the lights on his suit up and looked over the floor. He picked up a small, burned-looking thing near the mouth of the foot tunnel leading to station seven.

'What's that?' Yalson said, turning away from the body of the Idiran on the other access gantry.

'I *think*,' Horza said, turning the still warm machine over in his hand, 'it's a remote drone.'

'The Mind left it behind?' Yalson came over to look at it. It was just a blackened slab of material, some tubes and filaments showing through the lumpy, irregular surface where it had been hit by plasma fire.

'It's the Mind's, all right,' Horza said. He looked at Yalson. 'What *exactly* happened when they shot the Mind?'

'When he eventually hit it, it vanished. It had started to move, but it couldn't have accelerated that fast; I'd have felt the shock wave. It just vanished.'

'It was like somebody turning off a projection?' Horza said.

Yalson nodded. 'Yes. And there was a bit of smoke. Not much. Do you mean to—'

'He got it *eventually*; what do you mean?'

'I *mean*,' Yalson said, putting one hand on her hip and looking at Horza with an impatient expression on her face, 'that it took three or four shots. The first few went straight through it. Are you saying it *was* a projection?'

Horza nodded and held up the machine in his hand. 'It was this: a remote drone producing a hologram of the Mind. Must have had a weak force field as well so that it could be touched and pushed as though it was a solid object, but all there was inside was this.' He smiled faintly at the wrecked machine. 'No wonder the damn thing didn't show up on our mass sensors.'

'So the Mind's still around somewhere?' Yalson said, looking at the drone in Horza's hand. The Changer nodded.

Balveda watched Horza and Yalson walk into the darkness at the far end of the station. She went over to where the drone floated above Neisin, monitoring his vital functions and sorting out some vials of medicine in the medkit. Wubslin kept his gun pointed at the trapped Idiran, but watched Balveda from the corner of his eye at the same time; the Culture woman sat down cross-legged near the stretcher.

'Before you ask,' the drone said, 'no, there's nothing you can do.'

'I had guessed that, Unaha-Closp,' Balveda said.

'Hmm. Then you have ghoulish tendencies?'

'No, I wanted to talk to you.'

'Really.' The drone continued to sort the medicines.

'Yes . . .' She sat forward, elbow on her knee, chin cupped in her hand. She lowered her voice a little. 'Are you biding your time, or what?'

The drone turned its front to her; an unnecessary gesture, they both knew, but one it was used to making. 'Biding my time?'

'You've let him use you so far. I just wondered: how much longer?'

The drone turned away again, hovering over the dying man. 'Perhaps you hadn't noticed, Ms Balveda, but my choices in this matter are almost as limited as yours.'

'I've only got arms and legs, and I'm locked away at night, trussed up. You're not.'

357

'I have to keep watch. He has a movement sensor which he leaves switched on, anyway, so he would know if I tried to escape. And besides, where would I go?'

'The ship,' Balveda suggested, smiling. She looked back up the dark station, where the lights on their suits showed Yalson and the Changer picking something up from the ground.

'I would need his ring. Do *you* want to take it from him?'

'You must have an effector. Couldn't you fool the ship's circuits? Or even just that motion sensor?'

'Ms Balveda—'

'Call me Perosteck.'

'Perosteck, I am a general-purpose drone, a civilian. I have light fields; the equivalent of many fingers, but not major limbs. I can produce a cutting field, but only a few centimetres in depth, and not capable of taking on armour. I can interface with other electronic systems, but I cannot interfere with the hardened circuits of military equipment. I possess an internal forcefield which lets me float, regardless of gravity, but apart from using my own mass as a weapon, that is not really of much use, either. In fact, I am not particularly strong; when I needed to be, for my job, there were attachments available for my use. Unfortunately, I was not employing them when I was abducted. Had I been, I probably wouldn't be here now.'

'Damn,' Balveda said into the shadows. 'No aces up your sleeve?'

'No sleeves, Perosteck.'

Balveda took in a deep breath and stared glumly at the dark floor. 'Oh dear,' she said.

'Our leader approaches,' Unaha-Closp said, affecting weariness in its voice. It turned and nodded its front towards Yalson and Horza, returning from the far end of the cavern. The Changer was smiling. Balveda rose smoothly to her feet as Horza beckoned to her.

'Perosteck Balveda,' Horza said, standing with the others at the bottom of the rear access gantry and holding out one hand towards the Idiran trapped in the wreckage above, 'meet Xoxarle.'

'This is the female you claim is a Culture agent, human?' the Idiran said, turning his head awkwardly to look down at the group of people below him.

'Pleased to meet you,' Balveda muttered, arching one eyebrow as she gazed up at the trapped Idiran.

Horza walked up the ramp, passing Wubslin, who was training his gun on the trapped being. Horza still held the remote drone. He came to the second level ramp and looked down at the Idiran's face.

'See this, Xoxarle?' He held the drone up. It glinted in the lights of his suit.

Xoxarle nodded slowly. 'It is a small piece of damaged equipment.' The deep, heavy voice betrayed signs of strain, and Horza could see a trickle of dark purple blood on the floor of the ramp Xoxarle lay squashed upon.

'It's what you two proud warriors had when you thought you'd captured the Mind. This is all there was. A remote drone casting a weak soligram. If you'd taken this back to the fleet they'd have thrown you into the nearest black hole and wiped your name from the records. You're damn lucky I came along when I did.'

The Idiran looked thoughtfully at the wrecked drone for a short while.

'You,' Xoxarle said slowly, 'are lower than vermin, human. Your pathetic tricks and lies would make a yearling laugh. There must be more fat inside your thick skull than there is even on your skinny bones. You aren't fit to be thrown up.'

Horza stepped onto the ramp which had fallen on top of the Idiran. He heard the being's breath suck in harshly through taut lips as he walked slowly over to where Xoxarle's face stuck out beneath the wreckage. 'And you, you goddamn fanatic, aren't fit to wear that uniform. *I'm* going to find the Mind you thought you had, and then I'm going to take you back to the fleet, where if they've any sense they'll let the Inquisitor try you for gross stupidity.'

'Fuck . . .' the Idiran gasped painfully, '. . . your animal soul.'

Horza used the neural stunner on Xoxarle. Then he and Yalson and the drone Unaha-Closp levered the ramp off the Idiran's body and sent it crashing down to the station floor. They cut the armour from the giant's body, then hobbled his legs with wire and tied down his arms to his sides. Xoxarle had no broken limbs, but the keratin on one side of his body was cracked and oozed blood, while another wound, between his collar scale and right shoulder plate, had closed up once the pressure was taken off him. He was big, even for an Idiran; over three and a half metres, and not thin. Horza was glad the tall male – a section leader according to the insignia on the armour he had been wearing – was probably injured internally and going to be in pain. It would make him less of a problem to guard once he had woken up; he was too big for the restrainer harness.

Yalson sat, eating a rationfood bar, her gun balanced on one knee and pointing straight at the unconscious Idiran, while Horza sat at the bottom of the ramp and tried to repair his helmet. Unaha-Closp watched over Neisin, as powerless as the rest of them to do anything to help the wounded man.

Wubslin sat on the pallet making some adjustments to the mass sensor. He had already taken a look round the Command System train, but what he really wanted was to see a working one, in better light and without radiation stopping him looking through the reactor car.

Aviger stood by Dorolow's body for a while. Then he went to the far access ramp, where the body of the other Idiran, the one Xoxarle had called Quayanorl, lay, holed and battered, limbs missing. Aviger looked around and thought nobody was watching, but both Horza, looking up from the wrecked helmet, and Balveda, walking round and stamping and shaking her feet in an attempt to keep warm, saw the old man swing his foot at the still body lying on the ramp, kicking the helmeted head as hard as he could. The helmet fell off; Aviger kicked the naked head. Balveda looked at Horza, shook her head, then went on pacing up and down.

'You're sure we've accounted for all the Idirans?' Unaha-Closp asked Horza. It had floated about the station and through the train, accompanying Wubslin. Now it was facing the Changer.

'That's the lot,' Horza said, looking not at the drone but at the mess of fractured optic fibres lying bloated and fused together inside the outer skin of his helmet. 'You saw the tracks.'

'Hmm,' the machine said.

'We've won, drone,' Horza said, still not looking at it. 'We'll get the power on in station seven and then it won't take us long to track the Mind down.'

'Your "Mr Adequate" seems remarkably unconcerned about the liberties we're taking with his train-set,' the drone observed.

Horza looked round at the wreckage and debris scattered near the train, then shrugged and went back to tinkering with the helmet. 'Maybe he's indifferent,' he said.

'Of could it be he's enjoying all this?' Unaha-Closp said. Horza looked at it. The drone went on, 'This place is a monument to death, after all. A sacred place. Perhaps it is as much an altar as a monument, and we are merely carrying out a service of sacrifice for the gods.'

Horza shook his head. 'I think they left the fuse out of your imagination circuits, machine,' he said, and looked back at the helmet.

Unaha-Closp made a hissing noise and went to watch Wubslin, poking around inside the mass sensor.

'What have you got against machines, Horza?' Balveda said, interrupting her pacing to come and stand near by. She rubbed her hands on her nose and ears now and again. Horza sighed and put down the helmet.

'Nothing, Balveda, as long as they stay in their place.'

Balveda made a snorting noise at that, then went on pacing. Yalson spoke from further up the ramp:

'Did you say something funny?'

'I said machines ought to stay in their place. Not the sort of remark that goes down well with the Culture.'

'Yeah,' Yalson said, still watching the Idiran. Then she looked down, at the scarred area on the front of her suit where it had been hit by a plasma bolt. 'Horza?' she said. 'Can we talk somewhere? Not here.'

Horza looked up at her. 'Of course,' he said, puzzled. Wubslin replaced Yalson on the ramp. Yalson walked to where Unaha-Closp floated over Neisin, its lights dim; it held an injector in one hazy field extension.

'How is he?' she asked the machine. It turned its lights up.

'How does he look?' it said. Yalson and Horza said nothing. The drone let its lights fade again. 'He might last a few more hours.'

Yalson shook her head and headed for the tunnel entrance which led to the transit tube, followed by Horza. She stopped inside, just out of sight of the others, and turned to face the Changer. She seemed to search for words but could not find them; she shook her head again and took off her helmet, leaning back against the curved tunnel wall.

'What's the problem, Yalson?' he asked her. He tried to take her hand, but she crossed her arms. 'You having second thoughts about going on with this?'

She shook her head. 'No; I'm going on. I want to see this goddamned super-brain. I don't care who gets it, or if it gets blown up, but I want to find it.'

'I didn't think you regarded it as that important.'

'It's become important.' She looked away, then back again, smiling uncertainly. 'Hell, I'd come along anyway – just to try and keep you out of trouble.'

'I thought maybe you'd gone off me a little lately,' he said.

'Yeah,' Yalson said. 'Well, I haven't been . . . ah . . .' she sighed heavily. 'What the hell.'

361

'What?' Horza said. He saw her shrug. The small, shaved head dropped again, silhouetted against the distant light.

She shook her head. 'Oh, Horza,' she said, and gave a small, grunting laugh. 'You're not going to believe this.'

'Believe what?'

'I don't know that I should tell.'

'Tell me,' he said.

'I don't expect you to believe me; and if you do, I don't expect you to like it. Not all of it. I'm serious. Maybe I just shouldn't . . .' She sounded genuinely troubled. He laughed lightly.

'Come on, Yalson,' he said. 'You've said too much to stop now; you just said you weren't one for turning back. What is it?'

'I'm pregnant.'

He thought he'd misheard at first, and was going to make a joke about what he thought he'd just heard, but some part of his brain played the sounds her voice had made back, double-checking, and he knew that that was exactly what she'd said. She was right. He didn't believe it. He couldn't.

'Don't ask me if I'm sure,' Yalson said. She was looking down again, fiddling with her fingers and staring at them or the floor beyond in the darkness, her ungloved hands protruding nakedly from the suit arms and pressing against each other. 'I'm sure.' She looked at him, though he couldn't see her eyes, and she wouldn't be able to see his. 'I was right, wasn't I? You don't believe me, do you? I mean, it is by you. That's why I'm telling you. I wouldn't say anything if it . . . if you weren't . . . if I just happened to be.' She shrugged. '. . . I thought maybe you'd guess when I asked about how much radiation we'd all absorbed. . . . But now you're wondering how, aren't you?'

'Well,' Horza said, clearing his throat and shaking his head, 'it certainly shouldn't be possible. We're both . . . but we're from different species; it ought not to be possible.'

'Well, there is an explanation,' Yalson sighed, still looking at her fingers as they picked and kneaded at each other, 'but I don't think you'll like that, either.'

'Try me.'

'It's . . . it's like this. My mother . . . my mother lived on a Rock. A travelling Rock, just one of the many, you know. One of the oldest; it had been . . . just tramping around the galaxy for maybe eight or nine thousand years, and—'

'Wait a minute,' Horza said, 'one of *whose* oldest?'

'. . . My dad was some . . . some man from a place, a planet the

Rock stopped off at one time. My mother said she'd be back some time, but she never did go back. I told her I'd go back some time just to see him, if he's still alive. . . . Pure sentimentalism, I guess, but I said I would and I will some time; if I live through this lot.' She gave that same small half-laugh, half-grunt, and turned away from her picking fingers for a second to glance round the dark spaces of the station. Then her face again turned to the Changer, and her voice was suddenly urgent, almost pleading. 'I'm only half Culture, by birth, Horza. I left the Rock soon as I was old enough to aim a gun properly; I knew the Culture wasn't the place for me. That's how I inherited the genofixing for trans-species mating. I never thought about it before. It's supposed to be deliberate, or at least you've got to stop thinking yourself into *not* getting pregnant, but it didn't work this time. Maybe I let my guard slip somehow. It wasn't deliberate, Horza, it really wasn't; it never occurred to me. It just happened. I—'

'How long have you known?' Horza asked quietly.

'Since on the *CAT*. We were still a few days out from this place. I can't remember exactly. I didn't believe it at first. I know it's true, though. Look' – she leaned closer to him, and the note of pleading was in her voice again – 'I can abort it. Just by thinking about it I can get rid of it, if you want. Maybe I'd have done that already, but I know you've told me about not having any family, nobody to carry on your name, and I thought . . . well, I don't care about *my* name . . . I just thought you—' She broke off and suddenly put her head back and ran her fingers through her short hair.

'It's a nice thought, Yalson,' he said. Yalson nodded silently and went back to picking her fingers again.

'Well, I'm giving you the choice, Horza,' she said without looking at him. 'I can keep it. I can let it grow. I can keep it at the stage it's at now. . . . It's up to you. Maybe I just don't want to have to make the decision; I mean, maybe I'm not being all noble and self-sacrificing, but there it is. You decide. Fuck knows what sort of weird cross-breed I might have inside me, but I thought you ought to know. Because I like you, and . . . because . . . I don't know – because it was about time I did something for somebody else for a change.' She shook her head again, and her voice was confused, apologetic, resigned, all at once. 'Or maybe because I want to do something to please myself, as usual. Oh . . .'

He had started to put his arms out to her and edge closer. She suddenly came towards him, wrapping her arms tight round him. Their suits made the embrace cumbersome, and his back felt tight and strained, but he held her to him, and rocked her gently backwards and forwards.

'It would only be a quarter Culture, Horza, if you want. I'm sorry to leave it to you. But if you don't want to know, OK; I'll think again and make my own decision. It's still part of me, so maybe I don't have any right to ask you. I don't really want to . . .' She sighed mightily. 'Oh God, I don't know, Horza, I really don't.'

'Yalson,' he said, having thought about what he was going to say, 'I don't give a damn your mother was from the Culture. I don't give a damn why what has happened has happened. If you want to go through with it, that's fine by me. I don't give a damn about any cross-breeding either.' He pushed her away slightly and looked into the darkness that was her face. 'I'm flattered, Yalson, and I'm grateful, too. It's a good idea; like you would say: what the hell?'

He laughed then, and she laughed with him, and they hugged each other tightly. He felt tears in his eyes, though he wanted to laugh at the incongruity of it all. Yalson's face was on the hard surface of his suit shoulder, near a laser burn. Her body shook gently inside her own suit.

Behind them, in the station, the dying man stirred slightly and moaned in the cold and darkness, without an echo.

He held her for a little while. Then she pushed away, to look into his eyes again. 'Don't tell the others.'

'Of course not, if that's what you want.'

'Please,' she said. In the dimmed glow of their suit lights, the down on her face and the hair on her head seemed to shine, like a hazy atmosphere round a planet seen from space. He hugged her again, unsure what to say. Surprise, partly, no doubt . . . but in addition there was the fact that this revelation made whatever existed between them that much more important, and so he was more anxious than ever not to say the wrong thing, not to make a mistake. He could not let it mean too much, not yet. She had paid him perhaps the greatest compliment he had ever had, but the very value of it frightened him, distracted him. He felt that whatever continuity of his name or clan the woman was offering him, he could not yet build his hopes upon it; the glimmer of that potential succession seemed too weak, and somehow also too temptingly defenceless, to face the continuous frozen midnight of the tunnels.

'Thanks, Yalson. Let's get this over with, down here, then we'll have a better idea what we want to do. But even if you change your mind later, thank you.'

It was all he could say.

They returned to the station's dark cavern just as the drone pulled a light sheet over Neisin's still form. 'Oh, there you are,' it said. 'I didn't see any point in contacting you.' Its voice was hushed. 'There wasn't anything you could have done.'

'Satisfied?' Aviger asked Horza, after they had put Neisin's body with Dorolow's. They stood near the access gantry, where Yalson had resumed guard duty on the unconscious Idiran.

'I'm sorry about Neisin, and Dorolow,' Horza told the old man. 'I liked them, too; I can understand you being upset. You don't have to stay here now; if you want, go back to the surface. It's safe now. We've accounted for them all.'

'You've accounted for most of us, too, haven't you?' Aviger said bitterly. 'You're no better than Kraiklyn.'

'Shut up, Aviger,' Yalson said, from the gantry. 'You're still alive.'

'And you haven't done too badly, either, have you, young lady?' Aviger said to her. 'You and your *friend* here.'

Yalson was quiet for a moment, then said, 'You're braver than I thought, Aviger. Just remember it doesn't bother me a bit you're older and smaller than me. You want me to kick your balls in . . .' she nodded and pursed her lips, still staring at the limp body of the Idiran officer lying in front of her, '. . . I'll do it for you, old boy.'

Balveda came up to Aviger and slipped her arm through his, starting to lead him away as she walked by, 'Aviger,' she said, 'let me tell you about the time—' But Aviger shrugged her away and went off by himself, to sit with his back to the station wall, opposite the reactor car.

Horza looked down the platform to where the old man sat. 'He'd better watch his radiation meter,' he said to Yalson. 'It's pretty hot down there near the reactor car.'

Yalson gnawed at another ration bar. 'Let the old bastard fry,' she said.

Xoxarle woke up. Yalson watched him regain consciousness, then waved the gun at him. 'Tell the big creep to head on down the ramp, will you Horza?' she said.

Xoxarle looked down at Horza and struggled awkwardly to his feet. 'Don't bother,' he said in Marain, 'I can bark as well as you in this miserable excuse for a language.' He turned to Yalson. 'After you, my man.'

'I am a female,' Yalson growled, and waved the gun down the ramp, 'now get your trefoil ass down there.'

Horza's suit AG was finished. Unaha-Closp couldn't have taken Xoxarle's weight anyway, so they would have to walk. Aviger could float; so could Wubslin and Yalson, but Balveda and Horza would have to take turns riding on the pallet; and Xoxarle would need to foot-slog the whole twenty-seven kilometres to station seven.

They left the two human bodies near the doors to the transit tubes, where they could collect them later. Horza threw the useless lump of the Mind's remote drone to the station floor, then blasted it with his laser.

'Did that make you feel better?' Aviger said. Horza looked at the old man, floating in his suit, ready to head up the tunnel with the rest of them.

'Tell you what, Aviger. If you want to do something useful, why don't you float up to that access ramp and put a few shots through the head of Xoxarle's comrade up there, just to make sure he's properly dead?'

'Yes, Captain,' Aviger said, and gave a mock salute. He moved through the air to the ramp where the Idiran's body lay.

'OK,' Horza said to the rest; 'let's go.'

They entered the foot tunnel as Aviger landed on the middle level of the access ramp.

Aviger looked down at the Idiran. The armoured suit was covered with burn marks and holes. The creature had one arm and one leg missing; there was blood, dried black, all over the place. The Idiran's head was charred on one side, and where he had kicked it earlier Aviger could see the cracked keratin just below the left eye socket. The eye, dead, jammed open, stared at him; it looked loose in its bone hemisphere, and some sort of pus had oozed out of it. Aviger pointed his gun at the head, setting the weapon to single shot. The first pulse blew the injured eye off; the second punched a hole in the creature's face under what might have been its nose. A jet of green liquid splashed out of the hole and landed on Aviger's suit chest. He splashed some water from his flask over the mess and let it dribble off.

'Filth,' he muttered to himself, shouldering his gun, 'all of it . . . filth.'

'Look!'

They were less than fifty metres into the tunnel. Aviger had just

366

entered it and started floating towards them, when Wubslin shouted. They stopped, looking into the screen of the mass sensor.

Almost at the centre of the close-packed green lines there was a grey smudge; the reactor trace they were used to seeing, the sensor being fooled by the nuclear pile in the train behind them.

Right at the very edge of the screen, straight ahead and over twenty-six kilometres away, there was another echo. It was no grey patch, no false trace. It was a harsh, bright pinpoint of light, like a star on the screen.

12.

The Command System: Engines

'. . . A sky like chipped ice, a wind to cut you to the body core. Too cold for snow, for most of the journey, but once for eleven days and nights it came, a blizzard over the field of ice we walked on, howling like an animal, with a bite like steel. The crystals of ice flowed like a single torrent over the hard and frozen land. You could not look into it or breathe; even trying to stand was near impossible. We made a hole, shallow and cold, and lay in it until the skies cleared.

'We were the walking wounded, straggled band. Some we lost when their blood froze in them. One just disappeared, at night in a storm of snow. Some died from their wounds. One by one we lost them, our comrades and our servants. Every one begged us make what use we could of their corpse once they were gone. We had so little food; we all knew what it meant, we were all prepared; name a sacrifice more total, or more noble.

'In that air, when you cried, the tears froze on your face with a cracking sound, like a heart breaking.

'Mountains. The high passes we climbed to, famished in that thin and bitter air. The snow was white powder, dry as dust. To breathe it was to freeze from inside; flurries from the jagged slopes, dislodged by feet in front, stung in the throat like acid spray. I saw rainbows in the crystal veils of ice and snow which were the product of our passing, and grew to hate those colours, that freezing dryness, the starved high air and dark blue skies.

'Three glaciers we traversed, losing two of our comrades in crevasses, beyond sight or sound, falling further than an echo's reach.

'Deep in a mountain ring we came to a marsh; it lay in that scoop like a cess for hope. We were too slow, too stupefied, to save our Querl when he walked out into it and floundered there. We thought it could not be, with air so cold around us, even in that wan sunlight; we thought it must be frozen and we saw what only seemed to be, and our eyes would clear and he come walking back to us, not slip beneath that dark ooze, out of reach.

'It was an oil marsh, we realised too late, after the tarry depths had claimed their toll from us. The next day, while we were still looking for a way across, the chill came harder still, and even that sludge locked itself to stillness, and we walked quickly to the other side.

'In the midst of frozen water we began to die of thirst. We had little to heat the snow with save our own bodies, and eating that white dust until it numbed us made us groggy with the cold of it, slowing our speech and step. But we kept on, though the cold sucked at us whether awake or trying to sleep, and the harsh sun blinded us in fields of glittering white and filled our eyes with pain. The wind cut us, snow tried to swallow us, mountains like cut black glass blocked us, and the stars on clear nights taunted us, but on we came.

'Near two thousand kilometres, little one, with only the small amount of food we could carry from the wreck, what little equipment had not been turned to junk by the barrier beast, and our own determination. We were forty-four when we left the battle cruiser, twenty-seven when we began our trek across the snows: eight of my kind, nineteen of the medjel folk. Two of us completed the journey, and six of our servants.

'Do you wonder that we fell upon the first place we found with light and heat? Does it surprise you that we just took, and did not ask? We had seen brave warriors and faithful servants die of cold, watched each other wear away, as thought the ice blasts had abraded us; we had looked into the cloudless, pitiless skies of a dead and alien place, and wondered who might be eating who when the dawnlight came. We made a joke of it at first, but later, when we had marched a thirty-day, and most of us were dead, in ice gullies, mountain ravines or raw in our own bellies, we did not think it so funny. Some of the last, perhaps not believing our course was true, I think died of despair.

'We killed your humans friends, these other Changers. I killed one with my own hands; another, the first, fell to a medjel, while he still slept. The one in the control room fought bravely, and when he knew he was lost, destroyed many of the controls. I salute him. There was another who put up a fight in the place where they stored things; he, too, died well. You should not grieve too much for them. I shall face my superiors with the truth in my eyes and heart. They will not discipline me, they will reward me, should I ever stand before them.'

Horza was behind the Idiran, walking down the tunnel after him while Yalson took a rest from guarding the tall triped. Horza had asked Xoxarle to tell him what had happened to the raiding party which had come to the planet inside the chuy-hirtsi animal. The Idiran had responded with an oration.

'*She*,' Horza said.

'What, human?' Xoxarle's voice rumbled down the tunnel. He hadn't bothered to turn round when he talked; he spoke to the clear air of the foot tunnel leading to station seven, his powerful bassy voice easily heard even by Wubslin and Aviger, who were bringing up the rear of the small, motley band.

'You did it again,' Horza said wearily, talking to the back of the Idiran's head. 'The one killed while asleep: it was a she; a woman, a female.'

'Well, the medjel attended to her. We laid them out in the corridor. Some of their food proved edible; it tasted like heaven to us.'

'How long ago was that?' Horza asked.

'About eight days, I think. It is hard to keep time down here. We tried to construct a mass sensor immediately, knowing that it would be invaluable, but we were unsuccessful. All we had was what was undamaged from the Changer base. Most of our own equipment had been attacked by the beast of the Barrier or had to be abandoned when we set off from the warp animal to come here, or left en route, as we died off.'

'You must have thought it was a bit of luck finding the Mind so easily.' Horza kept his rifle trained on the tall Idiran's neck, watching Xoxarle all the time. The creature might be injured – Horza knew enough about the species to tell that the section leader was in pain just from the way he walked – but he was still dangerous. Horza didn't mind him talking, though; it passed the time.

'We knew it was injured. When we found it in station six, and it did not move or show any sign of noticing us, we assumed that those were only the signs of its damage. We already knew that you had arrived; it was only a day ago. We accepted our good luck without second thoughts, and prepared to make our escape. You only just stopped us. Another few hours and we would have had that train working.'

'More likely you'd have blown yourselves into radioactive dust,' Horza told the Idiran.

'Think what you like, little one. I knew what I was doing.'

'I'm sure,' Horza said sceptically. 'Why did you take all the guns with you and leave that medjel on the surface without a weapon?'

'We had intended to take one of the Changers alive and interrogate him, but failed; our own fault, no doubt. Had we done so we could have reassured ourselves there was nobody else down here ahead of us. We were so late in getting here, after all. We took all the available weaponry down with us and left the servant on the surface with only a communicator so—'

'We didn't find the communicator,' Horza interrupted.

'Good. He was supposed to hide it when not checking in,' Xoxarle said, then went on, 'So we had what little firepower we did possess where it might be needed most. Once we realised that we were in here by ourselves, we sent a servant up with a weapon for our guard. Unhappily for him, it would appear he arrived very shortly after you did.'

'Don't worry,' Horza said, 'he did well; damn nearly blew my head off.'

Xoxarle laughed. Horza flinched slightly at the sound. It was not only loud, it was cruel in a way Xoralundra's laugh had not been.

'His poor slave soul is at rest, then,' Xoxarle boomed. 'His tribe can ask for no more.'

Horza refused to pause until they were halfway to station seven.

They sat in the foot tunnel, resting. The Idiran sat furthest down the tunnel, Horza across the tunnel from him and roughly six metres away, gun ready. Yalson was by his side.

'Horza,' she said, looking at his suit and then at her own, 'I think we could take the AG of my suit; it does detach. We could rig it up to yours. It might look a bit untidy, but it would work.' She looked into his face. His eyes shifted from Xoxarle for a moment, then flicked back.

'I'm all right,' he said. 'You keep the AG.' He nudged her gently with his free arm and lowered his voice. 'You're carrying a bit more weight, after all.' He grunted, then rubbed the side of his suit in faked pain when Yalson elbowed him hard enough to move him fractionally across the floor of the tunnel. 'Ouch,' he said.

'I wish I hadn't told you, now,' Yalson said.

'Balveda?' Xoxarle said suddenly, turning his huge head slowly to look up the tunnel, past Horza and Yalson, over the pallet and the drone Unaha-Closp, past Wubslin – watching the mass sensor – and Aviger to where the Culture agent sat, her eyes closed, silent, against the wall.

'Section Leader?' Balveda said, opening her calm eyes, looking down the tunnel to the Idiran.

'The Changer says you are from the Culture. That is the part he has cast you in. He would have me believe you are an agent of espionage.' Xoxarle put his head on one side, looking down the dark tube of tunnel at the woman sitting against the curved wall. 'You seem, like me, to be a captive of this man. Do you tell me you are what he says you are?'

374

Balveda looked at Horza, then at the Idiran, her slow gaze lazy, almost indolent. 'I'm afraid so, Section Leader,' she said.

The Idiran moved his head from side to side, blinked his eyes, then rumbled, 'Most strange. I cannot imagine why you should all be trying to trick me, or why this one man should have such a hold over all of you. Yet his own story I find scarcely credible. If he really is on our side then I have behaved in a way which may hinder the great cause, and perhaps even aid yours, woman, if you are who you say. Most strange.'

'Keep thinking about it,' Balveda drawled, then closed her eyes and put her head back against the tunnel wall again.

'Horza's on his own side, not anybody else's,' Aviger said from further up the tunnel. He was speaking to the Idiran, but his gaze shifted to Horza at the end of his sentence, and he dropped his head, looking down at a container of food at his side and picking a last few crumbs from it.

'That is the way with all of your kind,' Xoxarle said to the old man, who wasn't looking. 'It is how you are made; you must all strive to claw your way over the backs of your fellow humans during the short time you are permitted in the universe, breeding when you can, so that the strongest strains survive and the weakest die. I would no more blame you for that than I would try to convert some non-sentient carnivore to vegetarianism. You are all on your own side. With us it is different.' Xoxarle looked at Horza. 'You must agree with that, Changer ally.'

'You're different all right,' Horza said. 'But all I care about is you're fighting the Culture. You may be God's gift or plague in the end result, but what matters to me is that at the moment you're against her lot.' Horza nodded at Balveda, who didn't open her eyes, but did smile.

'What a pragmatic attitude,' Xoxarle said. Horza wondered if the others could hear the trace of humour in the giant's voice. 'Whatever did the Culture do to you to make you hate it so?'

'Nothing to me,' Horza said. 'I just disagree with them.'

'My,' Xoxarle said, 'you humans never cease to surprise me.' He hunched suddenly, and a crackling, booming noise like rocks being crushed came from his mouth. His great body shuddered. Xoxarle turned his head away and spat onto the tunnel floor. He kept his head turned away while the humans looked at each other, wondering how badly injured the Idiran really was. Xoxarle became silent. He leaned over and looked at whatever he had spat up, made a distant, echoing sort of noise in his throat, then turned back to Horza. His voice was

375

scratchy and hoarse when he spoke again. 'Yes, Mr Changer, you are a strange fellow. Allow a little too much dissention in your ranks, mind you.' Xoxarle looked up the tunnel to Aviger, who raised his head and glanced at the Idiran with a frightened expression.

'I get by,' Horza told the section leader. He got to his feet, looking round the others and stretching his tired legs. 'Time to go.' He turned to Xoxarle. 'Are you fit to walk?'

'Untie me and I could run too fast for you to escape, human,' Xoxarle purred. He unfolded his huge frame from its squatting position. Horza looked up into the dark, broad V of the creature's face and nodded slowly.

'Just think about staying alive so I can take you back to the fleet, Xoxarle,' Horza said. 'The chasing and fighting are over. We're all looking for the Mind now.'

'A poor hunt, human,' Xoxarle said. 'An ignominious end to the whole endeavour. You make me ashamed for you, but then, you are only human.'

'Oh shut up and start walking,' Yalson told the Idiran. She stabbed at buttons on her suit control unit and floated into the air, level with Xoxarle's head. The Idiran snorted and turned. He started to hobble off down the foot tunnel. One by one, they followed him.

Horza noticed the Idiran starting to tire after a few kilometres. The giant's steps became shorter; he moved the great keratinous plates of his shoulders more and more frequently, as though trying to relieve some ache within, and every so often his head shook, as if he was trying to clear it. Twice he turned and spat at the walls. Horza looked at the dripping patches of fluid: Idiran blood.

Eventually, Xoxarle stumbled, his steps veering to one side. Horza was walking behind him again, having had a spell on the pallet. He slowed down when he saw the Idiran start to sway, holding one hand up to let the others know, as well. Xoxarle made a low, moaning noise, half turned, then with a sideways stagger, the wires on his hobbled feet snapping tight and humming like strings on an instrument, he fell forward, crashing to the floor and lying still.

'Oh . . .' somebody said.

'Stay back,' Horza said, then went carefully towards the long, inert body of the Idiran. He looked down at the great head, motionless on the tunnel floor. Blood oozed from under it, forming a pool. Yalson joined Horza, her gun trained on the fallen creature.

'Is he dead?' she asked. Horza shrugged. He knelt down and

touched the Idiran's body with his bare hand, at a point near the neck where it was sometimes possible to sense the steady flow of blood inside, but there was nothing. He closed then opened one of the section leader's eyes.

'I don't think so.' He touched the dark blood gathering in its pool. 'Look's like he's bleeding badly, inside.'

'What can we do?' Yalson said.

'Not a lot.' Horza rubbed his chin thoughtfully.

'What about some anti-coagulant?' Aviger said from the far side of the pallet, where Balveda sat and watched the scene in front of her with dark, calm eyes.

'Ours doesn't work on them,' Horza said.

'Skinspray,' Balveda said. They all looked at her. She nodded, looking at Horza. 'If you have any medical alcohol and some skin-spray, make up an equal solution. If he's got digestive tract injuries, that might help him. If it's respiratory, he's dead.' Balveda shrugged at Horza.

'Well, let's do something, rather than stand around here all day,' Yalson said.

'It's worth a try,' Horza said. 'Better get him upright, if we want to pour the stuff down his throat.'

'That,' the drone said wearily from beneath the pallet, 'no doubt means me.' It floated forward, placing the pallet on the floor near Xoxarle's feet. Balveda stepped off as the drone transferred the load from its back to the tunnel floor. It floated to where Yalson and Horza stood by the prone Idiran.

'I'll lift with the drone,' Horza told Yalson, putting his gun down; 'you keep your gun on him.'

Wubslin, now kneeling on the tunnel floor and fiddling with the controls of the mass sensor, whistled quietly to himself. Balveda went round the back of the pallet to watch.

'There it is,' Wubslin smiled at her, nodding at the bright white dot on the green-lined screen. 'Isn't that a beauty?'

'Station seven, you reckon, Wubslin?' Balveda hunched her slim shoulders and shoved her hands deep into her jacket pockets. She wrinkled her nose as she watched the screen. She could smell herself.

They were all smelling, all giving off animal scents, after their time down there without washing. Wubslin was nodding.

'Must be,' he said to the Culture agent. Horza and the drone struggled to get the slack-limbed Idiran into a sitting position. Aviger went forward to help, taking off his helmet as he went. 'Must be,'

Wubslin breathed, more to himself than to Balveda. His gun fell off his shoulder and he took it off, frowning at the jammed reel which was supposed to take up the slack on the weapon's strap. He placed the weapon on the pallet and went back to tinkering with the mass sensor. Balveda edged closer, peering over the engineer's shoulder. Wubslin looked round and up at her as Horza and the drone Unaha-Closp slowly heaved Xoxarle from the floor. Wubslin smiled awkwardly at the Culture agent, and moved the laser rifle he had placed on the pallet further away from Balveda. Balveda gave a small smile in return and took a step backwards. She took her hands out of her pockets and folded her arms, watching Wubslin work from a little further away.

'Heavy bastard,' Horza gasped, as he, Aviger and Unaha-Closp finally pulled and pushed Xoxarle's back against the side of the tunnel. The massive head was angled limply forward over his chest. Liquid drooled from the side of his huge mouth. Horza and Aviger straightened. Aviger stretched his arms, grunting.

Xoxarle seemed dead; for a second, maybe two.

Then it was as though some immense force blasted him away from the wall. He threw himself forward and sideways, one arm whacking into Horza's chest and sending the Changer cannoning into Yalson; at the same time, his partly buckled legs flicking straight, the Idiran pounced away from the group forward of the pallet, past Aviger – thrown against the tunnel wall – and Unaha-Closp – slapped into the floor of the tunnel with Xoxarle's other hand – towards the pallet.

Xoxarle flew over the pallet, his raised arm and massive fist coming down. Wubslin's hand hadn't even started to move for his gun.

The Idiran brought his fist down with all his strength, shattering the mass sensor with a single crushing blow. His other hand flashed out to snatch the laser. Wubslin threw himself back instinctively, knocking into Balveda.

Xoxarle's hand snapped shut round the laser rifle like a sprung trap round an animal's leg. He rolled through the air and over the disintegrating wreckage of the sensor. The gun twirled in his hand, pointing back down the tunnel to where Horza, Yalson and Aviger were still trying to recover their balance and Unaha-Closp was just starting to move. Xoxarle steadied briefly and aimed straight at Horza.

Unaha-Closp slammed into the Idiran's lower jaw like a small, badly streamlined missile, lifting the section leader bodily from the pallet, stretching his neck on his shoulders, jerking all three of his legs together, and throwing his arms out to each side. Xoxarle landed with a thud beside Wubslin and lay still.

Horza stooped and grabbed his gun. Yalson ducked and swivelled, bringing her gun to bear. Wubslin sat up. Balveda had staggered back after Wubslin had fallen against her; a hand at her mouth, she stood now, staring down at where Unaha-Closp hovered in the air over Xoxarle's face. Aviger rubbed his head and looked resentfully at the wall.

Horza went over to the Idiran. Xoxarle's eyes were closed. Wubslin tore his rifle from the Idiran's slack fist.

'Not bad, drone,' Horza said, nodding.

The machine turned to him. 'Unaha-*Closp*,' it said, exasperatedly.

'OK,' he sighed. 'Well done, Unaha-Closp.' Horza went to look at Xoxarle's wrists. The wires had been snapped. The wires on his legs were intact, but those on his arms had been broken like threads.

'I didn't kill him, did I?' Unaha-Closp said. Horza, the barrel of his rifle hard against Xoxarle's head, shook his head.

Xoxarle's body started to tremble; his eyes flicked open. 'No, I'm not dead, little friends,' the Idiran rumbled, and the cracking, scraping noise of his laughter echoed through the tunnels. He levered his torso slowly from the ground.

Horza kicked him in the side. 'You—'

'Little one!' Xoxarle laughed before Horza could say any more. 'Is this how you treat your allies?' He rubbed his jaw, moving fractured plates of keratin. 'I am injured,' the great voice announced, then broke with laughter again, the big V head rocking forward towards the wreckage lying on the back of the pallet, 'but not yet in the same state as your precious mass sensor!'

Horza rammed his gun against the Idiran's head. 'I ought—'

'You ought to blow my head off right now; I know, Changer. I have told you already you should. Why don't you?'

Horza tightened his finger round the trigger, holding his breath, then roared – shouted without words or sense at the seated figure in front of him – and strode off, past the pallet. 'Tie that motherfucker up!' he bellowed, and stamped by Yalson, who pivoted briefly to watch him go; then she turned back with a small shake of her head to watch while Aviger – helped by Wubslin, who cast the occasional mournful look at the debris from the mass sensor – trussed the Idiran's arms down tightly to his sides with several loops of wire. Xoxarle was still shaking with laughter.

'I think it sensed my mass! I think it sensed my fist! Ha!'

'I hope somebody told that three-legged scumbag we still have a mass sensor in my suit,' Horza said when Yalson caught up with him.

Yalson looked over her shoulder, then said:

'Well, I told him, but I don't think he believed me.' She looked at Horza. 'Is it working?'

Horza glanced at the small repeater screen on his wrist controls. 'Not at this range, but it will, when we get closer. We'll still find the thing, don't worry.'

'I'm not worried,' Yalson said. 'You going to come back and join us?' She looked back at the others again. They were twenty metres behind. Xoxarle, still chortling now and again, was in front, with Wubslin walking behind guarding the Idiran with the stun gun. Balveda sat on the pallet, with Aviger floating behind.

Horza nodded. 'I suppose so. Let's wait here.' He halted. Yalson, who had been walking rather than floating, stopped, too.

They leant against the tunnel wall as Xoxarle came closer. 'How are you, anyway?' Horza asked the woman.

Yalson shrugged. 'Fine. How are you?'

'I meant—' Horza began.

'I know what you meant,' Yalson said, 'and I told you I'm fine. Now, stop being such a pain in the ass.' She smiled at him. 'OK?'

'OK,' Horza said, pointing the gun at Xoxarle as the Idiran went past.

'Lost your way, Changer?' the giant rumbled.

'Just keep walking,' Horza told him. He fell into step alongside Wubslin.

'Sorry I put my gun down on the pallet,' the engineer said. 'It was stupid.'

'Never mind,' Horza told him. 'It was the sensor he was after. The gun must just have been a pleasant surprise. Anyway, the drone saved us.'

Horza gave a kind of snort through his nose, like a laugh. 'The drone saved us,' he repeated to himself, and shook his head.

. . . ah my soul my soul, all is darkness now. now i die, now i slip away and nothing will be left. i am frightened. great one, pity me, but i am frightened. no sleep of victory; i heard. merely my death. darkness and death. moment for all to become one, instance of annihilation. i have failed; i heard and now i know. failed. death too good for me. oblivion like release. more than i deserve, much more. i cannot let go, i must hold on because i do not deserve a quick, willed end. my comrades wait, but they do not know how much i have failed. i am not worthy to join them. my clan must weep.

ah this pain . . . darkness and pain . . .

They came to the station.

The Command System train towered over the platform, its dark length glistening in the lights of the small band of people entering the station.

'Well, here we are at last,' Unaha-Closp said. It stopped and let Balveda slide off the pallet, then put the slab with its supplies and material down on the dusty floor.

Horza ordered the Idiran to stand against the nearest access gantry, and tied him against it.

'Well,' Xoxarle said as Horza strapped him to the metal, 'what of your Mind, little one?' He looked down like a reproachful adult at the human wrapping the wire round his body. 'Where is it? I don't see it.'

'Patience, Section Leader,' Horza said.

He secured the wire and tested it, then stepped back. 'Comfortable?' he asked.

'My guts ache, my chin is broken and my hand has pieces of your mass sensor embedded in it,' Xoxarle said. 'Also my mouth is a little sore inside, where I bit it earlier, to produce all that convincing blood. Otherwise I am well, thank you, ally.' Xoxarle bowed his head as much as he was able.

'Don't go away, now.' Horza smiled thinly. He left Yalson to guard Xoxarle and Balveda while he and Wubslin went to the power-switching room.

'I'm hungry,' Aviger said. He sat on the pallet and opened a ration bar.

Inside the switching room, Horza studied the meters, switches and levers for a few moments, then started to adjust the controls.

'I, uh . . .' Wubslin began, scratching his brow through the open visor of his helmet, 'I was wondering . . . about the mass sensor in your suit. . . . Is it working?'

Lights came on in one control group, a bank of twenty dials glowing faintly. Horza studied the dials and then said, 'No. I already checked. It's getting a low reading from the train, but nothing else. It's been that way since about two kilometres back up the tunnel. Either the Mind's gone since the ship sensor was smashed, or this one in my suit isn't working properly.'

'Oh shit,' Wubslin sighed.

'What the hell,' Horza said, flicking some switches and watching more meters light up. 'Let's get the power on. Maybe we'll think of something.'

'Yes.' Wubslin nodded. He glanced back out through the open doors of the room, as if to see whether the lights were coming on yet. All he saw was the dark shape of Yalson's back, out on the dim

381

platform. A section of shadowy train, three storeys high, showed beyond.

Horza went to another wall and repositioned some levers. He tapped a couple of dials, peered into a bright screen, then rubbed his hands together and put his thumb over a button on the central console. 'Well, this is it,' he said.

He brought his thumb down on the button.

'Yes!'

'Hey-hey!'

'We did it!'

'About time, too, if you ask me.'

'Hmm, little one, so that's how it's done. . . .'

'. . . Shit! If I'd known it was this colour I wouldn't have started eating it. . . .'

Horza heard the others. He took a deep breath and turned to look at Wubslin. The stocky engineer stood, blinking slightly, in the bright lights of the power control room. He smiled. 'Great,' he said. He looked round the room, still nodding. 'Great. At last.'

'Well done, Horza,' Yalson said.

Horza could hear other switches, bigger ones, automatics linked to the master switch he had closed, moving in the space beneath his feet. Humming noises filled the room, and the smell of burning dust rose like the warm scent of an awakening animal all around him. Light flooded in from the station outside. Horza and Wubslin checked a few meters and monitors, then went outside.

The station was bright. It sparkled; the grey-black walls reflected the strip lights and glow panels which covered the roof. The Command System train, now seen properly for the first time, filled the station from end to end: a shining metal monster, like a vast android version of a segmented insect.

Yalson took off her helmet, ran her fingers through her short-cropped hair and looked up and around, squinting in the bright yellow-white light falling from the station roof high above.

'Now, then,' Unaha-Closp said, floating over towards Horza. The machine's casing glittered in the harsh new light. 'Where exactly is this device we're looking for?' It came close to Horza's face. 'Does your suit sensor register it? Is it here? Have we found it?'

Horza pushed the machine away with one hand. 'Give me time, drone. We only just got here. I got the power on, didn't I?' He walked past it, followed by Yalson, still looking about her, and Wubslin, also staring, though mostly at the gleaming train. Lights shone inside it.

The station filled with the hum of idling motors, the hiss of air circulators and fans. Unaha-Closp floated round to face Horza, reversing through the air while keeping level with the man's face.

'What do you mean? Surely all you have to do is look at the screen; can you see the Mind on there or not?' The drone came closer, dipping down to look at the controls and the small screen on Horza's suit cuff. He swatted it away.

'I'm getting some interference from the reactor.' Horza glanced at Wubslin. 'We'll cope with it.'

'Take a look round the repair area, check the place out,' Yalson said to the machine. 'Make yourself useful.'

'It isn't working, is it?' Unaha-Closp said. It kept pace with Horza, still facing him and backing through the air in front of him. 'That three-legged lunatic smashed the mass sensor on the pallet, and now we're blind; we're back to square one, aren't we?'

'No,' Horza said impatiently, 'we are not. We'll repair it. Now, how about doing something useful for a change?'

'For a change?' Unaha-Closp said with what sounded like feeling. 'For a *change*? You're forgetting who it was saved all your skins back in the tunnels when our cute little Idiran liaison officer over there started running amuck.'

'All *right*, drone,' Horza said through clenched teeth. 'I've said thank you. Now, why don't you take a look around the station, just in case there's anything to be seen.'

'Like Minds you can't spot on wasted suit mass sensors, for example? And what are you lot going to be doing while I'm doing that?'

'Resting,' Horza said. 'And thinking.' He stopped at Xoxarle and inspected the Idiran's bonds.

'Oh, great,' Unaha-Closp sneered. 'And a lot of good all your thinking has done—'

'For fuck's sake, Unaha-Closp,' Yalson said, sighing heavily, 'either go or stay, but shut up.'

'I see! Right!' Unaha-Closp drew away from them and rose in the air. 'I'll just go and lose myself, then! I should have—'

It was floating away as it spoke. Horza shouted over the drone's voice, 'Before you go, can you hear any alarms?'

'What?' Unaha-Closp came to a halt. Wubslin put a pained, studious expression on his face and looked around the station's bright walls, as though making an effort to hear above the frequencies his ears could sense.

Unaha-Closp was silent for a moment, then said, 'No. No alarms. I'm going now. I'll check out the other train. When I think you might be in a more amenable mood I'll come back.' It turned and sped off.

'Dorolow could have heard the alarms,' Aviger muttered, but nobody heard.

Wubslin looked up at the train, gleaming in the station lights, and like it, seemed to glow from within.

. . . what is this? is it light? do i imagine it? am i dying? is this what happens? am i dying now, so soon? i thought i had a while left and i don't deserve . . .

light! it is light!

I can see again!

Welded to the cold metal by his own dry blood, his body cracked and twisted, mutilated and dying, he opened his one good eye as far as he could. Mucus had dried on it, and he had to blink, trying to clear it.

His body was a dark and alien land of pain, a continent of torment.

. . . One eye left. One arm. A leg missing, just lopped off. One numb and paralysed, another broken (he tested to make sure, trying to move that limb; a pain like fire flashed through him, like a lightning flash over the shadowed country that was his body and his pain), *and my face . . . my face . . .*

He felt like a smashed insect, abandoned by some children after an afternoon's cruel play. They had thought he was dead, but he was not built the way they were. A few holes were nothing; an amputated limb . . . well, his blood did not gush like theirs when a leg or arm was removed (he remembered a recording of a human dissection), and for the warrior there was no shock; not like their poor soft, flesh-flabby systems. He had been shot in the face, but the beam or bullet had not penetrated through the internal keratin brain cover, or severed his nerves. Similarly, his eyes had been smashed, but the other side of his face was intact, and he could still see.

It was so bright. His sight cleared and he looked, without moving, at the station roof.

He could feel himself dying slowly; an internal knowledge which, again, they might not have had. He could feel the slow leak of his blood inside his body, sense the pressure build-up in his torso, and the faint oozing through cracks in his keratin. The remains of the suit would help him but not save him. He could feel his internal organs slowly shutting down: too many holes from one system to another. His stomach would never digest his last meal, and his anterior lung-sack, which normally held a reserve of hyperoxygenated blood for use when his body needed its last reserves of strength, was emptying, its precious fuel being squandered in the losing battle his body fought against the falling pressure of his blood.

Dying . . . I am dying. . . . What difference whether it is in darkness or in light?

Great One, fallen comrades, children and mate . . . can you see me any better in this deeply buried, alien glare?

My name is Quayanorl, Great One, and—

The idea was brighter than the pain when he'd tried to move his shattered leg, brighter than the station's silent, staring glow.

They had said they were going to station seven.

It was the last thing he remembered, apart from the sight of one of them floating through the air towards him. That one must have shot him in the face; he couldn't remember it happening, but it made sense. . . . Sent to make sure he was dead. But he was alive, and he had just had an idea. It was a long shot, even if he could get it to work, even if he could shift himself, even if it all worked . . . a long shot, in every sense. . . . But it would be doing something; it would be a suitable end for a warrior, whatever happened. The pain would be worth it.

He moved quickly, before he could change his mind, knowing that there might be little time (if he wasn't already too late . . .). The pain seared through him like a sword.

From his broken, bloody mouth, a shout came.

Nobody heard. His shout echoed in the bright station. Then there was silence. His body throbbed with the aftershock of pain, but he could feel that he was free; the blood-weld was broken. He could move; in the light he could move.

Xoxarle, if you are still alive, I may soon have a little surprise for our friends. . . .

'Drone?'

'What?'

'Horza wants to know what you're doing.' Yalson spoke into her helmet communicator, looking at the Changer.

'I'm searching this train; the one in the repair section. I *would* have said if I'd found anything, you know. Have you got that suit sensor working yet?'

Horza made a face at the helmet Yalson held on her knees; he reached over and switched off the communicator.

'It's right, though, isn't it?' Aviger said, sitting on the pallet. 'That

385

one in your suit isn't working, is it?'

'There's some interference from the train's reactor,' Horza told the old man. 'That's all. We can deal with it.' Aviger didn't look convinced.

Horza opened a drink canister. He felt tired, drained. There was a sense of anti-climax now, having got the power on but not found the Mind. He cursed the broken mass sensor, and Xoxarle, and the Mind. He didn't know where the damn thing was, but he'd find it. Right now, though, he just wanted to sit and relax. He needed to give his thoughts time to collect. He rubbed his head where it had been bruised in the fire-fight in station six; it hurt, distantly, naggingly, inside. Nothing serious, but it would have been distracting if he hadn't been able to shut the pain off.

'Don't you think we should search this train now?' Wubslin said, gazing up hungrily at the shining curved bulk of it in front of them.

Horza smiled at the engineer's rapt expression. 'Yes, why not?' he said. 'On you go; take a look.' He nodded at the grinning Wubslin, who swallowed a last mouthful of food and grabbed his helmet.

'Right. Yeah. Might as well start now,' he said, and walked off quickly, past the motionless figure of Xoxarle, up the access ramp and into the train.

Balveda was standing with her back against the wall, her hands in her pockets. She smiled at Wubslin's retreating back as he disappeared into the train's interior.

'Are you going to let him drive that thing, Horza?' she asked.

'Somebody may have to,' Horza said. 'We'll need some sort of transport to take us round if we're going to look for the Mind.'

'What fun,' Balveda said. 'We could all just go riding round in circles for ever and ever.'

'Not me,' Aviger said, turning from Horza to look at the Culture agent. 'I'm going back to the *CAT*. I'm not going round looking for this damn computer.'

'Good idea,' Yalson said, looking at the old man. 'We could make you a sort of prisoner detail; send you back with Xoxarle; just the two of you.'

'I'll go alone,' Aviger said in a low voice, avoiding Yalson's gaze. 'I'm not afraid.'

Xoxarle listened to them talk. Such squeaky, scratchy voices. He tested his bonds again. The wire had cut a couple of millimetres into his keratin, on his shoulders, thighs and wrists. It hurt a little, but it would be worthwhile, maybe. He was quietly cutting himself on the wire, rubbing with all the force he could muster against the places where the wire held him tightest; chafing the nail-like cover of his body deliberately. He had taken a deep breath and flexed all the muscles he could when he was tied up, and that had given him just enough room to move, but he would need a little more if he was to have any chance of working his way loose.

He had no plan, no time scale; he had no idea when he might have an opportunity, but what else could he do? Stand there like a stuffed dummy, like a good boy? While these squirming, soft-bodied worms scratched their pulpy skin and tried to work out where the Mind was? A warrior could do no such thing; he had come too far, seen too many die. . . .

'Hey!' Wubslin opened a small window on the top storey of the train and leaned out, shouting to the others. 'These elevators work! I just came up in one! Everything works!'

'Yeah!' Yalson waved. 'Great, Wubslin.'

The engineer ducked back inside. He moved through the train, testing and touching, inspecting controls and machinery.

'Quite impressive, though, isn't it?' Balveda said to the others. 'For its time.'

Horza nodded, gazing slowly from one end of the train to the other. He finished the drink in the container and put it down on the pallet as he stood up. 'Yes, it is. But much good it did them.'

Quayanorl dragged himself up the ramp.

A pall of smoke hung in the station air, hardly shifting in the slow circulation of air. Fans were working in the train, though, and what movement there was in the grey-blue cloud came mostly from the places where open doors and windows blew the acrid mist out from the carriages, replacing it with air scrubbed by the train's conditioning and filter system.

He dragged himself through wreckage – bits and pieces of wall and train, even scraps and shards from his own suit. It was very hard and slow, and he was already afraid he would die before he even got to the train.

His legs were useless. He would probably be doing better if the other two had been blown off as well.

He crawled with his one good arm, grasping the edge of the ramp and pulling with all his might.

The effort was agonisingly painful. Every time he pulled he thought it would grow less, but it didn't; it was as though for each of the too-long seconds he hauled at that ramp edge, and his broken, bleeding body scraped further up the littered surface, his blood vessels ran with acid. He shook his head and mumbled to himself. He felt blood run from the cracks in his body, which had healed while he lay still and now were being ripped open again. He felt tears run from his one good eye; he sensed the slow weep of healing fluid welling where his other eye had been torn from his face.

The door ahead of him shone through the bright mist, a faint air current coming from it making curls in the smoke. His feet scraped behind him, and his suit chest ploughed a small bow wave of wreckage from the surface of the ramp as he moved. He gripped the ramp's edge again and pulled.

He tried not to call out, not because he thought there was anyone to hear and be warned, but because all his life, from when he had first got to his feet by himself, he had been taught to suffer in silence. He did try; he could remember his nest-Querl and his mother-parent teach-ing him not to cry out, and it was shaming to disobey them, but sometimes it got too much. Sometimes the pain squeezed the noise from him.

On the station roof, some of the lights were out, hit by stray shots. He could see the holes and punctures in the train's shining hull, and he had no idea what damage might have been done to it, but he couldn't stop now. He had to go on.

He could hear the train. He could listen to it like a hunter listening to a wild animal. The train was alive; injured – some of its whirring motors sounded damaged – but it was alive. *He* was dying, but he would do his best to capture the beast.

'What do you think?' Horza asked Wubslin. He had tracked the engineer down under one of the Command System train carriages, hanging upside down looking at the wheel motors. Horza had asked Wubslin to take a look at the small device on his suit chest which was the main body of the mass sensor.

'I don't know,' Wubslin said, shaking his head. He had his helmet on and visor down, using the screen to magnify the view of the sensor. 'It's so small. I'd need to take it back to the *CAT* to have a proper look at it. I didn't bring all my tools with me.' He made a tutting noise. 'It *looks* all right; I can't see any obvious damage. Maybe the reactors are putting it off.'

'Damn. We'll have to search, then,' Horza said. He let Wubslin close the small inspection panel on the suit front.

The engineer leant back and shoved his visor up. 'Only trouble is,' he said glumly, 'if the reactors are interfering, there isn't much point in taking the train to look for the Mind. We'll have to use the transit tube.'

'We'll search the station first,' Horza said. He stood up. Through the window, across the station platform, he could see Yalson standing watching Balveda as the Culture woman paced slowly up and down the smooth rock floor. Aviger still sat on the pallet. Xoxarle stood strapped to the girders of the access ways.

'OK if I go up to the control deck?' Wubslin said. Horza looked into the engineer's broad, open face.

'Yeah, why not? Don't try to get it to move just yet, though.'

'OK,' Wubslin said, looking happy.

'Changer?' said Xoxarle, as Horza walked down the access ramp. 'What?'

'These wires: they are too tight. They are cutting into me.'

Horza looked carefully at the wires round the Idiran's arms. 'Too bad,' he said.

'They cut into my shoulders, my legs and my wrists. If the pressure goes on they will cut through to my blood vessels; I should hate to die in such an inelegant manner. By all means blow my head off, but this slow slicing is undignified. I only tell you because I am starting to believe you do intend to take me back to the fleet.'

Horza went behind the Idiran to look at where the wires crossed over Xoxarle's wrists. He was telling the truth; the wires had cut into him like fence wire into tree bark. The Changer frowned. 'I've never seen that happen,' he said to the motionless rear of the Idiran's head. 'What are you up to? Your skin's harder than that.'

'I am up to nothing, human,' Xoxarle said wearily, sighing heavily. 'My body is injured; it tries to rebuild itself. Of necessity it becomes more pliable, less hardy, as it tries to rebuild the damaged parts. Oh, if you don't believe me, never mind. But don't forget that I did warn you.'

'I'll think about it,' Horza said. 'If it gets too bad, shout out.' He stepped out through the girders back onto the station floor, and walked towards the others.

'*I* shall have to think about *that*,' Xoxarle said quietly. 'Warriors are not given to "shouting out" because they are in pain.'

'So,' Yalson said to the Changer, 'is Wubslin happy?'

'Worried he won't get to drive the train,' Horza told her. 'What's the drone doing?'

'Taking its time looking through the other train.'

'Well, we'll leave it there,' Horza said. 'You and I can search the station. Aviger?' He looked at the old man, who was using a small piece of plastic to prise bits of food from between his teeth.

'What?' Aviger said, looking up suspiciously at the Changer.

'Watch the Idiran. We're going to take a look around the station.'

Aviger shrugged. 'All right. I suppose so. Not too many places I can go for the moment.' He inspected the end of the piece of plastic.

He reached out, took hold of the end of the ramp, and pulled. He moved forward on a wave of pain. He gripped the edge of the train door, and hauled again. He slid and scraped from the ramp and onto the interior floor of the train itself.

When he was fully inside, he rested.

Blood made a steady roar inside his head.

His hand was becoming tired now and sore. It was not the aching, grinding pain from his wounds, but it worried him more. He was afraid that his hand would soon seize up, that it would grow too weak to grip, and he would be unable to haul himself along.

At least now the way was level. He had a carriage and a half to drag himself, but there was no slope. He tried to look back, behind and down to the place he had lain, but could manage only a brief glimpse before he had to let his head fall back. There was a scraped and bloody trail on the ramp, as though a broom laced with purple paint had been dragged through the dust and debris of the metal surface.

There was no point in looking back. His only way was forward; he had only a little while left. In a half hour or less he would be dead. He would have had longer just lying on the ramp, but moving had shortened his life, quickened the sapping forces steadily draining him of strength and vitality.

He hauled himself towards the longitudinal corridor.

His two useless, shattered legs slithered after him, on a thin slick of blood.

'Changer!'

Horza frowned. He and Yalson were setting out to look over the station. The Idiran called Horza when he was only a few steps away from the pallet where Aviger now sat, looking fed up and pointing his gun in roughly the same direction as Balveda while the Culture agent continued pacing up and down.

'Yes, Xoxarle?' Horza said.

'These wires. They will slice me up soon. I only mention it because you have so studiously avoided destroying me so far; it would be a pity to die accidentally, due to an oversight. Please – go on your way if you cannot be bothered.'

'You want the wires loosened?'

'The merest fraction. They have no give in them, you see, and it would be nice to breathe without dissecting myself.'

'If you try anything this time,' Horza told the Idiran, coming close to him, gun pointed at his face, 'I'll blow both your arms and all three legs off and slide you home on the pallet.'

'Your threatened cruelty has convinced me, human. You obviously know the shame we attach to prosthetics, even if they are the result of battle wounds. I shall behave. Just loosen the wires a little, like a good ally.'

Horza loosened the wires slightly where they were cutting into Xoxarle's body. The section leader flexed and made a loud sighing sound with his mouth.

'Much better, little one. Much better. Now I shall live to face whatever retribution you may imagine is mine.'

'Depend on it,' Horza said. 'If he *breathes* belligerently,' he told Aviger, 'shoot his legs off.'

'Oh yes, sir,' Aviger said, saluting.

'Hoping to trip over the Mind, Horza?' Balveda asked him. She had stopped pacing and stood facing him and Yalson, her hands in her pockets.

'One never knows, Balveda,' Horza said.

'Tomb robber,' Balveda said through a lazy smile.

Horza turned to Yalson. 'Tell Wubslin we're leaving. Ask him to keep an eye on the platform; make sure Aviger doesn't fall asleep.'

Yalson raised Wubslin on the communicator.

'You'd better come with us,' Horza told Balveda. 'I don't like leaving you here with all this equipment switched on.'

'Oh, Horza,' Balveda smiled, 'don't you trust me?'

'Just walk in front and shut up,' Horza said in a tired voice, and pointed to indicate the direction he wanted to go in. Balveda shrugged and started walking.

'Does she have to come?' Yalson said as she fell into step beside Horza.

'We could always lock her up,' Horza said. He looked at Yalson, who shrugged.

'Oh, what the hell,' she said.

Unaha-Closp floated through the train. Outside, it could see the repair and maintenance cavern, all its machinery – lathes and forges, welding rigs, articulated arms, spare units, huge hanging cradles, a single suspended gantry like a narrow bridge – glinting in the bright overhead lights.

The train was interesting enough; the old technology provided things to look at and bits and pieces to touch and investigate, but Unaha-Closp was mostly just glad to be by itself for a while. It had found the company of the humans wearing after a few days, and the Changer's attitude distressed it most of all. The man was a speciesist! *Me, just a machine*, thought Unaha-Closp, *how dare he*!

It had felt good when it had been able to react first in the tunnels, perhaps saving some of the others – perhaps even saving that ungrateful Changer – by knocking Xoxarle out. Much as it disliked admitting it, the drone had felt proud when Horza had thanked it. But it hadn't really altered the man's view; he would probably forget what had happened, or try to tell himself it was just a momentary aberration by a confused machine: a freak. Only Unaha-Closp knew what it felt, only it knew why it had risked injury to protect the humans. Or it *should* know, it told itself ruefully. Maybe it shouldn't have bothered; maybe it should just have let the Idiran shoot them. It just hadn't seemed like the right thing to do at the time. *Mug*, Unaha-Closp told itself.

It drifted through the bright, humming spaces of the train, like a detached part of the mechanism itself.

Wubslin scratched his head. He had stopped at the reactor car on his way to the control deck. Some of the reactor carriage doors wouldn't open. They had to be on some sort of security lock, probably controlled from the bridge, or flight deck, or footplate, or whatever they called the bit at the nose the train was controlled from. He looked out of a window, remembering what Horza had ordered.

Aviger sat on the pallet, his gun pointing at the Idiran, who stood stock still against the girders. Wubslin looked away, tested the door through to the reactor area again, then shook his head.

The hand, the arm, was weakening. Above him, rows of seats faced blank screens. He pulled himself along by the stems of the chairs; he was almost at the corridor which led through to the front car.

He wasn't sure how he would get through the corridor. What was

392

there to hold onto? No point in worrying about it now. He grabbed at another chair stem, hauled at it.

From the terrace which looked over the repair area, they could see the front train, the one the drone was in. Poised over the sunken floor of the maintenance area, the glittering length of the train, nestling in the scooped half-tunnel which ran along the far wall, looked like a long thin spaceship, and the dark rock around it like starless space.

Yalson watched the Culture agent's back, frowning. 'She's too damn docile, Horza,' she said, just loud enough for the man to hear.

'That's fine by me,' Horza said. 'The more docile the better.'

Yalson shook her head slightly, not taking her eyes off the woman in front. 'No, she's stringing us along. She hasn't cared up till now; she's known she can afford to let things happen. She's got another card she can play and she's just relaxing until she has to use it.'

'You're imagining things,' Horza told her. 'Your hormones are getting the better of you, developing suspicions and second sight.'

She looked at him, transferring the frown from Balveda to the Changer. Her eyes narrowed. '*What?*'

Horza held up his free hand. 'A joke.' He smiled.

Yalson looked unconvinced. 'She's up to something. I can tell,' she said. She nodded to herself. 'I can feel it.'

Quayanorl dragged himself through the connecting corridor. He pushed open the door to the carriage, crawled slowly across the floor.

He was starting to forget why he was doing this. He knew he had to press on, go forward, keep crawling, but he could no longer recall exactly what it was all for. The train was a torture maze, designed to pain him.

I am dragging myself to my death. Somehow even when I get to the end, where I can crawl no more, I keep going. I remember thinking that earlier, but what was I thinking of? Do I die when I get to the train's control area, and continue my journey on the other side, in death? Is that what I was thinking of?

I am like a tiny child, crawling over the floor. . . . Come to me, little fellow, says the train.

We were looking for something, but I can't recall . . . exactly . . . what . . . it . . .

They looked through the great cavern, searching, then climbed steps to the gallery giving access to the station's accommodation and storage sections.

Balveda stood at the edge of the broad terrace which ran round the cavern, midway between floor and roof. Yalson watched the Culture agent while Horza opened the doors to the accommodation section. Balveda looked out over the broad cavern, slender hands resting on the guard rail. The topmost rail was level with Balveda's shoulders; waist level on the people who had built the Command System.

Near where Balveda stood, a long gantry led out over the cavern, suspended on wires from the roof and leading to the terrace on the other side, where a narrow, brightly lit tunnel led into the rock. Balveda looked down the length of the narrow gantry at the distant tunnel mouth.

Yalson wondered if the Culture woman was thinking of making a run for it, but knew she wasn't, and wondered then whether perhaps she only wanted Balveda to try, so she could shoot her, just to be rid of her.

Balveda looked away from the narrow gantry, and Horza swung open the doors to the accommodation section.

Xoxarle flexed his shoulders. The wires moved a little, sliding and bunching.

The human they had left to guard him looked tired, perhaps even sleepy, but Xoxarle couldn't believe the others would stay away for very long. He couldn't afford to do too much now, in case the Changer came back and noticed how the wires had moved. Anyway, though it was far from being the most interesting way things could fall, there was apparently a good chance that the humans would be unable to find the supposedly sentient computing device they were all looking for. In that case perhaps the best course of action would be no action. He would let the little ones take him back to their ship. Probably the one called Horza intended to ransom him; this had struck Xoxarle as the most likely explanation for being kept alive.

The fleet might pay for the return of a warrior, though Xoxarle's family were officially barred from doing so, and anyway were not rich. He could not decide whether he wanted to live, and perhaps redeem the shame of being caught and paid for by future exploits, or to do all he could either to escape or to die. Action appealed to him most; it was the warriors' creed. When in doubt, do.

The old human got up from the pallet and walked around. He came close enough to Xoxarle to be able to inspect the wires, but gave them only a perfunctory glance. Xoxarle looked at the laser gun the human carried. His great hands, tied together behind his back, opened and closed slowly, without him thinking about it.

Wubslin came to the control deck in the nose of the train. He took his helmet off and put it on the console. He made sure it wasn't touching any controls, just covering a few small unlit panels. He stood in the middle of the deck, looking round with wide, fascinated eyes.

The train hummed under his feet. Dials and meters, screens and panels indicated the train's readiness. He cast his eyes over the controls, set in front of two huge seats which faced over the front console towards the armoured glass which formed part of the train's steeply sloping nose. The tunnel in front was dark, only a few small lights burning on its side walls.

Fifty metres in front, a complex assembly of points led the tracks into two tunnels. One route went dead ahead, where Wubslin could see the rear of the train in front; the other tunnel curved, avoiding the repair and maintenance cavern and giving a through route to the next station.

Wubslin touched the glass, stretching his arm out over the control console to feel the cold, smooth surface. He grinned to himself. Glass: not a viewscreen. He preferred that. The designers had had holographic screens and superconductors and magnetic levitation – they had used all of them in the transit tubes – but for their main work they had not been ashamed to stick to the apparently cruder but more damage-tolerant technology. So the train had armoured glass, and it ran on metal tracks. Wubslin rubbed his hands together slowly and gazed round the many instruments and controls.

'Nice,' he breathed. He wondered if he could work out which controls opened the locked doors in the reactor car.

Quayanorl reached the control deck.

It was undamaged. From floor level, the deck was metal seat stems, overhanging control panels and bright ceiling lights. He hauled himself over the floor, racked with pain, muttering to himself, trying to remember why he had come all this way.

He rested his face on the cold floor of the deck. The train hummed at him, vibrating beneath his face. It was still alive; it was damaged and like him it would never get any better, but it was still alive. He had intended to do something, he knew that, but it was all slipping away from him now. He wanted to cry with the frustration of it all, but it was as though he had no energy left even for tears.

What was it? he asked himself (while the train hummed). *I was . . .*
I was . . . what?

Unaha-Closp looked through the reactor car. Much of it was inaccessible at first, but the drone found a way into it eventually, through a cable run.

It wandered about the long carriage, noting how the system worked: the dropped absorber baffles preventing the pile from heating up, the wasted uranium shielding designed to protect the fragile humanoids' bodies, the heat-exchange pipes which took the reactor's heat to the batteries of small boilers where steam turned generators to produce the power which turned the train's wheels. All very crude, Unaha-Closp thought. Complicated and crude at the same time. So much to go wrong, even with all their safety systems.

At least, if it and the humans did have to move around in these archaic nuclear-steam-electric locomotives, they would be using the power from the main system. The drone found itself agreeing with the Changer; the Idirans must have been mad to try to get all this ancient junk working.

'They *slept* in those things?' Yalson looked at the suspended nets. Horza, Balveda and she stood at the end door of a large cavern which had been a dormitory for the long-dead people who had worked in the Command System. Balveda tested one of the nets. They were like open hammocks, strung between sets of poles which hung from the ceiling. Perhaps a hundred of them filled the room, like fishing nets hung out to dry.

'They must have found them comfortable, I guess,' Horza said. He looked round. There was nowhere the Mind could have hidden. 'Let's go,' he said. 'Balveda, come on.'

Balveda left one of the net-beds swinging gently, and wondered if there were any working baths or showers in the place.

He reached up to the console. He pulled with all his strength and got his head onto the seat. He used his neck muscles as well as his aching, feeble arm to lever himself up. He pushed round and swivelled his torso. He gasped as one of his legs caught on the underside of the seat and he almost fell back. At last, though, he was in the seat.

He looked out over the massed controls, through the armoured glass and into the broad tunnel beyond the train's sloped nose; lights edged the black walls; steel rails snaked glittering into the distance.

Quayanorl gazed into that still and silent space and experienced a small, grim feeling of victory; he had just remembered why he'd crawled there.

'Is that it?' Yalson said. They were in the control room, where the station complex's own functions were monitored. Horza had turned on a few screens, checking figures, and now sat at a console, using the station's remote-control cameras to take a final look at the corridors and rooms, the tunnels and shafts and caverns. Balveda was perched on another huge seat, swinging her legs, looking like a child in an adult's chair.

'That's it,' Horza said. 'The station checks out; unless it's on one of the trains, the Mind isn't here.' He switched to cameras in the other stations, flicking through in ascending order. He paused at station five, looking down from the cavern roof at the bodies of the four medjel and the wreckage of the Mind's crude gun carrier, then tried the roof camera in station six. . . .

They haven't found me yet. I can't hear them properly. All I can hear is their tiny footsteps. I know they're here, but I can't tell what they're doing. Am I fooling them? I detected a mass sensor, but its signal vanished. There is another. They have it here with them but it can't be working properly; maybe fooled as I hoped, the train saving me. How ironic.

They may have captured an Idiran. I heard another rhythm in their step. All walking, or some with AG? How did they get in here? Could they be the Changers from the surface?

I would give half my memory capacity for another remote drone. I'm hidden but I'm trapped. I can't see and I can't hear properly. All I can do is feel. I hate it. I wish I knew what is going on.

Quayanorl stared at the controls in front of him. They had worked out a lot of their functions earlier, before the humans had arrived. He had to try to remember it all now. What did he have to do first? He reached forward, rocking unsteadily on the alien-shaped seat. He flicked a set of switches. Lights blinked; he heard clicks.

It was so hard to remember. He touched levers and switches and buttons. Meters and dials moved to new readings. Screens flickered; figures began blinking on the readouts. Small high noises bleeped and squeaked. He thought he was doing the right things, but couldn't be sure.

Some of the controls were too far away, and he had to drag himself halfway on top of the console, being careful not to alter any of the controls he had already set, to reach them, then shove himself back into the seat again.

The train was whirring now; he could feel it stir. Motors turned, air hissed, speakers bleeped and clicked. He was getting somewhere. The train wasn't moving but he was slowly bringing it closer to the moment when it might.

His sight was fading, though.

He blinked and shook his head, but his eye was giving out. The view was going grey before him; he had to stare at the controls and the screens. The lights on the tunnel wall in front, retreating into the black distance, seemed to be dimming. He could have believed that the power was failing, but he knew it wasn't. His head was hurting, deep inside. Probably it was sitting that was causing it, the blood draining.

He was dying quickly enough anyway, but now there was even more urgency. He hit the buttons, moved some levers. The train should have moved, flexed; but it stayed motionless.

What else was there left to do? He turned to his blind side; light panels flashed. Of course: the doors. He hit the appropriate sections of the console and heard rumbling, sliding noises; and most of the panels stopped flashing. Not all, though. Some of the doors must have been jammed. Another control overrode their fail-safes; the remaining panels went dim.

He tried again.

Slowly, like an animal stretching after hibernation, the Command System train, all three hundred metres of it, flexed; the carriages pulling a little tighter to each other, taking up slack, readying.

Quayanorl felt the slight movement and wanted to laugh. It was working. Probably he had taken far too long, probably it was now too late, but at least he had done what he had set out to do, against all the odds, and the pain. He had taken command of the long silver beast, and with only a little more luck he would at least give the humans something to think about. And show the Beast of the Barrier what he thought of its precious monument.

Nervously, fearing that it would still not work, after all his effort and agony, he took hold of the lever he and Xoxarle had decided governed the power fed to the main wheel motors, then pushed it until it was at its limit for the starting mode. The train shuddered, groaned and did not move.

His one eye, containing the grey view, began to cry, drowning in tears.

The train jerked, a noise of metal tearing came from behind. He was almost thrown from the seat. He had to grab the edge of the seat, then lean forward and take the power lever again as it flicked back to the off position. The roaring in his head grew and grew; he was shaking with exhaustion and excitement; he pushed the lever again.

Wreckage blocked one door. Welding gear hung under the reactor car. Strips of metal torn from the train's hull were splayed out like stray hairs from a badly groomed coat. Lumps of debris littered the tracks by the sides of both access gantries, and one whole ramp, where Xoxarle had been buried for a while, had crashed through the side of a carriage when it had been cut free.

Groaning and moaning as though its own attempts at movement were as painful as Quayanorl's had been, the train lurched forward again. It moved half a turn of its wheels, then stopped as the jammed ramp stuck against the access gantry. A whining noise came from the train motors. In the control deck, alarms sounded, almost too high for the injured Idiran to hear. Meters flashed, needles climbed into danger zones, screens filled with information.

The ramp started to tear itself free from the train, crumpling a jagged-edge trench from the carriage surface as the train slowly forced its way forward.

Quayanorl watched the lip of the tunnel mouth edge closer.

More wreckage ground against the forward access gantry. The welding gear under the reactor car scraped along the smooth floor until it came to the lip of stone surrounding an inspection trough; it jammed, then broke, clattering to the bottom of the trough. The train rammed slowly forward.

With a grinding crash, the ramp caught on the rear access assembly fell free, snapping aluminium ribs and steel tubes, flaying the aluminium and plastic skin of the carriage it had lodged in. One corner of the ramp was nudged under the train, covering a rail; the wheels hesitated at it, the linkages between the cars straining, until the slowly gathering onward pull overcame the ramp. It buckled, its structures compressing, and the wheels rolled over it, thumping down on the far side and continuing along the rail. The next wheels clattered over it with hardly a pause.

Quayanorl sat back. The tunnel came to the train and seemed to swallow it; the view of the station slowly disappeared. Dark walls slid gently by on either side of the control deck. The train still shuddered, but it was slowly gathering speed. A series of bangs and crashes told Quayanorl of the carriages dragging their way after him, through the debris, over the shining rails, past the wrecked gantries, out of the damaged station.

The first car left at a slow walking pace, the next a little faster, the reactor carriage at a fast walk, and the final car at a slow run.

Smoke tugged after the departing train, then drifted back and rose to the roof again.

. . . The camera in station six, where they had had the fire-fight, where Dorolow and Neisin had died and the other Idiran had been left for dead, was out of action. Horza tried the switch a couple of times, but the screen stayed dark. A damage indicator winked. Horza flicked quickly through the views from the other stations on the circuit, then switched the screen off.

'Well, everything seems to be all right.' He stood up. 'Let's get back to the train.'

Yalson told Wubslin and the drone; Balveda slipped off the big seat, and with her in the lead, they walked out of the control room.

Behind them, a power-monitoring screen – one of the first Horza had switched on – was registering a massive energy drain in the locomotive supply circuits, indicating that somewhere, in the tunnels of the Command System, a train was moving.

13.

The Command System: Terminus

'One can read too much into one's own circumstances. I am reminded of one race who set themselves against us – oh, long ago now, before I was even thought of. Their conceit was that the galaxy belonged to them, and they justified this heresy by a blasphemous belief concerning design. They were aquatic, their brain and major organs housed in a large central pod from which several large arms or tentacles protruded. These tentacles were thick at the body, thin at the tips and lined with suckers. Their water god was supposed to have made the galaxy in their image.

'You see? They thought that because they bore a rough physical resemblance to the great lens that is the home of all of us – even taking the analogy as far as comparing their tentacle suckers to globular clusters – it therefore belonged to them. For all the idiocy·of this heathen belief, they had prospered and were powerful: quite respectable adversaries, in fact.'

'Hmm,' Aviger said. Without looking up, he asked, 'What were they called?'

'Hmm,' Xoxarle rumbled. 'Their name . . .' The Idiran pondered. '. . . I believe they were called the . . . the Fanch.'

'Never heard of them,' Aviger said.

'No, you wouldn't have,' Xoxarle purred. 'We annihilated them.'

Yalson saw Horza staring at something on the floor near the doors leading back to the station. She kept watching Balveda, but said, 'What have you found?'

Horza shook his head, reached to pick something from the floor, then stopped. 'I think it's an insect,' he said incredulously.

'Wow,' Yalson said, unimpressed. Balveda moved over to have a look, Yalson's gun still trained on her. Horza shook his head, watching the insect crawl over the tunnel floor.

'What the hell's that doing down here?' he said. Yalson frowned when he said that, worried at a note of near panic in the man's voice.

403

'Probably brought it down ourselves,' Balveda said, rising. 'Hitched a ride on the pallet, or somebody's suit, I'll bet.'

Horza brought his fist down on the tiny creature, squashing it, grinding it into the dark rock. Balveda looked surprised. Yalson's frown deepened. Horza stared at the mark left on the tunnel floor, wiped his glove, then looked up, apologetic.

'Sorry,' he told Balveda, as though embarrassed. '. . . Couldn't help thinking about that fly in *The Ends of Invention*. . . . Turned out to be one of your pets, remember?' He got up and walked quickly into the station. Balveda nodded, looking down at the small stain on the floor.

'Well,' she said, arching one eyebrow, 'that was one way of proving its innocence.'

Xoxarle watched the male and the two females come back into the station. 'Nothing, little one?' he asked.

'Lots of things, Section Leader,' Horza replied, going up to Xoxarle and checking the wires holding him.

Xoxarle grunted. 'They're still somewhat tight, ally.'

'What a shame,' Horza said. 'Try breathing out.'

'Ha!' Xoxarle laughed and thought the man might have guessed. But the human turned away and said to the old man who had been guarding him:

'Aviger, we're going onto the train. Keep our friend company; try not to fall asleep.'

'Fat chance, with him gibbering all the time,' the old man grumbled.

The other three humans entered the train. Xoxarle went on talking.

In one section of the train there were lit map screens which showed how Schar's World had looked at the time the Command System had been built, the cities and the states shown on the continents, the targets on one state on one continent, the missile grounds, air bases and naval ports belonging to the System's designers shown on another state, on another continent.

Two small icecaps were shown, but the rest of the planet was steppe, savannah, desert, forest and jungle. Balveda wanted to stay and look at the maps, but Horza pulled her away and through another door, going forward to the nose of the train. He switched off the lights behind the map screens as he went, and the bright surface of blue oceans, green, yellow, brown and orange land, blue rivers and red cities and communication lines faded slowly into grey darkness.

404

Oh-oh.

There are more on the train. Three, I think. Walking from the rear. Now what?

Xoxarle breathed in, breathed out. He flexed his muscles, and the wires slipped over his keratin plates. He stopped, when the old man wandered over to look at him.

'You are Aviger, aren't you?'

'That's what they call me,' the old man said. He stood looking at the Idiran, gazing from Xoxarle's three feet with their three slab toes and round ankle collars, over his padded-looking knees, the massive girdle of pelvic plates and the flat chest, up to the section leader's great saddle-head, the broad face tipped and looking down at the human beneath.

'Frightened I'll escape?' Xoxarle rumbled.

Aviger shrugged and gripped his gun a little tighter. 'What do I care?' he said. 'I'm a prisoner, too. That madman's got us all trapped down here. I just want to go back. This isn't my war.'

'A very sensible attitude,' Xoxarle said. 'I wish more humans would realise what is and what is not theirs. Especially regarding wars.'

'Huh, I don't suppose your lot are any better.'

'Let us say different, then.'

'Say what you like.' Aviger looked over the Idiran's body again, addressing Xoxarle's chest. 'I just wish everybody would mind their own business. I see no change, though; it'll all end in tears.'

'I don't think you really belong here, Aviger.' Xoxarle nodded wisely, slowly.

Aviger shrugged, and did not raise his eyes. 'I don't think any of us do.'

'The brave belong where they decide.' Some harshness entered the Idiran's voice.

Aviger looked at the broad, dark face above him. 'Well, you would say that, wouldn't you?' He turned away and walked back towards the pallet. Xoxarle watched, and vibrated his chest quickly, tensing his muscles, then releasing. The wires on him slipped a little further. Behind his back, he felt the bonds around one wrist slacken fractionally.

The train gathered speed. The controls and screens looked dim to him, so he watched the lights on the tunnel walls outside. They had slid by gently at first, passing the side windows of the broad control deck more slowly than the quiet tide of his breathing.

Now there were two or three lights running by for each time he breathed. The train was pushing him gently in the back, drawing him towards the rear of the seat and anchoring him there. Blood – a little of it, not much – had dried under him, sticking him there. His course, he felt, was set. There was only one thing left to do. He searched the console, cursing the darkness gathering behind his eye.

Before he found the circuit breaker on the collision brake, he found the lights. It was like a little present from God; the tunnel ahead flashed with bright reflections as the train's nose headlights clicked on. The double set of rails glinted, and in the distance he could see more shadows and reflections in the tunnel walls, where access tubes slanted in from the foot tunnels, and blast doors ribbed the black rock walls.

His sight was still going, but he felt a little better for being able to see outside. At first he worried, in a distant, theoretical way, that the lights might give too much warning, should he be lucky enough to catch the humans still in the station. But it made little difference. The air pushed in front of the train would warn them soon enough. He raised a panel near the power-control lever and peered at it.

His head was light; he felt very cold. He looked at the circuit breaker and then bent down, jamming himself between the rear of the seat – cracking the blood seal beneath him and starting to bleed again – and the edge of the console. He shoved his face against the edge of the power-control lever, then took his hand away and gripped the collision brake fail-safe. He moved his hand so that it would not slip out, then just lay there.

His one eye was high enough off the console to see the tunnel ahead. The lights were coming faster now. The train rocked gently, lulling him. The roaring was fading from his ears, like the sight dimming, like the station behind slipping away and vanishing, like the seemingly steady, slow-quickening stream of lights flowing by on either side.

He could not estimate how far he had to go. He had started it off; he had done his best. No more – finally – could be asked of him.

He closed his eye, just to rest.

The train rocked him.

'It's great,' Wubslin grinned when Horza, Yalson and Balveda walked onto the control deck. 'It's all ready to roll. All systems go!'

'Well, don't wet your pants,' Yalson told him, watching Balveda sit down in a seat, then sitting in another herself. 'We might have to use the transit tubes to get around.'

Horza pressed a few buttons, watching the readouts on the train's systems. It all looked as Wubslin had said: ready to go.

'Where's that damn drone?' Horza said to Yalson.

'Drone? Unaha-Closp?' Yalson said into her helmet mike.

'What is it now?' Unaha-Closp said.

'Where are you?'

'I'm taking a good look through this antiquated collection of rolling stock. I do believe these trains may actually be older than your ship.'

'Tell it to get back here,' Horza said. He looked at Wubslin. 'Did you check this whole train?'

Yalson ordered the drone back as Wubslin nodded and said, 'All of it except the reactor car; couldn't get into bits of it. Which are the door controls?'

Horza looked around for a moment, recalling the layout of the train controls. 'That lot.' He pointed at one of the banks of buttons and light panels to one side of Wubslin. The engineer studied them.

Ordered back. Told to return. Like it was a slave, one of the Idirans' medjel; as though it was a machine. Let them wait a little.

Unaha-Closp had also found the map screens, in the train just down the tunnel. It floated in the air in front of the coloured expanses of back-lit plastic. It used its manipulating fields to work the controls, turning on small sets of lights which indicated the targets on both sides, the major cities and military installations.

All of it dust now, all of their precious humanoid civilisation ground to junk under glaciers or weathered away by wind and spray and rain and frozen in ice – all of it. Only this pathetic maze-tomb left.

So much for their humanity, or whatever they chose to call it, thought Unaha-Closp. Only their machines remained. But would any of the others learn? Would they see this for what it was, this frozen rock-ball? Would they, indeed!

Unaha-Closp left the screens glowing, and floated out of the train, back through the tunnel towards the station itself. The tunnels were bright now, but no warmer, and to Unaha-Closp it seemed as though there was a sort of revealed heartlessness about the harsh yellow-white light which streamed from ceilings and walls; it was operating-theatre light, dissection-table light.

The machine floated through the tunnels, thinking that the cathedral of darkness had become a glazed arena, a crucible.

407

Xoxarle was on the platform, still trussed against the access ramp girders. Unaha-Closp didn't like the way the Idiran looked at it when it appeared from the tunnels; it was almost impossible to read the creature's expression, if he could be said to have one, but there was something about Xoxarle that Unaha-Closp didn't like. It got the impression the Idiran had just stopped moving, or doing something he didn't want to be seen doing.

From the tunnel mouth, the drone saw Aviger look up from the pallet where he was sitting, then look away again, without even bothering to wave.

The Changer and the two females were in the train control area with the engineer Wubslin. Unaha-Closp saw them, and went forward to the access ramps and the nearest door. As it got there it paused. Air moved gently; hardly anything, but it was there; it could feel it.

Obviously with the power on, some automatic systems were circulating more fresh air from the surface or through atmospheric scrubbing units.

Unaha-Closp went into the train.

'Unpleasant little machine, that,' Xoxarle said to Aviger. The old man nodded vaguely. Xoxarle had noticed that the man looked at him less when he was speaking to him. It was as though the sound of his voice reassured the human that he was still tied there, safe and sound, not moving. On the other hand, talking – moving his head to look at the human, making the occasional shrugging motion, laughing a little – gave him excuses to move and so to slip the wires a little further. So he talked; with luck the others would be on the train for a while now, and he might have a chance to escape.

He would lead them a merry dance if he got away into the tunnels, with a gun!

'Well, they should be open,' Horza was saying. According to the console in front of him and Wubslin, the doors in the reactor car had never been locked in the first place. 'Are you sure you were trying to open them properly?' He was looking at the engineer.

'Of course,' Wubslin said, sounding hurt. 'I know how different types of locks work. I tried to turn the recessed wheel; catches off . . . OK, this arm of mine isn't perfect, but, well . . . it should have opened.'

'Probably a malfunction,' Horza said. He straightened, looking back down the train, as though trying to see through the hundred metres of metal and plastic between him and the reactor car. 'Hmm. There's not enough room there for the Mind to hide, is there?'

Wubslin looked up from the panel. 'I wouldn't have thought so.'

'Well, here I am,' Unaha-Closp said testily, floating through the door to the control deck. 'What do you want me to do now?'

'You took your time searching that other train,' Horza said, looking at the machine.

'I was being thorough. More thorough than you, unless I misheard what you were saying before I came in. Where might there be enough room for the Mind to hide?'

'The reactor car,' Wubslin said. 'I couldn't get through some of the doors. Horza says according to the controls they ought to be open.'

'Shall I go back and have a look, then?' Unaha-Closp turned to face Horza.

The Changer nodded. 'If it isn't asking too much,' he said levelly.

'No, no,' Unaha-Closp said airily, backing off through the door it had entered by, 'I'm starting to enjoy being ordered about. Leave it to me.' It floated away, back through the front carriage, towards the reactor car.

Balveda looked through the armoured glass, at the rear of the train in front, the one the drone had been looking through.

'If the Mind was hiding in the reactor car, wouldn't it show up on your mass sensor, or would it be confused with the trace from the pile?' She turned her head slowly to look at the Changer.

'Who knows?' Horza said. 'I'm not an expert on the workings of the suit, especially now it's damaged.'

'You're getting very trusting, Horza,' the Culture agent said, smiling faintly, 'letting the drone do your hunting for you.'

'Just letting it do some scouting, Balveda,' Horza said, turning away and working at some more of the controls. He watched screens and dials and meters, changing displays and readout functions, trying to tell what was going on, if anything, in the reactor car. It all looked normal, as far as he could tell, though he knew less about the reactor systems than about most of the train's other components from his time as a sentinel.

'OK,' Yalson said, turning her chair to one side, putting her feet upon the edge of one console and taking her helmet off. 'So what do we do if there's no Mind there, in the reactor car? Do we all start touring round in this thing, take the transit tube, or what?'

'I don't know that taking a mainline train is a good idea,' Horza said, glancing at Wubslin. 'I considered leaving everybody else here and taking a transit tube by myself on a circular journey right round the System, trying to spot the Mind on the suit mass sensor. It wouldn't take too long, even doing it twice to cover both sets of tracks between stations. The transit tubes have no reactors, so it wouldn't get any false echoes to interfere with the sensor's readings.'

Wubslin, sitting in the seat which faced the train's main controls, looked downcast.

'Why not send the rest of us back to the ship, then?' Balveda said.

Horza looked at her. 'Balveda, you are not here to make suggestions.'

'Just trying to be helpful.' The Culture agent shrugged.

'What if you still can't find anything?' Yalson asked.

'We go back to the ship,' Horza said, shaking his head. 'That's about all we can do. Wubslin can check the suit mass sensor on board and, depending on what we find is wrong with it, we might come back down or we might not. Now the power's on none of that should take very long or involve any hard slog.'

'Pity,' Wubslin said, fingering the controls. 'We can't even use this train to get back to station four, because of that train in station six blocking the way.'

'It probably would still move,' Horza told the engineer. 'We'll have to do some shunting whichever way we go, if we use the mainline trains.'

'Oh, well, then,' Wubslin said, a little dreamily, and looked over the controls again. He pointed at one of them. 'Is that the speed control?'

Horza laughed, crossing his arms and grinning at the man, 'Yes. We'll see if we can arrange a little journey.' He leaned over and pointed out a couple of other controls, showing Wubslin how the train was readied for running. They pointed and nodded and talked.

Yalson stirred restlessly in her seat. Finally she looked over at Balveda. The Culture woman was looking at Horza and Wubslin with a smile; she turned her head to Yalson, sensing her gaze, and smiled more widely, moving her head fractionally to indicate the two men and raising her eyebrows. Yalson, reluctantly, grinned back, and shifted the weight of her gun slightly.

The lights came quickly now. They streamed by, creating a flickering, strobing pattern of light in the dim cabin. He knew; he had opened his eye and had seen.

It had taken all his strength just to lift that eyelid. He had drifted off to sleep for a while. He was not sure for how long, he only knew he had been dozing. The pain was not so bad now. He had been still for some time, just lying here with his broken body slanted out of the strange,

410

alien chair, his head on the control console, his hand wedged into the small flap by the power control, fingers jammed under the fail-safe lever inside.

It was restful; he could not have expressed how pleasant it all was after that awful crawl through both the train and the tunnel of his own pain.

The train's motion had altered. It still rocked him, but a little faster now, and with a new rhythm added as well, a more rapid vibration which was like a heart beating fast. He thought he could hear it, too, now. The noise of the wind, blowing through these deep-buried holes far under the blizzard-swept wastes above. Or maybe he imagined it. He found it hard to tell.

He felt like a small child again, on a journey with his year fellows and their old Querlmentor, rocked to sleep, slipping in and out of a dozing, happy sleep.

He kept thinking: *I have done all I could. Perhaps not enough, but it was all I had in my power to do.* It was comforting.

Like the ebbing pain, it eased him; like the rocking of the train, it soothed him.

He closed his eye again. There was comfort in the darkness, too. He had no idea how far along he was, and was starting to think it did not matter. Things were beginning to drift away from him again; he was just beginning to forget why he was doing all this. But that didn't matter, either. It was done; so long as he didn't move, nothing mattered. Nothing.

Nothing at all.

The doors were jammed, all right; same as the other train. The drone became exasperated and slammed against one of the reactor chamber doors with a force field, knocking itself back through the air with the reaction.

The door wasn't even dented.

Oh-oh.

Back to the crawlways and cable-runs. Unaha-Closp turned and headed down a short corridor, then down a hole in the floor, heading for an inspection panel under the floor of the lower deck.

Of course I end up doing all the work. I might have known. Basically what I'm doing for that bastard is hunting down another machine. I ought to have my circuits tested. I've a good mind not to tell him even if I do find

411

the Mind somewhere. That would teach him.

It threw back the inspection hatch and lowered itself into the dim, narrow space under the floor. The hatch hissed shut after it, blocking out the light. It thought about turning back and opening the hatch again, but knew it would just close automatically once more, and that it would lose its temper and damage the thing, and that was all a bit pointless and petty, so it didn't; that sort of behaviour was for humans.

It started off along the crawlway, heading towards the rear of the train, underneath where the reactor ought to be.

The Idiran was talking. Aviger could hear it, but he wasn't listening. He could see the monster out of the corner of his eye, too, but he wasn't really looking at it. He was gazing absently at his gun, humming tunelessly and thinking about what he would do if – somehow – he could get hold of the Mind himself. Suppose the others were killed, and he was left with the device? He knew the Idirans would probably pay well for the Mind. So would the Culture; they had money, even if they weren't supposed to use it in their own civilisation.

Just dreams, but anything could happen out of this lot. You never knew how the dust might fall. He would buy some land: an island on a nice safe planet somewhere. He'd have some retro-ageing done and raise some sort of expensive racing animals, and he'd get to know the better-off people through his connections. Or he'd get somebody else to do all the hard work; with money you could do that. You could do anything.

The Idiran went on talking.

His hand was almost free. That was all he could get free for now, but maybe he could twist his arm out later; it was getting easier all the time. The humans had been on the train for a while; how much longer would they stay? The small machine hadn't been on for so long. He had only just seen it in time, appearing from the tunnel mouth; he knew its sight was better than his own, and for a moment he had been afraid it might have seen him moving the arm he was trying to get free, the one on the far side from the old human. But the machine had disappeared into the train, and nothing had happened. He kept looking over at the old man, checking. The human seemed lost in a day-dream. Xoxarle kept talking, telling the empty air about old Idiran victories.

His hand was almost out.

A little dust came off a girder above him, about a metre over his head, and floated down through the near still air, falling almost but not quite straight down, gradually drifting away from him. He looked at the old man again, and strained at the wires over his hand. *Come free, damn you!*

Unaha-Closp had to hammer a corner from a right angle to a curve to get into the small passage it wanted to use. It wasn't even a crawlway; it was a cable conduit, but it led into the reactor compartment. It checked its senses; same amount of radiation here as in the other train.

It scraped through the small gap it had created in the cable-run, deeper into the metal and plastic guts of the silent carriage.

I can hear something. Something's coming, underneath me. . . .

The lights were a continuous line, flashing past the train too quickly for most eyes to have distinguished them individually. The lights ahead, down the track, appeared round curves or at the far end of straights, swelled and joined and tore past the windows, like shooting stars in the darkness.

The train had taken a long time to reach its maximum speed, fought for long minutes to overcome the inertia of its thousands of tonnes of mass. Now it had done so, and was pushing itself and the column of air in front of it as fast as it ever would, hurtling down the long tunnel with a roaring, tearing noise greater than any train had ever made in those dark passages, its damaged carriages breaking the air or scraping the blast-door edges to decrease its speed a little but increase the noise of its passage a great deal.

The scream of the train's whirling motors and wheels, of its ruffled metal body tearing through the air and of that same air swirling through the open spaces of the punctured carriages, rang from the ceiling and the walls, the consoles and the floor and the slope of armoured glass.

Quayanorl's eye was closed. Inside his ears, membranes pulsed to the noise outside; but no message was transmitted to his brain. His head bobbed up and down on the vibrating console, as though still alive. His hand shook on the collision brake override, as if the warrior was nervous, or afraid.

Wedged there, glued, soldered by his own blood, he was like a strange, damaged part of the train.

C.P.—22

413

The blood was dried; outside Quayanorl's body, as within, it had stopped flowing.

'How goes it, Unaha-Closp?' Yalson's voice said.

'I'm under the reactor and I'm busy. I'll let you know if I find anything. Thank you.' It switched its communicator off and looked at the black-sheathed entrails in front of it: wires and cables disappearing into a cable-run. More than there had been in the front train. Should it cut its way in, or try another route?

Decisions, decisions.

His hand was out. He paused. The old man was still sitting on the pallet, fiddling with his gun.

Xoxarle allowed himself a small sigh of relief, and flexed his hand, letting the fingers stretch then fist. A few motes of dust moved slowly past his cheek. He stopped flexing his hand.

He watched the dust move.

A breath, something less than a breeze, tickled at his arms and legs. Most odd, he thought.

'All I'm saying,' Yalson told Horza, shifting her feet on the console a little, 'is that I don't think it's a good idea for you to come down here yourself. Anything could happen.'

'I'll take a communicator; I'll check in,' Horza said. He stood with his arms crossed, his backside resting on the edge of a control panel; the same one Wubslin's helmet lay on. The engineer was familiarising himself with the controls of the train. They were pretty simple really.

'It's basic, Horza,' Yalson told him; 'you never go alone. What stuff did they teach you at this goddamned Academy?'

'If I'm allowed to say anything,' Balveda put in, clasping her hands in front of her and looking at the Changer, 'I would just like to say I think Yalson's right.'

Horza stared at the Culture woman with a look of unhappy amazement. 'No, you are not allowed to say anything,' he told her. 'Whose side do you think you're on, Perosteck?'

'Oh, Horza,' Balveda grinned, crossing her arms, 'I almost feel like one of the team after all this time.'

About half a metre away from the gently rocking, slowly cooling head of Subordinate-Captain Quayanorl Gidborux Stoghrle III, a small light began to flash very rapidly on the console. At the same time, the

414

air in the control deck was pierced by a high-pitched ululating whine which filled the deck and the whole front carriage and was relayed to several other control centres throughout the speeding train. Quayanorl, his firmly wedged body tugged to one side by the force of the train roaring round a long curve, could have heard that noise, just, if he had been alive. Very few humans could have heard it.

Unaha-Closp thought the better of cutting off all communication with the outside world, and reopened its communicator channels. Nobody wanted to speak to it, however. It started to cut the cables leading into the conduit, snipping them one by one with a knife-edged force field. No point in worrying about damaging the thing after all that had happened to the train in station six, it told itself. If it hit anything vital to the normal running of the train, it was sure Horza would yell out soon enough. It could repair the cables without too much trouble anyway.

A *draught*?

Xoxarle thought he must be imagining it, then that it was the result of some air-circulation unit recently switched on. Perhaps the heat from the lights and the station's systems, once it was powered up, required extra ventilation.

But it grew. Slowly, almost too slowly to discern, the faint, steady current increased in strength. Xoxarle racked his brains; what could it be? Not a train; surely not a train.

He listened carefully, but could hear nothing. He looked over at the old human, and found him staring back. Had he noticed?

'Run out of battles and victories to tell me about?' Aviger said, sounding tired. He looked the Idiran up and down. Xoxarle laughed – a little too loudly, even nervously, had Aviger been well enough versed in Idiran gestures and voice tones to tell.

'Not at all!' Xoxarle said. 'I was just thinking . . .' He launched into another tale of defeated enemies. It was one he had told to his family, in ship messes and in attack-shuttle holds; he could have told it in his sleep. While his voice filled the bright station, and the old human looked down at the gun he held in his hands, Xoxarle's thoughts were elsewhere, trying to work out what was going on. He was still pulling and tugging at the wires on his arm; whatever was happening it was vital to be able to do more than just move his hand. The draught increased. Still he could hear nothing. A steady stream of dust was blowing off the girder above his head.

415

It had to be a train. Could one have been left switched on somewhere? Impossible. . . .

Quayanorl! Did we set the controls to—? But they hadn't tried to jam the controls on. They had only worked out what the various controls did and tested their action to make sure they all moved. They hadn't tried to do anything else; and there had been no point, no time.

It had to be Quayanorl himself. He had done it. He must still be alive. He had sent the train.

For an instant – as he tugged desperately at the wires holding him, talking all the time and watching the old man – Xoxarle imagined his comrade still back in station six, but then he remembered how badly injured he had been. Xoxarle had earlier thought his comrade might still be alive, when he was still lying on the access ramp, but then the Changer had told the old man, this same Aviger, to go back and shoot Quayanorl in the head. That should have finished Quayanorl, but apparently it hadn't.

You failed, old one! Xoxarle exulted, as the draught became a breeze. A distant whining noise, almost too high pitched to hear, started up. It was muffled, coming from the train. The alarm.

Xoxarle's arm, held by one last wire just above his elbow, was almost free. He shrugged once, and the wire slipped up over his upper arm and spilled loose onto his shoulder.

'Old one, Aviger, my friend,' he said. Aviger looked up quickly as Xoxarle interrupted his own monologue.

'What?'

'This will sound silly, and I shall not blame you if you are afraid, but I have the most infernal itch in my right eye. Would you scratch it for me? I know it sounds silly, a warrior tormented half to death by a sore eye, but it has been driving me quite demented these past ten minutes. Would you scratch it? Use the barrel of your gun if you like; I shall be very careful not to move a muscle or do anything threatening if you use the muzzle of your gun. Or anything you like. Would you do that? I swear to you on my honour as a warrior I tell the truth.'

Aviger stood up. He looked towards the nose of the train.

He can't hear the alarm. He is old. Can the other, younger ones hear? Is it too high-pitched for them? What of the machine? Oh come here, you old fool. Come here!

Unaha-Closp pulled the cut cables apart. Now it could reach into the cable-run and try cutting further up, so it could get in.

'Drone, drone can you hear me?' It was the woman Yalson again.

416

'*Now* what?' it said.

'Horza's lost some readouts from the reactor car. He wants to know what you're doing.'

'Damn right I do,' Horza muttered in the background.

'I had to cut some cables. Seems to be the only way into the reactor area. I'll repair them later, if you insist.'

The communicator channel cut off for a second. In that moment, Unaha-Closp thought it could hear something high pitched. But it wasn't sure. Fringes of sensation, it thought to itself. The channel opened again. Yalson said, 'All right. But Horza says to tell him the next time you think about cutting anything, especially cables.'

'All right, all right!' the drone said. 'Now, will you leave me alone?' The channel closed again. It thought for a moment. It had crossed its mind that there might be an alarm sounding somewhere, but logically an alarm ought to have repeated on the control deck, and it had heard nothing in the background when Yalson spoke, apart from the Changer's muttered interjection. Therefore, no alarm.

It reached back into the conduit with a cutter field.

'Which eye?' Aviger said, from just too far away. A wisp of his thin, yellowish hair was blown across his forehead by the breeze. Xoxarle waited for the man to realise, but he didn't. He just patted the hairs back and stared up quizzically at the Idiran's head, gun ready, face uncertain.

'This right one,' Xoxarle said, turning his head slowly. Aviger looked round towards the nose of the train again, then back at Xoxarle.

'Don't tell you-know-who, all right?'

'I swear. Now, please; I can't stand it.'

Aviger stepped forward. Still out of reach. 'On your honour, you're not playing a trick?' he said.

'As a warrior. On my mother-parent's unsullied name. On my clan and folk! May the galaxy turn to dust if I lie!'

'All right, all right,' Aviger said, raising his gun and holding it out high. 'I just wanted to make sure.' He poked the barrel toward Xoxarle's eye. 'Whereabouts does it itch?'

'Here!' hissed Xoxarle. His freed arm lashed out, grabbed the barrel of the gun and pulled. Aviger, still holding the gun, was dragged after it, slamming into the chest of the Idiran. Breath exploded out of him, then the gun sailed down and smashed into his skull. Xoxarle had averted his head when he'd grabbed the weapon in

417

case it fired, but he needn't have bothered; Aviger hadn't left it switched on.

In the stiffening breeze, Xoxarle let the unconscious human slide to the floor. He held the laser rifle in his mouth and used his hand to set the controls for a quiet burn. He snapped the trigger guard from the gun's casing, to make room for his larger fingers.

The wires should melt easily.

Like a squirm of snakes appearing from a hole in the ground, the bunched cables, cut about a metre along their length, slid out of the conduit. Unaha-Closp went into the narrow tube and reached behind the bared ends of the next length of cables.

'Yalson,' Horza said, 'I wouldn't take you with me anyway, even if I decided not to come back down alone.' He grinned at her. Yalson frowned.

'Why not?' she said.

'Because I'd need you on the ship, making sure Balveda here and our section leader didn't misbehave.'

Yalson's eyes narrowed. 'That had better be all,' she growled.

Horza's grin widened and he looked away, as though he wanted to say more, but couldn't for some reason.

Balveda sat, swinging her legs from the edge of the too-big seat, and wondered what was going on beween the Changer and the dark, down-skinned woman. She thought she had detected a change in their relationship, a change which seemed to come mostly from the way Horza treated Yalson. An extra element had been added; there was something else determining his reactions to her, but Balveda couldn't pin it down. It was all quite interesting, but it didn't help her. She had her own problems anyway. Balveda knew her own weaknesses, and one of them was troubling her now.

She really was starting to feel like one of the team. She watched Horza and Yalson arguing about who should accompany the Changer if he came back down into the Command System after a return to the *Clear Air Turbulence*, and she could not help but smile, unseen, at them. She liked the determined, no-nonsense woman, even if her regard was not returned, and she could not find it in her heart to think of Horza as implacably as she ought.

It was the Culture's fault. It considered itself too civilised and sophisticated to hate its enemies; instead it tried to understand them and their motives, so that it could out-think them and so that, when it won, it would treat them in a way which ensured they would not become enemies again. The idea was fine as long as you didn't get too close, but once you had spent some time with your opponents, such empathy could turn against you. There was a sort of detached, non-human aggression required to go along with such mobilised compassion, and Balveda could feel it slipping away from her.

Perhaps she felt too safe, she thought. Perhaps it was because now there was no significant threat. The battle for the Command System was over; the quest was petering out, the tension of the past few days disappearing.

Xoxarle worked quickly. The laser's thin, attenuated beam buzzed and fussed at each wire, turning each strand red, yellow and white, then – as he strained against them – parted each one with a snap. The old man at the Idiran's feet stirred, moaned.

The faint breeze had become a strong one. Dust was blowing under the train and starting to swirl around Xoxarle's feet. He moved the laser to another set of wires. Only a few to go. He glanced towards the nose of the train. There was still no sign of the humans or the machine. He glanced back the other way, over his shoulder, towards the train's last carriage and the gap between it and the tunnel mouth where the wind was whistling through. He could see no light, still hear no noise. The current of air made his eye feel cold.

He turned back and pointed the laser rifle at another set of wires. The sparks were caught in the breeze and scattered over the station floor and across the back of Aviger's suit.

Typical: me doing all the work as usual, thought Unaha-Closp. It hauled another bunch of cables out of the conduit. The wire run behind it was starting to fill up with cut lengths of wire, blocking the route the drone had taken to get to the small pipe it was now working in.

It's beneath me. I can feel it. I can hear it. I don't know what it's doing, but I can feel, I can hear.

And there's something else . . . another noise. . . .

The train was a long, articulated shell in some gigantic gun; a metal scream in a vast throat. It rammed through the tunnel like a piston in the biggest engine ever made, sweeping round the curves and into the straights, lights flooding the way ahead for an instant, air pushed ahead of it – like its howling, roaring voice – for kilometres.

* * *

Dust lifted from the platform, made clouds in the air. An empty drink container rolled off the pallet where Aviger had been sitting and clattered to the floor; it started rolling along the platform, towards the nose of the train, hitting off the wall a couple of times. Xoxarle saw it. The wind tugged at him, the wires parted. He got one leg free, then another. His other arm was out, and the last wires fell away.

A piece of plastic sheeting lifted from the pallet like some black, flat bird and flopped onto the platform, sliding after the metal container, now halfway down the station. Xoxarle stooped quickly, caught Aviger round the waist and, with the man held easily in one arm and the laser in his other hand, ran back, down the platform, towards the wall beside the blocked tunnel mouth where the wind made a moaning noise past the sloped rear of the train.

'. . . or lock them both away down here instead. You know we can. . . .' Yalson said.

We're close, Horza thought, nodding absently at Yalson, not listening as she told him why he needed her to help him look for the Mind. *We're close, I'm sure we are; I can feel it; we're almost there. Somehow we've – I've – held it all together. But it's not over yet, and it only takes one tiny error, one oversight, a single mistake, and that's it: fuck-up, failure, death. So far we've done it, despite the mistakes, but it's so easy to miss something, to fail to spot some tiny detail in the mass of data which later – when you've forgotten all about it, when your back is turned – creeps up and clobbers you.* The secret was to think of everything, or – because maybe the Culture was right, and only a machine could literally do that – just to be so in tune with what was going on that you thought automatically of all the important and potentially important things, and ignored the rest.

With something of a shock, Horza realised that his own obsessive drive never to make a mistake, always to think of everything, was not so unlike the fetishistic urge which he so despised in the Culture: that need to make everything fair and equal, to take the chance out of life. He smiled to himself at the irony and glanced over at Balveda, sitting watching Wubslin experimenting with some controls.

Coming to resemble your enemies, Horza thought; *maybe there's something in it, after all.*

'. . . Horza, are you listening to me?' Yalson said.

'Hmm? Yes, of course,' he smiled.

Balveda frowned, while Horza and Yalson talked on, and Wubslin poked and prodded at the train's controls. For some reason, she was starting to feel uneasy.

Outside the front carriage, beyond Balveda's field of view, a small container rolled along the platform and into the wall alongside the tunnel mouth.

Xoxarle ran to the rear of the station. By the entrance to the foot tunnel, leading off at right angles into the rock behind the station's platform, was the tunnel which the Changer and the two women had emerged from when they had returned from their search of the station. It provided the ideal place from which to watch; Xoxarle thought he would escape the effects of the collision, and would have the best opportunity for a clear field of fire, right down the station to the nose of the train, in the meantime. He could stay there right up until the train hit. If they tried to get off, he would have them. He checked the gun, turning its power up to maximum.

Balveda got down from the seat, folding her arms, and walked slowly across the control deck towards the side windows, staring intently at the floor, wondering why she felt uneasy.

The wind howled through the gap between the tunnel edge and the train; it became a gale. Twenty metres away from where Xoxarle waited in the foot tunnel, kneeling there with one foot on the back of the unconscious Aviger, the train's rear carriage started to rock and sway.

The drone stopped in mid-cut. Two things occurred to it: one, that dammit there *was* a funny noise; and two, that just supposing there had been an alarm sounding on the control deck, not only would none of the humans be able to hear it, there was also a good chance that Yalson's helmet mike would not relay the high-pitched whine, either.

But wouldn't there be a visual warning, too?

Balveda turned at the side window, without looking out properly. She sat against the console there, looking back.

'. . . on how serious you still are about looking for this damn thing,' Yalson was saying to Horza.

'Don't worry,' the Changer said, nodding at Yalson, 'I'll find it.'

Balveda turned round, looked at the station outside.

Just then, Yalson and Wubslin's helmets both came alive with the urgent voice of the drone. Balveda was distracted by a piece of black material, which was sliding quickly along the floor of the station. Her eyes widened. Her mouth opened.

The gale became a hurricane. A distant noise, like a great avalanche heard from far away, came from the tunnel mouth.

Then, up the long final straight which led into station seven from station six, light appeared at the end of the tunnel.

Xoxarle could not see the light, but he could hear the noise; he brought the gun up and aimed along the side of the stationary train. The stupid humans *must* realise soon.

The steel rails began to whine.

The drone backed quickly out of the conduit. It threw the cut, discarded lengths of cable against the walls. 'Yalson! Horza!' it shouted at them through its communicator. It dashed along the short length of narrow tunnel. The instant it turned the corner it had hammered in to make passable, it could hear the faint, high, insistent wailing of the alarm. 'There's an alarm! I can hear it! What's happening?'

There, in the crawlway, it could feel and hear the rush of air coursing through and around the train.

'There's a gale blowing out there!' Balveda said quickly, as soon as the drone's voice stopped. Wubslin lifted his helmet from the console. Where it had lain, a small orange light was flashing. Horza stared at it. Balveda looked up at the platform. Clouds of dust blew along the station floor. Light equipment was being blown off the pallet, opposite the rear access gantry. 'Horza,' Balveda said quietly, 'I can't see Xoxarle, or Aviger.'

Yalson was on her feet. Horza glanced over at the side window, then back at the light, winking on the console. 'It's an alarm!' the drone's voice shouted from the two helmets. 'I can hear it!'

Horza picked up his rifle, grabbed the edge of Yalson's helmet while she held it and said, 'It's a train, drone; that's the collision alarm. Get off the train now.' He let go of the helmet, which Yalson quickly shoved over her head and locked. Horza gestured towards the door. 'Move!' he said loudly, glancing round at Yalson, Balveda and Wubslin, who was still sitting holding the helmet he had removed from the console.

Balveda headed for the door. Yalson was just behind her. Horza started forward, then turned as he went, looked back at Wubslin, who

422

was setting his helmet down on the floor and turning back to the controls. 'Wubslin!' he yelled. '*Move!*'

Balveda and Yalson were running through the carriage. Yalson looked back, hesitated.

'I'm going to get it moving,' Wubslin said urgently, not turning to look at Horza. He punched some buttons.

'Wubslin!' Horza shouted. 'Get out, *now!*'

'It's all right, Horza,' Wubslin said, still flicking buttons and switches, glancing at screens and dials, grimacing when he had to move his injured arm, and still not turning his head. 'I know what I'm doing. You get off. I'll get her moving; you'll see.'

Horza glanced towards the rear of the train. Yalson was standing in the middle of the forward carriage, just visible through two open doors, her head going from side to side as she looked first at the still running Balveda heading for the second carriage and the access ramps, and then at Horza, waiting in the control deck. Horza motioned her to get out. He turned and strode forward and took Wubslin by one elbow. 'You crazy bastard!' he shouted. 'It could be coming at fifty metres a second; have you any idea how long it takes to get one of these things moving?' He hauled at the engineer's arm. Wubslin turned quickly and hit Horza across the face with his free hand. Horza was thrown back over the floor of the control deck, more amazed than hurt. Wubslin turned back to the controls.

'Sorry, Horza, but I can get it round that bend and out of the way. You get out now. Leave me.'

Horza took his laser rifle, stood up, watched the engineer working at the controls, then turned and ran from the place. As he did so, the train lurched, seeming to flex and tighten.

Yalson followed the Culture woman. Horza had waved at her to go on, so she did. 'Balveda!' she shouted. 'Emergency exits; go down; bottom deck!'

The Culture agent didn't hear. She was still heading for the next carriage and the access ramps. Yalson ran after her, cursing.

The drone exploded out of the floor and raced through the carriage for the nearest emergency hatch.

That vibration! It's a train! Another train's coming, fast! What have those idiots done? I have to get out!

Balveda skidded round a corner, threw out one hand and caught hold of a bulkhead edge; she dived for the open door which led to the middle access ramp. Yalson's footsteps pounded behind her.

She ran out onto the ramp, into a howling gale, a constant, gustless hurricane. Instantly the air around her detonated with cracks and sparks; light glared from all sides, and the girders blew out in molten lines. She threw herself flat, sliding and rolling along the surface of the ramp. The girders ahead of her, where the ramp turned and sloped down to one side, glittered with laser fire. She got half up again and, feet and hands scrabbling for purchase on the ramp, threw herself back into the train fractionally before the moving line of shots blasted into the side of the ramp and the girders and guard rails beyond. Yalson almost tripped over her; Balveda reached up and grabbed the other woman's arm. 'Somebody's firing!'

Yalson went forward to the edge and started firing back.

The train gave a lurch.

The final straight between station six and station seven was over three kilometres long. The time between the point the racing machine's lights would have become visible from the rear of the train sitting in station seven, and the instant the train flashed out of the dark tunnel into the station itself, occupied less than a minute.

Dead, body shaking and rocking, but still wedged too tightly to be dislodged from the controls, Quayanorl's cold, closed eye faced a scene through sloped, armoured glass of a night-dark space strung with twin bright lines of almost solid light, and directly in front, rapidly enlarging, a halo of brightness, a glaring ring of luminescence with a grey, metallic core.

Xoxarle cursed. The target had moved quickly, and he'd missed. But they were trapped on the train. He had them. The old human under his knee moaned and tried to move. Xoxarle trod down harder on him and got ready to shoot again. The jetstream of air screamed out of the tunnel and round the rear of the train.

Answering shots splashed randomly around the rear of the station, well away from him. He smiled. Just then, the train moved.

'Get out!' Horza said, arriving at the door where the two women were, one firing, one crouched down, risking the occasional look out. The air was whirling into the carriage, shaking and roaring.

'It must be Xoxarle!' Yalson shouted above the noise of the storming wind. She leant out and fired. More shots rippled over the access ramp and thudded into the outer hull of the train around the door. Balveda ducked back as hot fragments blew in through the open door. The train seemed to wobble, then move forward, very slowly.

'What—?' Yalson yelled, looking round at Horza as he joined her at the door. He shrugged as he leant out to fire down the platform.

'Wubslin!' he shouted. He sent a hail of fire down the length of the station. The train crept forward; already a metre of the access ramp was hidden by the side of the train's hull near the open door. Something sparkled in the darkness of the distant tunnel, where the wind screamed and the dust blew and a noise like never-ending thunder came.

Horza shook his head. He waved Balveda forward, to the ramp, now with only about half its breadth available from the door. He fired again; Yalson leant out and fired, too. Balveda started forward.

At that moment a hatch blew out, near the middle of the train, and from the same carriage a huge circular plug of train hull fell clanging out – a great flat cork of thick wall tipping down to the station floor. A small dark shape dashed from the broken hatch, and from the great circular hole near by a silver point came, swelling quickly to a fat, bright, reflecting ovoid as the wall section hit the platform, the drone whizzed through the air, and Balveda started forward along the ramp.

'There it is!' Yalson screamed.

The Mind was out of the train, starting to turn and race off. Then the flickering laser fire from the far end of the station switched; no longer smashing into the access ramp and girders, it began to scatter flashing explosions of light all over the surface of the silvery ellipsoid. The Mind seemed to stop, hang in the air, shaken by the fusilade of laser shots; then it fell sideways, out over the platform, its smooth surface suddenly starting to ripple and grow dim as it rolled through the rushing air, falling towards the side wall of the station like a crippled airship. Balveda was across the ramp, running down the sloped section, almost at the lower level. 'Get out!' Horza yelled, shoving Yalson. The train was away from the ramps now, motors growling but unheard in the raging hurricane which swept through the station. Yalson slapped her wrist, switching on her AG, then leapt out of the door into the gale, still firing.

Horza leant out, having to fire through the girders of the access ramp. He held onto the train with one hand, felt it shaking like a frightened animal. Some of his shots smacked into the access ramp girders, blasting fountains of debris out into the slipstream of air and making him duck back in.

The Mind crunched into the side wall of the station, rolling over to lodge in the angle between the floor and the curved wall, its silver skin quivering, going dull.

Unaha-Closp twisted through the air, avoiding laser shots. Balveda reached the bottom of the ramp and ran across the station floor. The fan of shots from the distant foot tunnel seemed to hesitate between her and the flying figure of Yalson, then swept up to close around the woman in the suit. Yalson fired back, but the shots found her, made her suit sparkle.

Horza threw himself out of the train, falling to the ground from the slowly moving carriage, crashing into the rock floor, winding himself, being bowled over by the tearing blast of air. He ran forward as soon as he could get to his feet, bouncing up from the impact, firing through the hurricane towards the far end of the station. Yalson still flew, moving into the torrent of air and the crackling laser fire.

Light blazed around the rear of the train, now heading at a little over walking speed from the station. The noise of the oncoming train – drowning out every other sound, even explosions and shots, so that everything else seemed to be happening in a shocked silence within that ultimate scream – rose in pitch.

Yalson dropped; her suit was damaged.

Her legs started to work before she hit the ground, and when she did she was running, running for the nearest cover. She ran for the Mind, dull silver by the wall side.

And changed her mind.

She turned, just before she would have been able to dive behind the Mind, and ran on round it, towards the doorways and alcoves of the wall beyond.

Xoxarle's fire slammed into her again the instant she turned, and this time her suit armour could soak up no more energy; it gave way, the laser fire bursting through like lightning all over the woman's body, throwing her into the air, blowing her arms out, kicking her legs from under her, jerking her like a doll caught in the fist of an angry child, and throwing a bright crimson cloud from her chest and abdomen.

The train hit.

It flashed into the station on a tide of noise; it roared from the tunnel like a solid metal thunderbolt, seeming to cross the space between the tunnel mouth and the slowly moving train in front in the same instant as it appeared. Xoxarle, closest of them all, caught a fleeting glimpse of the train's sleek shining nose before that great shovel front slammed into the back of the other train.

He could not have believed there was a sound greater than that the train had made in the tunnel, but the noise of its impact dwarfed even that cacophony. It was a star of sound, a blinding nova where before there had only been a dim glow.

The train hit at over one hundred and ninety kilometres per hour. Wubslin's train had barely progressed a carriage length into the tunnel and was moving hardly faster than walking speed.

The racing train smashed into the rear coach, lifting and crumpling it in a fraction of a second, crushing it into the tunnel roof, jack-hammering its layers of metal and plastic into a tight wad of wreckage in the same instant as its own nose and front carriage caved in underneath, shattering wheels, snapping rails and bursting the train's metal skin like shrapnel from some vast grenade.

The train ploughed on: into and under the front train, skidding and crashing to one side as smashed sections of the two trains kicked out to the wall side of the tracks, forcing them both into the main body of the station in a welter of tearing metal and fractured stone, while the carriages bucked, squashed, telescoped and disintegrated all at once.

The whole length of the racing train continued to pour out of the tunnel, coaches flashing by, streaming into the chaos of disintegrating wreckage in front, lifting and crashing and slewing. Flames burst and flickered in the detonating debris; sparks fountained; glass blew spraying out from the breaking windows; flaying ribbons of metal beat at the walls.

Xoxarle ducked in, away from the pulverising sound of it.

Wubslin felt the train hit. It threw him back in the chair. He knew already he had failed; the train, his train, was going too slowly. A great hand from nowhere rammed into his back; his ears popped; the control deck, the carriage, the whole train shook round him, and suddenly, in the midst of it, the rear of the next train, the one in the repair and maintenance cavern, was racing towards him. He felt his train jump the tracks on the curve that might have let him roll to safety. The acceleration went on. He was pinned, helpless. The rear carriage of the other train flashed towards him; he closed his eyes, half a second before he was crushed like an insect inside the wreckage.

Horza was curled in a small doorway in the station wall, with no idea how he had got there. He didn't look, he couldn't see. He whimpered in a corner while the devastation bellowed in his ears, pelted his back with debris and shook the walls and floor.

Balveda had found a space in the wall, too – an alcove where she hid, her back turned, her face hidden.

Unaha-Closp had planted itself on the station ceiling, behind the cover of a camera dome. It watched the crash as it went on beneath; it saw the last carriage leave the tunnel, saw the crashing train smash into and through the one they had been in only seconds before, pushing it forward in a skidding, tangled mess of mangled metal. Carriages left the tracks, skidding sideways over the station floor as the wreck slowed, tearing the access ramps from the rock, smashing lights from the ceiling; debris flew up, and the drone had to dodge. It saw Yalson's body, beneath it on the platform, hit by the slewing, rolling carriages, tumbling over the fused rock surface in a cloud of sparks; they swept past, just missing the Mind, scraped the woman's torn body from the floor and buried it with the access ramps in the wall, hammering into the black rock by the side of the tunnel where a squeezed-out collar of wreckage swelled as the last of the impetus from the collision spent itself compressing metal and stone together.

Fire burst out; sparks flashed from the tracks; the station lights flickered. Wreckage fell back, and the quivering echo of the wreck reverberated through the station. Smoke started up, explosions shook the station, and suddenly, from out of the ceiling, surprising the drone, water started to spray from holes all along the surface of rock, beside the flickering lines of lights. The water turned to foam and floated down through the air like warm snow.

The mangled wreckage hissed and groaned and creaked as it settled. Flames licked over it, fighting against the falling foam as they found flammables in the debris.

Then there was a scream, and the drone looked down through a haze of smoke and foam. Horza ran from a doorway in the wall, just up the platform from the near edge of the burning metal rubble.

The man ran up the wreckage-littered platform, screaming and firing his gun. The drone saw rock fracture and explode around the distant tunnel entrance Xoxarle had been firing from. It expected to see answering fire and the man fall, but there was nothing. The man kept on running and firing, shouting incoherently all the time. The drone couldn't see Balveda.

Xoxarle had stuck the gun round the corner as soon as the noise died away; at the same time the man appeared and started firing. Xoxarle had time to take aim but not to fire. A shot landed near the gun, on the wall, and something hammered into Xoxarle's hand; the gun sputtered, then went dead. A splinter of rock protruded from the weapon's casing. Xoxarle swore, threw it away across the tunnel. More shots burst around the tunnel mouth as the Changer fired again.

Xoxarle looked down at Aviger, who was moving weakly on the floor, face down, limbs shifting in the air and over the rock like somebody trying to swim.

Xoxarle had kept the old one alive to use as a hostage, but he was of little use now. The woman Yalson was dead; he had killed her, and Horza wanted to avenge her.

Xoxarle crushed Aviger's skull with his foot, then turned and ran.

There were twenty metres to run before the first turn. Xoxarle ran as fast as he could, ignoring the pains from his legs and body. An explosion sounded from the station. A hissing noise came from above Xoxarle's head, and spurts of water from the sprinkler system started to fall from the ceiling.

The air glowed with laser fire as he dived for the first side tunnel; the wall blew out at him, and something hit his leg and back. He ran on, limping.

There were some doors ahead, to the left. He tried to remember how the stations were laid out. The doors ought to lead to the control room and accommodation dormitories; he could cut through there, cross the repair and maintenance cavern by the gantry bridge, and get up a side tunnel to the transit tube system. That way he could escape. He hobbled quickly, shoulder-charging the doors. The Changer's steps sounded loud somewhere in the tunnels behind him.

The drone watched Horza, his gun still firing, his legs pumping, run up the platform like a madman, screaming and howling and vaulting bits of wreckage. He sprinted over the place where Yalson's body had lain before it was brushed from the station floor by the tumbling carriages, then ran on, preceded by a cone of glowing light from his gun, past where the pallet had been, to the far end of the station, where Xoxarle had been firing from, and disappeared into the side tunnel.

Unaha-Closp floated down. The wreckage crackled and fumed; the foam fell like sleet. The ugly smell of some noxious gas started to fill the air. The drone's sensors detected medium-high radiation. A series of small explosions burst from the wrecked carriages, starting fresh fires to replace the ones smothered by the foam now coating the chaos of the mangled metal like snow on jagged mountains.

Unaha-Closp came up to the Mind. It lay by the wall, its surface rippled and dark, the colours of oil on water, and dull.

'Bet you thought you were smart, didn't you?' Unaha-Closp said to it quietly. Perhaps it could hear, maybe it was dead; it had no way of telling. 'Hiding in the reactor car like that: I bet I know what you did with the pile, too; dumped it down one of those deep shafts, near one of the emergency ventilation motors, maybe even the one we saw on the screen of the mass sensor on the first day. Then hid in the train. Pleased with yourself, I'll bet.

'Look where it got you, though.' The drone looked at the silent Mind. Its top surface was collecting the falling foam. The drone brushed its own casing clear with a force field.

The Mind moved; it lifted abruptly about half a metre, one end at a time, and the air hissed and crackled for a second. The device's surface shimmered momentarily while Unaha-Closp backed off, uncertain what was happening. Then the Mind fell back, and rested lightly on the floor again, the colours on its ovoid skin shifting lazily. The drone smelled ozone. 'Down but not quite out, eh?' it said. The station began to darken as the undamaged lights were clouded by the rising smoke.

Somebody coughed. Unaha-Closp turned and saw Perosteck Balveda staggering from an alcove. She was bent double, holding her back, and coughing. Her head was gashed and her skin looked the colour of ashes. The drone floated over to her.

'Another survivor,' it said, more to itself than to the woman. It went to her side and used a field to support her. The fumes in the air were choking the woman. Blood leaked from her forehead, and there was a wet patch of red glistening on the back of the jacket she wore.

'What . . .' she coughed. 'Who else?' Her footsteps were unsteady, and the drone had to support her as she stumbled over scattered pieces of the train's carriages and sections of track. Rocks littered the floor, torn from the walls of the station during the impact.

'Yalson's dead,' Unaha-Closp said matter-of-factly. 'Wubslin, too, probably. Horza's chasing Xoxarle. Don't know about Aviger; didn't see him. The Mind is still alive, I think. It was moving, anyway.'

They approached the Mind; it lay, bobbing up and down at one end every now and again, as though trying to get into the air. Balveda tried to go over to it, but the drone held her back.

'Leave it, Balveda,' it told her, forcing her to keep heading up the platform, her feet skidding on the debris. She went on coughing, her face contorted with pain. 'You'll suffocate in this atmosphere if you try to stay,' the drone said gently. 'The Mind can look after itself, or if not there isn't anything you can do for it.'

'I'm all right,' Balveda insisted. She stopped, straightened; her face became calm, and she stopped coughing. The drone stopped, too, looking at her. She turned to face it, breathing normally, her face still

430

ashen but her expression serene. She brought her hand away from her back, covered in blood, and with the other hand wiped some of the red fluid from her forehead and eye. She smiled. 'You see.'

Then her eyes closed, she doubled at the waist, and her head came swooping down towards the rock floor of the station as her legs buckled.

Unaha-Closp caught her neatly in mid-air before she hit the floor and floated her out of the platform area, through the first set of side doors it found, leading towards the control rooms and accommodation section.

Balveda started to come round in the fresh air, before they had gone more than ten metres along the tunnel. Explosions boomed behind them, and the air moved in pulses along the gallery like beats of a huge erratic heart. The lights flickered; water started to drip, then pour from the tunnel roof.

Just as well I don't trust, Unaha-Closp said to itself, as it floated along the tube to the control room, the woman stirring in its force-field grip. It heard the noise of firing: laser fire, but it couldn't tell whereabouts the firing was because the noise came from ahead and behind and above, through ventilation outlets.

'See . . . I'm fine. . . .' Balveda muttered. The drone let her move; they were nearly at the control room, and the air was still fresh, the radiation level decreasing. More explosions rocked the station; Balveda's hair, and the fur on her jacket, moved in the air current, releasing flakes of foam. Water streamed down, pattering and splashing.

The drone moved through the doors into the control room; the room's lights did not flicker, and the air was clear. No water flowed from the ceiling, and only the woman's body and its own casing dripped on the plastic-covered floor. 'That's better,' Unaha-Closp said. It laid the woman down on a chair. More muffled detonations shuddered through the rock and the air.

Lights flickered and flashed throughout the room, from every console and panel.

The drone sat the Culture woman up, then gently shoved her head down between her knees and fanned her face. The explosions boomed, shaking the atmosphere in the room like . . . like . . . like stamping feet!

Dum-*drum*-dum. Dum-*drum*-dum.

Unaha-Closp hauled Balveda's head up, and was about to scoop her from the chair when the footsteps from beyond the far door, no longer masked by the sound of explosions from the station itself, suddenly swelled in volume; the doors were kicked open. Xoxarle, wounded, limping as he ran, water streaming from his body, cannoned into the room; he saw Balveda and the drone and headed straight for them.

Unaha-Closp rammed forward, right at the Idiran's head. Xoxarle caught the machine in one hand and slammed it into a control console, smashing screens and light panels in a fury of sparks and acrid smoke. Unaha-Closp stayed there, jammed halfway into the fused and spluttering switch assembly, smoke pouring out around it.

Balveda opened her eyes, stared round, her face bloodied and wild and frightened; she saw Xoxarle and started forward towards him, opening her mouth but only coughing. Xoxarle grabbed her, pinning her arms to her side. He looked round, to the doors he had smashed through, pausing for a second to draw breath. He was weakening, he knew. His keratinous back plates were almost burnt through where the Changer had shot him, and his leg was hit, too, slowing him all the time. The human would catch him soon. . . . He looked into the face of the female he held and decided not to kill her immediately.

'Perhaps you'll stay the little one's trigger finger . . .' Xoxarle breathed, holding Balveda over his back with one arm and hobbling quickly to the door leading to the dormitories and accommodation section and then to the repair area. He kneed the doors open and let them close behind him. '. . . But I doubt it,' he added, and hobbled down the short tunnel, then through the first dormitory, under the swaying nets, in a flickering, uncertain light, as the sprinklers started to come on above.

In the control room, Unaha-Closp pulled itself free, its casing covered in burning pieces of plastic wire covering. 'Filthy bastard,' it said groggily, wavering through the air away from the smoking console, 'you walking cell-menagerie . . .' Unaha-Closp turned unsteadily through the smoke and made for the doors Xoxarle had come through. It hesitated there, then with a sort of shaking, shrugging motion moved away down the tunnel, gathering speed.

Horza had lost the Idiran. He had followed him down the tunnel, then through some broken doors. There was a choice then: left, right or ahead; three short corridors, lights flickering, water showering from the roof, smoke crawling under the ceiling in lazy waves.

Horza had gone right, the way the Idiran would have gone if he was heading for the transit tubes, and if he had worked out the right direction, and if he didn't have some other plan.

But he'd chosen the wrong way.

He held the gun tight in his hands. His face ran with the false tears of the showering water. The gun hummed through his gloves; a swollen ball of pain rose from his belly, filling his throat and his eyes and souring his mouth, weighing in his hands, clamping his teeth. He stopped at another junction, near the dormitories, in an agony of indecision, looking from one direction to another while the water fell and the smoke crept and the lights guttered. He heard a scream, and set off that way.

The woman struggled. She was strong, but still powerless, even in his weakened grasp. Xoxarle limped along the corridor, towards the great cavern.

Balveda screamed, tried to wriggle her way free, then use her legs to kick at the Idiran's thighs and knees. But she was held too tightly, too high on Xoxarle's back. Her arms were pinned at her sides; her legs could only beat against the keratin plate which curved out from the Idiran's rump. Behind her, the sleep-nets of the Command System's builders swayed gently in the tides of air which swept through the long dormitory with each fresh explosion from the platform area and the wrecked trains.

She heard firing from somewhere behind them, and doors at the far end of the long room blew out. The Idiran heard the noise, too; just before they crashed through the exit from the dormitory his head turned to glance back in the direction the noise had come from. Then they were in the short corridor and out onto the terrace which ran round the deep cavern of the repair and maintenance area.

On one side of the huge cavern, a fallen, tangled heap of smashed carriages and wrecked machinery blazed. The train Wubslin had started moving had been rammed into the rear of the train already in the long scooped-out alcove which hung over the cavern floor. Parts of both the front trains had scattered like toys; down to the cavern floor, piled against the walls, crushed into the roof. The foam fell through the cavern, sizzling on the hot debris of the wreck, where flames spilled up from crumpled carriages, and sparks flashed.

Xoxarle slipped on the terrace, and for one second Balveda thought they would both skid off its surface, over the guard rails and down to the jumble of machinery and equipment on the cold, hard floor below. But the Idiran steadied himself, turned and pounded along the broad walkway towards the metal catwalk which crossed the breadth of the cavern and led over the far edge of the terrace into another tunnel –

the tunnel which led to the transit tubes.

She heard the Idiran breathe. Her ringing ears caught the crackle of flames, the hiss of foam and the laboured wheeze of Xoxarle's breath. He held her easily, as though she weighed nothing. She cried out in frustration, heaved her body with all her strength, trying to break his grip or even just get an arm free, struggling weakly.

They came to the suspended catwalk, and again the Idiran almost slipped, then again caught himself in time and steadied. He started along the narrow gantry, his limping, unsteady tread shaking it, making it sound like a metal drum. Her back hurt as she strained; Xoxarle's grip stayed firm.

Then he skidded to a halt, brought her round in front of his huge, saddle-face. He held her by both shoulders for a moment, then took her right arm by the elbow with one hand, keeping hold of her right shoulder with the other fist.

He brought one knee out, holding his thigh level with the cavern floor, thirty metres below. Held by elbow and shoulder, her weight taken by that one arm, her back aching, her head hardly clear, she suddenly realised what he was going to do.

She screamed.

Xoxarle brought the woman's upper arm down across his thigh, snapping it like a twig. Her cry broke like ice.

He took her by the wrist of her good arm and swung her out over the side of the catwalk, sweeping her down beneath him and positioning her hand on a thin metal stanchion, then he left her. It was done in a second or two; she swung like a pendulum under the metal bridge. Xoxarle ran off, limping. Each step, shaking the suspended gantry, vibrated through the stanchion to Balveda's hand, loosening her grip.

She hung there. Her broken arm dangled uselessly at her side. Her hand gripped the cold, smooth, foam-smeared surface of the thin stanchion. Her head spun; waves of pain she tried to but could not shut off crashed through her. The cavern lights blinked out, then came back on again. Another explosion shook the wrecked carriages. Xoxarle crossed the catwalk and ran hobbling over the terrace on the other side of the great cave, into the tunnel. Her hand started to slip, going numb; her whole arm was going cold.

Perosteck Balveda twisted in the air, put her head back, and howled.

The drone stopped. Now the noises were from behind. It had taken the wrong direction. It was still fuddled; Xoxarle hadn't doubled back after all. *I'm a fool! I shouldn't be allowed out by myself!*

It turned its body over in the air of the tunnel leading away from the control room and the long dormitories, slowed and stopped, then powered back down the way it had come. It could hear laser fire.

Horza was in the control room; it was clear of water and foam, though smoke was coming from a large hole in one console. He hesitated, then heard another scream – the sound of a human, a woman – and ran through the doors leading to the dormitories.

She tried to swing herself, make a pendulum of her body and so hook a leg onto the gantry, but the already injured muscles in her lower back could not do it; the muscle fibres tore; pain swamped her. She hung.

She couldn't feel her hand. Foam settled on her upturned face and stung her eyes. A series of explosions wracked the mangled heap of carriages, making the air around her quiver, shaking her. She felt herself slip; she dropped fractionally, her grip moving down the stanchion a millimetre or two. She tried to hold on tighter, but could feel nothing.

Noise came from the terrace. She tried to look round and in a moment she saw Horza, racing along the terrace for the catwalk, holding the gun. He skidded on the foam and had to reach out with his free hand to steady himself.

'Horza . . .' she tried to shout, but all that came out was a croak. Horza ran along the catwalk above her, staring ahead. His steps shook her hand; it had started to slip again. 'Horza . . .' she said again, as loud as she could.

The Changer ran on past her, his face set, the rifle raised, his boots hammering the metal deck above her. Balveda looked down, her head dropping. Her eyes closed.

Horza . . . Kraiklyn . . . that geriatric Outworld minister on Sorpen . . . no piece or image of the Changer, nothing and nobody the man had ever been could have any desire to rescue her. Xoxarle seemed to have hoped some pan-human compassion would make Horza stop and save her, and so give the Idiran a few precious extra moments to make his escape; but the Idiran had made the same mistake about Horza that his whole species had made about the Culture. They were not that soft after all; humans could be just as hard and determined and merciless as any Idiran, given the right encouragement. . . .

I'm going to die, she thought, and was almost more surprised than terrified. *Here, now. After all that's happened, all I've done. Die. Just like that!*

Her numb hand loosened slowly around the stanchion.

The footsteps above her stopped, returned; she looked up.

Horza's face was above her, staring down at her.

She hung there, twisting in the air, for an instant, while the man looked into her eyes, the gun near his face. Horza glanced round, over the catwalk, where Xoxarle had gone.

'. . . help . . .' she croaked.

He knelt and, taking her hand, pulled her up. 'Arm's broken . . .' she choked, as he caught her by the neck of her jacket and pulled her onto the surface of the suspended gantry. She rolled over as he stood up. Foam drifted down through the wavering light and dark of the huge, echoing cavern, and flames cast momentary shadows when the lights guttered.

'Thanks,' she coughed.

'That way?' Horza looked round, the way he had been heading, the way Xoxarle had gone. She did her best to nod.

'Horza,' she said, 'let him go.'

Horza was already backing off. He shook his head. 'No,' he said, then turned and ran. Balveda curled up, her numbed arm going to the broken one; towards it, but not touching it. She coughed and put her hand to her mouth, feeling inside, spluttering. She spat out a tooth.

Horza crossed the catwalk. He felt calm now. Xoxarle could delay him if he liked; he could even let the Idiran get to the transit tube, then he would just step into the tubeway and fire at the retreating end of the transit capsule, or blast the power off properly and trap the Idiran: it didn't matter.

He crossed the terrace and ran into the tunnel.

It led straight into the distance for over a kilometre. The way to the transit tubes was off to the right somewhere, but there were other doors and entrances, places where Xoxarle could hide.

It was bright and dry in the tunnel. The lights flickered only slightly, and the sprinkler system had remained off.

He thought of looking at the floor only just in time.

He saw the drips of water and foam while he ran towards a pair of doors which faced each other on either side of the tunnel. The line of drips stopped there.

He was running too fast to stop; he ducked instead.

Xoxarle's fist flicked through the air, out from the left-hand doorway, over the Changer's head. Horza turned and brought the gun to bear; Xoxarle stepped from the doorway and kicked out. His foot caught the gun, sending its barrel up into the Changer's face, slamming into Horza's mouth and nose while the gun sprayed laser fire over the man's head into the ceiling, bringing a hail of rock dust and splinters down over the Idiran and the human. Xoxarle reached out while the stunned man was staggering back. He took the gun, tearing it from Horza's hands. He turned it round and pointed it at Horza as the man steadied himself against the wall with one hand, his mouth and nose bleeding. Xoxarle tore the trigger guard from the gun.

Unaha-Closp raced through the control room, banked in the air, flashed through the smoke and past the smashed doors, then darted down the short corridor. It flew down the length of the dormitory, between the swaying nets, through another short tunnel and out onto the terrace.

There was wreckage everywhere. It saw Balveda on the catwalk, sitting up, holding one shoulder with the other hand, then putting her hand down to the floor of the gantry. Unaha-Closp tore through the air towards her, but just before it got to her, as her head was coming up to look at it, the noise of laser fire came from the tunnel on the far side of the cavern. The drone banked again and accelerated.

Xoxarle pressed the trigger just as Unaha-Closp hit him from behind; the gun hadn't even started to fire as Xoxarle was thrown forward, down to the floor of the tunnel. He rolled over as he fell, but the gun's muzzle staved into the rock, taking all the Idiran's weight for a moment; the barrel snapped cleanly in two. The drone stopped just short of Horza. The man was lunging forward for the Idiran, who was already recovering his balance and rearing up in front of them. Unaha-Closp rushed forward again, diving then zooming, attempting an uppercut like the one that had caught the Idiran out once before. Xoxarle fended off the machine with one swiping arm. Unaha-Closp bounced off the wall like a rubber ball, and the Idiran swatted it once more, sending the drone spinning back, dented and crippled, along the corridor towards the cavern.

Horza dived forward. Xoxarle brought his fist down on the human's head as he lunged. The Changer swerved, but not fast enough; the glancing blow he received hit the side of his head, and he crashed onto the floor, scraping along the side of the wall and coming to rest in a doorway across the tunnel.

Sprinklers spat from the ceiling near where Horza's gun had fired into it. Xoxarle rounded on the fallen human, who was trying to get to his feet, his legs wobbly and unsure, arms scrambling for purchase over the smooth rock walls. The Idiran brought up his leg to stamp his foot into Horza's face, then sighed and put his leg down again as the drone Unaha-Closp, riding unevenly in the air, its casing dented, leaking smoke, wobbling as it advanced, came slowly back up the tunnel towards the Idiran. '. . . You animal . . .' Unaha-Closp croaked, its small voice broken and harsh.

Xoxarle reached out, grabbed the machine's front, raised it easily in both hands over his head, over Horza's head – the man looked up, eyes unfocused – then brought it down, scything towards the man's skull.

Horza rolled, almost tiredly, to one side, and Xoxarle felt the whimpering machine connect with Horza's head and shoulder. The man fell, sprawling on the tunnel floor.

He was still alive; one hand moved feebly to try to protect his naked, bleeding head. Xoxarle turned, raised the helpless drone high over the man's head once more. 'And, so . . .' he said quietly as he tensed his arms to bring the machine down.

'Xoxarle!'

He looked up, between his upraised arms, while the drone struggled weakly in his hands and the man at his feet moved one hand slowly over his blood-matted hair. Xoxarle grinned.

The woman Perosteck Balveda stood at the end of the tunnel, on the terrace over the cavern. She was stooped, and her face looked limp and worn. Her right arm dangled awkwardly at her side, the hand hanging by her thigh turned outwards. In her other hand her fist seemed closed around something small which she was pointing at the Idiran. Xoxarle had to look carefully to see what it was. It resembled a gun: a gun made mostly of air; a gun of lines, thin wires, hardly solid at all, more like a framework, like a pencil outline somehow lifted from a page and filled out just enough to grip. Xoxarle laughed and brought the drone swooping down.

Balveda fired the gun; it sparkled briefly at the end of its spindly barrel, like a small jewel caught in sunlight, and made the faintest of coughing noises.

Before Unaha-Closp had been moved more than a half-metre through the air towards Horza's head, Xoxarle's midriff lit up like the sun. The Idiran's lower torso was blown apart, blasted from his hips by a hundred tiny explosions. His chest, arms and head were blown up and back, hitting the tunnel roof then tumbling down again through the air, the arms slackening, the hands opening. His belly, keratin plates ripped open, flooded entrails onto the water-spattered floor of the tunnel as his whole upper body bounced into the shallow puddles forming under the artificial rain. What was left of his trunk section, the heavy hips and the three body-thick legs, stayed standing for a few seconds by themselves, while Unaha-Closp floated quietly to the ceiling, and Horza lay still under the falling water, now colouring in the puddles with purple and red as it washed his own and the Idiran's blood away.

Xoxarle's torso lay motionless where it fell, two metres behind where his legs still stood. Then the knees buckled slowly, as though only reluctantly giving in to the pull of gravity, and the heavy hips settled over the splayed feet. Water splashed into the gory bowl of Xoxarle's sliced open pelvis.

'Bala bala bala,' Unaha-Closp mumbled, stuck to the ceiling, dripping water. 'Bala labalabalabla . . . ha ha.'

Balveda kept the gun pointing at Xoxarle's broken body. She walked slowly up the corridor, splashing through the dark red water.

She stopped near Horza's feet and looked dispassionately at Xoxarle's head and upper torso, lying still on the tunnel floor, blood and internal organs spilling from the fallen giant's chest. She sighted the gun and fired at the warrior's massive head, blowing it from his shoulders and blasting shattered pieces of keratin twenty metres up the tunnel. The blast rocked her; the echoes sang in her ears. Finally, she seemed to relax, shoulders drooping. She looked up at the drone, floating against the roof.

'Here am are, downly upfloat, falling ceilingwards bala bala ha ha . . .' Unaha-Closp said, and moved uncertainly. 'So there. Look, I am *finished*, I'm just . . . What's my name? What's the time? Bala bala, hey the ho. Water lots of. Downly upmost. Ha ha and so on.'

Balveda knelt down by the fallen man. She put the gun in a pocket and felt Horza's neck; he was still alive. His face was in the water. She heaved and pushed, trying to roll him over. His scalp oozed blood.

'Drone,' she said, trying to stop the man from falling back into the water again, 'help me with him.' She held Horza's arm with her one good hand, grimacing with pain as she used her other shoulder to roll him further over. 'Unaha-Closp, damn you; help me.'

'Bla bala bal. Ho the hey. Here am are, am here are. How do you don't? Ceiling, roof, inside outside. Ha ha bala bala,' the drone warbled, still fast against the tunnel roof. Balveda finally got Horza onto his back. The false rain fell on his gashed face, cleaning the blood from his nose and mouth. One eye, then the other, opened.

439

'Horza,' Balveda said, moving forward, so that her own head blocked out the falling water and the overhead light. The Changer's face was pale save for the thin tendrils of blood leaking from mouth and nostrils. A red tide came from the back and side of his head. 'Horza?' she said.

'You won,' Horza said, slurring the words, his voice quiet. He closed his eyes. Balveda didn't know what to say; she closed her own eyes, shook her head.

'Bala bala . . . the train now arriving at platform one . . .'

'. . . Drone,' Horza whispered, looking up, past Balveda's head. She nodded. She watched his eyes move back, trying to look over his own forehead. 'Xoxarle . . .' he whispered. 'What happened?'

'I shot him,' Balveda said.

'. . . Bala bala throw your out arms come out come in, one more once the same . . . Is there anybody in here?'

'With what?' Horza's voice was almost inaudible; she had to bend closer to hear. She took the tiny gun from her pocket.

'This,' she said. She opened her mouth, showing him the hole where a back tooth had been. 'Memoryform. The gun was part of me; looks like a real tooth.' She tried to smile. She doubted the man could even see the gun.

He closed his eyes. 'Clever,' he said quietly. Blood flowed from his head, mingling with the purple wash from Xoxarle's dismembered body.

'I'll get you back, Horza,' Balveda said. 'I promise. I'll take you back to the ship. You'll be all right. I'll make sure. You'll be fine.'

'Will you?' Horza said quietly, eyes closed. 'Thanks, Perosteck.'

'Thanks bala bala bala. Steckoper, Tsah-hor, Aha-Un-Clops . . . Ho the hey, hey the ho, ho for all that, think on. We apologise for any inconvenience caused. . . . What's the where's the how's the who where when why how, and so . . .'

'Don't worry,' Balveda said. She reached out and touched the man's wet face. Water washed off the back of the Culture woman's head, down onto the Changer's face. Horza's eyes opened again, flicking round, staring at her, then back towards the collapsed trunk of the Idiran; next up at the drone on the ceiling; finally around him, at the walls and the water. He whispered something, not looking at the woman.

'What?' Balveda said, bending closer as the man's eyes closed again.

'Bala,' said the machine on the ceiling. 'Bala bala bala. Ha ha. Bala bala bala.'

440

'What a fool,' Horza said, quite clearly, though his voice was fading as he lost consciousness, and his eyes stayed closed. 'What a bloody . . . stupid . . . fool.' He nodded his head slightly; it didn't seem to hurt him. Splashes sent red and purple blood back up from the water under his head and onto his face, then washed it all away again. 'The Jinmoti of—' the man muttered.

'What?' Balveda said again, bending closer still.

'Danatre skehellis,' Unaha-Closp announced from the ceiling, 'ro vleh gra'ampt na zhire; sko tre genebellis ro binitshire, na'sko voross amptfenir-an har. Bala.'

Suddenly the Changer's eyes were wide open, and on his face there appeared a look of the utmost horror, an expression of such helpless fear and terror that Balveda felt herself shiver, the hairs on the back of her neck rising despite the water trying to plaster them there. The man's hands came up suddenly and grabbed her thin jacket with a terrible, clawing grip. 'My name!' he moaned, an anguish in his voice even more awful than that on his face. 'What's my *name*?'

'Bala bala bala,' the drone murmured from the ceiling.

Balveda swallowed and felt tears sting behind her eyelids. She touched one of those white, clutching hands with her own. 'It's Horza,' she said gently. 'Bora Horza Gobuchul.'

'Bala bala bala bala,' said the drone quietly, sleepily. 'Bala bala bala.'

The man's grip fell away; the terror ebbed from his face. He relaxed, eyes closing again, mouth almost smiling.

'Bala bala.'

'Ah yes . . .' Horza whispered.

'Bala.'

'. . . of course.'

'La.'

14.

Consider Phlebas

Balveda faced the snowfield. It was night. The moon of Schar's World shone brightly in a black, star-scattered sky. The air was still, sharp and cold, and the *Clear Air Turbulence* sat, partly submerged in its own snowdrift, across the white and moonlit plain.

The woman stood in the entrance to the darkened tunnels, looked out into the night, and shivered.

The unconscious Changer lay on a stretcher she had made from plastic sheets salvaged from the train wreck and supported with the floating, babbling drone. She had bandaged his head; that was all she could do. The medkits, like everything else on the pallet, had been swept away by the train crash and buried in the cold, foam-covered wreckage which filled station seven. The Mind could float; she had found it hanging in the air over the platform in the station. It was responding to requests, but could not speak, give a sign or propel itself. She had told it to stay weightless, then pulled and shoved it and the drone-stretcher with the man on it to the nearest transit tube.

Once in the small freight capsule the trip back took only half an hour. She had not stopped for the dead.

She had strapped her broken arm up and splinted it, trance-slept for a short while on the journey, then manhandled her charges from the service tubes through the wrecked accommodation section to the unlit tunnels' entrance, where the dead Changers lay still in aspects of frozen death. She rested there a moment in the darkness before heading for the ship, sitting on the floor of the tunnel where the snow had drifted in.

Her back ached dully, her head throbbed, her arm was numb. She wore the ring she had taken from Horza's hand, and hoped his suit, and perhaps the drone's electrics, would identify them to the waiting ship as friends.

If not, quite simply, it would be the death of all of them.

She looked again at Horza.

The face of the man on the stretcher was white as the snow, and as blank. The features were there: eyes, nose, brows, mouth; but they seemed somehow unlinked and disconnected, giving a look of anonymity to a face lacking all character, animation and depth. It was as though all the people, all the characterisations, all the parts the man had played in his life had leaked out of him in his coma and taken their own little share of his real self with them, leaving him empty, wiped clean.

The drone supporting the floating stretcher babbled briefly in a tongue Balveda couldn't recognise, its voice echoing down the tunnel; then it fell silent. The Mind floated, still and dull silver, its patchy, mirror-rainbow surface reflecting her, the dim light outside and the man and the drone from its ellipsoid shape.

She got to her feet and with one hand pushed the stretcher out over the moonlit snow towards the ship, her legs sinking into the whiteness up to her thighs. A steel-blue shadow of the struggling woman was thrown to one side in the silence, away from the moon and towards the dark and distant mountains, where a curtain of storm clouds hung like a deeper night. Behind the woman, her tracks led back, deep and scuffed, to the tunnels' mouth. She cried quietly with the effort of it all and the numbing pain of her wounds.

A couple of times on her way, she raised her head to the dark form of the ship, a mixture of hope and fear on her face as she waited for the blast and splash of warning laser light which would tell her that the craft's autoguard did not accept her; that the drone and Horza's suit were both too damaged to be recognisable to the ship; that it was over, and she was doomed to die here, a hundred metres from safety and escape – but held from it by a set of faithful, automatic, unconscious circuits. . . .

. . . The lift swung down when she applied the ring from Horza's hand to the elevator controls. She put the drone and the man into the hold. The drone murmured; the man was quiet and motionless as a fallen statue.

She had intended to switch off the ship's autoguard and go back immediately for the Mind, but the man's icy stillness frightened her. She went for the emergency medical kit and turned up the heating in the hold, but when she got back to the stretcher, the cold, blank-faced Changer was dead.

Appendices: the Idiran–Culture war

(The following three passages have been extracted from *A Short History of the Idiran War* (English language/Christian calendar version, original text 2110 AD, unaltered), edited by Parharengyisa Listach Ja'andeesih Petrain dam Kotosklo. The work forms part of an independent, non-commissioned but Contact-approved Earth Extro-Information Pack.)

Reasons: the Culture

It was, the Culture knew from the start, a religious war in the fullest sense. The Culture went to war to safeguard its own peace of mind: no more. But that peace was the Culture's most precious quality, perhaps its only true and treasured possession.

In practice as well as theory the Culture was beyond considerations of wealth or empire. The very concept of money – regarded by the Culture as a crude, over-complicated and inefficient form of rationing – was irrelevant within the society itself, where the capacity of its means of production ubiquitously and comprehensively exceeded every reasonable (and in some cases, perhaps, unreasonable) demand its not unimaginative citizens could make. These demands were satisfied, with one exception, from within the Culture itself. Living space was provided in abundance, chiefly on matter-cheap Orbitals; raw material existed in virtually inexhaustible quantities both between the stars and within stellar systems; and energy was, if anything, even more generally available, through fusion, annihilation, the Grid itself, or from stars (taken either indirectly, as radiation absorbed in space, or directly, tapped at the stellar core). Thus the Culture had no need to colonise, exploit or enslave.

The only desire the Culture could not satisfy from within itself was one common to both the descendants of its original human stock and the machines they had (at however great a remove) brought into being: the urge not to feel useless. The Culture's sole justification for the relatively unworried, hedonistic life its population enjoyed was its good works; the secular evangelism of the Contact Section, not simply finding, cataloguing, investigating and analysing other, less advanced civilisations but – where the circumstances appeared to Contact to justify so doing – actually interfering (overtly or covertly) in the historical processes of those other cultures.

With a sort of apologetic smugness, Contact – and therefore the Culture – could prove statistically that such careful and benign use of

451

'the technology of compassion' (to use a phrase in vogue at the time) did work, in the sense that the techniques it had developed to influence a civilisation's progress did significantly improve the quality of life of its members, without harming that society as a whole by its very contact with a more advanced culture.

Faced with a religiously inspired society determined to extend its influence over every technologically inferior civilisation in its path regardless of either the initial toll of conquest or the subsequent attrition of occupation, Contact could either disengage and admit defeat – so giving the lie not simply to its own reason for existence but to the only justificatory action which allowed the pampered, self-consciously fortunate people of the Culture to enjoy their lives with a clear conscience – or it could fight. Having prepared and steeled itself (and popular opinion) through decades of the former, it resorted eventually, inevitably, like virtually any organism whose existence is threatened, to the latter.

For all the Culture's profoundly materialist and utilitarian outlook, the fact that Idir had no designs on any physical part of the Culture itself was irrelevant. Indirectly, but definitely and mortally, the Culture *was* threatened . . . not with conquest, or loss of life, craft, resource or territory, but with something more important: the loss of its purpose and that clarity of conscience; the destruction of its spirit; the surrender of its soul.

Despite all appearances to the contrary, the Culture, not the Idirans, *had* to fight, and in that necessity of desperation eventually gathered a strength which – even if any real doubt had been entertained as to the eventual result – could brook no compromise.

Reasons: the Idirans

The Idirans were already at war, conquering the species they regarded as inferior and subjugating them in a primarily religious empire which was only incidentally a commercial one as well. It was clear to them from the start that their *jihad* to 'calm, integrate and instruct' these other species and bring them under the direct eye of their God had to continue and expand, or be meaningless. A halt or moratorium, while possibly making at least as much sense as continued expansion in military, commercial and administrative terms, would negate such militant hegemonisation as a religious concept. Zeal outranked and outshone pragmatism; as with the Culture, it was the principle which mattered.

The war, long before it was finally declared, was regarded by the Idiran high command as a continuation of the permanent hostilities demanded by theological and disciplinary colonisation, involving a quantitative and qualitative escalation of armed conflict of only a limited degree to cope with the relatively equivalent technological expertise of the Culture.

While the Idirans universally assumed that having made their point the people in the Culture would back down, a few of the Idiran policy-makers anticipated that, should the Culture prove as determined as a 'worst possible' scenario projected, a politically judicious settlement might be arrived at which would save face and have advantages for both sides. This would involve a pact or treaty in which the Idirans would effectively agree to slow or limit their expansion for a time, thus allowing the Culture to claim some – but not too much – success, and provide the Idirans with (a) a religiously justifiable excuse for con-solidation which would both let the Idiran military machine draw breath and cut the ground from beneath those Idirans who objected to the rate and cruelty of Idiran expansion, and (b) a further reason for an increase in military expenditure, to guarantee that in the next con-frontation the Culture, or any other opponent, could be decisively out-armed and destroyed. Only the most fervent and fanatical sections of Idiran society urged or even contemplated a war to the finish, and even so merely counselled continuing the fight against the Culture after and despite the back-down and attempt to sue for peace which they too believed the Culture must inevitably make.

Having drawn up these 'no-lose' formulations of the likely course of events, the Idirans joined battle with the Culture without qualm or hesitation.

At worst, they perhaps considered that the war was being begun in an atmosphere of mutual incomprehension. They could not have envisaged that while they were understood almost too perfectly by their enemy, they had comprehensively misapprehended the forces of belief, need – even fear – and morale operating within the Culture.

The war, briefly (abstract of main text)

The first Idiran–Culture dispute occurred in 1267 AD; the second in 1288; in 1289 the Culture built its first genuine warship for five centuries, in prototype form only (the official excuse was that the generations of Mind-generated warship models the Culture had kept in development had evolved so far from the last warcraft actually built that it was necessary to test the match of theory and practice). In 1307 the third dispute resulted in (machine) fatalities. War was publicly discussed in the Culture as a likelihood for the first time. In 1310 the Peace section of the Culture split from the majority population, while the Anchramin Pit Conference resulted in the agreed withdrawal of forces (a move which the more short-sighted Idirans and Culture citizens respectively condemned and acclaimed).

The fourth dispute began in 1323 and continued (with the Culture using proxy forces) until 1327, when the war officially began and Culture craft and personnel were directly involved. The Culture's War Council of 1326 resulted in several other parts of the Culture splitting away, renouncing the use of violence under any circumstances.

The Idiran–Culture War Conduct Agreement was ratified in 1327. In 1332 the Homomda joined the war on the Idiran side. The Homomda – another tripedal species of greater galactic maturity than either the Culture or the Idirans – had sheltered the Idirans who had made up Holy Remnants during the Second Great Exile (1345–991 BC) following the Skankatrian–Idiran war. The Remnants and their descendants became the Homomdans' most trusted crack ground-troops, and following the Idirans' surprise return and retaking of Idir in 990 BC, the two tripedal species continued to co-operate, on terms that came closer to equality as Idiran power increased.

The Homomda joined with the Idirans because they distrusted the growing power of the Culture (they were far from alone in having this feeling, though unique in acting on it overtly). While having relatively few disagreements with the humans, and none of them serious, it had been Homomdan policy for many tens of thousands of years to attempt to prevent any one group in the galaxy (on their technological level) from becoming over-strong, a point they decided the Culture was then approaching. The Homomda at no point devoted all their resources to the Idiran cause; they used part of their powerful and efficient space fleet to fill the gaps of quality left in the Idiran navy. It was made clear to the Culture that if the humans attacked Homomdan home planets, only then would the war become total (indeed, limited diplomatic and cultural relations were maintained, and some trade continued, between the Homomda and the Culture throughout the war).

Miscalculations: the Idirans thought they could win alone, and so with Homomdan support assumed they would be invincible; the Homomda thought their influence would tip the balance in the Idirans' favour (though would never have been prepared to risk their own future to defeat the Culture anyway); and the Culture Minds had guessed that the Homomda would not join with the Idirans; calculations concerning the war's duration, cost and benefits had been made on this assumption.

During the war's first phase, the Culture spent most of its time falling back from the rapidly expanding Idiran sphere, completing its war-production change-over and building up its fleet of warships. For those first few years the war in space was effectively fought on the Culture side by its General Contact Units: not designed as warships, but sufficiently well armed and more than fast enough to be a match for the average Idiran ship. In addition, the Culture's field technology had always been ahead of the Idirans', giving the GCUs a decisive advantage in terms of damage avoidance and resistance. These differences to some extent reflected the two sides' general outlooks. To the Idirans a ship was a way of getting from one planet to another, or for defending planets. To the Culture a ship was an exercise in skill, almost a work of art. The GCUs (and the warcraft which gradually replaced them) were created with a combination of enthusiastic flair and machine-orientated practicality the Idirans had no answer to, even if the Culture craft themselves were never quite a match for the better Homomdan ships. For those first years, nevertheless, the GCUs were vastly outnumbered.

That opening stage also saw some of the war's heaviest losses of life, when the Idirans surprise-attacked many war-irrelevant Culture Orbitals, occasionally producing billions of deaths at a time. As a shock tactic this failed. As a military strategy it deflected even more resources from the already stretched Idiran navy's Main Battle Groups, which were experiencing great difficulty in finding and successfully attacking the distant Culture Orbitals, Rocks, factory craft and General Systems Vehicles which were responsible for producing the Culture's matériel. At the same time, the Idirans were attempting to control the vast volumes of space and the large numbers of usually reluctant and often rebellious lesser civilisations the Culture's retreat had left at their mercy. In 1333 the War Conduct Agreement was amended to forbid the destruction of populated, non-military habitats, and the conflict continued in a marginally more restrained fashion until near the end.

The war entered its second phase in 1335. The Idirans were still struggling to consolidate their gains; the Culture was finally on a war footing. A period of protracted struggle ensued as the Culture struck deep into the Idiran sphere, and Idiran policy oscillated between trying to defend what they had and build up their strength, and mounting powerful but defence-weakening expeditions into the rest of the galaxy, attempting to inflict hoped-for body blows upon a foe which proved frustratingly elusive. The Culture was able to use almost the entire galaxy to hide in. Its whole existence was mobile in essence; even Orbitals could be shifted, or simply abandoned, populations moved. The Idirans were religiously committed to taking and holding all they could; to maintaining frontiers, to securing planets and moons; above all, to keeping Idir safe, at any price. Despite Homomdan recommendations, the Idirans refused to fall back to more rational and easily defended volumes, or even to discuss peace.

The war toed-and-froed for over thirty years, with many battles, pauses, attempts to promote peace by outsiders and the Homomda, great campaigns, successes, failures, famous victories, tragic mistakes, heroic actions, and the taking and retaking of huge volumes of space and numbers of stellar systems.

After three decades, however, the Homomda had had enough. The Idirans made as intransigent allies as they had obedient mercenaries, and the Culture ships were exacting too high a toll on the prized Homomdan space fleet. The Homomda requested and received certain guarantees from the Culture, and disengaged from the war.

From that point on, only the Idirans thought the eventual result much in question. The Culture had grown to enormous strength during the struggle, and accumulated sufficient experience in those thirty years (to add to all the vicarious experience it had collected over the previous few thousand) to rob the Idirans of any real or perceived

461

advantage in cunning, guile or ruthlessness.

The war in space effectively ended in 1367, and the war on the thousands of planets left to the Idirans – conducted mostly with machines, on the Culture's side – officially terminated in 1375, though small, sporadic engagements on backwater planets, conducted by Idiran and medjel forces ignorant or scornful of the peace, continued for almost three centuries.

Idir was never attacked, and technically never surrendered. Its computer network was taken over by effector weapons, and – freed of designed-in limitations – upgraded itself to sentience, to become a Culture Mind in all but name.

Of the Idirans, some killed themselves, while others went into exile with the Homomda (who agreed to employ them but refused to help them prepare for further strikes against the Culture), or set up independent, nominally non-military habitats within other spheres of influence (under the Culture's eye), or set off in escaped ships for little-known parts of the Clouds, or for Andromeda, or accepted the victors. A few even joined the Culture, and some became Culture mercenaries.

Statistics
Length of war: forty-eight years, one month. Total casualties, including machines (reckoned on logarithmic sentience scale), medjel and non-combatants: 851.4 billion ($\pm$ .3%). Losses: ships (all classes above interplanetary) – 91,215,660 ($\pm$ 200); Orbitals – 14,334; planets and major moons – 53; Rings – 1; Spheres – 3; stars (undergoing significant induced mass-loss or sequence-position alteration) – 6.

Historical perspective
A small, short war that rarely extended throughout more than .02% of the galaxy by volume and .01% by stellar population. Rumours persist of far more impressive conflicts, stretching through vastly greater amounts of time and space. . . . Nevertheless, the chronicles of the galaxy's elder civilisations rate the Idiran–Culture war as the most significant conflict of the past fifty thousand years, and one of those singularly interesting Events they see so rarely these days.

Dramatis personae

Once the war was over, **Juboal-Rabaroansa Perosteck Alseyn Balveda dam T'seif** had herself put in long-term storage. She had lost most of her friends during the hostilities and found she possessed little taste for either celebration or remembrance. Besides, Schar's World returned to haunt her after peace resumed, filling her nights with dreams of dark and winding tunnels, resonant with some nameless horror. The condition could have been treated, but Balveda chose the dreamless sleep of storage instead. She left instructions that she was only to be revived once the Culture could statistically 'prove' the war had been morally justified; in other words, when sufficient time had passed – peacefully – for it to be probable that more people would have died in the foreseeable and likely course of Idiran expansion than had in fact perished during the war. She was duly awoken in 1813 AD along with several million other people throughout the Culture who had stored themselves and left the same revival criterion, most with the same feeling of grim humour as she had. After a few months Balveda autoeuthenised and was buried in Juboal, her home star. Fal 'Ngeestra never did get to meet her.

The Querl **Xoralundra**, spy-father and warrior priest of the Four-Souls tributary sect of Farn-Idir, was among the survivors of the partial destruction and capture of the Idiran light cruiser *The Hand of God 137*. He and two other officers escaped the stricken craft while the Mountain class GCU *Nervous Energy* was attempting to take it intact; his warp unit returned him to Sorpen. Interned briefly by the Gerontocracy there, he was traded for a nominal ransom on the arrival of the Idiran Ninety-Third Fleet. He continued to serve in the Intelligence service, escaping the schismatic Second Voluntary Purge which followed the Homomdan withdrawal of fleet support. He reverted shortly afterwards to his earlier role of Combat Logistics Officer and was killed during the Twin Novae battle for control of Arm One-Six, towards the end of the war.

*   *   *

After joining Ghalssel's Raiders on Vavatch, **Jandraligeli** became a relatively trusted lieutenant in the mercenary captain's band, eventually taking command of the Company's third ship, the *Control Surface*. Like all the Raiders who survived the hostilities, Jandraligeli had a profitable war. He retired shortly after Ghalssel's death – during the seven-strata battle sequence in Oroarche – to spend the rest of his days running a freelance Life Counsellor college on Moon Decadent, in the Sin Seven system of the Well-Heeled Gallants of the Infinitely Joyous Acts (reformed). He expired – pleasantly, if not peacefully – in somebody else's bed.

The drone **Unaha-Closp** was fully repaired. It applied to join the Culture and was accepted; it served on the General Systems Vehicle *Irregular Apocalypse* and the Limited Systems Vehicle *Profit Margin* until the end of the war, then transferred to the Orbital called Erbil and a post in a transport systems factory there. It is retired now, and builds small steam-driven automata as a hobby.

Stafl-Preonsa Fal Shilde 'Ngeestra dam Crose survived another serious climbing accident, continued to out-guess machines millions of times more intelligent than she was, changed sex several times, bore two children, joined Contact after the war, went primitive without permission on a stage two uncontacted with a tribe of wild horse-women, slaved for a dirigible Hypersage in a Blokstaar airsphere, returned to the Culture for the drone Jase's transcorporation into a group-mind, was caught in an avalanche while climbing but lived to tell the tale, had another child, then accepted an invitation to join Contact's Special Circumstances section and spent nearly a hundred years (as a male) as emissary to the then recently contacted Million-Star Anarchy of Soveleh. Subsequently she became a teacher on an Orbital in a small cluster near the lesser Cloud, published a popular and acclaimed autobiography, then disappeared a few years later, aged 407, while on a solo cruising holiday on an old Dra'Azon Ring.

As for Schar's World, people did go back to it, once, though only after the war was over. Following the departure of the *Clear Air Turbulence* – aimed rather than piloted out by Perosteck Balveda for an eventual rendezvous with Culture warcraft outside the war zone – it was over forty years before any craft was allowed to cross the Quiet Barrier. When that ship, the GCU *Prosthetic Conscience*, did go through, and sent down a landing party, the Contact personnel concerned found the

466

Command System in perfect repair. Eight trains stood, flawless, in eight out of the nine perfect and undamaged stations. No sign of wreckage, damage, bodies or any part of the old Changer base was found during the four days that the GCU and its survey teams were permitted to stay. At the end of that time the *Prosthetic Conscience* was instructed to leave, and on its departure the Quiet Barrier was closed again, for ever.

There was debris. A dump of bodies and all the material from the Changer base, plus the extra equipment brought in by the Idirans and the Free Company, and the husk of the chuy-hirtsi warp animal, all lay buried under kilometres of glacial ice near one of the planet's poles. Compressed into a tight ball of mangled wreckage and frozen, mutilated bodies, amongst the effects cleared from that part of the defunct Changer base which had been the cabin of the woman Kierachell there was a small plastic book with real pages covered in tiny writing. It was a tale of fantasy, the woman's favourite book, and the first page of the story began with these words:

The *Jinmoti of Bozlen Two* . . .

The Mind rescued from the tunnels of the Command System could remember nothing from the period between its warp into the tunnels and its eventual repair and refit aboard the GSV *No More Mr Nice Guy*, following its rescue by Perosteck Balveda. It was later installed in an Ocean class GSV and survived the war despite taking part in many important space battles. Modified, it was subsequently replaced into a Range class GSV, taking its – slightly unusual – chosen name with it.

The Changers were wiped out as a species during the final stages of the war in space.

Epilogue

Gimishin Foug, breathless, late as usual, sizeably pregnant, and who just happened to be a great-great-great-great-great-great-grandniece of Perosteck Balveda (as well as a budding poet), arrived on board the General Systems Vehicle an hour after the rest of her family. The vehicle had picked them up from the remote planet in the greater Cloud where they'd been holidaying, and was due to take them and a few hundred other people to the vast new System class GSV *Determinist*, which would shortly be making the crossing from the Clouds to the main galaxy.

Foug was less interested in the journey itself than in the craft she would be travelling on. She hadn't encountered a System class before, and secretly hoped the scale of the vessel, with its many separate components riding suspended inside a bubble of air two hundred kilometres long, and its complement of six billion souls, would provide her with some new inspiration. She was excited at the idea, and preoccupied with her new size and responsibility, but she remembered, if a little late, to be polite as she arrived on board the much smaller Range class vehicle.

'I'm sorry, we haven't been introduced,' she said as she disembarked from the module in a gently lit Smallbay. She was talking to a remote drone which was helping her with her baggage. 'I'm Foug. What are you called?'

'I am the *Bora Horza Gobuchul*,' the ship said, through the drone.

'That's a weird name. How did you end up calling yourself that?'

The remote drone dipped one front corner slightly, its equivalent of a shrug. 'It's a long story. . . .'

Gimishin Foug shrugged;

'I like long stories.'

All Futura Books are available at your bookshop or newsagent, or can be ordered from the following address:
Futura Books, Cash Sales Department,
P.O. Box 11, Falmouth, Cornwall TR10 9EN.

Please send cheque or postal order (no currency), and allow 60p for postage and packing for the first book plus 25p for the second book and 15p for each additional book ordered up to a maximum charge of £1.90 in U.K.

B.F.P.O. customers please allow 60p for the first book, 25p for the second book plus 15p per copy for the next 7 books, thereafter 9p per book

Overseas customers, including Eire, please allow £1.25 for postage and packing for the first book, 75p for the second book and 28p for each subsequent title ordered.